SERVANTS AT KELDACROSS:
John Bailley 1280–1349
Cuthbert Constable b. 1293
Gilbert Falkoner b. 1298
Joan Falkoner b. 1300

KELDA VILLAGE FAMILIES

Simon Thornrigg —— *Hawisa Woodward*   Thomas Reeve —— Martha
b. 1285   b. 1287   b. 1290   1290–1349

Edwin ———————————————— *Mary Reeve*
1316–1348   1319–1349

Adam Bradback, miller; his son Thomas (m. Edith Brewer)
Wat Cottar; his wife Ragenhilda

MASTERS AND STUDENTS AT OXFORD
Robert Treng, warden of Merton College (d. 1349)
Alexander ("the Scot" or "the Screws"), principal of Chimney Hall
Goodram ("Agrestis") of Scarra (d. 1349)
Uthred ("the Puler") (d. 1349)
Stephen of Melcombe (d. 1349)
Miles Spottiswoode
Iago ap Rhys ("Lyra") (d. 1349)
Cyan the Harp

CISTERCIAN BROTHERS AT RIEVAULX
Abbot William de Langeton
Stephen, Novice master
Gilbert of Kerby, novice; later hospitaler

OTHER RELIGIOUS AND CLERGY
Bonaventure Thaxby, Franciscan
Oswin of Urra, parson of Keldacross

LAYPEOPLE IN OXFORD
Judith the cordwainer
John Hand, her journeyman

THE THRESHING FLOOR

A Novel By

JENNIFER RUSSELL

PAULIST PRESS ◇ NEW YORK ◇ MAHWAH

Acknowledgments
I would like to thank the following people for their encouragement, literary advice, or invaluable source materials.

The author of *The Cloud of Unknowing* and his commentators
David Darwazeh
Samuel Garrett
Barbara Hanawalt
Ann Mora
Pamela Morgan
Julie Naidich
Carmen Tapia
Philip Ziegler

Book design by Theresa M. Sparacio.

Copyright © 1987
by Jennifer Russell

Library of Congress Cataloging-in-Publication Data

Russell, Jennifer Ellen, 1957-
 The threshing floor.

 I. Title.
PS3568.U7667T4   1987   813'.54   87-9203
ISBN 0-8091-0394-X

Published by Paulist Press
997 Macarthur Boulevard
Mahwah, New Jersey 07430

Printed and bound in the
United States of America

---- ✴ ----

His winnowing fork is in his hand, and
he will clear his threshing floor.

MATTHEW 3:12

When I sey derknes, I mene a lacking
of knowing; as all that thing that thou
knowest not, or elles thou hast forgeyten.

THE CLOUD OF UNKNOWING

---- ✴ ----

✳ In loving gratitude
　　to my grandmother, whose enthusiasm gave me courage to begin
　　to my mother, whose support gave me courage to continue
　　to my father, for his labors on behalf of this book.

✳ 1

Prologue
The Manor of Keldacross,
in Yorkshire, the North Riding

"**K**eld" is what the old Danes had called a spring, and the wellspring at Keldacross was holy, because St Godrich of Finchale had come there in the old days and drawn a demon out of it. The villeins thought he had planted the great dark yew there as well, the tree that dropped its red berries in the water and buckled the stones set round the spring so that the carven lid would not fit over it any more, but lay to one side, mossy, in the grass. Wilfrid the parson doubted the tree was that old, for the hermit had lived in the ancient days, "when St Ailred was abbot of Rievaulx nearby," said Wilfrid, "when all the white monks were saints, before they were so fond of acquiring sheep pasture." But the villeins looked at him blankly when he said this, and went on calling the yew holy tree, and burnt its needles in their hearths for good smoke and good health. Wilfrid saw no harm in it. If the tree weren't the one planted by Godrich's hand, it could well be its seedling, and besides, it took its drink from the well. That, he supposed, was blessing enough.

Every season before ploughing, Wilfrid sprinkled the fields with well water, and after ploughing he tramped them all over again and sprinkled the furrows. It was the custom. It had been done since the beginning. And, as the old geezers pointed out, it worked. Even in the great famines of their young days Keldacross had never failed a harvest, though people in other villages might eat dogs and dead children. Gaunt beggars had straggled up to the hall in those days and the lady had doled out bread like Joseph in Egypt without mind for where they came from. The villagers had kept what was theirs to themselves. You never knew when you might need what you had put aside.

The one who was lady now came from Wherne in Coverdale to the west. Although she was from a foreign place, she honored Godrich's well.

1

Everyone knew how after her third miscarriage, she'd struggled down from the hall in the dead of winter and got down on her knees in the hard, broken snow. She was not a woman to bewail her sonlessness before the priest, but she knelt long and silent by the black well in the gripping cold. Whatever vows or penances she made there proved the well's power, for in the two years following she had borne two healthy sons.

Now the lady was thinking of having a new lid made for the well. Last summer, William, her younger son, the small terror of the village, the one everyone called "Will of the Wisp," had fallen in, and it was only God's grace that Wilfrid priest was there to fish him out.

Part One

Of sondry folk, by aventure y-falle
In felawshipe, and pilgrims were they alle.
PROLOGUE TO THE CANTERBURY TALES

✳ 2

Keldacross
November 1331

Hawisa the woodward's daughter had been married to Simon Thornrigg the ploughman for years, but she had never loved him nor cared for him, because he neither loved nor cared for her. Besides, he was dark and hairy. She loved and cared for her son Edwin, who was fair. Simon did what work he could not avoid on his own strips and on Sir Gervase's. He did his week work and his boon work; he paid his fees and tithes and tillage. But as for mending his own tools or his own roof or his own fence, or caring for his own cattle, or threshing his own corn—all that he left to Hawisa, and to Win, from the day Win was big enough to heft a pitchfork.

One evening Hawisa said to Simon, who sat by the fire eating a bowl of black beans, "Man, we are nearly out of firewood."

Simon scraped the bowl with his wooden spoon and replied, "Cook me some more of this."

Hawisa thought: The black bear gorges himself while his son goes about like a beanpole. She said, "There's more in the pot. If you want it, get it yourself." Another man would have beaten her for that, but wife-beating was too much work for Simon. She pulled up her hood and went out of the cottage. A sharp wind met her at the door. She found Win outside, plastering mud into cracks in the wall that Simon had not bothered to repair.

Hawisa said, "Leave that now, Win. I am going to the wood for kindling."

Win shook his hands to get off the mud and wiped the rest on the front of his tunic. "Let me get the axe," he said, and went back into the house. Hawisa waited, hugging herself, shivering in the seeping cold. Win came out again with the axe. "Sitting on his arse," he said. Win was fifteen and had no use for his father.

5

The copse that belonged to the village was beyond Kelda beck, across the common pasture from Simon's house. Simon's grandfather had cut a little outfield at the foot of Kelda fell, and built his cottage there. That is why he was called Thornrigg, and his son and grandson after him, for he lived in the shadow of the ridge, and in his time the place had been thorny and wild. Now there were several other cottages nearby, and most of the land around was cleared.

The common was mucky. Halfway across it, women were gathered by the pond. The thatcher's wife was carrying on about something. When Hawisa and Win drew closer, they saw that she was scolding Hereswith the gooseherd, who scowled and sneered and twitched her switch. The gooseherd was a little odd. Most people tried to avoid her, even when she let the geese run all over the pasture, covering it with their unwholesome green dung, which was what the thatcher's wife was screaming about now. Once Garth the shepherd's boy had set his dog to chasing Hereswith's goslings. Hereswith had set her ganders on Garth. The shepherd had beaten Garth black and blue afterward too, for you could ruin a dog by giving him a taste for chasing, even if it were only goslings.

"I'll not have your stinking birds dropping their muck all over the pasture," the thatcher's wife was screaming. "I'll not have another of my ewes die of liver rot!"

"Geese's got as much right at the pond as sheep," Hereswith retorted. "You want to change that, see John Bailley, not me."

"You hear that?" The thatcher's wife turned to Martha the reeve's wife. "You hear the way she talks to me? Am I not a freewoman? Is she not a goosegirl?"

"Th'art a free woman but a loud one," Win observed to his mother out of the side of his mouth. Hawisa snickered. They passed the skirmish by, waving to Martha, who had lifted her voice over the shrieking: "Cold evening, 'Wisa! Bitter wind!"

Win and his mother cut between Jack Thatcher's pig fence and the reeve's big cowbarn. They crossed the village street and went down by the mill to go over Keldabeck on Mucklebridge. Mucklebridge was not muckle, but it was made of stone, and bigger at least than the plank bridge set from bank to bank farther upstream. Beyond the plank bridge, where the beck broke in two, rose the low hump of hill that bedded Old Keep and the Hall.

"Beck looks cold," observed Hawisa. "She has t'look of greywinter now."

"Soon she'll be Icebeck," said Win, and they crossed.

It had rained cold rain all the night before, but the high branches

6

were as dry and brittle as bones. It was as if the wind had whipped out all their dampness. But the moss on the stumps and fallen logs was fat and juicy, and Wisa and Win could hear the rushing of the stream behind them as it ran high and full over round green stones.

Win picked up a stick and threw it at an oak branch. He felled a knot of acorns.

"What are you doing that for?" Hawisa chided him mildly. "Haven't you got enough to do without doing old Hob swineherd's work for him?"

"I like to do it," said Win. "I like to try my aim."

"You've a good eye," said Hawisa. Even the knight had noticed his skill.

Win smiled and stooped to find another stone. His eyes might be sharp, but they were pink around the rims; his hair was pale, almost white, and the lads called him Rabbit, which he hated. Hawisa went to pick up an alder stick lying at her feet. Win said, "I'll go lop those dead branches off that elm behind wolfhead stump. Don't lift anything heavy. Leave it for me and save your back."

Hawisa puttered about. For this short time she was not unhappy. Simon was out of earshot and out of mind. Win's axe echoed like a bell under the grey trees.

They collected as much wood as they could strap on their backs and started home again. When they came to Mucklebridge they could not cross on it, for Cuthbert the constable was on it with the knight's two sons. The three of them sat high on the broad back of Sir Gervase's great warhorse Maccabeus. Flaxheaded William sat before fat Cuth in the saddle, clutching at the reins and beating his little heels against the brawny horse's flanks. Browneyed Nicholas sat behind, quiet, straight backed, looking ahead; William and Cuth leaned sideways, peering down into the clattering beck. Cuthbert looked up. "Even, Wisa, Rabbit. Bitter wind." But he showed no sign of budging, so they had to trudge upstream to the plank bridge and cross there.

"Why couldn't he ford the beck?" Win grumbled. "That tall horse affeared of water?"

"Think he might be more affeared the bridge'd crack under them. I wonder who weighs more, the horse or Cuth Constable?"

Win laughed. They skirted the pond. Hereswith and the shrieking women had gone in, and the common was empty and faded under the leaden sky.

"That little William," Hawisa remarked, "isn't near as fair as you."

They heard Simon singing one of his loud songs inside the cottage, and as they entered they set their faces against him.

Great Maccabeus carried the knight's sons and Cuthbert across the stone bridge and up the track that climbed toward the hall. The big house was at the top of the rise, surrounded by a high wall, and the gate in the wall was open. They rode through. Once within the manorhouse court, Cuth Constable dismounted, with grace for so large a man. He lifted William from the great heights of Maccabeus and set him in the low and muddy regions of the yard. "There you are, Will o' the Wisp," said Cuthbert. He reached up for Nicholas, who ignored his arms. Nicholas would stay on the warhorse as long as he could.

"FAT CUTHBERT!" William bellowed, down below. He tried to hug Cuth around the waist. Then he peered around Cuth's girth with a wild, inquiring look in his eyes and demanded, "What if Maccabeus was a pig and not a horse?"

Cuthbert did not know how to answer such a question. "Well, now," he said helplessly. Then he turned back to Nicholas. "You've got your wish, Master Nicholas, and set your rump on the great black's back, but now it's time to touch your toes to earth."

Nicholas addressed William. "Our father would never ride on a pig."

William nodded. "No, because his feet would drag on the ground. Unless it was a giant pig. A giant pig! A giant pig who did a jig!"

Nicholas looked at him patiently. "Not even a giant pig."

When Nicholas was finally set to earth, he took William by the hand. Nicholas was eight years old and William two years younger, and their mother always said, "Look after your brother when you play, for he is full of mischiefs." Obedient to her now, Nicholas pulled William across the yard. William wanted to squat by a mud puddle to look at wriggling things, but Nicholas hauled him up. "No, no." Not too impatiently, because William regarded him with worship and always did whatever he told him. Nicholas thought that it was good to have a brother, instead of a sister only, especially an older sister who bossed and raged like their sister Katharine. In return for William's fealty Nicholas felt obliged to tolerate and protect him. Katherine sometimes ordered William, "Don't say 'Nickless;' say Nich-O-las. If our father wanted 'Nickless' he wouldn't have put an 'o' in the name." Nicholas would interrupt: "He can call me what he wants."

Nicholas and William climbed the stairs to Old Keep door, which opened into the great hall of their father's house. When they came into the hall, they saw their father standing way down at the other end before the screens, talking loudly to John his bailiff.

"Well, tell the thatcher if he don't pay his mill fee you'll take it out of his barley bags. You know how to get it out of him. Why bother me about it?"

The bailiff scowled. "You asked for news of manor court. You want it, sir, or not?" Since John had been bailiff under Sir Gervase's father and Gervase trusted him to look after his interests, John Bailley could talk to the knight almost any way he wanted. They were of one mind.

"Hell, yes, but take care of that one yourself. What I want to know is what's this gossip about Simon Thornrigg's son doing all his threshing for him the whole month long? Goddam it, how many times do I have to say it? I want that lad's arm saved for shooting this winter. I want him out with Mark Fletcher, not wrecking his elbow with a goddam thrastle." Gervase's face flushed. His rage grew the more he thought about it. "Goddam it to hell! I go out of my way to take him on as an archer when he's only sixteen . . ."

"Fifteen or thereabouts," interrupted the bailley.

"Damn it!" Gervase exploded.

"Aye, aye, aye. Dame Magdalen said as much to Hawisa. But Wisa's a stubborn old sow. Says they'll starve if Win don't thrash. Of course that's tripe. Simon would get off his arse soon enough if the two of them didn't rush out to do his labor every time he hoisted a mug of beer."

Gervase began to reply but interrupted himself because he saw his sons barreling down the hall. Immediately a look of paternal devotion spread over his face. He had the pale hair, red complexion, and cold blue eyes of his Danish ancestors, and it was not easy for him to look benign. Three beings only had this effect on him: occasionally his old friend Ralph Torbeck, sometimes his wife Magdalen, and always his son Nicholas.

"Oho!" Gervase bent his knee and held out his arms. He knew that Nicholas felt too old to be greeted in this manner, but since Gervase had been two months away in service he chose to forget it. Nicholas stopped short of his reach and told him, "I rode Maccabeus today."

William meanwhile lunged into Gervase's arms, shouting "BLACK MACCABEUS! Me and Nickless rode BLACK MACCABEUS!"

"What?" Gervase turned an anxious frown on Nicholas. "By yourself?"

"No, sir, with Cuth. But I could have, by myself."

"No doubt, for you are a valorous fellow." Gervase rested his left hand on William's head and held out his right for Nicholas, who did not come closer.

"I wouldn't tell him that if I were you, Sir Gervase," warned the bailley. "Cuthbert says he loiters in the stables all day long. I wouldn't be surprised if he took it into his head to mount up some day when Cuth's back is turned."

"Na, Nick'll never do that. And do you know why? Because he's a man who keeps his word. Are you not, Nicholas?"

"Yes sir." Nicholas assumed an honorable, noble expression.

"Me!" William said. "Me too." But Gervase set William aside and pulled Nicholas to him, crushing him against his belt and kissing him on the cheek.

The bailley grunted. He did not like it that his master had only two sons and that the little one was already marked for uselessness, at least so far as the manor was concerned. Sir Gervase should not have buckled in to Dame Magdalen on this matter. She was wise in most things but misguided in this, and Sir Gervase could not afford to squander sons, not even for the sake of monkish piety. The matter of their sons was the only one in which the bailley found Dame Magdalen unreasonable and Sir Gervase, well, weak headed.

John glowered at Gervase, who was still squeezing Nicholas against his side and promising him all manner of great things when he went up to be a page at Helmsley not four months from now. John thought: Look at the little one, the Wisp, beaming away like a fool without even the sense to be jealous.

✳ 3

Keldacross
December 1331

Every morning Dame Magdalen took William by the hand and walked him down the hill to St Godrich's to hear mass, for she was a devout lady. Afterward, they would cross the churchyard to Wilfrid priest's, and there she would leave William a while to learn how to be a monk. If the day was fine, he and Wilfrid would sit on benches under the yew by the well; usually they sat inside Wilfrid's house at his big, scarred oaken table. William liked it there except when Wilfrid beat him, but that was rare, for William was quick at lessons. Nicholas came sometimes, but Nicholas was not quick at schoolwork. He stuck out his lip and twitched his elbows and breathed loudly through his nose with the labor of it. Then William would act dull too ("Out of courtesy?" Wilfrid queried), or worse, he would play the fool, pulling clownish faces and making stupid errors. So Wilfrid did not mourn that Nicholas was going soon to live at Helmsley.

"Your elder son is not created for booklearning," Wilfrid told Dame Magdalen. "Yet it appears that the Lord has fit each brother admirably to his own estate."

"Indeed," said Magdalen, pleased. Wilfrid was her cousin, an old man and learned: she thought much of his opinion.

There was one thing Wilfrid taught him that Nicholas did love, and that was stories of the ancient days of Northumbria. He liked King Edwin and pagan Penda, and Oswin and Oswy, and Ella Bretwalda who threw Ragnor the Dane into a pit of serpents. He also liked to hear about Aethelraed Unraed and Alfred of Wessex, except that his sense of justice was offended by the existence of the old Danelaw. "Why did Alfred put the Danemen here in the North, on *us?*" he demanded. "We should not have let him."

Wilfrid was ironic. "Us? We? Who is that? You have a good bit of Danish blood in you, Nicholas, as do most of us in Yorkshire."

"My father's kin were here in these dales before the Dane came. Cuthbert says it."

"And it is so. You may be proud of that. Your mother's kin cannot boast it. Even Lord Henry de Ros cannot boast it."

Nicholas looked astonished. "He can't?"

"No." Then Wilfrid implied that he might tell them tales of the Norman Conqueror who laid the North in smouldering ruins until the rebellion of Hereward the Wake was finally put down. "If," Wilfrid said, "we make sufficient progress in the lesson I have set for you."

"CREDO!" William bellowed. "CREDO IN UNUM DEUM!"

"William, sit silently. Now, Nicholas, repeat it to me."

Nicholas, morosely obedient, knit his brows. "Credo in unum Deum . . ."

"Yes?"

"Pa—pater om—omp . . ."

"Patrem omnipotentem. Begin again."

"Credo in unum Deum, patrem omnipotentem . . ."

William rocked his bench rhythmically as Nicholas struggled through his prayer.

Nicholas halted at "Deum de Deo."

"Lumen de lumine," William whispered, and could not hold it in any longer. "LU-men de LU-mine!" He toppled the bench backward in his enthusiasm and knocked his head on the floor. This enraged Wilfrid, but at least Nicholas was off the hook.

After he had chastised William, Wilfrid let them go; he was too irritated to teach any more. William, redfaced and gulping, tagged after Nicholas. "Ego sum Tostig," he declared, "et quis es?"

"What?" Nicholas refused any dealings with Latin unless Wilfrid forced him. The brothers walked under Godrich's yew and over villein graves to the lychgate. They left the churchyard and stood on the beaten path to Keldabeck.

"I'm treacherous Tostig," said William.

"Why do you want to be *him*?"

"Because he was bad. You be my good brother, Harold Godwinson." That Harold had been the hero of Stamford Bridge, not far distant from Keldacross. He was also the king shot with an arrow on Hastings Field. Nicholas had no desire to be anyone so ill fated. "Race you to Mucklebridge," he said. He added generously: "You start ahead of me."

"HARALD HARDRADA!" William yelled senselessly, rolling out the r's. "ELLA BRETWALDA! RAGNOR LODBOK!"

Nicholas overlooked this. William liked to repeat words and names just to hear the sound of saying them. "Go on," Nicholas urged. "Run to Mucklebridge." He let William start ten paces in advance, and then slowed his own pace so that William would think they had tied. "Now, Adam's mill!" said Nicholas, and they raced again. Keldabeck rushed and tumbled over stones as they ran by her, through hoary trunks of oak and ash, and brown and brittle leaves of alder.

They passed Win Thornrigg as they ran. He was down in the streambed, picking up rocks with chapped fingers for his slingshot. It was said that Win Thornrigg had killed more crows in the village than all the farmers put together since Cain ploughed sod at the beginning of the world.

✳ 4

Keldacross and Helmsley Castle
March 1332

Nicholas did not cry when he left Keldacross for Helmsley to serve Lord Ros. The night before, he was frightened, but it was William who wet the bed. The warm, scratchy feel of it crept across the sheet. "Nickless," William blubbered. "Nickless." And Dame Magdalen had to come in sternly. "You are six years old, William," she reproved him.

Even she could not stop William from howling, crimson faced, next morning when Nicholas was set astride Gervase's palfrey and all his belongings tied onto the mule that Mark Fletcher would lead behind them. When Magdalen went over to kiss him goodbye, William howled even louder. The tears ran down his cheeks in streams and dribbled under his chin. He stood with Joan the falconer's wife on the steps before the great door, and Joan twisted his ear to make him stop bawling. "Hush," she scolded, but his sister Katharine who stood with them said, "Shut up." She was angry at William. "Shut up," she said again, but he didn't even hear her.

Nicholas was vaguely embarrassed by William, but he was too excited to care much. His father mounted behind him and reached his arms around him to take the reins. Nicholas chafed at that because he knew he could ride the palfrey by himself.

"You shall be a Helmsley man next time I see you," Dame Magdalen said, looking up at him. "Now don't forget the manners I taught you. Don't let me be ashamed before Lady Ros when I come to see you."

Nicholas nodded. Dame Magdalen looked him over one more time. His brown eyes were solemn under the brim of his hat, a small copy of his father's green one. It grieved her that they would knock all the sweetness out of him at Helmsley, but she knew there was no help for it. "God bless you, my Nicholas," she told him. "Think of your mother and pray for her as she will pray for you."

He nodded again, but without listening. He kicked the palfrey's flanks so that Gervase had to say, "Whoa! Let me kiss your mother." He leaned sideways to get a peck on the lips. "See you by your nameday, Maudlin," he said. (That was the feast of Mary Magdalene in late July.) "Unless some goddam thing happens."

"God forbid," said Magdalen. She patted him stiffly on the knee of his boot. She was not a woman who liked these farewells, because she felt her own passions in danger of exposure.

At last Gervase slapped his palfrey's reins and nudged him with his heels. They clattered out of the courtyard into the shadow of the gate and into the dull sunlight beyond. Mark Fletcher followed with the mule, and Gib Faulkoner and Cuth Constable pulled the gates shut behind them.

Magdalen turned to face the house—and William bellowing on the steps. Tall, thin, and russet haired, she regarded him with calm grey eyes. "For shame," she said in a grieved voice. "You should be proud that your brother is going to serve Lord Ros. Some day you may be glad of his protection."

"Nooooa!" William roared, his face like a beet, his hands balled up and crammed into his eyes. "I want Nickless!"

"You shall have Nicholas. He will come home perhaps for Christmas, and you'll also no doubt see him one day at Helmsley." Magdalen picked up her skirts and came up to him. "Now stop this weeping. You are far too old to carry on so."

William had to stop, since she was there, standing over him. But when he looked up at her, gulping and sniffling, he knew, even without understanding it, that Nicholas might come back, but Nickless would not, and they would never see him again.

Nicholas forgot about Keldacross almost as soon as he got to Helmsley. He slept in a cot with an older boy, a page named Hugh Cliderhou of Eskmere. Nicholas had always been the older boy. Now he was the younger, and Hugh filled him with awe, admiration—and some undefined uneasiness. In the morning Gervase came and took him to Lord Ros, who let him try to lift his iron broadsword off the floor and smacked him in the rear when he fell backward doing so. "Keep at it, boy," Lord Ros said, pinching Nicholas' thin arm between thumb and forefinger. "There's the making of muscle here."

Gervase glowed. "Aye," he said. "He's a charger, is this one."

The lord of Helmsley stood six feet tall. He had cropped brown hair, a short brown beard, and sharp blue eyes that squinted. He valued his vassal Gervase highly. Lord Ros also liked Dame Magdalen. He considered her admirable, though she was the daughter and the wife of plain knights only. "Tell you what, fellow," he said now, addressing Nicholas. "This is what we do at Helmsley. First time you can lift your sword and swing it, I tell your father, and he's obliged to ask me for a present for you. Your own choice: within reason, of course." He raised a brow at Gervase, who winked at Nicholas.

"Aye, he'll make his father proud, and his mother too," said Gervase, "or I'll know the reason why."

Gervase watched his son disappear through the doorway, following Hugh Cliderhou. He had to clear his throat twice before speaking. "Walt Cliderhou's boy has grown up fast. We'll see him squiring before long."

"Aye, and then he's leaving my service for my Uncle Godfrey's." Gervase looked surprised.

"At my lady's request," the lord explained dryly. "She dislikes Hugh—says his manners are low."

Gervase grunted. "Well, his father's a rough character. Maudlin don't like to give him hospitality."

Lord Ros smiled. "Never bien-aimés among the ladies, the Clider-hous. But the family have always been fine warriors. In any case, my lady will be pleased to have had a lad like your Nicholas about her. Proud, courteous fellow, isn't he? The mark of his mother is strong in him."

Gervase coughed. Lord Ros added, "No doubt he'll show his father's prowess in due time."

In a small chamber adjoining the hall, Hugh Cliderhou stopped, turned, and regarded Nicholas speculatively. The expectant baby face provoked him somehow, and an amusing thought struck him. He gestured toward a tall man plainly dressed in brown and engaged in conversation. "See that steward over there?" he asked Nicholas. "It is custom here for such a man to fetch guests a cup of wine. Go tell him your father is in the hall and requires a cup."

Nicholas' face lit. He would show how well he could serve! Glancing once over his shoulder at Hugh's encouraging face, he marched up to the man with an air of command. "My father, Sir Gervase of Kelda, is in the hall with your master. Pray go quickly and fetch him a cup of wine."

The plain brown man turned and, with an expressionless face, whacked Nicholas hard across the chest. Nicholas fell back against the wall, gasping. The brown man's companion guffawed. Nicholas looked wildly around for Hugh: the brown man turned casually back to his conversation. Hugh was nowhere to be seen.

Shrinking against the wall, Nicholas turned hot, then cold, then hot again. It was suddenly and terribly plain to him that the brown man was some great baron, and that Hugh had for some reason done this to make him look like a clown. He thought of running back to his father, but no, the lord would see him; the lord would know that the boy Hugh Cliderhou had made Nicholas look like a clown.

Nicholas hated Hugh, but he did not know where to go without him, so he stood rigidly against the wall while the noblemen ignored him. He wished and wished that his father would come. But what if the brown nobleman were to say to Gervase, "Is this your son? He is insolent," and his father were ashamed of him.

At length the noblemen went away. Still Nicholas stood against the wall. Despair held him motionless; it seemed as if long hours passed. He almost wept. But what if someone saw him weeping? The tears were about to come in spite of him; but then great, beefy laughter sounded outside, and Nicholas' heart leapt at the familiarity of it. A burly man lumbered into the room. It was Gervase's great friend Ralph Torbeck.

But he did not see Nicholas! He was walking by him, without

noticing him, and Nicholas was ashamed to call out in case it was not done at Helmsley for a page to call out to a knight. But fear whelmed over him as Sir Ralph's back receded into the hall. He choked out, "I'm Nicholas!"

Sir Ralph turned, peered, and spotted him. He came back exclaiming, "Why! It's my friend Nicko!" He squatted, bulky, in front of Nicholas. "What are you doing here all alone, Nicko, eh? Eh? What's wrong, lad?"

Nicholas's face went crooked, and he said, "Hugh Cliderhou went away."

"He did, did he?" Sir Ralph squinted in kindly consternation. "Well," he said at last, "I'm damned if I can't find you a better friend than that! Guess who I've brought up with me on purpose the very week you've come up to Helmsley with your father?"

"Rabbie?" Sir Ralph's only living son, of an age with Nicholas.

"You've guessed it, but you must call him Rab from this day forward. You and he are Helmsley men now." Sir Ralph laid his big hand on Nicholas' shoulder and took him away from the place of his humiliation.

Outside in the bailey they found sturdy, beaming Rab Torbeck. As soon as he saw Nicholas he braced his feet, stuck out his chest, and demanded, "Punch my belly. It's hard as rock."

Nicholas obliged him, and then Rab obliged Nicholas in the same way. He waggled his fist and blew in his knuckles. "Aye, yours too. Hard as a rock."

"I hate this boy named Hugh Cliderhou," Nicholas informed him, and Rab said, "So do I," although he had never yet seen Hugh Cliderhou.

Sir Ralph swatted them on their backsides and left them in the care of a tolerant squire, who showed them the stables and the lord's destriers and many other great things. For the rest of the morning Nicholas was happy and forgot Hugh Cliderhou.

That afternoon Sir Gervase and Sir Ralph were riding away to meet the lord's Uncle Godfrey up Durham way, where there had been some small trouble with Scots. Gervase's heart was heavy at leaving Nicholas, and he wanted to say goodbye, but Nicholas could not be found. After Gervase had gone, the lord's eldest daughter found him, with Rab, up on the barbican turrets. They were yelling, spitting, and dropping stones.

"You! Nicholas of Kelda!" the lady cried, shading her eyes. "Your father wanted to take leave of you, but now he is already gone. Come down."

Her name was Lady Ursula de Ros; she was twelve years old and imposing, but Nicholas ignored her, and so was cuffed about by her when he at last did come down. But that was not so bad, because afterward he got to ride with Rab at the pages' swinging quintain, the post and target at which they learned to ride and tilt.

But the night was different. Then, sharing a blanket with Hugh Cliderhou, it finally came to Nicholas that his father was really gone, and not only his father but even Sir Ralph also. And they would not let him sleep with Rab; Rab, too, had to sleep with an older boy. Hugh's breath was hot in the dark against Nicholas's ear. "If you cry for your mam I'll knock you out of bed."

So Nicholas lay motionless in the dark, listening to Hugh's slow sleepbreathing and hoping desperately that he would not wake.

Nicholas himself dared not close his eyes. Whenever they closed of their own accord, he saw one of the dogs at Kelda whom he specially loved, and his chest tightened and his throat ached painfully. He tried not to think of the dog. He clenched his teeth and balled his fists to keep back his breath, but in the end three loud squeaking gasps burst out. More followed. The harder he tried to keep them in, the louder they burst out, and finally, inevitably, he felt Hugh stir, and the hot breath in his ear:

"Crying for your mammy? Does mammy love her perfect little Nicky?"

Back at Keldacross Katharine said to William, her eyes narrowed, "Now you have to follow *me* and do what *I* say." Unhappily, Katharine resembled her mother's kin in looks and not her father's. Her face was blotched with freckles, her eyes pale and set too wide, her hair red and rough. Her nose was straight, and her mouth would be well enough, Dame Magdalen told her, if she did not always keep it puckered in a rage. Katharine was often in a rage.

"You must do what I tell you," she informed William. "If I want to play siege, you must play siege. If I want to shoot targets, you must shoot targets. If I want to ride out, you must ride out. If our mother will let us."

"Aye," said William, beaming with rosy face and round, agreeable eyes.

Katharine stared at him, taken aback, somewhat disappointed at her easy victory. She had expected some kind of resistance. "What*ever* I say you have to do," she repeated. "What*ever* I say." William was foolish. He believed every stupid story the villeins told him. He fell into wells. At mass, when he should be silent, he sang at the top of his lungs. "Saecula saeculoooorum," he would chant through his nose like Wilfrid priest, grinning at Katharine. "Shut your mouth," she would hiss when he did that.

"Whatever I say," she said now.

"Aye," William roared, jumping up and down. "Say cuLORum, Katie is a WHORum!"

Katharine shouted, "You white head pimple! You don't even know what that means. You runaway coward!"

She shouted this last because he was rushing out of the room to take refuge behind their mother, who would protect him, as usual, because she loved him best. Anyone could see that. She turned from her loom. "Oh, William, what's amiss?"

"Katharine's chasing me."

"Children, don't vex each other," Magdalen said firmly. But of course she reached out to touch William's hair.

✳ 5

Keldacross
December 1332

On the fourth Wednesday of Advent Wilfrid made William put his pen down early. "You have done well, William." He scanned the work. "I am pleased."

William beamed. His mouth was rimmed with ink. He enjoyed sucking on pens.

"I am ending our lessons early today, because it is almost Christmas, and I remember how boys are at Christmastime."

"I am going to eat and eat until I am fatter than Cuth Constable," said William, "and my father might give me a brown pony."

"It will not be happy for the pony if you are fatter than Cuth Constable," Wilfrid replied. "Before I dismiss you, William, tell me. Have you practiced those antiphons I've been teaching you all Advent long? Can you sing them to me in full?" William had certainly practiced them, loudly and interminably, in every part of the manor house.

"Yes, Wilfrid priest."

"Then do so."

The Seven O's. William loved them. He loved the way the words rolled off his tongue. He began straightaway.

"O sapientia, quae ex ore Altissimi prodiisti, O Wisdom, that comest out of the mouth of the Most High . . . O Adonai et dux domus Israel,

18

qui Moysi in igne flammae rubi apparuisti, O Adonai and ruler of the house of Israel, who appeared to Moses in the flame of the burning bush . . . "

"Wait," Wilfrid said. He went over to his bed, behind which, on the wall, hung a nine-stringed psaltery. Lovingly Wilfrid brought it down. He smiled at the psaltery and then at William. "Now! Let's try that again. I shall play five tones below you; that is called organum. I don't know whether the white monks will tinker with such things at Rievaulx. According to Rule, they ought not, but simplicity means nothing to them nowadays. In any event, there is no harm enjoying ourselves here. Come, William, sing. Canta mihi."

O Radix; O Clavis; O Oriens, O Root; O Key; O Dayspring. William did them all without error, and Wilfrid lifted his old deep voice and sang with him. Wilfrid was unaccountably merry this morning. His fingers plucked the psaltery strings, and once he even winked at William as they sang. "Veni et illumina sedentes in tenebris et umbra mortis, Come illumine them that sit in darkness and in the shadow of death."

Wilfrid did not tell William that a surprise awaited him up at the house, but Cuth Constable was standing watch at the gate as William came toiling up the hill. "What think you, Master Wisp?" he bellowed down at the skinny, red faced little fellow who ran up to him, muffled in scarves. "Your brother's home for Christmas!" William was so overjoyed that he punched Cuth in the stomach before rushing into the court. There was his father in his battered green hat and thick brown cloak, and Nicholas standing by him all in russet with Lord Ros' colours on his sleeve. William ran across the yard. "Nickless!" he cried. He slipped on a slimy place on the cobbles and had to scramble up out of the mud. Nicholas, embarrassed, turned away coldly and asked Gervase, "Is that a new mare Wat's leading?"

In the hall Nicholas stood about with Katharine and told her all about Helmsley, about Lord Ros' Uncle Godfrey with his face so scarred he could barely raise three hairs on it, and how Ingram Tarn of Tunnersgil knocked a smith's head against an anvil because he'd shod his horse wrong, and how their cousin Mun Wydclif who'd come up to the castle last Easter always got unhorsed at the quint but Nicholas never did. Finally Katharine went out to fetch the sparrowhawk her godmother had given her last Easter, and William, taking the opportunity, approached Nicholas reverently with a bit of parchment. "This is for you, Nickless."

Nicholas looked, but did not take. "What is it?"

"It's a writing I did for you." William stepped back a little. "Wilfrid priest says I do right well."

19

"So?" Nicholas turned to watch Katharine come in with her hawk. "God's death!" he exclaimed, manly, father-like. "There's a beauty, that is." He went to stroke the bird. "When do I get my own hawk?"

"His name's Dart," Katharine told him. "Do you want to see me fly him?"

"Sure enough!" The two of them left the hall together. William stood holding his parchment, looking after them.

Nicholas est frater meus
Est puer in Helmsley
Erit miles grandissimus et fortissimus in Tewisdale
Et sum frater eius Gulielmus

Nicholas is my brother. He is a page at Helmsley. He will be the biggest, strongest knight in Tewisdale. And I am his brother William. There was a picture in the margin of a tall knight on a horse with overlarge feet, and a squiggly little boy figure below, with arms outstretched, admiring.

✳ 6

Keldacross
June 1333

June again. They were mowing the meadow down by Keldabeck. Sir Gervase stood on the spur of the fell they called the Knee, watching. John Bailey stood by, thumbs tucked in his belt. They breathed in the grassy smell of haying and smiled, as if they had brought about the sweet sun and mild air by their own special munificence. The scythes flashed in the meadow. Hawisa Thornrigg's big rough voice lifted to them on the breeze. She was singing to the mowers, to keep up the swing of their arms.

"Good June weather, Sir Gervase," said the bailley. "No spoilt hay this year."

Gervase nodded.

"Good building weather too," the bailley added. "Those York glaziers should finish the windows in the solar before long."

"If those bastards aren't finished with those windows before I'm down to Helmsley," said Gervase, "I'll bury them alive in the moor."

"Maiden on the moor-e lay," sang Hawisa.

"Maiden on the moor-e lay," sang the mowers.

"Maiden on the moor-e lay," sang Hawisa, "seven nicht fulle."

"Speaking of York," said the bailley, "what of the woolmerchant? Before we know it it'll be shearing time."

"He'd better give us a better price than he gave us last year," Gervase replied. "Last year he as good as had our wool as gift, and we can't afford to hand him gifts."

"It's all this uncertainty about the Staple. If the king would quit changing his mind about trading with the Low Countries, the merchants might be surer of profit and buy the wool higher."

"Ah," said Gervase dismissively. "Moneymen. They're all cheats and thieves." He swung around and started back to the hall in his odd, abrupt stride. Walking, not riding, was second nature to him.

"Well was her drink-e," sang Hawisa.

"What was her drink-e?" sang the mowers.

"Well was her drink-e, seven nicht fulle."

John took leave of his master and went down into the hayfield. "See it done well, Thomas Reeve," he called, over the singing.

✳ 7

The City of York
July 1333

Alice Eycot hated the bailiff of Keldacross. "Nasty, grasping old villein," she said. "Though he gives himself such airs." She knew all about that kind. Her father was one of them—a crusty old freeman who'd made his way to York from the wold twenty odd years ago. Alice hated him too. But since her master Andrew Comyn the stapler was the busy merchant he was, there was always a great coming and going of bailiffs and stewards and such, along with the woolsacks from the abbeys and manors. Alice watched them with disgust, served them with bad grace, and railed at them behind their backs, before the other maidservants. She had heard plenty about the manors from her father and had to admire the old fart for squeezing his way out when he could. "As my old sire always says," she told the kitchen, " 'City air stinks; but it's free.' "

She was a fierce one, was Alice. She was never happier than when shoving her way down a jostling street, screaming over her shoulder at scrawny prentices, or haggling mercilessly with crow voiced goodwives.

21

Furiously she struggled in the Shambles for a good rib of beef or leg of mutton for her mistress. Awful was her black brow as she battled, deadly her elbows, terrible her tongue. All the journeymen in York knew and avoided her. Master Comyn said that she was as brawny as a boy, so he let his little Marion go along with her to gaze in wonder at all the shops and booths in Goodramgate, or to watch the holy plays on the Minster porch. One day they had watched the demons tumbling and leaping on the stage before Our Good Lord came to bind them in hell, and Marion had laughed and clapped, but afterward she asked Alice with knit brows, "Poor demons, did they have to stay in hell forever?"

Alice was Marion Comyn's own special maidservant, and Marion was Andrew Comyn's only child. He had remarried soon after Marion's mother died, but his new wife Alison was barren and showed no sign of approaching death. So Marion, please God, would be a rich woman some day. Marion was a sweet bairn, a browneyed darling who scarcely gave a soul a moment's trouble. Alice Eycot loved her almost as much as she loved York itself, its shops, its crooked streets, its clatter and noise, its smell, its air.

Alice and Marion happened to be in Petergate when a party of men who had set out against the Scots last month returned through Bootham bar, with prisoners. There was a sound of horns and hooves, and everyone in the street had to duck away into stalls and houses.

"See those?" Alice lifted Marion up by the armpits so that she could see over the counter they had scuttled behind. "Those are Scots."

Prentices were hissing and catcalling and throwing clots of gutter-muck at the prisoners.

"You may thank God and St Mary that we have such a fine strong chivalry to save us from those beasts," said a clerc who had packed into the goldsmith's stall with them. "For they would not stick at taking a little maid like you and tossing her on their lances, or dashing her head against a stone, or splitting her down the middle like a pig."

"Me," said the goldsmith, "I'd as soon spit a Scot as spit *on* him. That's what I say. Did you hear what they did in Ripon? How they tore babies out of their living mothers' wombs? How they drew the wakeman's guts out through his nostrils? St Mary, they're worse than the Dane ever was."

"Na," said a fellow beside them. "That's lies. I'm of Ripon, and none of what you say is true. All that happened was . . . "

The goldsmith scowled him into silence. "All I say is that I'd as soon spit a Scot as look at him. That's what I say."

"I heard tell of a manor up in the Bishopric," said Alice, "where the Scots came by night and burnt the place to black ashes: village and fields and church and house. And raped all the women, were they never so young as this little maid here, and hacked up all the men and boys. And that rather than look on her son being cut up alive, the lady of the manor tore out her eyes—her very eyes, right out of her own skull; that's what I heard."

Marion listened hard. A sick feeling grew in her stomach. "But that won't happen in York, will it, Alice?"

The goldsmith shook his head. "Only by the grace of God are we kept safe."

"And by the might of the Chivalry of the North," added the clerc. "My very own brothers lost their lives at Bannockburn, and John but newly belted. Ai, how we wept."

"Aye," agreed the goldsmith forebodingly. "Bannockburn."

Then the street was clear, and Alice and Marion could go home.

"Listen." The Ripon fellow began again. "What you heard about Ripon was false. Only six men lost their lives, for it was only a piddling raid, and . . ."

"Have you had a chance to look at my wares?" said the goldsmith to Alice. "You'll not see finer craftsmanship in all the city. Why, I'm making a great chalice for the archbishop himself this very month, I am."

" . . . the wakeman is hale and hearty, and all the aldermen as well."

"Master," said Alice, "I am only a maidservant and cannot buy no rich cup."

"Well, speak to your mistress about it. Tell her I'm making a chalice for the archbishop himself."

" . . . and there weren't no babes torn from no wombs, neither."

"I might, I might," said Alice. "Come along, pudding pie." She tugged on Marion, who was still staring in horror down the street where the Scots had passed.

"Now you take heed of all that was said," Alice warned as they went back up Goodramgate. "You keep apraying your hardest, morning, noon and night, that the Scots don't get in, for if they do, that's the end of us. You think they'll take pity on you because you're a bonny wee bairn, and rich? Ha! It'll be all the worse for you."

For many weeks after that day Marion passed her nights in sweaty terror.

Once she woke from a dream of fire and gaunt, staggering figures, and she sat up screaming. Mistress Alison came in with her hair hanging all witchy about her face. Marion took one look and cowered back in her bed against the wall, gibbering. For it seemed that Mistress Alison had no eyes.

23

"There, there! Darling, curdie pie!" Mistress Alison sat down on the bed. "What's amiss? It's only your very own stepmother. Sweetheart, you were dreaming."

"Scots!" Marion sobbed. "Scots might come!"

"Scots? Now how should Scots get into York with all the stout wall around us, and the bars with their barbicans and portcullises, and our brave men, and the castle and the minster church here as well? No, only be a good girl, and you'll have nowt to fear from any Scot, nor any other man neither." And after kissing and cuddling, Mistress Alison went back to bed.

If only you are a good girl.

Marion thought of the picture of the flaming city in the big Book at Holy Trinity, and the poem parson John had once read her:

Also in the days of Lot befelle
Men ete and drank, shortly to tell,
Married with each other, solde and boght
And planted and begetted and houses wroght.

"If God could have found but ten good folks in that city," Parson John had told her, explaining the picture, "He would have spared it for their sake."

"Lord Jesu!" Marion prayed feverishly, shaking in her bed.

Jhesu at thy wille I pray that I might be;
That I have don ill, Jhesu forgive thou me.

That was a prayer of Master Richard the hermit that Parson John had taught her. Master Richard was a good man. He lived in the woods all alone, and prayed for the world day in and day out, never ceasing. That is what Parson John said.

✳ 8

Keldacross
July 1333

William was terribly ill, lying in the small bare sickroom in Old Keep, whimpering for his mother. His eyes burned in their sockets. He could see them in his mind, red coals in black smokepits. Then he would scream, "Mother, Mother!" Or he would think he had screamed it, but no one heard.

This had been going on for three days. Dame Magdalen would stay with him as long as she could bear it and then run downstairs to see to the maidservants' mending and cleaning, or do anything that would blot out the image of her suffering child. Neither Hawisa Thornrigg, who was handy with cures, nor Wilfrid priest, who had read some Galen, could do anything about it. At last Magdalen would collect herself and run upstairs again, sick with dread. She would dip long linen cloths in bowls of God-richwater and lay them on William's cheeks and forehead. Mother of God, it was as if she could hear them sizzle he was so hot. Then he would say something she could not understand, and she would lean her ear to him and say, "Yes, love?" And he would say, "There's knives in my throat." Then she would run downstairs again, covering her mouth with her hands.

Her mother Emma was visiting from her home at Wherne in Cov-erdale. She was on her way home from watching Magdalen's fourth brother, Roger, be priested in York. She had hoped for a happy visit at Keldacross, for she had not seen Magdalen for some time. But the visit was a disappointment, because her daughter, usually so tough, was puling like a milkmaid over the child.

"I thought I raised you up a gentlewoman, not some frantic fishwife," she barked, when Magdalen sat down and sobbed in the solar. She was sobbing because Wilfrid had just gone up Old Keep stairs wearing his stole and carrying the sacrament.

"I am amazed at you, Maudlin," Dame Emma continued. "This is not like you. Look, girl, you know as well as I do. Children come and children go. God gives 'em and takes 'em at will, and there's nothing we can do about it. I lost four of my own, not counting the miscarried ones. So sit up and for God's sake stop pitying yourself."

Magdalen did sit up. She was ashamed before her mother, but she could not stop pitying herself. "That is well enough for you to say. You had your ten. I have but three, and I'll not be having any more, that's plain. And it's *this* one." She wept into her hands. "It's *this* one."

"Maudlin," Dame Emma said, "I am ashamed. I am tempted to ride for Coverdale straightaway."

Magdalen sat straight again. "Oh no, Mother, please. Don't leave me."

But William did not die. Wilfrid priest sat by the bed, holding William's small hands between his long ones. He stood up, smiling, when Magdalen came in.

"Deo gratias," he said. "The fever's broken. The body of Christ is the best medicine of all."

25

"Oh," she gasped. And she had to lean against the wall.

The next day William was well enough to sit up against the bolster and eat clear mutton broth. Magdalen tried to feed it to him, but he said, "No! I'm not a baby," and set the bowl on his knees and fed himself. But his spoon wobbled, and she leaned forward to wipe his chin with her napkin. He grinned at her. "If I died," he said, "would you cut off all your hair?"

The following day Katharine was admitted to the sickroom.

"If I had died," William told her, "you and our mother and our grandmother and all the women of the village would have cut off your hair and rolled in ashes."

"The hell I would," said Katharine.

"God did not want you with him yet, William," said Dame Magdalen. "He wanted you to be here, to do good things for him in this world."

"Na," said Katharine, glowering. "If he'd've died, he'd've gone straight to Satan."

Magdalen sent her a pale, fell look. Katharine withered. William smirked and said, "Aye. Because I'm bloated with Pride and Self-love, that's why." He made a sickening sweet drooly face at their mother. She clutched him to her. "Oh, my little William."

Katharine stormed out of the room. Who loved her? No one loved her.

She met her grandmother on the stairs. "Is the mewling and sopping still going on?" Dame Emma demanded.

Katharine nodded, admiration for her grandmother swelling within her.

"God's Body," Dame Emma swore. "God's Blood. Enough is enough."

✳ 9

York
August 1333

Marion Comyn was called before Alison her stepmother in the master bedchamber because Master Comyn was conducting great wool business today, and she must know how to behave.

"Your father is meeting with the masters in the hall," Mistress Alison informed her. "So you stay away from there and don't bother them. I will send you to Mistress Whewell's. You may play with Cis and Agnes all morning, but don't come wandering into the house." She appointed Alice to usher Marion across the lane to the Whewells'.

Alice led Marion up the Whewells' steps and knocked on their door, but she left right away before anyone answered. She had some disagreeable chores she wanted to get out of the way, and besides, she had no reason to think the door would not be answered. Mistress Comyn and Mistress Whewell had arranged for Marion's visit early in the day. "Be good, curdie pie," Alice said, and hastened back to her master's house to strip the beds.

Marion stood on the step for what seemed a long time. Nobody came to answer the door. Marion heard people moving and talking in the recesses of the house, but she was too shy to knock again herself. What if they really didn't want her and hoped that she would go away?

She turned and faced her father's house. Two great masters in fur trimmed gowns were just arriving. Marion felt hot to imagine what they would think if they turned around and saw her: Who is that silly looking girl? But the masters did not look around or see her. They climbed up to Andrew's great wide door and were welcomed into the house.

A few moments later Marion saw thin Adam Scawe hurrying out the door. Adam served Andrew Comyn as an accountant and a personal man-servant rolled into one; right now he had in his hand a ring of Andrew's keys that jingled against his knee as he ran down the steps two at a time. Marion watched him go round to the ironbound door of Andrew's store-room, a dark place sunk below the level of the street. Adam rattled the keys in the heavy iron padlock. A notion entered Marion's head.

"I am magic Queen Lilliflour," she said aloud. "I am looking for my bright-thimble-full-of-song that the witches stole from me. I have to go down into the deep dungeonhouse to find it."

Adam swung the storeroom door open and went down into the darkness, leaving the door ajar. Vaguely, Marion picked up her skirts, climbed down the Whewells' steps, and crossed the cobbles. She peeked round the doorway into the dungeon. The Keeper must not see her.

Adam had his back to her, so she tiptoed down the shallow steps leading to the cold stone floor. The cellar was a perfect prison with its small barred window and moldy darkness. Lumpy shapes of woolsacks hulked from racks under the low vaulting. Marion stepped behind a pillar. She watched Adam, half believing he was an ogre. Adam had a kindly smile (even though he was missing half his teeth) and he was always nice to her, but now he was the monstrous Keeper of the Evil Dungeon. He took a small book from his belt and began to flip the pages with moistened thumb. He kept glancing up from the book to a particular rack of woolsacks, then down at the little book again, nodding to himself and muttering.

Those are the bones of all the people he has eaten in this prison. A deliciously horrible thrill ran through Marion's body. She chanted under her breath, "Bricht thimbel ful of songe, Come by me, do not be long!" Bright Thimble would make an enchanted light and drive the Keeper away.

Suddenly the Keeper swung round and looked as if he were staring at her, right through the pillar! She pulled her chin down to her chest and scrunched herself as little as she could. Her heart pounded in her throat when the Keeper stopped right before her hiding place and stood there for a long time. She could not imagine what he was doing. She shivered.

But in the next moment real horror overtook her, because Adam quickly strode off and ran up the shallow steps. Before she could think, he had slammed the door and clicked the padlock behind him.

She was locked in her father's cellar.

At first she was too shocked to do anything. Then she leaped up, screaming, "No, no! Adam! Adam!" She plunged toward the door, treading on her hems, and threw herself against the studded boards. "Adam! Adam! Let me out, oh let me out!"

Frantic with terror of the dank darkness behind her, she burst into tears. She beat her fists against the door. "Adam, Adam, ADAM!" Then: "Mother, I want my mother."

The door opened outward, and Marion fell into Adam's arms.

"Did you think Adam would leave you in there when you called to him?" he told her, sitting down on his haunches to dry her eyes with his sleeve. "Silly lass and bad lass for creeping in there like a thief. Why didn't you tell me you were there?"

Marion could not possibly tell him about Lilliflour and the monstrous Keeper of the Bones.

Adam led her back to the Whewells' house. He knocked loud and hard on the door and waited till a manservant answered.

"Mistress Marion is here to pay her call on Mistress Agnes," he said formally, winking at the Whewells' man.

It wasn't long before Marion was happily playing Magic queens with Agnes, running in and out of the Whewells' chambers and out into the close and back again. Agnes was cross with Cecily Noye who lived at the end of the close, and since Agnes was the one who always said what to do, Marion had to act cross with Cis too. Marion's heart hurt for Cis when she stuck her sad, peaky face over her mother's garden wall, but she was too timid to go against Agnes.

Andrew Comyn heard the voices in the lane and got up, stretching, from his guests and his account book. He went to the window looking out on the narrow courtyard where he and two other staple merchants had their houses. Fine houses they were, built of oak and plaster and stone. Andrew had made the plasterer mould a row of sheep and scales over the door that faced Goodramgate ("Which cost no piddling sum, let me tell you"). Andrew's house had no fewer than five glazed windows, through whose thickness glowed the rosy light of fires on crisp evenings, or the faint yellow of a candle before it was snuffed out for bed. Matthew Whewell and Thomas Noye had not so much glass. Their grandfathers had built their houses in the days before there were so many comforts for mere woolsellers; Andrew had built his own house, during more comfortable times.

Two little girls were telling secrets in the lane. Andrew rubbed his beard, smiling. Agnes Whewell was whispering in his daughter's ear, pulling Marion's dark head to her own fair one. Cecily Noye must be in disfavor today. "Close as coneys," his wife Alison always said, "and quarrelsome as squirrels."

Agnes let go Marion's neck, and they both went scurrying out of sight under the gable that was Andrew's counting room.

"Cissy Noye is a weasel!" rose shrilly from below. "She can't be Lilliflour, and *I'm* Queen Philippa!"

An invisible child answered from across the lane. "Do I care? Do I lose? Drown your baby in the Ouse!"

Andrew watched a great, silver rimmed cloud come sailing over the wet rooftops and sail away again. Puddles in the cobbles shone up blue at the watery sky, a gable or two shimmering in their shallows. Matthew Whewell's bedroom shutters rattled, then flew open. Mistress Whewell looked out to take the air. She caught sight of Andrew and nodded cheerfully. Andrew raised his hand.

"Don't you work too hard, Andrew."

"Ai, Edith, don't you count on that."

"Pooh!" said she, "menfolk. Always with your noses in your ledgers." Then she disappeared into the house.

Andrew turned back to his guests. Matthew Whewell drummed his fingers on the table. Jack Comyn said, "Well, brother, what say you?" Andrew went slowly to the table. He peered at the lines and scores and neat black script in the thick, leather bound account book, feeling his brother's impatience and enjoying it. He ran his finger down a column, frowning. "What's this? Oh. Aye. Keldacross. Good fat sheep and good thick wool up there, and lots of it."

Jack made a loud, impatient sigh. Adam Scawe came in with a basket of white cheese and Alison's wheat bread. Marion tagged behind, peeking round the doorway at the masters and ducking back when Master Noye winked at her. Andrew saw, and summoned her. "Sweetheart," he said, "come in."

She obeyed shyly, eyes on the floor, sucking on one of her braids. Andrew held out his arms, and she went to be enveloped in the rich broad folds of his dark gown.

"Sweet lass, bonny lass," the guests chanted dutifully.

"Sweetheart," said Andrew Comyn, "show the masters what you can do."

Marion took the quill he held out for her and looked round at her Uncle Jack, who stood with his arms folded, grinning. She did not know that the grin came from fretfulness and boredom, so she smiled back and bent her head over the parchment her father had laid out for her. The others who had come to confer with Andrew grinned the same grin as Jack Comyn, and played with the ends of their sleeves or slid their cups from one hand to the other on the table. Marion chewed on her upper lip and bore down on her pen, scattering ink. Laboriously she scrawled out her name: Marion Comyn, then slid the paper to her father. He held it up so that they could all see.

"Clever lass, bonny lass," they chanted, nodding.

She blushed harder and stuffed the ends of both her plaits into her mouth. Andrew pulled her close and kissed the top of her head. "This lass of mine," he said, "is a bright treasure."

"Yes, yes," muttered Jack Comyn, his impatience growing. "That she surely is. Now tell us. Will you go down to Hull for us or not? And if not, why not?"

Andrew pushed Marion gently away. "Go find your stepmother, sweetheart. Go tell her we want some more wine."

Marion ran out of the room. Andrew gazed after her. "A treasure," he repeated.

"Brother!" Jack exploded, bringing his cup down hard on the table. A treasure she certainly was. All the merchants in York speculated over their beer on her dowry. Andrew would never say a word on it. As always, he bided his time. As always, he would decide, when he did decide, to his own great advantage.

"Hmmmm?" said Andrew, smiling sweetly. Aye, thought his brother, behind that sweet smile a grip on profits like a vise.

Marion ran into the kitchen garden, where Mistress Alison was directing the planting of a new bed of herbs. "Stepmother! I wrote my name for all the masters!"

"Did you?" Alison replied abruptly. "Martin Eycot, watch out! You need not plant your foot in the middle of the sage."

"Yes, Stepmother, and they said it was the best thing they ever saw. They said I wrote like a queen, or a lady." For the length of the moment she said it, it seemed the truth.

Alison said, "I wish we had a bank. Rosemary grows best on a bank." She turned to Marion. "Well then," she said, "the lady of Goodramgate surely has a dirty face. And her hair is falling out of her plaits." She scrutinized Marion. Marion shifted uncomfortably and dropped her eyes. She thought Mistress Alison was finding out the untruth. "Stepmother," she said hastily, "my father sent me to tell you they want more wine."

"Why me? Why not Adam? Is he not there? Am I to be in all parts of the house at once?" Alison was in a foul mood; it was her time of the month. She glared at Marion. "Well! Don't stand there gaping. Find Adam Scawe and tell him to hop to work." She turned back to Martin Eycot. "No, no! You're planting them too close! Marry, I know not why I don't do everything myself." She dropped to her knees in the hoed mud. "Here! Give it to me." Martin handed her the trowel and sat back on his haunches, rolling his eyes up at the sky. *Let* her get down in the mud then.

Alison glared over her shoulder. "Well? What are you gawping for? Do as I say."

Marion went back into the house. "It's not my fault," she whispered. "Not my fault." Adam was not in the kitchen nor in the big hall, nor anywhere she looked. Her father would think she had forgotten; he would be angry. She had better go up there now and tell him that she hadn't forgotten but that Mistress Alison wouldn't do it. But Alice Eycot was coming down the stairs under a great bulk of dirty linens, followed by Nan, with a basket, and they took up the whole stair. Something trailed off the top of Alice's load and tripped her. She lurched, shrieking "St William!" and sat backward on her rump. The laundry tumbled over the stairs and onto the floor. "Damn the stinking things!" Alice cursed. "The rotten, lousy bastards!" Nan sniggered behind her.

"Alice," said Marion, "have you seen Adam Scawe?"

Alice stood up, rubbing her hindquarters. "He's in serving the masters. Where else should he be?"

"Oh," said Marion vaguely. She made toward the stairs.

"Well don't tread all over the laundry!" Marion halted. Alice swung round on Nan. "Shut up your snorting and help me gather up this dungy

31

stuff again." She glowered as Marion attempted to squeeze by. "What are you up to?"

"I'm up to tell my father summat."

"Oh no you're not, not with a face like that! What've you been playing at? Swineherd's daughter? Here," she said to Nan. "You muck about with that lousy stuff. I'm going to take this bairn into the kitchen and scrub her good."

"Oh aye," said Nan. "Anything to get out of washing sheets."

"Just wait a little, can't you?" Alice flung back at Nan. She yanked Marion into the kitchen and stood her on a stool. She dipped into a bucket of water and scrubbed the child's face with a harsh cloth. "What in the name of Beelzie's pig is this black spot all over your chin? Ink? I can't budge it."

"Ow! ow!" Marion wept. "Stop! It hurts! It's not my fault!"

✳ 10

Keldacross
September 1334

Wat the cottar trudged in the drizzle, harrowing Sir Gervase's strips, the only strips he had to harrow, for he had none of his own. He plodded along before the harrow with a goad and one of Sir Gervase's brown oxen. His son Gabriel ran about with a slingshot to keep off the crows. The rain turned from drizzle to downpour, but still Wat trudged on, sullen, for fear of the reeve. Them as had their own strips, them as had their own oxen, they could scuttle off under a tree if they liked, but not a cottar, not poor Wat. The rain let up again, and the black clouds dashed southward to drench some other poor cottar down at Wydclif.

"All we need," said Simon Thornrigg, coming up alongside him, "is to drown our rye before it's planted, eh, Wat?"

Wat plodded on, patched shoes squelching in the mud. He made Simon no answer. Simon had four fine fat cows, and a son who did all his work, and still he whined about having to pay for the use of the knight's stud bulls. If Wat had four fine cows he wouldn't be whining about no piddling fees.

"Weather's bad," grunted old Winfrith atte-Beck, on Wat's other side. "Gets colder earlier every year, and stays cold longer. It wasn't like this in my day."

"Ah, that's what the geezers always say." Wat's ox balked for no reason. Wat cursed and prodded him viciously with the goad.

"Here!" Thomas Reeve picked his way over the furrows. "Drive the beast, you scum, don't butcher him!"

Wat ground his teeth and blamed God—for the weather, for the balking ox, for his poor lot, and for Thomas Reeve.

"Kindliest reeve we ever had," said the geezers, "but that's not saying much."

While the villagers harrowed, Wilfrid priest stood on his threshold and gazed blearily into the churchyard while William scratched out his lessons. The rain had let up; the day turned yellow, dull, and hazy.

"In . . . ipso . . . vita . . . erat," William muttered, bearing down on his pen. "Et . . . vita . . . erat . . . lux . . . hominum . . . Et lux . . . in tenebris . . . lucet, In him was life, and the life was the light of men, and the light shines in darkness . . . "

Wilfrid said, "Write in silence, boy. Learn not to disturb others with your studies." He scowled. Ragenhilda, Wat Cottar's wife, was coming round the churchyard wall, dragging a child by his skinny arm. The child was howling; Ragenhilda was cursing. Martha Reeve and Hawisa Thornrigg followed, scolding and clucking at her like angered hens. They came through the gate and made toward Wilfrid. He wished he could duck into the house and slam the door against them. He had a good bolt, and stores enough in his loft to withstand a prolonged siege. But no, he gritted his teeth and stood his ground.

"Wilfrid priest!" Ragenhilda shrieked. "She's bewitched him! She's bewitched my son!"

"Bewitched!" Martha squawked. "I've bewitched him surely, indeed I have! I've bewitched him by darning his hosen and plucking the lice from his scalp and feeding his poor little belly on something better than bean juice!"

"She's got no sons of her own," Ragenhilda sobbed, "so she's got to witch one of mine away from me. Stop her, Wilfrid priest! Stop her!"

"I should think you would be glad to be relieved of one child, Ragenhilda," Wilfrid remarked dryly. "You have—how many living? Seven?"

Ragenhilda ignored this. "She's stolen my son!"

"You hold your noise, Ragenhilda," William commanded from the recesses of the cottage. "You are disturbing me at my studies."

Wilfrid sighed and stepped out, shutting the door behind him. "Wives," he said wearily, "quit your quarreling and let us see what we may do about this in a quiet and seemly manner."

"I hate her!" Ragenhilda wept. "I hope her cows die before the week is out."

33

Martha snarled back: "You sorry scarecrow of a mother."

Hawisa agreed wholeheartedly. "Martha and I know how to raise our children."

Ragenhilda turned on Hawisa. "You're in on this witchcraft too, you and your herbs!"

When Wilfrid came back again, William had stopped writing. He was sprawled over the table in an unlikely position, cheek resting on the pages of the great Book, one hand scratching his hindparts, the other making long slow loops and curlicues around the margins of his work. When he saw Wilfrid he scrambled back onto his stool. "I finished what you gave me," he said.

Wilfrid took up the work and squinted at it. "What's this?" he said in a crabbed voice. "You call this Latin? What's wrong with you, boy, can't you even copy fair? And what's all this scribbling around it? If I'd have wanted you to illuminate your work I would have said so." He clipped William on the ear.

William turned red and screwed his eyes.

Wilfrid relented. "Ah well," he muttered. He went over to the window where he kept his books. "Here," he said, pulling out a small, frayed volume. He thumbed through the book and laid it open on the table. "Read to me, from here to here. That's right. Good." Wilfrid sat down on the stool opposite and leaned his elbows on the table. He shut his eyes. His head ached. William did not notice, for he loved this book, and he had already begun to read. "Cum Caedmon corpus somno dedisset, angelus Domini ei dormienti . . . when Caedmon had settled himself to sleep, an angel of the Lord came to him as he dreamt."

Wilfrid sat forward and clapped his hand down on the page. "Boy," he snapped, "tell me. Are there angels?"

William looked up, startled and offended. "Why certainly there are angels."

"How do you know this?"

William narrowed his eyes and observed Wilfrid suspiciously. What was the catch this time?

"Do you taste them, smell them, hear them, touch them?"

"No, Father Wilfrid."

"Do you see them?"

William replied cautiously, "After a fashion."

"Ah good," Wilfrid said wryly. "At long last Keldacross has its own vision seer. In what manner do you see angels, Master Vision Seer?"

"In my mind's eye I see angels." Then, quickly: "And Holy Scripture says there are angels."

"Revelation is one way of knowing, yes. Why didn't you say so at first? But how else might you know there are angels?"

William thought for a moment. Then he said, "Because it stands to reason that there would be angels."

Wilfrid crooked his eyebrow. "Go on."

"Why would there be stones, and trees, and beetles, and dogs, and us, and then, suddenly, GOD! with nothing in between?"

Wilfrid sat back, smiling a little. Then he sat forward again and rumpled William's hair. " 'Not an Angle,' " he quoted, " 'but an angel.' You little Lucifer." Then he sat back once more. "Read."

William continued. " 'Caedmon,' inquit angelus, 'canta mihi principium creaturam.' Et statim coepit cantare in laudem Dei creatoris versus quos numquam audiverat. 'Caedmon,' said the angel, 'sing to me of the first creation.' And immediately he began to sing in praise of God the creator verses that he had never heard."

Wilfrid brooded. "Ah," he said aloud. "This boy. If he were not bound for the abbey, I should prophesy for him a sojourn in the schools. Though much good that did me. Ah well. A dose of humility never hurt a soul, I suppose. I never dreamt *this* would be my ending place, back in those days at Merton." He looked sadly at William. "God does not give second chances," he said. "If a man does not take the opportunity when God offers it, God will not offer it again."

William looked up uncomprehendingly. He did not know what "Merton" or "the schools" were. When he asked, Wilfrid only said, "Ah, that concerns not you, William, nor me any longer." William concluded that Merton must be some fine and distant market town that Wilfrid had visited once, for whenever he spoke of it, it was in the same longing voice.

✳ 11

Helmsley Castle
September 1334

Hugh Cliderhou, now fourteen, was three years older than Nicholas. He had been made the squire of Godfrey Scarface, the lord's uncle, and now he bullied the pages ferociously, as if he had never been one of them. He burst into the inner court where Nicholas and Rab Torbeck and Edmund Wydclif were sitting on a bench, polishing bits of armour.

"Right, right," he bawled. "Who's got Sir Godfrey's heaume?"

Nicholas stood up sullenly. "I've got it. It's here." He held out the great tourney helmet.

"I've got it here, *sir*," Hugh corrected him.

"You're no sir," Nicholas muttered.

"What did you say?" Hugh loomed. He was tall, trim, and broad shouldered, and he could narrow his eyes into terrifying slits.

"I've got it here, sir."

Hugh continued to stare at him. "What have you got there?"

"Sir Godfrey's heaume, *sir*."

"Good," said Hugh. "Hand it over." Nicholas obeyed, and Hugh took the helmet back into the castle hall, letting the long panache of scalloped cloth float out behind him.

When he was well out of earshot, Rab got up and swaggered wildly, shoving his nose into the air. "I'm handsome Hugh of Eskmere," he said in a stupid, arrogant voice. "And I think I'm something great. I have a face like a pimply arse, and when I fart, men listen."

"No, they faint," said Nicholas, and Edmund fell off the bench laughing.

Someone poked his head out from a window high above them. "Hey you puppies, what're you doing? Get to work."

They set to polishing again.

"Know what we should do?" said Rab.

"What?" asked Nicholas.

"Next time Hugh's making minstrel eyes at that Ursula of his, we should hide behind him and make farting noises so she'll think it's him."

"I wish there was such a thing as rotted leek perfume," said Mun, "so we could pour it out over his clothes."

"I know what," said Rab. "Listen. One of us could go into the kitchen and steal a pot of leek soup. Then we could all go up into the barbican turrets, see, and when Hugh Shittenhou rides out after Scarface, we could pour it over his head."

"Scalding leek soup." Nicholas rubbed fiercely at one of Scarface's cuisses. "*Boiling* leek soup."

"Na, we couldn't keep it hot that long."

"If we cover it."

"But what," Mun fell off the bench again, "if we hit Sir Godfrey by mistake?"

"Ah, he'll be mailed. It'd run right off him."

They discussed this strategy for a while. They each of them knew that none of them dared carry it out.

36

Someone came out of the hall and bellowed that it was near dinner and they had better come in and serve.

"I have another plan," said Rab. They collected the polished mail. "One of us can go to him and say that Lady Ursula bids him meet her at the outer gate at midnight. Then, while he's standing there like a fool, we can drop the portcullis on him. Creak, clang, ar-r-r. He'd be dead."

They went into the hall to find their tunics with the lord's arms embroidered on sleeves and breast—not the things to wear while sitting in a muddy bailey messing with grease-polish.

"I hate Hugh Cliderhou," said Nicholas, pulling his tunic over his head. "I really hate him. Someday I'm going to cut his head off."

✳ 12

Keldacross and Coverdale
March 1335

In March Dame Magdalen desired to see her mother in Coverdale. Gervase turned wounded and truculent when she mentioned it. "Dammit, Maudlin, I've just come home."

"For two months I've seen to your manor," she replied calmly. "Now I would like to see my mother."

"Well, damn it, I would like to stay home."

"I'm not asking you to come with me, though all at Wherne would be glad of your visit. But I will go alone if you prefer."

"Who'd protect you?" The journey to Coverdale passed through long stretches of wild waste country.

"Gib Faulkoner perhaps."

"Gib Faulkoner? Who will look to my hawks?"

Magdalen sighed. "Send whom you like. But I would take William and Katharine, for they do not know their uncles."

Gervase looked aggrieved for some time, but eventually he surrendered to Magdalen's cool politeness. He told John Bailley to scare up a couple of stout, sharp eyed villeins to carry bows and cudgels.

The sowers sang returning from the fields. Win Thornrigg tramped through Kelda village with the others; they had just come from sowing the springfield. Win had twelve dead blackbirds hanging over his shoulder on a cord. "Thought they'd get a bellyful of oats," he quipped, "but we'll get a bellyful of them."

"Were it not Lent, you mean," said Harry atte-Beck, tramping along beside him. "Too bad you can't change 'em into herrings."

"Ai, I forgot." Ash Wednesday had been three days ago. Still, Win bore his blackbirds like a trophy.

Harry wiggled his elbow. "Ee, what an ache I have."

"That's bad broadcasting. Cast gentler and you won't suffer."

Harry was irritated. "Who made you my granddad, Rabbit?"

Win replied amicably. "The same One who made you a bad sower." He whistled the tune they'd been singing: "Spring is come with love to town." March was meatless but hopeful, promising joy. Spring hinted at an early coming this year. The air was brisk, but the sun was bright. Fat white clouds sped through deep blue spaces above Kelda rigg. The trees quickening by Mucklebridge bowed their branches before the breeze, and among them small birds hopped and chittered.

"West wind," observed one of the sowers. "We've an early April." Win touched the wood of Jack thatcher's pig fence as they went by. "Doan't speak it *aloud*, you mule's arse," muttered Harry-atte-Beck.

He and Win broke away from the others to cut across the common between the pig fence and the house of Thomas Reeve. Just as they were about to pass the end of the reeve's, one of the doors cracked open (for the reeve possessed the rarity of two doors, one at either end of his house) and a voice said, "Ssst." It was a giggly voice.

"What the—" said Harry.

Young Mary Reeve thrust her round brown head out the door. Her bright eyes peeked at them; she was plainly in a tipsy way. Her cheeks were even redder than usual. "E, Win, you thirsty?" she whispered, and giggled again.

Win stopped in his tracks.

"How'd you like a taste of something lovely?"

Harry made a noise like a bull calf, but Win asked, grinning, "What might that be?"

"Tell that mucky friend of yours to go away with his foul britches. I'm offering *you* a taste of my father's blackberry wine."

At the mention of the blackberry wine, waters welled up under Win's tongue, and he swallowed. Wine of any sort was something he was lucky to get even at Christmas.

"They're all out of the house and I've had a bit. It's lovely."

At that Win said, "Lass, are you touched?"

"Come in and have a little bit of drink."

"A little bit of dead, you mean. T'reeve finds me in there tippling with you and I'm a goner."

"My father likes you, Edwin."

"Not that much he don't."

"Aye he does! Says you're one of the best workers in Kelda."

The whole time Mary was twinkling at Win, Win was leaning his elbow against the pig fence and swinging his sling against his knee, and Harry atte-Beck was feeling more and more belligerent. He held his empty seedpouch at his hip and tugged at its strap. "Come on, Rabbit. Going to jaw all day?"

"I hear my mam coming," said Mary suddenly, and slammed the door.

"What's she playing Eve with you for?" Harry grumbled as they came near the duck pond. "Pouring out her dad's wine, and it's Lent to boot. Anyhow, she should be teasing Tom Bradback if she's teasing any man."

"Maybe she don't fancy him."

"Gaw! He's t'miller's son. What's good about you? You ain't rich, nor free."

"Ah, free yourself." Win went sauntering on ahead, the dead birds swinging jauntily from his shoulder.

"Where're you going? You said you'd help me pull down that shed."

"Changed my mind."

"You stringy hare! Last time I ever help you stick swine at Hallowtide."

"Aye, tell that to your mam when she don't get one of our hams."

"*My* mam? *You're* the one wrapped up in your mother's smock!" Harry bellowed this while stomping around the long way, along the opposite side of the pond. But he didn't remain angry for long. Next day he came at cockcrow to walk with Win to the furrows, and that afternoon Win helped him pull down his shed. It was a treat ripping down the rotted thing. They bashed in the old daub and wattle and knocked down the old spongy beams, and then they chopped up the beams for firewood. Kelda rigg echoed their axefalls and the sound of their rough singing.

Win came back to Simon's house tired but happy, with a load of chopped up cowshed in his arms. Hawisa was waiting for him at the door. She had an anxious look on her face. "You're wanted up at the hall," she said.

"Why? What for?"

"I don't know. T'reeve just came by and said John Bailley wanted you."

"Scabby owd fart," Simon grunted inside the house. "He's come up with some piddling thing I done wrong so he can fine me for it."

"If it was you he wanted, he'd call for you," Hawisa snapped. "You'd best go, Win. Have dinner when you come back."

"St Godrich," Win cursed. He didn't feel like slogging up the hill, and he couldn't think what the bailley might want him for.

John Bailley met him in the manor house kitchen. "There you are. Where's your gear?"

Win shook his head. "No one said owt—"

The bailley's brows beetled, and the sour lines around his mouth deepened. "Well, you'll have to go down again and fetch it. Bow, quiver, the whole gear. You're sleeping up here tonight and leaving at the crack of dawn with Dame Magdalen. She's riding for Coverdale."

"But—" said Win. He didn't want to go to no foreign place.

"What?" snapped the bailley.

"It's planting time."

The bailley snorted. "Think we can't do without you? Now look sharp. Mark Fletcher is going too."

So Win had to go all the way down the hill and come all the way up again, without his supper. "They'd better give you summat at t'hall," Hawisa worried.

Next morning Sir Gervase started out with them, intending to go no further than Rievaulx Abbey. But once they came to Rievaulx he could not stand the idea of Maudlin's crossing the wastelands without real protection, so he ended by going the whole way to Coverdale after all. It was wonderful for William and Katharine, for they rarely had their father's full attention. Now he flew hawks with Katharine and laid mock wagers on whose would stoop first. He let William take command of his palfrey while he got off to stretch his legs.

"I'm Robert the Bruce," William blurted aloud, and felt his head get fat and hot when his father squinted up at him. "What the hell?" But William could not explain to his father how it was that he felt like "that damn fell Scot," nor why it should be pleasurable.

The earth of March on the moor was still dry and cold, hard under the horses' hooves. But still the west wind blew and the jocund clouds raced across a rainless sky. Win shot a hare as it sprang across the road a hundred feet ahead of them. "Better and better, Rabbit," Mark Fletcher allowed, somewhat grudgingly, for he was feeling middle aged and did not appreciate the competition.

Win nodded and said, "Aye." He ran to skin his hare and left the rest for the birds of the air, for they did not keep Lent.

Gervase, too, enjoyed himself, until they reached Coverdale, where Dame Emma stomped around her domain like a field marshal, barking orders right and left. Dame Emma was a little woman with thin, papery skin and watery eyes. But she had a voice like a battle horn and a mouth (Gervase maintained) like a sewer. Gervase admired her, but the tall, red-haired sons who surrounded her, cursing constantly but doing whatever she commanded, irked him. Every one of them called him by a different name: "Geoffrey," "George," "Jack," and once, inexplicably, "Dick." By evening the first day it got too much for Gervase, and he made a scene at the table. "It's Gervase!" he snapped at the eldest brother, Edward. "Gervase of Kelda! Holy Death of God, sir, I'm your sister's husband and have been for years! Gervase! What's so damn difficult about that?"

"Shush, husband, shush!" said Dame Magdalen under her breath. She hated these displays of temper, particularly at table.

All the brothers looked taken aback. They apologized profusely to Gervase, but went back to calling him Jack, George, or Geoffrey the very next morning. Finally he could suffer no more of it. He made excuses to Dame Emma. "They expect me at manor court," he told her.

"Well, go along, man. Daughter Magdalen can do without you for a fortnight. I'll send Ned back with her then. He's going to York in any event." Then Uncle Edward asked whether Maudlin had been told the news about Roger. Roger was the youngest Coverdale uncle, and Nicholas' godfather.

"Forgot all about it," Dame Emma admitted. "Tell her now, Ned."

"Roger's come back to Yorkshire. He was so well reputed down in Oxenford that they've made him a canon of the minster straightaway. They say that Archbishop Zouche likes him well."

"Indeed?" said Magdalen. "Maybe he will be the next archbishop. Archbishop Wherne, Mother: how like you that?" She was teasing. She smiled over at Gervase, who managed to conjure up a grumpy "Mmmph."

"Well enough," Dame Emma replied, "but I'll be skewered before I'll kiss his ring."

William spoke up brightly. "Wilfrid priest my tutor was at Oxenford."

Uncle Edward smiled at him. "Aye, old cousin Wilfrid. He was down there, wasn't he?"

"Got tossed out, as I recall," Dame Emma mused. "Some sort of scandal."

Magdalen cleared her throat, indicating William with her head. Dame Emma forged on regardless. "Aye, they tossed him out of his college. Been stuck at Kelda ever since."

William looked at his grandmother with baffled, disbelieving eyes. Magdalen quickly changed the subject. "Lord Ros has promised his eldest girl to a Westmoreland Dacre." The conversation turned to the barbarity of Cumberland and Westmoreland, and whether it was possible for any Yorkshire lady to live there without terrible self-sacrifice and mortification.

"I'd do it, to be a Dacre," Katharine declared, and all the uncles laughed. "Young Katharine's one of us, a Wherne woman, tough as nails." She glowed in their praise but added hotly that Kelda blood was just as good. They chuckled and approved of her and told Gervase, "That's a real little war falcon you've got there, George."

"Aye," said Gervase drily, rising from his chair. "See you in a fortnight, Maudlin. Enjoy yourself." He nodded curtly at the brothers and thanked Dame Emma for her hospitality. Within a quarter of an hour he was riding back to Keldacross with Win and Mark Fletcher loping along on foot behind him. Win whistled as they went. His mam would be glad to see him back early.

✳ 13

Keldacross
October 1335

"Now," said Gilbert the falconer. "Lay the net so, over the kill."
Nicholas did as he was shown.

"That's right. Now. Behind the clump. And wait." Gib needn't tell Nicholas to keep silent. The boy was a natural hunter. Gib refused to take the Wisp trapping, for no matter how the boy swore he'd keep still, he always ended by twiddling about, snapping twigs, and saying, "How long is it going to *be*, Gib? When is she going to *come*?" in a voice shrill enough to raise the dead. The second (and last) time Gib had suffered him to "help," William had scared away a fine goshawk just as it was stooping for its netted rabbit. But it was a pilgrim falcon Gib was after this time, a passenger peregrine. Nicholas remained respectfully silent, as intent and serious as Gib himself. They lay on their bellies in the stickery bushes, under the low branches of a scarlet berried whitebeam.

"Let me pull the cord," Nicholas whispered, almost mouthing it.

Gib replied in the same way. "You'll pull only when I say? Not before or after?"

Nicholas nodded, and crossed himself. Gib looked at him gravely and handed over the cord. Then he set one fist upon the other and his chin on that, and waited, gazing out onto the rusty moor. He was long and thin as a reed; his hair was the color of russet. Nicholas wore a dun colored overtunic with a green capuchon hood. He stretched his legs behind him and set his face to watch. They were one with the autumn thicket.

Rainclouds scudded overhead. A curlew called from somewhere in the east; they could hear faint, busy shouting from the village below. They waited.

She came, brown wings outstretched in grey sky, round eyes fierce, talons curved out to bind to her prey.

"Now!" Gib hissed, and Nicholas pulled.

"Aye!" Gib cried. "We've got her!" He sprang up on his stringy legs. "Well done, young Nicholas, *well* done!" Nicholas returned him one of his little half smiles. "And it's no tercel neither," said Nicholas.

"No, sir, she's a true falcon. A noble lady." The male hawk, the tercel, was only two thirds her size. "Now you stay here; I'll go and get her. Does no good to have more folks than needed crowding round her while she's in such a rage." The bird was beating her great wings inside the net, tearing at it with her curved beak.

Nicholas watched Gib untangle her from the net with care and skill, and attach to her legs the leather things called jesses, and cover her eyes with the rufter, a soft leather hood. "There you are, lady," Gib crooned. "Aye, there you are. Now, young Nicholas, come out and admire our catch."

Nicholas scrambled up and came over. He put out his forefinger, gingerly, to stroke the ruffled plumage.

They wandered back over the moor, talking quietly, mostly to the falcon. They made their way down one of the steep footpaths that crisscrossed the haunch of Kelda, and clambered out onto the Knee. They stopped there and examined their prize again.

"She's far better than that eyas merlin Hugh Cliderhou brags about all day long," said Nicholas.

"She's a sweetheart, she is, a very warrior."

"My father will wish she were his."

"No, but she's yours. I'll keep her at hack for you and train her. If you come back at Christmas I'll give you a full trained peregrine for a present." The falcon thrashed and tore at Gilbert's glove with her beak, but he had already bound her fast.

"I wish I could train her myself," said Nicholas.

"It's a delicate thing, training a hawk," said Gib, and they climbed down the Knee into the field below, which lay fallow that year.

But for all the rest of his stay Nicholas was allowed to carry the falcon on his gloved fist and croon to her and stroke her feathers with a quill. And to feed her, bound to her perch in the hawkhouse, her bits of bloody meat.

"May I feed her now?" William begged, shuffling his feet in the white-splotched straw.

"No," said Nicholas.

"What's her name?" asked Katharine.

"I haven't thought of one yet. What do you think?"

"Hmmm. What about 'Thunderbolt'?"

"Na. Every third peregrine's named that."

"Well, I never heard of one, except that one of Ingram Tarn's over in Tunnersgil, that got strangled in the fowler's net that time."

"You don't live at Helmsley. Every third peregrine's named 'Thunderbolt.' "

"I know," William piped up. " 'Windiscry.' "

" 'Windiscry.' " Nicholas tried it out. "The wind's cry. Aye. That's her name: Windiscry. Here you are, Windiscry. Snap up your bit of hare." Windiscry snapped, and almost took off his finger.

"Let me feed her now, Nickless, then, please?" William grabbed at the bag of tidbits hanging from Nicholas' wrist. Nicholas swung his arm away, slamming the bag flat across William's nose. "I said no," he said, in a nasty voice.

William stood holding his nose, face crimson, eyes wet and sparkling. "I hate you, you pig face," he shouted, "and I hate your shitten peregrine too. I'm going to come in the middle of the night with a bootlace and strangle her to death, like Ingram Tarn's."

"You do, Pimple, and I'll string your guts all over Kelda village." Nicholas stepped forward, eyes cold, nostrils white, hand on knife hilt. "I can do it, too."

"Aye, Pimple," Katharine agreed. "He can do it."

William drew himself up and stared from one to the other of them. "You'll both be sorry," he said, "when I'm dead tomorrow." Then he ran out of the hawkhouse.

Nicholas turned back to Windiscry. "One more bit, lady, and you've et your supper." Katharine went to fetch her own bird from his perch.

In bed that night Nicholas tossed and turned. Usually he could not make the Pimple shut his mouth at night, but now there was an uncanny silence from the other side of the bed, and a cold stiffness there too.

Finally, "William," he said, "William, answer me."

No answer.

"William, you're not going to strangle my bird, are you, when I'm away?"

Silence.

"I swear, William, I'm sorry for what I said."

Nothing.

"You can feed her all the time I'm gone, Wisp. You can pull the lures for her too; I'll tell Gib Faulkoner."

Silence.

Nicholas grew frightened, and not only on account of Windiscry.

"William!" he jabbed the skinny little back with his elbows. "William, answer me!"

Nothing.

"William! In God's name I'm sorry. That was a fine name you picked for her, truly. I'll tell you what. I'll catch another hawk for you. Gib's shown me how. I'll catch one for you and train it too, and give it to you at Christmas."

Finally, a voice. "What do I want with a shitten old hawk? I hope yours pecks your eyes out."

"Go to hell then!" Nicholas rolled over violently, yanking the blankets.

William yanked back. "I hate you. I hope you die by the sword!" He did not know yet that such words are better not spoken, for it is written that you shall not tempt the Lord your God.

✳ 14

Keldacross
December 1335

It was worse than Magdalen had thought, sending William away. They had planned to wait until after Twelfth Night so that he would enjoy one last Christmas at Keldacross. But there was a new prioress at Rosedale, and the cellarer of Rievaulx was her cousin, so he had gone up to see her take office. On his way home he and the three monks traveling with him spent the night at Keldacross. And "Since they are already there," said Sir Gervase, "why not send the boy over with them? It'll save me two days of travel in dead winter."

"I promised him he would keep Christmas here," Dame Magdalen protested, "and we've got nothing ready."

"Well then, *make* ready, damn it."

"It's nothing to *you*, is it," she snapped back, "sending this one away?"

"God damn it, wife, it's nothing to *you* that I freeze my arse on the way to Rievaulx when I need not go there at all!"

The cellarer was easily persuaded to spend another day toasting his toes by the fire while they made ready. But they did not tell William when they planned to send him away. He lurked about the hall, peering at the shorn, black and white Cistercians from behind the solar screens. Win Thornrigg came in with a tall ladder and leaned it against a wall. His nose was red and his eyes running from the cold. Mary Reeve came in with a basket of sharp-leaved holly. She handed up the pricking branches, which Win cursingly wound around the roofbeams.

The monks watched and laughed and talked among themselves.

William watched them.

Joan Faulkoner knelt in the Long Chamber with Dame Magdalen, helping her pack a trunk. Magdalen was silent, her mouth tight and strangely shaped.

"Men are cruel things," observed Joan.

"My little William will never be cruel," said Magdalen. "He will be my own holy monk at Rievaulx." And she put her proud chin in her hand, to hide the shaking of it.

That afternoon she came to William with a set face. He thought she was angry with him for something, so he leapt away, protecting his backside. But "Come, William," she said, reaching out her hand.

He took her long, cold fingers and went out of the hall with her, across the courtyard, through the gate, and down the hill. The world was gray and drained of color. They walked through the frozen courtyard, their feet crunching on the brittle snow. William shivered and said, "It's *damn* cold, Mother, isn't it?" The "damn" was a boast: he thought it made him sound masterful like his father. They went into St Godrich's, which was no less cold than without, but darker. A red light burned in the sanctuary, before the Sacrament in the hanging pyx. From the dimness of the walls stared six-winged angels, fiery eyed seraphim.

Magdalen pushed William to his knees. "You stay here and pray," she said. "I shall go and fetch Wilfrid."

He did not know what he was to pray for. The stone was hard under his knees. He lifted his head and peered up at the seraphim. The Watchers. He did not know why, but that was the name he had always given them. "Watchers," he said, "let me stay for Christmas." For it was just beginning to break on him.

His mother came back with Wilfrid. Wilfrid said prayers over him and blessed him in a cracked voice. Finally his mother pulled him up from the flags and held him to her skirts. A hoarse sound came out of her. She pushed him away from her and hurried out of the church, leaving him alone with Wilfrid priest.

Wilfrid, drying his eyes on the back of his hand, said, "Your poor mother is sore grieved to let you go, William."

William's eyes filled with horror. "She said I could have Christmas," he cried. "She said!"

"Mother!" sobbed William all night long in the bed he shared at Rievaulx with a boy named Gilbert Kerby. "Mother, Mother. Wilfrid priest."

Nothing Stephen the novice master could do would calm him; neither soothing words nor threat of the strap availed. Finally he took the boy over to the infirmarian, because William had worked himself into a fit and been sick all over the bed.

I wish, Stephen thought dolefully, that we had remained true to the wisdom of our fathers of Cîteaux, who did not admit child oblates.

Part Two

God sendeth the kow, bot not by the horne.

THE CLOUD OF UNKNOWING

✳ 15

Helmsley Castle
March 1338

Robert and Edmund and Nicholas were all rolled up in blankets on the straw in Helmsley great hall, before the embers of the huge chimney. Nicholas was asleep. The other two were not, because Nicholas was dreaming. It was always the same. First he would twitch all over, like a dog, and whimper under his breath. Then he'd give a great gasp, and sit up staring. He would never tell them what he had dreamed of in the morning. At night they told him to lie down and shut up.

Tonight was different. He twitched, he whimpered, and he gasped, but then he screamed and made a fist and struck out, catching Rab right across the lip.

"Damn it, Nick," Rab yelled. "Wake the hell up. You're dreaming."

"Quiet over there!" Gruff voices grunted from all over the hall.

Nicholas sat up, sweating and trembling. "Oh St Godrich," he mumbled into his hands. "Oh St Mary."

"Lie down, Nick. You were only dreaming."

Nicholas would not lie down. "Oh, that face," he said. "That face."

"Must've been some face." Rab nursed his lip and rolled over, muttering.

Nicholas finally lay down again, but he would not close his eyes, for fear of what he might see behind them. He stared up into the dark vaulting of the hall, propping his eyelids open with his fingers, for they ached with heaviness. To his wild horror the next thing he knew he was crossing the moor again. He was a knight already, but he was walking, not riding, and his feet were heavy as lead. The moor was very bright, yellow with broom and daffodil and purple with heather all at once. The sky was blue and cloudless. Nothing was in it but the sun, which burned high and small and stark up in the naked dome. The moor rose up to a ridge, like the rigg of Kelda, but it was not Kelda moor but someplace vaster and wilder and utterly silent. Nicholas kept dragging toward the ridge, where the gaudy moor and the harsh sky came together. Everything in his bones and blood cried, "Turn; run!" But still he trudged forward, sweltering, laden. There was another knight at the top of the ridge, with his back to the moor. He was tall and broad. There was something horrible about the way his helm set on his great hunched shoulders. He wore a tabard like a herald's, glaring white, with a black device on it that Nicholas could not make out. And now Nicholas went faster and faster until he was standing only a few feet below the top of the ridge, staring up. The insigne was a crooked black triangle on a white field. The knight turned and faced him. The knight lifted his hands to raise his helm. Nicholas' tongue dried up. He could not turn his eyes or close them. They burned. The knight lifted his helm. Under it was the head of an owl, huge. The round eyes stared into the glaring sun. The curved beak opened once, twice, and shut again with a clacking sound. Nicholas reached heavily for his sword. The beak opened again, wider and wider, and inside the blackness was a red flickering tongue like a serpent's—or a flame. Nicholas struck—and suddenly there was no more darkness, no more tongue, but only a black crow sweeping crazily away over the moor.

Nicholas opened his eyes. Above him was the castle vaulting, dim and gray in the morning light, not the black emptiness of night. His friends were stirring. Rab stretched and yawned. Mun sat up and said, "Hey! Today's the day the armourers come from York! They'd better have it right this time or the lord'll have their guts out."

"Aye, and curse at us all day too. I hate it when he's pissed. And speaking of piss . . . " Rab got up and made his way outside.

Having done his business, he came back into the hall. Hugh Cliderhou shouldered past him on his own way out—tall, muscular, seventeen, and sneering. "Your little friend dream bad dreams again, Rabbie? Was that game we ate last night too strong for his digestion?"

"Seeing your bastardly face was too strong for his digestion," Rab muttered when Hugh was out of earshot. He dared not say it aloud—not yet. He returned to Nick and Mun. "When we're knighted," he told them, "we'll knock the innards out of Hugh Cliderhou."

Mun stood up. He nudged Nicholas with his foot. "That was a terror you gave us last night, Nick. What was the nightmare, that you had to smash Rab's nose in?"

"What?" said Nicholas, staring into the vaulting. "I don't know." He clenched his teeth. "I don't remember."

✳ 16

York
April 1338

Marion woke with a start in the small hours of the morning. The wind was blowing hard. It rushed round the corners of her father's house, rattling the windows and toppling something heavy with a crash, down lane. After that she could not sleep again. It was not an unhappy kind of wakefulness, though, not the kind filled with nagging griping things— what she ought to have said when Agnes had done such and such, or how hot she felt on account of making a clown of herself last Michaelmas, or the writhing guilt over the spilt ink in her father's counting book, for which Alice took the strap, or what would happen if the Scots came down on York the way they had come down on Durham.

Now instead she lay thinking gentle thoughts that ran through her mind like deer: lithe, fleeting, one following close upon another, disappearing behind the thickets of her mind, only to appear again, later, in an altogether unexpected spot. Little things from her childhood flashed upon her, and dimmed away again. Oh! that little wooden mouse with the painted fur. I'd forgotten. That round window with the curly X in it that made an X on the floor when the sun came through. Where was that? Those three moles my mother had on her wrist, in the shape of a little hat. I'd forgotten. Forgotten. Somewhere with long grass and sky, and a great white cloud rising over the edge of the world. Where, oh where was that?

A dog barked, distantly.

The abbey bell of great St Mary's rang out to call the brothers to Matins. Other bells answered from the priories all over town. Dawn was breaking, breathing pearly light against her windowpanes. Marion heard someone running down Goodramgate. His feet pounded and echoed in the street. She climbed out of her blankets and snaked on her belly to the foot of the bed, where she could lean her cheek on the windowsill and look out, just in time to see the fellow disappear, dimly, round the corner of Petergate. She wondered mildly what he was running for. Two stars burned, one in the Shepherd in the west, one dimmer, in the Swan, toward the east. Then a light flared and shone yellow in the window across from her own, and she saw Master Whewell stumbling about in his shirt. She giggled. He took the candle out of his room, and that window grew dark again. The candle reappeared in the next window. She saw him sit down at his counting table with a pen. At work so early? He was worse than her father. The chestnut tree in the Noyes' kitchen garden made a tracery of black branches against a sky that had turned egg blue. The Minster towers were black, too, above the roofs, but as she watched they grew greyer and greyer, until she could make out the very stones. Thin rosy clouds shifted and spread in the rushing sky. Marion gasped. Suddenly the clouds turned a red-orange-gold so bright that she knew it must be a color of heaven, for you never saw it anywhere else, or any time else, but daybreak.

Folk were moving about in the street now. A cart rolled and clattered on the cobbles, and the carter whistled as he went: Dic nobis, Maria, tell us, Mary, what did you see on the road? He was carrying cheese and butter and milk from Yorkiswold. People began to move in earnest now. Loud yawns and grumbles, father noises, came through the wall at the head of Marion's bed, and the softer, higher noises of Mistress Alison. Someone shouted over Thomas Mercer's garden wall. Alice's voice answered, "Marry, you halfwit! Out in Walmgate! What did you think?"

Already the feeling of dawn was fading from Marion's mind. She never afterward remembered those strange things she had remembered that night. Not, at least, until the very end.

St Mary's Abbey rang out for Prime. The others answered. Ros lucis est ros tuus, et terram gigantum detrahes in ruinam; Anima mea desider-avit te in nocte. Your dew is a shining dew, and you bring the land of the shades to naught; my soul has desired you in the night.

✴ 17

Rievaulx Abbey
April 1338

In the abbey parlor Father Stephen the novice master was telling them again of the founding of Rievaulx.

"It was in the reign of the first Henry," he said, "when Thurston, archbishop of York, sent to the blessed Bernard, for he was eager to have an abbey founded for the new order in his diocese. So holy Bernard sent to England a handful of his own monks of Clairvaux under the leadership of our father William, and a letter with them." Stephen read from his book: " 'Wherein he prayed the king to assist these messengers of the Lord to reclaim those who had been taken captive in the toils of Satan.' And then what happened?"

William leaned forward on his bench.

"Tell us what happened, William."

William stood up. "At the royal court of King Henry the First, Abbot William met one Walter Espec, the lord of Helmsley, a nobleman of prowess and devotion. And it was that nobleman who gave Abbot William nine curacates of land and a bit of forest in loco horroris et vastae solitudinis, in a frightful place of great loneliness."

"Well said." Stephen motioned for William to sit again. William pretended not to see. "And then came Fountains, not a year after. And then Byland, then Jervaulx, then Salley, then Roche and Kirkstall, then Meaux." He sat down with a satisfied thump. The others glowered at him.

"You have said rightly, William, but you have also said proudly. Beware the sin of pride."

William tried to look humble.

"I shall now read you from what our great St Aelred says of Walter Espec."

William sat forward again, listening intently.

"St Aelred calls him 'an old man, full of days, quick witted, prudent in council, moderate in peace, circumspect in war; a true friend, a loyal subject. His stature was passing tall, his limbs of just a size as not to exceed their just proportions, and yet well matched to his great height. His hair was still black, his beard long and flowing, his forehead wide and noble, his eyes large and bright, his face broad but well featured, his voice like the sound of a trumpet, setting off his natural eloquence of speech with a certain majesty of sound . . . "

William sat back. It seemed to him that old Lord Walter had leapt out of the book and strode into the room, tossing back his black hair, swinging his great two-handed sword, and crying: "Here shall live my holy monks of Rievaulx."

"Poor Lord Walter." Stephen closed the book and set it gently aside. "His only son fell from a horse and died. But you see how God brings good out of evil. For it was on that account that Lord Walter founded Kirkham Priory and Warden and Rievaulx, to the memory of that son. So you see that we must always praise God, who brings great good out of what may seem to us great evils."

William chewed his fingernails. He considered what his father might do if Nicholas died. He did not think Gervase would found any abbeys. But then neither could William imagine the present abbot of Rievaulx hacking thistles from the moorside, or eating messes of boiled beech leaves, as had the brethren who had come over, so long ago, from the abbey of Clairvaux.

Father Stephen set William copywork as a check to his intellectual pride. He established him at a scriptorium with inkpot, pen, parchment, and the prophet Isaiah. He gave William his lesson by signs and made him understand that it was to be completed in perfection by the time he returned, shortly before the office of Terce.

William sat in the long light of a window whose tracery cast bright quatrefoils on the pages of the great Book. He dipped his pen in and out of the inkwell, considering the chapter from which he must copy. It was dark and holy.

I saw the Lord, high and exalted.

And the hem of his robe filled the temple.

About him were seraphim, and each had six wings.

One pair covered his face, another pair his feet

And the third was spread in flight.

And they were calling ceaselessly to one another.

A chill pricked William's spine. He saw St Godrich's nave on a winter night with red lights in the sanctuary and the Watchers on the walls crying out: Sanctus, sanctus, sanctus, Dominus Deus Sabaoth!

But the verse that Father Stephen said he must copy, and do it seven times, was:

You will hear, and hear again, and not understand;

You will look, and look again, and yet not see.

Immediately, William felt the reproof, and it stung! Unfair! He was *not* proud! Wilfrid priest had never called him so. Wilfrid had been *glad* when he asked questions, *glad* when he understood. William jabbed his pen into the inkwell and copied the offending verse. He copied it a second time, cramming the pen down so that the ink blobbed on the page. He disobeyed Father Stephen and dropped his pen before he finished. Why shouldn't he understand? And if he looked and looked again, why shouldn't he know? He read on to where Isaiah cries, "How long, O Lord?" and felt an indignant sympathy with the prophet. He turned the heavy pages, seeking justification, or at least edification.

Beware, the Lord will empty the earth,

Split it open and turn it upside down.

Then it will be the same for priest and people,

Master and servant, mistress and maid, seller and buyer.

The earth is emptied and stripped clean bare.

The nations stand aghast.

What was all this? How could it be that God cared so little for people as to answer Isaiah thus?

If a man runs from the noise of the hunters,
He will fall into the pit.
If he climbs out of the pit,
He will be caught in the trap.

William jerked his elbow and overturned the inkpot. "Damn!" he blurted, just as Father Stephen came in, early and unexpected, through the door. Stephen caught him across the mouth with the back of his hand.

Soaking up the spilled ink with a rag, William wept longer than the blow warranted and ended by sobbing hopelessly. In the end Stephen sat down with him in a way that said, What troubles you? William pointed at the Book.

Stephen glanced at the words. After considering for a moment, he judged it proper in charity to break silence. After all, if they foolishly relaxed the rule to admit children like this, they must allow for your dealing with them. "What you read there," he said, "is the destruction of Judah. It happened long ago."

William retorted, "Sir, last week you read from St Augustine, and he shows that all times are Now."

The boy was troubled; it was plain he did not mean to be impertinent. "It is as you say, William. In God, all times are Now. And death is at all times at the root of creation."

William sat bewildered, accusatory. Death he could accept, insofar as he could grasp it. But why this savage terror dealt out to his people by God himself? "He did *not* have to do it," said William. "He could at least have made it so that I could understand it."

"Your mind cannot contain it."

"Why did he make my mind, then? What's the good of it?"

" 'Will the babe say to his father, What are you begetting? Or the infant to his mother, What are you bringing to birth?' "

Isaiah again. It answered nothing. It justified nothing. William struggled for words. "Non est . . . It's not rational."

"What," said Stephen mildly, "a little schoolman in our midst." He warmed to the child. Few at Rievaulx, grown or otherwise, would have cared enough to be so outraged. "You may look and look for reasons, William. Find as many as you hope may satisfy. But the Lord God of Hosts will surpass them all." And he decided that the boy should play a while outdoors with his friend, later, after common prayer.

That afternoon, William and Gilbert Kerby struggled up a green hill, digging their toes into the turf, hitching up their habits, and clutching at gorse and grass with their free hands, for the hill was steep. A shepherd, driving his flock along the path below, glanced up, saw them, and thought, Doves in green sky.

William and Gilbert had escaped the abbey, or rather they had been given permission to go out with the cellarer's greyhound, which was almost as good. They were not to go out of sight of the abbey; they were to return for the midday office of None. They had already gone out of sight of the abbey, though they would see it again when they climbed higher—which was William's justification for it—and now William said, "What would they do to us if we were not back for None?"

"They will cut off our arms and legs and feed them to the dogs," said Gib.

"They will flay us alive and use our skins for vellum," said William. "And then the words of holy Bernard will truly be written in us forever."

The greyhound darted between them to make its third ascent of the slope. It reached the top, ran around barking, and charged down again. Gilbert rested, balancing himself against a trunk. "I wish I were a greyhound." Sweat slid over his freckled forehead, and he breathed hard. They watched the dog tear back and forth after some invisible little beast. They could now see the top of Rievaulx choir above the trees. William boasted, "My brother Nicholas could run up this hill faster than the dog, and he wouldn't be tired."

"So could my brothers," said Gilbert.

"Nicholas would beat them."

"Say *you*."

"Say I."

"Say *you*."

"What will happen if we're not back for None?"

"Ow."

"What would happen if we weren't back for Vespers?"

"Ow! Ow!"

"What if we weren't back for Compline?"

"Jesu Christe Domine, dona nobis requiem, Lord Jesus Christ, grant our soul repose."

William tore up some grass and threw it in Gilbert's face. "You're a coward."

Gilbert shook it off. "I am not."

"Yes you are. You would have denied Our Lord."

58

"So would you!"

"No, but then I would have come back with a mace and smashed their faces in."

"What good would that do?" Gilbert argued. "He would only have healed them up again."

They toiled upward, arguing breathlessly.

"Besides," Gilbert maintained, "he came to die. If he didn't die, how could we get free of Satan?"

"All the same," said William, "if we were there we ought to try to stop it."

"Why?"

William wiped his forehead and stared. "Why, because you ought always to fight against evil things."

"But that evil thing must happen, or there would be even worse evil."

"You ought still to fight against it." William glanced over his shoulder. He whistled, feebly, for the greyhound, wet his lips, and tried again. "Whip! Come on, Whip!" The dog's thin grey rump stuck ridiculously out of an animal hole. The dog paid William no heed. William turned back to Gilbert. "Besides," he continued in a low voice, "I never understood it. I always think: Why does he have to die with so much suffering? Can't he do it some other way? He's God, isn't he?"

"I think," said Gilbert, "because *we* suffer."

"I don't understand it." William made one last scramble and achieved the summit. "Hoy, Gib, look!"

Gilbert joined him, shading his eyes. The other side of the hill was a gentle slope, broken here and there by a grey rock or stumpy tree. It folded down into a tiny valley that lay like a still green pond in the hollow of the wooded hills, the hallow of hills holy for their silence under the blue sky. Nothing stirred in the small valley but a single black crow. The boys looked at each other and then, furtively, back over their shoulders. They peered once more into the valley. The temptation was too much. They tucked their smocks into their belts and galloped wildly down the slope, brandishing imaginary weapons and screaming bloody war cries.

The meadow, unfortunately, was boggy. William's shoe came off in the mud. He bent, pulled it out, and hurled it at Gib. It smacked Gib flat in the chest, leaving a big brown blotch. Gilbert bellowed, grabbed up the shoe, and chased squelchingly after his foe. He aimed the shoe at William's head, and missed. "You bastard!"

William laughed maniacally, and wheeled around. "Pray, Robert Bruce!" he yelled, "for this is your dying hour!"

"Say *you*, King Edward!" Gilbert charged him. They collided and rolled in the mud, pummeling and kicking each other. Then Gilbert sat up, wrinkling his nose. "Oh no!" William howled, laughing and wallowing. "It's Bannockburn!"

"Will," said Gilbert in a strange voice, "It's sheep dung."

William sniffed hard. His nose was stuffed, and he could not smell very well. "Marry," he said, "it is?" They surveyed one another. "We had better climb down to Rye and wash this off," William suggested soberly.

"What will we tell them at the abbey? We'll miss Office, and we'll be sodden."

"We can tell Father Stephen we saw wolves in the woods and had to crawl on our bellies in the mud to get away from them."

"He won't believe us."

"We can tell him that a man came and threw mud all over us, and we had to bathe in the river to get it off."

"You tell," said Gilbert. "He'll not believe us."

They trudged up the slope and topped the ridge. Gilbert squinted. "Where's the greyhound?"

The greyhound was nowhere in sight.

It was long past None when they finally skulked in through the abbey gate, tugging the greyhound by William's belt. They crept to the fountain and washed themselves as best they could. They decided on the story of the madman who hated monks.

It was not successful.

✳ 18

York
June 1338

Marion's father returned home from business in Hull on the twenty-fourth of June, the feast of John the Baptist. The business had not gone well. He rode into the lane, soaked and spattered and surly. When he was settled in his chair by the fire, Marion brought down dry hosen and shoes and handed them to him, smiling. He looked right through her. "These aren't warmed," he said, and threw them at the hearth. Marion stooped to gather them up and set them on the fender, and Mistress Alison came in with a cup of steaming mulled wine. He said he wanted none of that, but plain cider, didn't she know that by now? But he took the wine and drank it.

"Go fetch the work we have been doing, Marion," said Alison. "The mulberry sleeves."

They were the long sleeves to Andrew's new gown. It would be his best gown. A tailor had fitted it and cut it out; Mistress Alison was doing the rest. "Why should I empty my purse into old Snipsnap's lap?" Andrew had pointed out. "You can do just as well." Alison had been horrified. He had no idea of the labor that would mean to her, nor how long it would take her to do it, even with the help of all the maidservants—and the not so helpful efforts of Marion. Old Snipsnap took it ill, too, but Andrew didn't give a fig for that. Marion went and got the sleeves.

"See," she said, "I hemmed this one." That was no easy thing, when they were so richly scalloped.

Andrew looked at it without interest and shoved it back at her. He turned on Alison. "Why are you letting her botch the work? Don't you know how much that mulberry cost me?"

Marion burst into tears. "Of course she knows! She bought it, didn't she? And I haven't botched it. My stepmother says I did it right well, but you won't even look at it." She fled upstairs.

"Jesu, woman!" she heard behind her. "If you cannot give me a son, you can at least see to it that the daughter I've got behaves herself mannerly."

Marion went into her bedchamber and slammed the door. She flung herself crosswise upon the bed and sulked. Then she got up and went to the window, because she heard Agnes' voice outside. Agnes was going down the lane carrying a small earthen pot in each hand, holding them away from her, gingerly.

"Hey, Agnes!" Marion called down. "Have you got spiders in those pots, or what?"

Agnes looked up. "Honey," she called back.

"Where are you taking it?"

"To Mistress Mercer. But after that, my mother says I'm free."

"Good! Come here and bring Cis, if her mother will let her."

Agnes made a bored face. "Aye," she said, and went out into the gate. She swung her yellow plait over her shoulder and twitched her hips as she walked.

61

"What game's she fixing to play? Princess Salome?"

Marion turned round. Alice was standing there, hands on her hips, sneering.

Marion frowned.

"Well, whatever," said Alice, "it's no games at all for you until the two of us go out to Aldwark and buy t'mistress a new kitchen knife, though I fear to hand it to her, the way that father of yours is behaving."

"You watch your tongue, Alice. You can't talk like that against my father."

"Not to mention the great boil I have on my foot, which gives me the agony of hell."

"Why do I have to go with you? I want to go out with Cis and Agnes. Why can't you go get it by yourself?"

"Oh, it's the pity of Peter you have, my love. I can't hobble to Aldwark without help! You're my crutch."

As they came downstairs, they heard Andrew fuming to Jack Comyn, loud enough for the whole house to hear. "Was that woman never taught the simplest lessons of housewifery? I tell you, brother, this house was otherwise in my wife Joan's day. We never lacked curdie pies then. A good wife should always be prepared for her husband's goings and comings. I notice that the hearth is unswept. A wife ought to be able to direct the men and maids in seemly quiet. A man does not like to hear her screeching at them in the kitchen. Why does she never prepare for anything? Surely she knew I would be returning this week, or the next! I tell you, brother, my other wife was able to perform these simple tasks with ease, and she was but a child."

Jack nodded and said nothing. As always, when Andrew had worked out his spleen on everyone around him, he would finally tell what had gone wrong in Hull, and then they would put their heads together to find a way to pull some profit out of it after all.

Alice and Marion crept past them and into the kitchen. Mistress Alison turned toward them with a hard face. "Well? What do you want? Didn't I tell you to get to Aldwark?"

"Yes, Mistress, but you forgot to give me the money for it." Alice spoke low and soothing.

"Oh, Jesu Christ," Alison swore, swiping her hand across her sweaty forehead. It was warm in the kitchen; they were madly baking curdie pies. She reached into the little purse by her knee and fished out a silver halfpenny. "Here." She smacked it into Alice's palm. "If it costs you more than that, he's cheating you." She glared at Marion. "Go! Before I slap that sullen face." She could just hear Andrew. "My other wife never found it necessary to strike the girl unless the girl had done some mischief. What mischief has she done? I thought not. If you cannot give me a son, mistress, you can at least refrain from beating my only daughter to death." As if Alison didn't love the girl as if she were her own. As if she weren't the ablest housewife in Goodramgate.

"Whew," breathed Alice, as she and Marion went out the door. "Glad to be out of *there!* What ails everybody today? Marry! As if we didn't have enough trouble with the Scots!" She walked on her heel and leaned heavily on Marion's shoulder. "It's seething with pus, is that boil," she said relishingly. "It'll have to be lanced."

After they'd bought the knife, Alice told the artisan's wife about it. "It's like a hill of pussy blackberries," she boasted. "You'd puke to look on it. Right on the ball of my foot, and marry, if it isn't a torment to tread upon. Yet my mistress tells me to get up and hobble all over town. The rich never has no pity on the poor."

"Eee," nodded the goodwife, "that's the truth of God."

"Aye. It'll have to be lanced." Alice grimaced.

"I'll tell you," said the goodwife. She was a thin little woman with needly black eyes. "I'm no poor hand at that. If you come back into my kitchen I can do that for you right now, and save you the walk home on it."

So Marion had to follow them through the stall into the low, dark house. She watched Alice sit on a stool and stick out her foot, rolling down her stocking. "See, Mistress Pudding, look there. Isn't he a fat fellow?"

Marion turned her face and said, "Ecch." The goodwife heated a long, sharp needle over the fire. Marion stared hard at a pile of dirty parsnips. When it was over, she and Alice went out in the street again. Alice limped harder and leaned harder and cursed, "Mary Mother, that hurt. God! St William!" Then, "Did you see all the stuff that came out of it? Pugh!"

When they came back to Goodramgate, Agnes and Cecily were crossing the cobbles. "Where were you?" asked Agnes. "You tell us to come, and then you're not there."

"My stepmother made me go out to Aldwark."

"Well, we're going to Ousegate to take more honey to Cis' granddam. Ask your stepmother if you can come."

Marion did not feel like asking Mistress Alison for anything today, so she said to Alice, "Tell my stepmother that I've gone with Cis and Agnes to see old Mistress Noye. Tell her we shall be back soon."

63

"Be back by None," said Alice in a choked voice. "Mind the bells."
She lurched in through the door.

"What ails her?" asked Agnes.

"She just had a boil lanced. It was the worst thing I ever saw."

"Good," said Agnes. "We can go alone. Let's get away from here before somebody stops us."

It was a long way from Andrew's house to old Mistress Noye's—halfway across town. They had to go all the way down Goodramgate, through the Shambles, a little way down the Stonebow, and then a way down high Ousegate to the narrow little house in sight of the great bridge of York. Agnes led.

"Ought we to do this?" Marion balked when they had to cross Petergate. "Why don't we go back and fetch Nan or someone to come with us?"

A hog came running up from the Shambles, grunting. A man in a bloody apron came after him. The girls pressed against the wall they were standing by, but were splashed by muck anyway. The butcher's man slipped in some slime and fell flat on his face. Agnes laughed loudly. "See the mighty boar hunter!"

"We'll be beaten when we get home," Marion went on.

"I think we should go back," said Cis.

Agnes stamped her foot. "Once we've come this far, we might as well go on."

And because it was Agnes that said so, they did.

Cis' granddam was not at home when they got there. The servant who opened the door said that she was at All Saints hearing mass, and that was where they might find her. But none of them wanted to go to church. They stood on the threshold, conferring.

"We should go home," Cis insisted. "We can come back later with Nan, or Alice, if she's better."

"Or we could wait here," said Marion. "Our mothers might not let us come out again."

"I know what I want to do," announced Agnes. "I want to go on to the bridge."

Cis stepped backward. "Oh, no," she shook her head. "Not me."

Marion gaped. "*Ousebridge?*" It was the boundary of the world to her.

"What other?"

"You two can do that if you like," said Cis, "but I stay here. My mother says the bridge teems with rogues and cutpurses."

Agnes rolled her eyes. "What have we got for them to steal?"

"Dare we?" asked Marion breathlessly.

"*I* dare," said Agnes. "I want to look at the water."

"Do what you like," said Cis virtuously. "Here I stay."

"You won't tell?" Agnes narrowed her blue eyes. "You won't tell, Cis, or I'll cut your tongue out."

"No, Cis," said Marion, "you won't tell?"

Cis puckered her mouth and shook her head. Agnes went switching down the street, looking back at them out of the corner of her eye. Marion hesitated. "Come, Cis. Don't be a timid minnow."

Cis shook her head stubbornly. "I don't want a whipping."

Agnes disappeared around the bend in low Ousegate. "She can't go alone," Marion explained to Cis and ran after Agnes.

"So you came," said Agnes. "At least I'm not the only one who's not craven."

The crowd pushed them forward onto the bridge. Someone shoved Marion. She grabbed hold of Agnes' plait. "Ow!" Agnes dug an elbow backward into Marion's chest. "Let go!"

"I hope no one sees us," said Marion. "What if someone sees us?"

When they were halfway across the span Agnes said, "There's a good place." She pointed to a narrow parapet between two of the sagging timber buildings that flanked the bridge. A stone bench was set there. They joined hands and dodged across the road. They crammed onto the bench. In front of one of the buildings a fishmonger was cleaning his wares, dumping the gelid waste into a pail. Marion twisted around to watch a barge slide under the great middle arch. Agnes peered out into the crowd.

"Look at that great ship!" Marion pointed at a tall shape drawing out of the mist downriver. "I wonder if that's Thomas Mercer's? My father said Thomas Mercer would be beggared if it didn't come in right soon."

"Margery Mercer's a fat sow," said Agnes absently.

Marion leaned over to watch the Ouse slide and ripple around the great piers.

"Caught you, Goslings!" said a rough voice behind them.

Marion whipped around, terrified. But it was no one's father. It was only two young men, grinning.

"I'm Peter, Peter Watson," said the one who had hailed them. He had curly hair and big teeth. He gestured at his friend. "He's Matthew. And who might you be?"

Agnes swung her buttery braid over her shoulder. "I might tell you if it was your business," she said.

"Oh, she's a pert one, is she," said Peter Watson, winking broadly at Marion. "Your friend's a pert one." He turned to the other boy. "What say you, Matt? Are they worth time away from old Warpwoof's looms?"

Matt grinned, scratching his pimples.

"We are Staplers' daughters," said Agnes. "We don't spend our time with dirty old journeymen." But she smirked when she said it, and tossed her braid backward again.

The journeymen moved forward, blocking the road and the passersby from their sight.

Marion hastily reminded Agnes, "Alice bade us return by None. I think it's near then now." She hated the way that Matt fellow was looking at her. It made her feel like hot, pasty pie. She picked at the hem of her apron.

"Tripe," said Agnes. "It's not half an hour since we left your house." Marion glared at her.

The Matthew fellow was moving closer and closer, grinning in that terrible way.

"If we've such scant time, goslings," said Peter Watson, "let's waste no more. Come on, gosling, give us a kiss." He reached for Agnes. Agnes laughed and skipped away. "On Doomsday maybe." She did not skip very far.

Suddenly Matt grabbed Marion and breathed turnip breath into her face. "What a darling *you* are," he said, hoarse and horrible.

"I'm not!" she said. "Let go me!" She crammed back as far as she could on the bench, but it did no good. Matt's hands were sweaty, his face close and stubbly. Marion wanted to jump off the bridge. "Agnes, help!" Agnes paid no attention.

If ever a man molest you, Alice always said, don't give it two thoughts. Give 'im the knee, where it hurts. Marion did so. Then she leaped up, thrust past Agnes, and rushed out onto the bridge, nearly colliding with a wheelbarrow. "Help! Help!" she screamed.

"Here, what's this?" People knotted about her.

"Vermin! Sheep dung! Move forward!" boomed a man on a horse.

Peter Watson, meanwhile, had jumped away from Agnes and was sauntering away across the bridge. Agnes glowered. Matthew crouched on the bench, groaning and cursing. Marion rubbed her mouth on her sleeve, sniveling.

The man on the horse came up alongside them, scowling down. "What's this?" he barked. It was John, the bailiff of Keldacross.

Marion was relieved, for she knew that the bailiff would get her off this horrible bridge—and horrified, because she knew he would tell the tale at home. Then Mistress Alison would give her a good beating. And so it happened, her only comfort being that Agnes, at least by her own lurid account, received a worse one. Her mother, she claimed, had chained her to a wall and lashed her with a horsewhip.

John Bailley had been sent down to York merely to drum up some more carpenters for Sir Gervase's new bedchamber. But he could also smell out a shrewd bargain—which was why his master was now a rich man. So he said to Andrew Comyn, with whom he had some small business of his own, "I'm thinking you'll be marrying off your daughter soon enough."

"No," said Andrew. "I'm biding my time."

John said nothing. He rolled a swallow of wine around in his mouth.

"She meant no harm on Ousebridge," said Andrew. "She's a good girl."

"Aye. All the same. Can't be too careful."

"Nay," Andrew replied sharply. "I say she's a good girl."

"No doubt. It's bad men I'm thinking on."

"She's well looked after," said Andrew.

"Aye. But a lass can't stay with her father all her days." John shot the stapler a pointed glance and looked down into his wine, swirling it gently in the cup.

"I'll marry her off when I'm good and ready. I've no lack of suitors."

"No, truly. Her looks will draw them if her dowry doesn't. Eh, Master Comyn?"

Andrew said, "Hmnh."

The bailley took more wine.

"I'm thinking of letting her enjoy a few more years of maidenhood," said Andrew at last.

"A few more years is what I was thinking on," said John.

"You?" Andrew thumped his cup on the table. "No offense, Master bailiff, but . . ."

"It wasn't me I was thinking of," John interrupted drily. "My master's son is squiring at Helmsley castle."

Andrew drew down the corners of his mouth. Then he said, "Did your master send you with this?"

"Noa," said the bailley.

"I thought not. Didn't believe he'd be thinking of a burgher's daughter for his only son."

"Two sons. One a monk."

"Mmm. Same thing."

"See. Master Comyn." John leaned forward. "I say my master has not spoken of it to me. Yet I know his mind is not wholly averse. To speak plain, Master Comyn: my master is a wealthy man; his flocks grow bigger year by year. Keldacross is a rich manor, and he now holds half the village of Tunnersgil as well, with Ingram Tarn, from Lord Ros."

Andrew raised his brows. This last was news.

"But all this building he's doing, now, it's a drain on his purse—not to mention the ordinary expenses of a knight, mounts, equipage, fees, and the like. He must soon think of the same for his son."

"A-ye?" Andrew spun his empty cup on the table. "A-ye?"

"I know well that it's not wealth that would make you think of such a match, Master Comyn. As you say, your daughter might have any of the great merchants of York. But Master Comyn, think of this: Kelda is an ancient manor. My master's folk have lived there since before the Dane. Sir Gervase rides in the tournaments at Middleham; Nevilles and Percies call him by name. What say you, Master Comyn?"

Andrew shuffled the pages of his counting book. He rubbed his beard with his free hand. Then he picked up his pen and called Adam Scawe to bring the moneybox. "Now what of this load you've brought me today, master bailley? Has it been weighed?"

"It's a shame," Alice scolded. Marion sat gingerly on the edge of her bed, humiliated and sore. Alice sat on Marion's clothes press, plaiting the girl's hair for bed. "Don't you ever let me catch you thinking about going out in the City alone again! Holy Rood and all angels! You're like to kill me!" She meant it. She, too, had caught the strap—in the kitchen, before the whole household—for negligence. But before Marion drew the bed-curtains, Alice turned back at the door. "Kicked him where it hurt, eh?" She grinned and went out.

✳ 19

Keldacross
October 1340

Adam the miller paced slowly across the common. Win Thornrigg fidgeted, plucking at the string of his great bow. Mark the fletcher stood by him, grinning fiercely. His own bow was flung casually on the ground. The gleaming yew wood showed dark against the grass. Adam finished his pacing.

"Sixty yards," he called back over the common. "Come set up the target."

"Na," Win called back. "Set it at seventy. I can hit it at seventy, easy."

"We said sixty!" Mark bawled. "Sixty yards!"

"What, fletcher," Hawisa jeered from behind him. "Afraid my lad'll shoot your tail off?"

"Shit," said the fletcher. "Seventy, then."

"Sixty is it?" shouted Adam.

"No, seventy," Mark Fletcher yelled back. He leered over his shoulder at his cronies. "Me, scared of this runt? Never fear."

"Teach t'lad a lesson, fletcher," said the hayward. "Teach him to honor his elders."

"Ye', Mark Fletcher," said Simon Thornrigg spitting on the ground. "Teach that worthless son of mine to respect them as is his elders and betters."

"Oh aye, dad." Win gritted his teeth.

The miller paced out the ten yards more, and his son Tom Bradback set up the target: a wooded post topped by a painted disk.

"Send 'em flying!" Adam bellowed, as Tom ran out of the way.

Win fixed his arrow to the string. He set his aim and pulled back his arm. Five years ago King Edward had commanded that simple men over the age of seventeen should practice no sport but archery, for he was preparing again for his war against King Philip of France. Nobody had taken that decree to heart as closely as Win Thornrigg. He had already outshot most of the older, burlier men of the village. Only the fletcher remained unconquered. That was to be remedied today.

"Bullseye," cried the miller.

The younger villagers cheered.

The fletcher chuckled harshly and drew back his string. The arrow shot out and ended alongside Win's, sending Win's quivering again.

The older men howled happily.

Win looked wild. "Move it farther!" he shrieked. "Ten yards more!"

Sir Gervase rode into the village with great Ralph of Torbeck. When they saw what was happening on the common, they reined in their horses and stopped to watch.

A child pranced out onto the green, pretending to be a horseman. "Shoot at me! Shoot at me!"

Win threw down his bow, glaring. Adam Bradback removed the child from the field. Sir Ralph guffawed. Win picked up his bow again. The fletcher tested his string.

"You know, I wish to hell that the damn pope would have kept his nose out of what don't concern him," said Sir Ralph. "Proclaiming a damned truce when we've got the Frogs on the run."

"What do you expect from a damn Frenchie pope?" Gervase shrugged. "He's just a creature of that coward Philip."

They fell silent. Gervase leaned forward on Hellfire's neck. Win was fixing his second arrow to the string, an arrow half as long as the bow itself. His face was grim and intent. He looked almost noble.

The arrow flew.

"Goddam it, *bullseye!*" The miller was amazed.

Win gloated. "Runt am I? Puny am I?"

The fletcher scowled; and tied him again.

"Did you hear that tale they were telling up at Middleham? About what happened after Sluys?" Gervase sat upright again to look at his friend.

Sir Ralph shook his head. "Don't know."

"Ah, you remember it. They said that after our ships won the battle all the Frenchies were shaking in their shoes to tell King Philip . . . "

"Craven, puling cowards," said Sir Ralph.

" . . . and so at last they sent in his fool . . . "

"What does he need a fool for? He's got *them* to laugh at."

" . . . and the fool says, 'Oh, those cowardly English.' "

"Then he was a fool indeed!"

"Na, listen. The fool says, 'Those cowardly English.' And Philip says, 'Why do you say so?' And the fool answers, 'They did not dare jump overboard like our brave French!' "

Sir Ralph drew his thick brows together. "What did he say *that* for? Of course they didn't jump overboard. They didn't *need* to jump overboard. What'd he say *that* for?"

"A joke, Ralph." Gervase slapped his glove against his thigh. "A *joke*. Ha ha."

"Oh, aye, I see it now." Sir Ralph laughed forcedly. "Ha ha, that's good."

"Christ," Gervase grunted. Sometimes he thought that Ralph had been dealt too many blows to the head, except that he had been like that ever since they were boys at Helmsley. "Look, they're finally going to shoot." They had been quarreling over the placement of the target. Or rather, Mark Fletcher had been niggling over it. Edwin had been tapping his foot, sighing loudly and muttering, "Set it anywhere you like. *Anywhere.*"

Win won the match when Mark's arrow missed the target at eighty yards, to the great delight of Hawisa. The men, even Fletcher's cronies, gathered round and slapped him on the back. Simon, suddenly friendly, took the credit for the skill of his son, in whose training he had taken no part. Mark Fletcher went growling home alone—his friends being of the fair weather kind.

"That's a good bowman, is that." Sir Ralph nodded toward Win.

"A *damn* good bowman," Gervase replied.

The two of them rode on up the hill.

"It'll be good to have our sons belted," Sir Ralph remarked.

"Aye. Thank God. For some years there I thought I was never going to have any sons."

"Hell, and now you've got two. And I, who'd got four, now have but one. The damn Sweat took the rest."

"I've only one that counts," said Gervase. "If Maudlin hadn't been so damn stubborn about sending the other to the damn white monks, I'd feel a lot easier in my boots."

"Hell, Gervie, you can always pull him out. He hasn't took his vows yet, has he?"

"Na. Maudlin would kill me in my bed. He's a singing sort of fellow anyway, is that one. Always was. Not fit to shoulder a sword, nor anything else useful."

They reached the manor house. The gate swung open, and the knights rode in.

✳ 20

The manor of Wydclif
November 1341

On Lord Ros' commendation Sir Gervase had been appointed one of the knights coroner for the North Riding. This was an honor for Gervase, but also a "pain in his arse" because it meant he had to ride out sometimes in hellish weather to purgatorial, woebegone places to look at sordid corpses and other results of unusual and unpleasant deaths. Other times it was well enough, especially when it took him to the manors of his friends. Then he would sit with them and stretch out his boots to their fires and say, "What's it come to, eh, sir? Ay, what's it all come to? Hell."

Now in this week he was called down to Wydclif to look into the death of a much hated miller who had been crushed by his machinery, either because he had fallen into it drunk or because someone had pushed him in. Sir Geoffrey thought it was murder; the villagers claimed it was drink. Apparently the whole village had been hopeful for years that someone would do the miller in.

Gervase took Nicholas with him on this inquest. "You'll have these duties one day, Nick," he said. "You'll benefit from the experience." It was a good excuse to spend some time alone with his son, for nowadays they rarely saw each other except in company.

Nicholas was not particularly interested in dead millers, but it was agreeable to ride with his father. They took their dogs and Windiscry and Gervase's peregrine, Plummet, to do some hawking on the way down.

"I'm aiming to fix you up with a good squire after your knighting." Gervase brought this up as they rode down the low, leafy road by rocky Woodenbeck. They held their hawks on their gloves. "Who'd you rather have, young Walt Cliderhou or Geoff Wydclif? Both their fathers are willing, and Lord Ros says aye to either."

Nicholas replied immediately. "Geoff Wydclif, no question."

"What's wrong with Walter?"

Nicholas looked astonished that Gervase didn't know. "I can't stand his brother," he explained.

"Hugh? I'll be damned. I thought you lads were cronies. He's a hell of a fighter, is Hugh."

"He has no courtesy."

"Nor have most of his family, I'll admit. But they're all good warriors. Now in Geoff Wydclif you'll find more courtesy, but wouldn't you say he's somewhat green and soft?"

Nicholas shook his head. "He'll get tougher. I'd rather have Mundo's brother than Hugh's."

"Right, then. I'll take it up with his father tonight. Old Geoff'll be glad of it. He and Ralph and I were like you and Mun and Rab when we were squires. Couldn't be parted. Slam a man's head into the wall before we'd hear him speak ill of one of our friends. Eh?"

Nicholas nodded, but looked self-conscious and intruded upon, so Gervase suggested, "Let's ride up on the rigg and fly the birds, what do you say?"

"Aye," said Nicholas, happier now that the talk had turned from matters of men to matters of hawks. Like his mother, Gervase thought, put off. So damn private. Well, well. Few words, fond heart.

Having lost Plummet on the moor and having spent a good two hours looking for her, they arrived at Wydclif later than they had expected. It was dusk, Wydclif house was moated, and they had just cranked up the bridge, so Gervase and Nicholas had to stand outside and bellow until someone recognized their voices. The bridge cranked down again; they rode over it into Wydclif courtyard. Stablemen came to take their reins. Sir Geoffrey strode out from the firelit door of his hall. "Grew dark; thought you weren't coming. What in hell took you so long?" The two knights clasped each other's arms, and then Sir Geoffrey nodded at Nicholas. "Welcome, Nick. Daughter Eleanor will be glad to see you. Come in, come in."

Wydclif was a snug place, gentler and more comfortable than Keldacross. Maybe comfort depended on the number of women that lived there. Edmund had six sisters, and the eldest, Eleanor, lent a high degree of gentillesse to Wydclif—so Nicholas thought—that his own sister, grand as she was, did not lend to Kelda.

Eleanor was sitting with her mother by the crackling fire in the solar, surrounded by a multitude of little sisters, all bent over some great common stitching. Dame Edith, round, plump, and rosy, stood up to greet the guests. "How welcome!" She kissed Gervase on the cheek and all the girls did likewise. Then it was Nicholas' turn. Eleanor hung back until the rest had done, then tiptoed to reach him. "Welcome, coz." They were indeed distant cousins, distant enough that their parents had seen no bar to discussing their betrothal. Sir Geoffrey had tried to pin Gervase down to it for years. "Aye, Geoff, next Christmas," Gervase would say, and then, "Aye, Geoff, Candlemas, next Candlemas we'll do it," and then, "Pentecost, Geoff, Pentecost." "God damn it," said Sir Geoffrey.

Eleanor was slim and shapely, blonde, with a broad forehead and dimples in her cheeks. She was altogether Nicholas' idea of a good-looking girl. "Ho, Eleanor," he said.

Dame Edith was speaking. "We've had our supper already, but we will sit down with you for some more victuals. Daughter, go tell them in the kitchen." Eleanor went off with her skirts rustling the rushes. Nicholas thought that he did not object to the idea of marrying her at all.

"Well, Gervie," said Sir Geoffrey, establishing his friend in his own chair and kicking a stool under his feet. "Coroner, eh? Soon or late you'll be sitting down with all those knights and burgesses down in Westminster, passing laws."

"I'd sooner pass wind in Edinburgh than laws down in London. Bunch of southron shopkeepers and tax makers."

"King's a southron."

"Na, but he's Edward Langshank's grandson, old Hammerscot's blood; he's all right. But I wish he'd settle it with these French bastards once and for all. This war's wrecking my bailiff's wool dealings."

"Aye, the advantage these woolmen take is not to be believed. Comyn of York and his ilk. Puny price he quoted me last was not to be believed."

"Yeh, well," said Gervase, suddenly reserved. "They are taking a risk these days, trading to Flanders."

Geoffrey grunted. Gervase had never been eager to excuse the woolmen before. "Well, I'd wish the king'd settle it."

"That's what I mean. Let Edward send over our northern chivalry. We'd get him back his Gascon fief in no time and smash Philip for him too. Have done with it is what I say."

"I wonder how much that dog Philip's paying the Scots to harass our borders. Egging them on like a French whoremaster."

"He's a cunning Froggie, is Philip. Knows the Marcher chivalry's the best. Keep us busy with Scots and he's covered half his arse."

Geoffrey and Gervase would have gone on happily for hours, getting red in the face and slapping the arms of their chairs, but Eleanor came back and said, "Mother, the table's ready." They got up and left the younger girls by the fire; Eleanor came with them to the hall and sat by Nicholas at table. She passed him plates of cold, sliced ginger duck and other collations. "Thanks," he told her, with one cheek full.

"How are you, coz?"

He swallowed. "Well. Mundo's well too. Said to greet you for him and to ask you whether you found that glove he left here last Whitsun."

"Tell him if that's all he can ask about, he's a no-good brother. I haven't found his glove, and now if I do, I'll lose it again." Eleanor dimpled. "All men are the same."

"Ay, well." Nicholas did not know what to say to that. "Where's your brother Geoff?"

"I don't know. He's usually here like quicksilver whenever food appears. He's probably prowling in the kennels vowing undying love to all the hounds. A man after your heart, coz."

"He's going to be my squire when the time comes."

Sir Geoffrey overheard and broke in. "What's this I hear? You've decided on that knave my Geoff?"

Gervase chuckled. "I asked Nick this very afternoon, and he said, 'Geoff Wydclif, no question.' Didn't you, son?"

Nicholas nodded.

"Oh, he'll be glad!" Eleanor exclaimed. So would she. Geoff was her favorite brother. She thought it would be pleasant if he were there when she went up to be lady of Keldacross.

Dame Edith instructed a servingman to fetch Geoff. "He doesn't know you're with us, or he'd have been here already," she told Gervase. "You know how much he thinks of Nicholas."

"Not just me," Nicholas said. "Rab and Mun too."

"Aye. Sticks to you fellows like a louse when he's at Helmsley, don't he?" Sir Geoffrey laughed. "It's 'Mundo says this' and 'Rab says that' and most of all 'Nicholas does thus and so.' You'll have a loyal squire in that rascal. He's already a fearless horseman, if I say it myself. He can spot and name you the arms of any house west of Whitby in an instant. Put me to shame twice last summer. And he can name you sires and dams of destriers back to Adam's stables."

Soon Geoff appeared, covered in dog hairs, looking strained, formal, and hopeful. He lit up when they told him the news. Nicholas smiled briefly at him. Geoff swallowed, honor and gratitude making him flush. Gervase considered him. He was skinny. That, and a certain softness about the mouth, made him seem green. But hell, he was only thirteen or thereabouts. At thirteen, Nicholas had been skinny, and look at him now! Geoff would develop. He had a promising square chin and a look of stubborn, mulish devotion that boded well for Nicholas. Yes, it was good Nicholas had chosen him. It might go a way in appeasing old Geoffrey about the marriage Gervase was working out for Nicholas with the woolman of York. He didn't look forward to breaking *that* news. It was better broken sooner than later—but Gervase wasn't yet quite sure: there was one more thing he needed to consider.

"Geoff will make you merry on the foulest winter days," Eleanor was telling Nicholas. "He's a wealth of songs."

In fact Geoff's music was no fountain of bubbling mirth. He liked songs about horrible tragedies, wicked betrayals of vassals by faithless lords and shameful betrayals of lords by faithless vassals; suicides; blood feuds; ignoble deaths; sorceries and curses. After supper, when they all went back to the fire, he sang them a long story about Morgan le Fey and her evil magics, and another one about an ominous green knight, and a third about a squire who killed himself when he learned that through the treachery of an enemy he had unwittingly murdered his own beloved master.

He set the sword agaynst hys brest

The pomel to a ston;

Through falsness of that lying manne

These gude lives were al gon.

They thanked Geoff, who bowed solemnly. Gervase got up and stretched, his eyes glistening. "God, I love a sad tale. Well, we'd better get some sleep if we're to see to this dead miller tomorrow morning."

The miller was laid out on the swept earth of his own cottage floor with bloody sacking over him. It had been two days since he died, and they tried to breathe through their mouths. Sir Geoffrey's reeve and his bailiff stood arguing over the corpse. Each had his own account to tell Gervase. The bailiff thought it murder; the reeve, drink.

"He was drunk seven night out of ten," the bailiff admitted. "He might well have fallen on his own. Problem is that Guth the cooper was heard threatening all kinds of things against him that very evening."

"Aye, and so?" The reeve spoke sharply. A villager himself, he saw the thing differently. He turned respectfully to Gervase. "Pardon, sir. But he was the meanest, thievingest awd dustbag we've ever known in Wydclif. Weighed false every time. Men've cursed and threatened him ever since he came here from Farndale. It was nowt new, what Guth said. Died of drink, did t' miller."

"What of the dent in the back of his skull, reeve?" Sir Geoffrey pointed out drily. "Think the miller put it there himself with an ale can?"

"Fell backward drunk in his cups, sir, and barked his head against a rock. He's done that sort of thing oft enough, sir."

Sir Geoffrey turned to Gervase. "The whole village is with my reeve, Gervie. Not one of them will give you a different story."

"Nobody killed t' miller, Sir Gervase," said the reeve. "But if somebody did, we'd be hard put not to shake his hand, for he was the thievingest owd . . ."

"Aye, aye," Gervase cut him off. "Let's have a look." The bailiff pulled back the sacking. Nicholas could not help making a face. "Christ," said Gervase.

"Done in good, eh, Gervie?"

Gervase shook his head. "Turn him over; let's see this dent."

Gervase stayed another day to examine the suspects, such as there were. The head wound appeared to be older, and it seemed to be explained by the testimony of one of the women Gervase questioned. She claimed she remembered hearing the miller stumble and fall backward in the night blackness outside her cottage a week before. His thuds and cursings had woken her husband and, she added sourly, her teething bairn. With no further evidence and no one to charge, Gervase had to declare the death accidental.

"What do you learn from this, Nick?" he asked as Wydclif bailiff inscribed the verdict in the manor record.

Nicholas shrugged. "Villeins have base ways of killing one another. And they lie about it."

76

"Aye. I must say I pity the bastard. Ground up in his own mill was no way to go. But some things just ain't worth pursuing."

Gervase and Nicholas stayed one more night at Wydclif, and the next morning they prepared to return to Helmsley.

"Do you stop at Kelda?" Dame Edith inquired. "Then give my love to Dame Magdalen. Tell her we look forward to her next visit." She and her daughters kissed Gervase and Nicholas turn by turn. Eleanor put her hand to Nicholas' cheek when she kissed him. Her father looked pointedly at Gervase. Gervase cleared his throat.

"Right. Let's be off. Lady, thanks for your hospitality. Friends, you know that Kelda's always open to you."

Sir Geoffrey nodded. "We'll be dining off your boards any day now, Gervie."

✳ 21

York
January 1342

Mistress Alison sent Alice across the way to fetch Marion back from Cissy Noye's. Alice ran across the close with her head bent and her hands in her armpits, for it was bitter cold.

Marion and Cis sat in one of Master Noye's bedchambers above his hall, their muffled feet against the wheeled iron brazier that warmed the room and their laps spread with fur lined blankets. They wore gloves with the fingertips cut off, for they were doing the finishing work on two close embroidered bench covers: Twelfth Night presents for their mothers. Kit, one of Cis' younger brothers, kept hanging about, tweaking threads and stealing scissors and singing a song that annoyed Marion very much.

"An hendy hap ichabbe y-hent
Ichot it is fram heavne me sent
Fram al wymmen ma love is lent
And licht on Marion!

A stroke of good luck has befallen me; I think it's sent from heaven; from all other women my love's withheld, and lighted on Marion."

"It's Alison, you stupid boy," Marion complained, snatching back her scissors. "That song is about 'Alison.' "

"But I don't care about your stepmother," the nuisance smirked. "I care about you." He was fourteen years old and thought of one thing only.

77

"Fayrest maiden under gore, herken to ma roune: Prettiest girl under a dress, listen to my song."

"If you don't leave us alone, I'll call Mother," Cis threatened.

The nuisance chuckled. "Then how'll you finish your stitchery? Her longe hair is fayr enogh, her browe broune, her eyen black, with lovesome chere she on me laugh, with midel small and well y-make."

"Here's my lovesome cheer," said Marion, and jabbed him in the rump with her scissors as he went dancing by.

"Ouch, I've been stung by lovis arrow!"

When they heard Mistress Noye's step on the stair they hid their presents under their behinds and tucked their blankets around them, giggling. Mistress Noye came in and chid them. "Sitting idle, girls? Kit, have you nothing better to do?" Then she said to Marion, "Sweetheart, Alice has come for you. Your father wants you straightaway, to greet a visitor."

Marion made a face. Since she'd grown up she hated it when her father showed her off to his guests. Last time she'd been displayed to a beaming Flanders merchant with a bald head. Again and again he had taken her cheek between his thumb and forefinger, saying over and over like a fool, "Ya, ya, yust zo is my little maidche home in Antwerpen." Marion had been glad when he went away.

"I wonder what it is this time?" she joked to Cis. "An old mercer with a muttony beard?"

"Now, girl, do as you are told without gripe," Mistress Noye reproved her. "You are a greatly blessed young woman. Go now, wrap up and run down to Alice."

Marion obeyed. She and Alice pulled their hoods over their faces and ran against the wind across the cobbles. Even that short distance reduced them to shivering and chattering teeth.

"Who would travel in such weather?"

"A knight staying at Clifford's tower," Alice replied. "Down from the moors."

"Well, why do I have to see a knight?"

"I can't tell you what I don't know, curdie pie." But Alice's voice sounded foreboding. "Come, hurry upstairs. The mistress wants you right quick."

Mistress Alison had made the maidservants lay out Marion's best winter gowns on her bed. "The raspberry surcotte, do you think, Alice," she said as they came in, "over the forest green?"

Alice nodded. "Yes, mistress. Lovely."

"Good, then. Come on, Marion, off with what you've got on now. Our guest hasn't got all day."

"But why do I have to meet this knight?"

"Nestlings chirp too many questions. Come, come. Alice, stand ready to do her hair. Get the red ribbon; we'll plait it in. Nan, come here and untie these points."

"I don't want to see this knight," Marion's voice came muffled through her undercotte as they pulled it over her head. No one paid any mind to her complaints.

When they had clothed and coiffed her to Alison's satisfaction, she was turned, inspected, and admired one last time, "Good, good." Mistress Alison patted her on the shoulder. "Go now. Your father is in the counting room."

The counting room. The most sacred room in the house, raised up by two steps from the level of the bedchambers above the hall in the gable overlooking Alison's herb garden. Marion never went in it except in her father's company, for it was padlocked, and the key hung at her father's belt was never used by anyone but him or honest Adam Scawe. Inside that room were two great ironbound coffers with carven lids and heavy locks, and in these coffers lay the profits of Andrew's trade. Each coffer was carven with an agnus-dei, complete with flying pennant and blood flowing from its side into a cup. This was an image Andrew loved because it expressed his piety and at the same time symbolized his livelihood. He had these lambs-of-God all over his house, painted onto walls, graven into chairs, and woven into hangings.

Andrew was standing before one of his most wonderful hangings when Marion came into the room. It showed the life of St William of York, in warm browns, reds, golds, and russets. There one saw the minster and its rose window, the clustered roofs of merchants' houses, the arches of Ousebridge span, and barges on the water. One saw the archbishop himself, performing miracles, confronting his persecutors, praying in a procession to St Mary's Without-the-Walls.

"Ah, daughter, here you are," said Andrew jovially. "Come in and curtsy to my guest."

The guest stood up from where he was sitting in front of the frosty window. The cold white light glared behind him so she could not see his face.

"Come greet Sir Gervase of Keldacross, Daughter. I know you remember hearing of Keldacross often."

"Yes, sir." Vaguely. There were so many manors her father had dealings with.

The guest came away from the window and stood across from her. He was a stocky man of middle height and yellow hair; he wore tall boots and a studded belt over a short surcotte of hunter's green. She did not look into his face because he made her nervous. All in all, she'd rather be forced to meet a Flanders clothmaker.

"Happy Christmastide to you," said the knight.

"Thank you, sir. A holy season to you also." Marion lifted her eyes. The knight was standing in front of the hanging Marion loved best of all the weavings in her father's house. It was in greens and blues and colors so bright it made summer in the room even in dead January. A ship sailed over a blue sea on its way to the Low Countries, away from a cliffy coast beyond which rose riggs, woods, and moorland. A little abbey lifted its tower above a copse; little manor houses and tiny thatched villages dotted the landscape. Small haymakers mowed a field, a band of little knights rode out of a crenellated keep, and grazing on the moor roamed the precious moorland sheep. When Marion was little, Andrew often held her up in front of the tapestry and let her laugh at the shepherd's dog with a hen in its mouth and at the two pairs of tiny feet sticking out of one of the haystacks. Sir Gervase was now blocking the largest figure in the weaving: a wool merchant on a horse, followed by his servants and a train of laden mules.

Andrew made pleasantries while the knight looked at Marion with a pleased, surprised expression on his rugged face. Once he even said, "Well, I'll be damned."

In a little while Andrew bade Marion go join her stepmother until dinner. As she went out the door she heard the knight say once more to Andrew, "Well, merchant, she's a fine girl. I'll be damned." She thought this very rude and wanted nothing more than to go back to Cis'.

At dinner in the hall she sat next to her stepmother directly across the table from the knight, and all through the meal he kept giving her sharp, pleased glances out of his frosty blue eyes. She had never known a person to have such yellow hair. She lowered her eyes and listened with embarrassment as Andrew and Alison managed to introduce one or another of Marion's accomplishments into every other sentence. Those cushions over there, embroidered by her; that cittern over there, played by her; that little book of lays and stories, read by her—yes, she could read and write a little, and it was Andrew's opinion that a man never knew when his wife's literacy might prove useful. Mistress Comyn herself knew how to keep accounts, but this was not mentioned as it would not have interested Sir Gervase.

Gervase chewed his meat and sipped his wine and nodded, making few comments, and still sending out those pleased, amazed glances. In a while he stood up. He must get back to Clifford's Tower. A jury was being assembled to try a Yorkiswold knight who had killed a nobleman's son in some quarrel over hunting rights. As one of the shire's coroners, Gervase was to present his findings and testimony.

"What a terrible thing, Sir Gervase!" Mistress Alison exclaimed. "Does the accused man plead innocent?"

"No," Gervase replied casually. "The fool left his own knife in the Percy's throat as if to prove his guilt, then came and threw himself on the mercy of Lord Harry Clifford. The only other way is if his son did it instead and he's protecting the boy. Some think so, since the boy cannot be found."

Marion blurted, "The son would sit and let his father do that?"

Gervase shrugged.

"Well, flesh is weak," Andrew remarked, rising with his guest. He frowned a little at Marion and hoped she had not made a bad impression with her forward speech.

After the knight had taken leave, Andrew called Marion to sit with him by the hall fire. He set her on a stool by his knee and twinkled down at her. "Well," he said, "what think you of Sir Gervase?"

Marion felt hot, and her throat tightened. A dread was slowly entering her breast.

"Hmm?" said Andrew.

"He's old."

"Old? Nestling, he's two or three years younger than I. A man in his prime! But why should Sir Gervase's age concern you?"

Marion looked into her lap and twisted her fingers.

"You don't think I'm considering you for his wife, do you? Why! what presumption!"

Marion looked up into his face with such grateful relief that Andrew had to laugh. "No, sweetheart, Sir Gervase is long married to a lady from Coverdale. I don't think he'd put her away, even for your sake."

Marion blushed sullenly. She hated to be teased like that. It made her sound vain and stupid.

"So you need not fret about Sir Gervase as a husband," Andrew went on. "But what if I told you to think of him as a father-in-law? How would you like to marry a handsome *young* gentleman?"

It had not occurred to Andrew that Marion could be anything but elated at the proposal. He was bewildered when she burst into tears.

"No! I don't want to leave Goodramgate."

Andrew was touched. "But, nestling! A woman has to marry some day. She can't stay with her father forever."

"Please, then, marry me to someone in Goodramgate." She didn't want to go out on the moors. The moors had no cozy walls encircling them; they had no minster blessing them. She did not know the people

81

who lived on them or understand them. She had never even thought that she might not stay in York.

Andrew grew disgruntled. He told her to go upstairs and wash her face. Jesu-Mary, he'd thought she'd be thrilled by the idea! It wasn't every burgher's daughter who attracted the attention of an old and knightly family. Well, the idea was new to her as yet. Andrew leaned forward and warmed his palms at the fire. "She'll get used to it," he told the crackling flames. "A year or two and she'll be proud to do her father so much honor."

"Hey Nicholas!" yelled Hugh Cliderhou. "Your father's here, and Lord Ros wants you in the hall."

"What's he here for? He's not due for his service for another month yet."

"I don't know, but they're waiting for you, so move your arse."

Nicholas jumped off the colt he was trying to break for the lord's daughter Ursula (the one Hugh loved). He threw the reins to a groom and stamped after Hugh, who jangled his spurs impressively. Hugh had been knighted last Michaelmas. Nicholas glared at his back and made curses with his lips. God, he hated Hugh Cliderhou.

"As I have said, Gervase," the lord was saying, "it's well enough with me. But I don't envy your breaking it to the boy. He's as proud as Lucifer."

They were sitting before the fire, drinking cups of mead, the lord in his carven chair, the knight across from him on a bench.

"My wife says the same," Gervase replied. "She would have me break him the bad news first and then pretty it up. Maudlin knows about such things. What say you, my lord?"

"Hell, I say break it gently."

"You know best. It's you that's had him under your roof all these years."

Nicholas came in. He bowed solemnly to Lord Ros. "My lord." And to Gervase. "Father?"

Gervase rose, holding out his arms. Nicholas embraced him stiffly and stepped back. What was this about? "My lord?"

"Stand, squire, and listen. Your father has a gift for you."

A gift? That splendid horse his father had won from Sir Edward Conyers last Christmas? Nicholas craved that horse.

"The best present a young man might hope for."

Nicholas stepped forward. "Knighting?"

The lord lifted his brows. "Hastening it rather, aren't you, boy?"

Nicholas blushed and scowled at the floor.

"This comes after your knighting, son, which is yet some months hence, I regret to say." Gervase winked at Lord Ros. "What I have done is get you a wife."

Oh. That. "Is it Eleanor Wydclif, sir?"

"Eleanor Wydclif is a curd compared to what I've got you." Talk up the girl's beauty, Maudlin had said.

Nicholas had seen few girls who made Eleanor Wydclif look like a curd—except certain great ladies one thought no more of marrying than of marrying the Blessed Virgin. He waited for his father to continue.

"She's er . . . got skin as white as lilies and eyes as dark as chestnuts, and braids as long and thick as hempen ropes. Let me tell you, son. If I were in your boots I'd be waiting for my wedding night as a bairn waits for Christmas pudding. She's a rare one, is she."

Nicholas observed him suspiciously. It was not like his father to go on like this. And in front of the lord. It was embarrassing.

Gervase looked at him expectantly.

"I thank you, sir. Who is she?"

Gervase shot Lord Ros a nervous glance and turned back to Nicholas. "Her name is Marion Comyn."

"Comyn? Are they of the North Riding?"

"They are of York."

Nicholas looked at him blankly.

"You must remember hearing of Master Andrew Comyn of York."

Nicholas swung round on the lord, who looked back with no expression at all.

"The *wool merchant?*" Nicholas exclaimed, aghast.

He went back to breaking the colt. At dinner, he would not speak to or look at his father, and when Gervase rode away, he was not there to say farewell.

✳ 22

Rievaulx
May 1342

In May Dame Magdalen rode with Joan Faulkoner and three stout villeins to see her mother in Coverdale. The first stop of the journey promised more joy than the last, for they stopped at Rievaulx the first afternoon where she could be near William. They lodged in the abbot's guesthouse.

"Lady," said the hospitaler, "we are about to sing Sext, but when we are done, I will tell your son you are here."

"No," she replied, "I would not disturb him."

"Lady!" cried Joan reproachfully. And since Dame Magdalen did not object, she told the monk to send William whenever he might. "We shall be walking in the orchard, by your leave, Hospitaler, for we would stretch our legs. Um! I'm stiff."

So they went walking out in the white orchard of apples and pears that lay in the outer precinct. The sun came down through scudding clouds and fell in shifting pools on the soft grass. The abbey bell rang. The women talked in low voices, picking up their skirts to keep their trailing hems from the damp.

A quarter of an hour passed. Then William broke in through the orchard gate, ducking his head under a low branch and racing across the grass. His blond hair curled round his ears and forehead. His eyes were as blue as the sky, and his mouth curved up like an angel's. Magdalen pressed her fingers to her mouth. William stopped short and looked at her.

She forced herself into composure, lowering her hands and folding them before her. "Well, my son," she said coolly. "How goes it with you? Are you doing God good service?"

At her severity his smile faded. He tucked his hands into his sleeves. "Yes, madam," he said, "I hope so."

"Are you obedient to your abbot and to my cousin the prior? Are you attentive in prayer, and do you do your copy work with a good will?"

"Lady, I try to."

She nodded. "Good."

He smiled again and took a step forward. "I am a good copyist, Mother, or shall be. I mean no pride, but Father Stephen (that's our novice master) says so. Would you like to see some of my work?"

"Yes," she said warmly, then checked herself. "Son, how should I do that? Would you have me tramping through cloister?"

"Oh," said William. "Aye." The smile faded again.

"Lady, perhaps he can bring it out here?" Joan suggested. "Or to the guesthouse?"

William nodded. "I'll get some of it."

Magdalen said, "I could not read it if you did. If Father Stephen says it is good, I believe him, and I am proud." She smiled with her eyes. He took another step forward.

"I am on my way to see your grandmother of Coverdale," she said quickly to keep him back. "Is there aught you would like me to say to her?"

William looked down at his shoes. "Tell her I pray for her daily."

"Good," she replied. "I will do so."

"Mother," he said, "I pray also for you, daily."

Her heart stopped. "Good," she said. "And I for you."

Joan looked up at the white branches, where a wren hopped, knocking off petals.

"Well," said Dame Magdalen. "I would not keep you from your work." She could not bear to send him away, and she could not bear to have him near.

"No," said William. He shifted his feet, then turned to go.

"William!" she cried, in spite of herself, when he had almost reached the gate. "You have forgotten to kiss me farewell!"

After that she did not go back to see him again, though Rievaulx was only a day's ride. She sent him Christmas and Easter presents, and letters in the beautiful hand of Wilfrid priest.

William wrote back and signed himself "Gulielmus Rivallis," William of Rievaulx, which pleased her very much.

✳ 23

Keldacross
September 1342

Win stood at the top of a wagonload of wheat. Sweat was running off his face and arms and down his bare, burnt chest, and he was calling for more sheaves.

"It's muckle high, Win!" Tom Bradback yelled back at him from way down below. "It's grand! We've got as much as the wagon can hold."

"Climb up and toss me another stook!"

"You're daft! You'll overturn us."

"It can take three more, easy."

Simon Thornrigg stood below in the shade of the wagon, leaning against the boards, chewing grass. "Falls and breaks his neck, his mam will have mine with her reapin' hook."

"Thinks he's got to prove summat," said Mark Fletcher, whose wagon stack wasn't nearly so high as Win's. He'd tied it off some time ago, and climbed down when it was prudent.

"Quail! Coney! Toss me up more corn!"

"Tie it, Win, just tie it. Look, here comes your mam."

Hawisa was coming up from the fields with the other women, gritty, scratcht, and bone sore. "Win!" she shrieked. "Get you down from there!" She turned on Simon. "What do you have him up there for? Why aren't *you* stacking?"

Simon spat out his grass. "He wanted to do it. Him and Tom."

"True, Mam," Win called from his lofty height.

"Well, get you down. Get down, I said!"

"Three more sheaves, Tom. What's holding you?"

Hawisa glared ferociously at Tom. "Take one more load up that ladder and I'll knock it down with you on it. I don't care if you are the miller's son."

Tom nodded. "I'm not bringing any more, Win, you mule's arse. I'm taking the ladder. Come on down now, unless you want to jump later. We've got the best wagon of the day anyhow."

"Not better than Harry atte-Beck's yesterday."

"Bugger Harry," said Tom. "I'm not bringing you more."

Young Mary Reeve was waiting at the foot of the ladder when Win climbed down. Although thwarted in his desire to outdo Harry atte-Beck, Win felt pleased with himself. He grinned at Mary.

"Ee, Win," she said. She offered him a skin of water. He squirted it all over his face before he drank it. "You're foolhardy," she told him admiringly.

"Na. I've got an eye for a load. But my mam's a worrier."

"You're good to your mam."

"Na."

"Oh aye," Mary disagreed. She looked at him with bright robin's eyes. Win ran his fingers through his hair. Suddenly Martha Reeve was there. "There's other men thirsty, Daughter. Don't pester Edwin." It wouldn't do to let those two be grinning at each other for long. Win was a good enough lad, but a plain ploughman and unfree. The reeve's family were villeins too, but rich ones. Thomas claimed a full thirty acres as well as his reeveship and its many benefits. Altogether, Martha would rather have Mary grinning at Tom Bradback, who was the miller's son and free to boot.

Evening settled on the fields. Work was done, and the harvesters straggled onto the common for some ale and a game or two for the young ones who could sweat all day and not be knackered out like their elders. Thomas Reeve, whose voice was rough from yelling at them all day long, was merry enough now to propose a winter's tune. "For it won't be long now," he said.

Hawisa groaned. "Don't say that, Reeve; it's only September."

"What's this baa-ing, you old ewe? Best harvest in years, and good harvest means good winter. Come January your husbandman can sit by his fire and fatten."

That was the wrong thing to say. "Hers does that already," someone remarked, and Hawisa looked grim. Simon didn't notice; he was busy putting down a pint of barley beer.

Ancient Winfrith atte-Beck chortled. "Aye, come January I'll sit by t'fire and gum ma beans, happy as cricket."

"You'll be hankering for spring before December's half out, y'owd geezer," Jack Thatcher laughed.

"Noa, why should I. Nobody wants to go in haystacks with me no more."

Adam Bradback laughed his great booming laugh. "Let's cheer up t'gaffer with a good rutting song." So they sang a song that belonged not to September or to winter but to April.

Wowes the wilde drakes
Males murgeth theyr makes
Ys no strem that striketh stille
Wormes woweth under cloude
Wymmen waxeth wounder proude
(So wel it wol them seme)
Yef me shall wonte will of on
This wunne woel y wole forgon
And wyght in wode be fleme!

The wild drakes woo; males make their mates merry; there is no stream that flows without chatter; worms woo under the clods; women become wondrous proud (so good all this seems to them). And if I don't get my will of one, this wealth of joy I'll forgo altogether and flee like a ghost in the wood.

"Poor old Winfrith," someone remarked loudly. "We won't let you wail in the wood come April. We'll find you a willing old crone."

"Doan't want no old crone. Had one for thirty years. Want a lass, and a young un."

"Out of luck, old man," some girls tittered. Winfrith menaced them: "If I were in my prime . . ."

Godrich's bells rang Vespers changes.

"Wilfrid priest's paying Wat Cottar's young Gabriel to learn bell ringing," Martha Reeve remarked to Edith Thatcher. "I wonder how Ragenhilda weasled that out of him."

"Paying him how?"

"Took some off of Wat's tithe."

"Wouldn't you know he'd let her off light. Why don't we all get our lads in to pull bells, and we'll none of us pay tithes. St Godrich, I'm vexed!"

The reeve got up regretfully. "Won't do to wait till nightfall; no moon tonight, and some here is tipsy." Simon Thornrigg and old Winfrith got weepy. They linked arms and swayed as they stumbled over the sheep-cropped stubble toward the village.

"Wynter wakeneth al ma care," Winfrith was warbling. "Now the leves waxeth bare, oft I sigh and mourne sare . . . "

"When it comes into my thought how this world's joy, it com to nowt," Simon joined him, slurry and out of tune.

"Look at that fool," Hawisa observed to Win. "Watch if he doan't fall into t'duck pond."

The hoarse, weepy voices wavered back to them in the dusk.

Nou it is, and nou it nys
As tho it never were, iwis.
That many saith, so it is:
All goth bot Goddis wille.

They heard Simon give a loud sob and then a splash as he fell into the duck pond. Win shook his head. He left his mother and ran across the common to help pull his father out of the mire.

Next morning, with his spade on his shoulder, Win took the customary cut between Jack Thatcher's pig fence and the reeve's house—because it was shorter, not because he'd had any notion of talking to the reeve's daughter. That had nothing to do with it.

But as he passed her door, she popped out on the threshold with a broom and sang out, "Where hasta been since I saw thee?"

Without meaning to, he sang back, "Upon t'moor bat'at!" Bare-headed on the moor. It was the refrain of a drinking song that Kelda attributed to Mary's grandfather. (Gib Faulkoner said they sang it over at Tunnersgil, and the constable said he'd heard it as far away as Ilkley, but "They must've had it o' the reeve's dad," the village maintained.)

"Tha'lt surely catch thy death of cold, upon the moor bat'at!" Mary continued the song, sweeping in time.

"Well, then tha'lt have to bury me, upon t'moor bat'at!"

"But *worms* will come and eat thee up!" Mary shrieked. She batted at him with her broom. "And look, you're already skin and bones! Now, don't deny it, Win Thornrigg, you've been with Hereswith the gooseherd. I can smell her on you."

"Oh, aye, her and me all night, upon the moor bat'at. Quit hitting at me!"

"Well, fight back, then."

"I'm weary from work."

"You think *I* do nowt but sit all morning? Fight like a man!" She swung at him again with the broom; he grabbed it, and they made a tug of war in front of the door.

Thomas Reeve came up the path. Win dropped his end of the broom. The reeve looked at him and said, "Get off into the house, Mary."

"Now then, Dad!"

"Now then yourself, lass," the reeve growled, ominous. "You speak to me respectful."

Mary looked sideways at Win and swung in through the door.

Thomas turned back to Win. "I'll talk to you."

In dread, Edwin bent to pick up his spade. Gaw, he felt the fool, and a scared fool too, having angered the reeve.

"Sit down here, on the bench." The reeve pointed Win to the seat before his door, then stood over him.

"Edwin," said the reeve at last, "you're a good lad, and I don't think I need tell you why not to play with my Mol."

"I meant no harm."

"I know that, son, because I know you. Nonetheless, I was a young man once, and I know it don't pay to look too hard at what you can't get."

Win looked embarrassed.

"Just a bit of wisdom, lad."

Win looked up, hoping to be dismissed, but the reeve cleared his throat. "There's another matter I'll speak to you on."

Win's spirits sank even lower.

"Your dad. Drunk three night in seven this week, as you know. This morning, didn't show for weekwork—I dragged him out of the tick where he was snoring before John Bailley noticed. That axle he broke of Harry-atte-Beck's on Tuesday? Still not fixed."

"I'll fix Harry's wheel."

Thomas shook his head. "No, son, it's on that I want to speak." He paused. "Your dad shames you, and that's too bad, but it's been that way a long time. Let Simon mend his own damages. Don't be stepping in for him every time."

"Reeve, I can't sit by and wait for him. He won't do owt till it's too late."

"He might act the man if you and your mam would let him tow his own load."

Win stuck his spade into the ground and wedged it down with his foot.

"Edwin!" Thomas barked. "Now you listen to what I say. I've spoke

89

to you friendly; now I tell you as your reeve. You fix Harry's wheel, and I'll have you in the stocks, do you hear me?"

Edwin smiled faintly, but Thomas looked him in the eye. "I'm not playing, lad. Summat's got to make you see reason and do what you're told."

"I'll do what you say, but I can't let my mam starve."

Thomas sighed gustily. "Hawisa won't starve. Leastways, not before you drop dead in your tracks from work."

Inside the cottage Mary was cheerily singing, "Ducks'll come and gobble up t'worms, and then we'll come and gobble up t'ducks . . . "

"Go then, Win. And don't forget my words."

But he'd forget them soon enough, Thomas reflected, and then the bailley'll be on my back for overworking the knight's good archer. Then, St. Godrich, I *will* clap the fellow in stocks, for all he thinks I'm playing.

"And then we'll have thee back again, upon t'moor bat'at," Mary was warbling as her father came in.

"Lass, I catch you diddling again with that ploughman, and you'll feel my belt."

"But, Dad . . . "

"You heed me, lass. I'm not playing."

But to Martha his wife he said, low, "I'm worried over Edwin Thornrigg. I've never known a day of freedom in my life, but *that* lad's double-thralled: once to the knight and once to his dam."

Martha, readying a batch of dough for baking, shook her head ruefully. She patted her last loaf into shape and called Mary to take the batch up to the ovens. "Here's to pay the bake-fee. Don't forget, girl, lest the bailley holler."

"Double thrall's too much for any man, that's all I'll say." The reeve settled down by his fire and stretched his hands out to the warmth, for it had turned sudden cold this morning, just as he'd predicted.

✴ 24

Keldacross and Emberthwaite
September 1342

Sir Gervase was always going on about how plain Katharine was and what a huge dowry he would have to offer in order to get rid of her. "Hell," he would say, why don't I just pack her off to Rosedale Abbey and have done with it; it'd spare my time and my purse. I've no doubt she'd make a grand prioress some day, riding roughshod over all those nuns." But actually he had never looked to marry her off before her eighteenth birthday, partly because he chafed at the bother, and partly because he liked the girl when he thought about her and was in no great haste to pack her off.

But Katharine did not know this. She stood by the solar windows with her back like a poker and a hard, pale face. Her freckles stood out on her skin like blemishes. She did not care about a husband, because she loved Kelda and did not hanker to live under some man's thumb in a strange place. But to be a nun? Never to ride or hunt? To sit inside all day long and pray? She'd be damned if she'd do it; she'd tell him so next time he said it. Let him swear, she thought, pressing her lips together. I'll swear and damn him for a lousy father. Does he care so little for me as to think of making me a nun?

"Husband," said Dame Magdalen finally, "would you have our only daughter die a spinster?" She had worried about Katharine's marriage for some time but had not mentioned it for months because she hated tempers and scenes.

"Don't push me, Maudlin!" Gervase retorted.

Magdalen flinched inwardly. Gervase was working himself into a rage. He burst out of the solar and stamped around the hall shouting, "Does she think I have nothing else to do? Mother of God! What do these women think? I fight, I work, I sleep on the cold ground for weeks on end, and they think I have nothing to do but dally in their trifles?" Then he went out hawking with Ingram Tarn of Tunnersgil.

But the next day he did his duty. He rode over to discuss marriage with a knight of Farndale whose second wife had died in childbed. "Oh good," Katharine snorted. "He's killed off two already; let's see how fast he can do me in."

Emberthwaite in Farndale lay some five miles east of Keldacross, near the River Dove. Its master, Sir Henry, was a kindly man in his thirties with thinning, mouse colored hair and a big pink nose. He was not much of a warrior. Not that he shirked his obligations, but neither did he fulfill them with the greatest zeal. He enjoyed standing with his shepherd on the moorside, talking long, slow talk about winter and spring and lambs and the scab. He always spoke in a quiet voice and was good at preventing quarrels. His friends thought him phlegmatic. Because of this Katharine disdained him, but she had scant choice in the matter. Gervase came home the same day he had ridden out and announced the betrothal at supper.

"I've found our daughter a husband," he said, "and after she thanks God she can thank me, for it was damn hard work."

The wedding itself was at Keldacross, but afterward they all rode over Rudland Rigg to Emberthwaite for the feast. William had not come from Rievaulx, because Dame Magdalen "did not wish to disturb him." But Nicholas came from Helmsley, and that pleased Eleanor Wydclif. She came up to Nicholas after the first round of Katharine's feast, when everyone was snoozing in the hall, and said, "Hey, cousin."

He sat up and rubbed his eyes. "Hey, cousin," he replied.

"Are you as heavy as I am? I feel like a stuffed goose." She rubbed her stomach.

"I've had to loosen my belt three notches," he agreed.

"I think the best way to settle digestion is to walk about, not lie about, don't you?"

"Well, I don't know."

"Our priest at Wydclif has a book that says so. You can ask Edmund."

"Why should I? I believe you."

She glanced around then and held out her hand. "Come, coz, let's walk out. I have something to tell you."

Something about her voice, and the way she looked at him, made his face feel red. He took her hand and got up.

They went out of the hall and into the courtyard, where villeins were jumping over barrels, singing raucously.

"Well, what?" asked Nicholas.

"They have a windmill here."

"Aye. So?"

"Let's go see it."

They went out the gate and down into the village. It was deserted: everyone was up at the manor house.

"There it is," said Eleanor, pointing. "Look at the great sails! Wouldn't you like to see them turning? Have you ever seen the sea, coz, and ships sailing?"

"Was up at Scarborough once." Something was making him mumble. He shrugged uncomfortably. "What did you want to tell me?"

"Let's go sit behind that beech," she said. "The grass looks green."

He turned red again. She pressed his arm, and he did as he was told.

She was very fair. Her hair was the color of daffodils, her forehead pure and broad, her eyes wide, the color of violets. She sat on the grass, against the tree, smiling at him. Then she pulled him down with her.

When it was over, she took him by the shoulders. "Remember what you've said, cousin. Remember what you have just sworn to me."

"Aye," he said, dazed.

"We mustn't wait too long." She fixed him with her blue gaze. "When will you tell them?" She shook him gently.

"I'll be up from Helmsley again at All Saints, to be fitted out for my gear. I'll tell them then."

She let him go, saying, "That will be well."

That evening, when the wedding couple were established in their bedchamber and the last rowdy guest finally routed out, Sir Henry spoke to Katharine and told her he hoped she would like Emberthwaite. "Since poor Adela died I have made changes in the hall and chambers to make them gentler and more comfortable for a lady."

Katharine replied in a hard voice. "I don't need comfort. I'm not soft."

Henry felt the cut but forgave it instantly. Poor girl, all stiff and frecklefaced. "Hard to leave your home at Kelda, eh?" He rubbed his pink nose sympathetically.

She shrugged. She was angry that he expected her to let him see into her heart. I'll be damned if I cry on his shoulder, she thought. Then she inquired bluntly, "Why are we gabbing? Is that what marriage is for? Let's get on with it."

Sir Henry, half chagrined, had to laugh at that. His nose turned several shades pinker, and he ran his fingers through his thinning hair. "Well," he chuckled, "I reckon I'll never have to guess what Dame Katharine is thinking."

"No," said Katharine, looking him in the eye. "You won't."

✳ 25

Rievaulx
October 1342

The bell rang for Sext. William did not budge except to thrust his nose deeper into St Aelred's *De spiritali amicitia, The Spiritual Friendship*. St Aelred was the pride of Rievaulx, and the nine handsome volumes of his works were the pride of Rievaulx library. William was leaning against a pillar in the cloister. The last bright sun of the year shone down warm on the back of his head. He preferred not to move.

Gilbert prodded him.

"Hmmm?"

"Hmm yourself," Gilbert whispered. An old monk glared balefully at them as he passed. They should be keeping the silence.

"I don't feel very well today," William whispered back. "My head aches. I think the sun has touched me."

"Aye, aye," said Gilbert, "you are always ill—or feigning to be so."

By the time he reached choir, William actually did feel queasy. Soon after they began to sing, everything went strange and hazy before him. The familiar faces in the opposite stalls receded sickeningly. The singing went mute. He heard a loud voice saying, "I'm going to faint," and the next thing he knew he was gazing up at the vaulting. For a moment he thought he was at Keldacross. Then he recognized Gilbert, pucker faced at having doubted his friend. The infirmarian loomed over him, so he sat up, head swimming.

"Can you walk?" the infirmarian asked.

"I think so," said William. His head felt muttony. He knew that some of them were vexed at the distraction and others glad of it. He did not know which was worse, so he leaned his head on the infirmarian's shoulder and thought of the bed he was going to lie in and the rich meat stew he was going to get. Usually when he went to the infirmary (and that was often) it was for vomiting, so he rarely got the stew.

Once he was in bed, the infirmarian let some blood from his arm, which made him feel even more wan. It was not an unpleasant feeling. He knew he would have nothing to do but loll in bed all day—and night. No Vigils. No Matins.

"I'm sorry, Infirmarian," he said in a sad, sickly voice.

"Indeed. Well, I don't suppose you could help it, though I cannot fathom what caused that swoon. You haven't the slightest fever, yet I doubt you're that good a mummer. Well, I'm back to cloister. Brother Hugh's about. Is there anything you'd like me to bring you when I return?"

"No, I thank you." But before the infirmarian quite reached the door, William sat up and said, "Oh, but sir. If I could have that volume of St Aelred, or perhaps the *Rhetorics*, to pass the hours, that would be charity."

The man turned and looked at him. One eyebrow lifted slightly. "Mmm hmm," he said, and went out.

William slumped back again, mournfully, and restfully.

When the infirmarian returned some hours later, he brought with him neither Aelred nor Cicero, but a small, battered volume of Holy Scripture. He set it firmly on William's knees: a plain little evangelium out of the austere olden days, bare of any illumination: only red capitals relieved the plain black script. St Aelred himself might have cherished the book between his palms, but William did not care. He sat up against the wall and made a face at the infirmarian's back. The wall was cold and hard. William thought, Don't I get enough Holy Writ in this place already? Could I not have something else, for once, even when I'm sick? He brimmed with self-pity. All afternoon he had slept pale afternoon sleep with a headache throbbing behind pale afternoon dreams. Everything was horrible. He did not even want the meat stew any more, because now he felt sick to his stomach. He opened the book and flipped the pages sullenly back and forth.

The words struck out at him, black and red. Deus meus, Deus meus, quare me dereliquisti, My God, my God, why have you forsaken me?

William slammed the book shut. His heart pounded; his face grew hot. He lay down again and stared at the ceiling. Leaf and light patterns moved across it, orange red in the westering sun. A hill, three gibbets, and night in the afternoon. William groaned. Shame poured over him, and fear, and horror. What was it that was demanded of him? Why wouldn't it leave him alone? Desperate to get away from whatever it was, he pushed the book down to the foot of the bed, rolled over, and covered his head with his blanket.

* 26

*Keldacross
November 1342*

Nicholas was to get his spurs shortly after Easter, so he was up at Keldacross being fitted out for armor and weapons and blazoned surcoat, and he was made much over by all.

"Well, brother," said Katharine as he stretched out his arms to be measured for his gambeson, the heavy quilted shirt that would go between him and his mail (and perhaps between him and an unlucky arrow). Katharine was up from Emberthwaite for the month, because Sir Henry was away at Helmsley, and she could not stand her mother-in-law. "Well, brother. Nobody will be able to say you do not make a knightly figure."

"Let us pray his deeds match his looks," said Dame Magdalen, around the pins in her mouth. Measuring strips dangled over her arm.

Nicholas twitched impatiently. "When do you think they'll be back? How long is it since they left?"

"I have told you, son, at least three times. They left two days ago, and I expect them back at any time."

Nicholas compressed his lips. Dame Magdalen smiled up at him. The reason for Gervase's riding out with Sir Ralph and Cuth Constable was no mystery to Nicholas or anyone else. They had gone out to buy a warhorse for Nicholas, Gervase boasting to Ralph that some men might scant their sons to spare their purses, but that was villainous stingy and he would never do it. Meantime everyone had to pretend ignorance of the errand so as to "surprise" Nicholas. In fact, Nicholas was twitching in excruciating suspense.

"Son, son," his mother admonished him. "Stand still a moment." She knelt and wound a cord around his narrow waist, snipping the cord where it met. Nicholas gazed over her head, out the solar windows, onto where Kelda rose, November bleak, under a low sky. He cracked his knuckles.

Magdalen rose again, somewhat stiffly. "There. That's all for now. Go out and ride off some of that impatience. You're trembling like a yearling colt."

Nicholas sprang off the stool and ran around the room twice.

"God's Nails," Katharine laughed. "Do you think you'll be able to stand still long enough to get your spurs?"

"At least he'll have no trouble keeping awake for his vigil," said Magdalen.

Nicholas flashed them one of his rare, broad grins, and bounded out of the room. They heard him crashing down the length of the hall.

Magdalen sighed. Yes, she truly loved this son. As always she tried to turn her mind firmly from the other who was given to God at Rievaulx. She draped the measuring strings over her great loom and marked them with a bit of charcoal: O for his waist, X for his arms, XX for his shoulders, XXX for his back.

"He's a beauty," said Katharine. "I am proud to have him for my brother."

"I'm thinking it would be a good thing if William could come see his brother knighted."

"Well, Mother, you may always call him home. I doubt the monks will refuse to let him out for this."

Dame Magdalen plied the loom shuttle. It rattled.

"And let me tell you about monks, Mother. We had two fine black monks of York come riding into Emberthwaite not a month since, one of them being a cousin of my husband's. They were on their way from a wedding, and they stayed at our house for nearly a week, eating and drinking and making very merry."

That was not a good thing to say. Dame Magdalen turned her back and set her jaw. "No, I mislike such things. A monk out of his house is like a fish out of water. I would not have my William made worldly."

"Oh, Mother," Katharine sighed.

That afternoon two things happened. The Wydclifs came to pass the rest of All Hallows, and Sir Gervase came riding down from wherever he'd been—with The Horse.

"Holy Rood!" cried Nicholas.

Gervase dismounted, came over, and slapped Nicholas in the rear. He smiled a foxy smile and beetled his brows. "Eh, boy? What do you think, eh?"

The horse gleamed like silver mail. He was as heavy boned and muscled as a warhorse must be, yet he moved his neck with marvelous grace, and he turned his great head to look full at Nicholas. His eyes were like fire; his nostrils flared; he breathed white steam into the chill air.

"Dragon," said Nicholas. "His name is Dragon."

"So be it," agreed Gervase. "He has been called Galahad, but Dragon he shall be. Now tell me, son, do you love me?"

"I love this horse," said Nicholas. He took the reins from Cuth Constable.

Later, after mass, Eleanor Wydclif came to Nicholas in the stable-yard, where he was walking round and round Dragon, running his hands along the smooth coat and talking to the horse in soft, admiring tones.

"Cousin," said Eleanor. "That is truly a wonderful horse. You are blessed to have a father who loves you so well. My brother Edmund's horse looks like a donkey compared with this one."

"Ay, he's fine," Nicholas agreed. "He's as fine as black Maccabeus."

Eleanor stood on the opposite side of Dragon, lifting her skirts above the muck with one hand. The other she ran along the destrier's lofty back. Nicholas looked up, caught her eye, and turned hot.

"Have you told your mother what we said?"

"No," he replied, "Not yet."

"Cousin! You swore to me!"

"I will, I will. Not tonight though. Tomorrow."

"You swore you would do it before All Hallows. *You gave your word.*"

Nicholas rubbed at a flawed spot in Dragon's coat. "Aye," he said, "I did." And he left the horse with Cuthbert and went into the house. He found his mother in the buttery. "Mother," he said, "I would speak to you alone." He gave her a strained look. She raised her brows and came out with him. She led him to the great bedchamber and closed the door.

"What is it?"

He told her.

"Oh, St Godrich," she groaned. "How could you do this to us, Nicholas, and *now*? Well, I shall have to fetch your father."

"I'll go out then," he said. "I'll go exercise my horse."

"Oh no you will not. You will stay right here." And she went and found Gervase in the hall, where he and Sir Geoffrey and Sir Ralph were quarreling happily by the fire.

"God have mercy on me, Maudlin," Gervase bellowed, when Nicholas told him, muttering the news to the floor with his eyes averted from his father. "God have mercy on me if I don't twist the little slut's head off!"

"Husband!" Magdalen flashed her eyes. "Lower your voice!" The door was shut and the walls were thick. But in a manor house the walls have ears.

"She's no slut," Nicholas whispered, "but a gentlewoman, and it's a gentlewoman I want to marry, not a shopgirl."

"Curse you, ungrateful villain," Gervase spat back. "I travel the whole North Riding to find you a horse fit for Earl Percy's arse. I empty my coffers to get you trapped out like a prince. And do you show me any love, or even the goddam obedience due a father? By God, if you think I'm such a doting fool as to break my contract with the merchant because you're too proud to marry his daughter, you're wrong, lad. Dead wrong."

"Then," said Nicholas, lifting his chin and feeling very noble, "I shall leave Yorkshire, for I cannot bear the dishonor of this."

"Then you can kiss your destrier and your knighthood farewell." Gervase spoke now in the hard, flat voice that meant what it said. "For I will have nothing more to do with you."

Nicholas turned to his mother.

"Son," she said, "what do you want me to say? I have never pretended to love this match, but it has been made. You cannot make your father forswear to the merchant. After all, the girl is not so very low. If she were low, would we betroth our son to her? As you know, your Uncle George of Coverdale made just such a marriage not two years since, and it has been all for the good."

"I swear I meant no jest, son," Gervase went on in the iron voice. "If you shame me in this, you may bid your horse and your spurs a long goodbye."

Nicholas cracked his knuckles. He looked at his father from under his brows. "Well, what about Eleanor?" he mumbled at last. "I did promise her."

"What about her? You had no business making such a promise."

"Well, what am I to say to her?"

"Tell her that if she knows what's good for her she'll keep her mouth shut and not go blabbing it about the country that she's a whore."

"And they are already irked enough with us at Wydclif," Magdalen added, "for not marrying you two as we always said we would."

Nicholas went out into the hall and beckoned to Eleanor. She lingered a little, then followed him out to the Old Keep, where he was waiting for her in the sickroom, as agreed. She went in and sat on the bed. He stood with his back to the door.

"They'll have none of it," he said.

"You told them everything?"

"Aye, and they'll have none of it."

She stared at him until he looked away. She had not believed for an instant that her plan would not work. She did not believe it now. "You can't have told them everything!"

"I tell you I did."

"But how . . . what did they say?"

"They'll just none of it, that's all."

Eleanor caught her breath. "We must ride to York or some place. We'll have a priest marry us there." She spoke with conviction and, still sitting on the bed, held out her hands.

He made no move toward her but instead found himself moving backward toward the door. "I won't disobey my father." A prodding feeling reminded him that this filial obedience had been less than honorably inspired. He shoved the thought aside. "My parents are willing to spare yours by saying nothing of this. We had best forget it."

He looked at Eleanor. Her eyes seemed purple, as if bruised. Staring at him, she withdrew her hands, then brought her feet up under her on the bed. "But what if I'm with child?"

It had never occurred to him. Now, the prospect offended him. "Why didn't you think of that before?" He swung out of the room, slamming the door behind him.

He ran down the steps three at a time. Was it his fault? Had he forced her? On the contrary, now that he thought of it, her behavior had really been whorish. A wife who acted like that would only bring a man shame in the end. Better to beg his father's pardon, marry the merchant's daughter, and keep his horse.

John Bailley recorded the price of the destrier in his big book of accounts. He winced as he did so. But then he thought of the rich dowry that would come with the stapler's daughter next summer. He thought, "If all goes well, we're home free."

✳ 27

York
November 1342

Andrew Comyn might scallop his sleeves; he might add an inch of fur to his hem; he might wear his capuchon atop his head, wound around with the end sticking up like a coxcomb. But his colors were always merchant sober, and his shoes of a seemly length and not too pointed. And he saw to it that his womenfolk dressed plainly to their station. Marion had two surcottes of good stuff, one of raspberry, the other of the same dark mulberry as her father's best gown. Her long cottes, worn under, were forest green or russet brown, her coverchiefs white and her collars high and modest. But now she must go down with Alice and Mistress Alison, to a tailor, to be fitted for the clothes of a lady.

They had already bought the stuff from Thomas Mercer: foreign cloths, of yellow and crimson and sky blue.

The woman's tailor was a big man with a huge deep voice, which everyone found hilarious because his work was considered effeminate. "Gentlewomen are wearing their cottes close fit, and their necks low," he said, "which I'm sure the gentlemen like right well." He winked at Mistress Alison, who stared back icily. "Watkin!" he bellowed. "Watkin! Get over here with that mannequin. Look at this surcotte, young mistress," he went on. "See how wide and low the armholes are cut? I think it far more comely than the old *bliaut*. I hear that the noblewomen of the court are wearing theirs cut way below the hip, to show their jeweled girdles. But you won't have that."

"Assuredly not," said Mistress Alison.

"You will need a pelisse, though," the tailor continued, "and perhaps a fur collar to go over it. Did you see the Lady Clifford when they rode in last month?" He whistled through his teeth.

"My stepdaughter is marrying a country knight, not Lord Clifford. I think we can manage without fur collars."

The tailor protested. "Why, no, Mistress Comyn. Just yesterday a gentlewoman from the Yorkiswold ordered a right fine one, not so wide off her shoulders as Lady Clifford's, but a right fine one all the same."

Coming home through the rain, Alice hefted an armload of wrapped oddments: a beaded belt, an embroidered bag, two gilt snoods, packets of spices to pack with the clothes, a little pearl-handled knife, a pair of tweezers, a damask coverchief—and a fur collar. (The furrier was the tailor's uncle.)

The cobbles were slick, and the women went gingerly. Someone backed a loaded handcart out of an alley and blocked the street. They edged past, and met Alice's brother Martin on the other side.

"They were doing a play of Jonah, were the fishmongers," he told them, as Alice shifted her load into his arms. "But the rain came and swallowed it up. Har har."

"Ho, ho," said Alice. "Quick! Before all this finery gets wet!" Alison and Marion hurried on ahead.

"Poor little curdie pie," said Alice. "My heart grieves for her, it truly does."

"She's as grey as the weather."

"So would you be, if you were going out to live on the manors, with bailiffs and clodhoppers. Purgatory for her. Remember what our old sire says about the manors."

"T'owd goat," said Martin cheerfully.

"Here, don't slosh that puddle all over me, gowp. And hurry!" Alice drew down her dark brows and stepped up her pace. Truly she grieved for her little mistress; she grieved sore. But if Master Comyn thought that Alice was going to leave York and go live with her out on the moors, even for a fortnight, well, he'd just gone mad.

That afternoon was dim, and the wives and daughters of Goodramgate were spending it in Master Comyn's hall, for it was the brightest room in the house. They were doing mending together so as to pass the tedium in gossip. Marion was darning her father's hosen; the toes had broken through. "I tell that man time and time again," Mistress Alison complained, "that if he would but trim his toenails he would not be so hard on his hosen."

"Why should he care?" Marion was in a churlish mood. "He doesn't have to mend them. It's me, always me." And she got a slap across the ear. Now she sat on a bench by the fire, absently drawing her needle in and out of the same spot and staring off with that distant expression Mistress Alison felt sure would one day drive her to distraction.

"Stepdaughter!" she snapped. "We are discussing matters of importance to housewives. Pay heed! If you're to be mistress of Keldacross you'll need to understand these skills."

Marion started. She lowered her head over the darning and then raised her eyes sullenly. "I *am* paying heed." She did not want to be mistress of Keldacross. She wanted to stay comfortably home in York.

"St William!" Mistress Alison turned to Mistress Noye. "The day you see a madwoman shrieking down Goodramgate tearing her hair, it will be me, driven crazy by that girl. St Peter, I know not what the lady of Keldacross will think of me, that I taught the lass neither manners nor wifery? Marry, she shames me. It's either walking down the street with her neck stuck out like a stork's, gawking at everybody she sees, or it's this—sitting pale and distant as a princess. As a queen she sits, yet she cannot take the trouble to wear her clothes with decent seemliness. Just yesterday I caught her about to go out in Goodramgate with the collar of her shift hanging out over her surcotte, all crumpled, like some sort of alehouse slattern. I know not what the lady of Keldacross will think of me, or of us wives of York, that we cannot teach our daughters to dress themselves! St Peter! I shall go mad."

"That's the way with maidens," said Mistress Noye soothingly. "Always in their world of dreams."

"It is? I never remember being so fey. Nor do I see Cis stumbling about like a halfwit. Do I, Cis?" Alison set down the sheet she was patching and looked at Cis, who peered hard at her own work and pretended not to have heard.

"Do I, Cis?" Alison repeated. "You don't behave yourself so."

Cis cast Marion a helpless little half glance and mumbled, "No, Mistress Comyn."

Mistress Whewell turned the talk back to the discussion to which Marion ought to have been paying heed. "Well. Goodwife Webbe may say what she will, but I have never known scattered alder leaves to make a whit of difference with fleas, and I cannot see how she should think so. I myself know of nothing better than a sheepskin spread over the bed. They will always hop onto it, and then you have them." She pinched her fingers quickly together and made a cracking sound.

"Aye," said Alison, "and as soon as you remove the sheepskin, they all hop back into the bed, and there they have *you*. Nay, that's no use."

"Well, Mistress Comyn," said Mistress Noye, "what's your secret, then, for getting rid of fleas?"

"Simple," Alison replied. "Soak two trenchers of bread in birdlime and set a lighted candle in the middle of each. The fleas will come and get stuck, and the birdlime—or turpentine if you prefer—kills them. That's the best way I've found."

"Well, I don't know," said Mistress Whewell. "I still say that if you lay out the sheepskin, and have a tub of soapy water at hand for to plunge it right in, you can drown most of them at once."

Marion's eyes glazed over. She wished she were far away from fear of wifery and talk of fleas. Bricht thimbel ful of song. . . . But she was too old to be Queen Liliflour, ever again.

✳ 28

Rievaulx
February 1343

William moaned, "Leave me alone. I'm sick." He was ill again. His eyelids ached with heavy gumminess; his throat rasped; his bones were one with the sheets. He sat up and put his legs out from under the blanket. His feet jarred on the cold floor. Painful shivers ran up from his soles into his knees. He hung his head, tucked his hands up under his armpits, and shuffled off after Gilbert and the others, to do his duty.

Once in choir he grew somewhat more awake. The cold moved up from his knees into his belly. He bent his neck, rubbed his eyes, sniffed up what was in his nose, and began to sing. A faint orange light flickered from the torch set in its sconce by the night stairs across the faces in the dark church. Red lights were burning in the sanctuary. The low voices rose and fell, answering back and forth. William thought of the white snow falling outside, and the poor people huddled in their freezing huts. But at least if any of them had wakened to the abbey bell, they could roll over and go to sleep again. For so it had tolled over all the turning years, as homely as the seasons and the fields that turned with the seasons. As long as it went on tolling, things were as well as they might be.

If only it weren't so dark. If only it weren't so cold. The wool of his habit scratched William's neck. His head hung heavy, and he slurred the syllables of the antiphon beyond recognition. Today was a holy day, Candlemas, so there would be two masses sung to the glory of God and for the good of his people.

If only it weren't so dark; if only it weren't so cold.

At breakfast in the frater William had to listen to the lector read from St Benedict: "And when they rise for night office, let them greatly encourage one another, on account of the excuses of the drowsy." Gilbert nudged William with his foot, grinning. William scowled. He made a swimming motion with one hand and plugged his nose with the other, indicating a dish of dried herring by Gilbert's elbow. Gilbert grinned wider and passed the dish.

Two hours later the sub-prior stepped into the warming room (they had lit the fire at the end of October; it would burn till April). He found William and touched him on the shoulder. He made the grim sign: Abbot.

William touched his chest. Me?

The sub-prior nodded his head for William to follow.

William's stomach rocked. It was all Giles Percy's fault. That fellow thought he had some kind of seigneurial right to everything he saw, just because of his name. William had only left cloister to go to the privy, and when he'd come back, Giles had taken his book. There had been a loud quarrel, breaking the silence and the peace, and William had ended with a swollen lip.

The subprior pushed open the heavy door to the abbot's parlor. Abbot Langeton sat at his carven table. The prior stood at his right elbow, the cellarer at his left. Father Stephen stood by the window, hands folded in his sleeves. The light fell in tracery patterns across his long face. The subprior pulled the door shut. The abbot looked up from the papers he had been studying. "Cellarer," he said, "go tell the woolmerchant that I will see him shortly. Make him comfortable." The cellarer bowed as he went out, glancing at William over his shoulder.

The abbot looked at William for a long time. William's knees turned to mud. He looked pleadingly at Stephen, who smiled, mysteriously.

"Well, my son," the abbot said at last. "We have two pieces of news for you. One great, one less. Which would you have first?"

William looked back at Father Stephen, incredulous hope rising within him that the summons had nothing to do with Giles Percy. William stuttered. "Lord Abbot, I would have the less."

"Good. The less is that your lady mother has asked that you might be present at your brother's knighting this spring, and we have agreed."

William opened his mouth. This was the *less?*

"Save your thanks for the great news, *fili*. Tell him, Stephen."

Father Stephen came forward. "You know that since our own Pope Benedict issued the bull *Fulgens* we Cistercians have been exhorted, nay required, to send our promising young men to the schools?"

"Yes, Father."

104

"And that we have a school in Oxford at Rewley Abbey?"

"Yes, Father."

"Well," said Stephen, "how would you like to go there?"

William stared speechless and amazed.

Abbot Langeton laughed.

Moments later, Andrew Comyn was striding across the great outer court, his brother Jack coming along beside him. They were at Rievaulx to stock up on wool from the abbey's rich flocks. Andrew glanced over his shoulder as he walked, shouting, "See that wool loaded tight and honest, Adam. Don't let the holy men cheat me." He nearly collided with a young novice leaping his way over the puddles toward the abbey gates.

"Ha! Pardon, little brother," Andrew said genially. "I should watch where I'm going." The boy lifted his face, and it was bright with what looked like fearful joy or joyful terror. Andrew laughed, startled. The boy ducked his head, swerved, and ran for the gates, splashing mud. He rammed past the men and mules at the gate and rushed out beyond the precinct wall.

"Marry!" said Jack Comyn. "What was that?"

The abbey bell rang for Terce.

"Skipping his prayers," Jack observed.

"He's going to catch it," Andrew observed, and he went in to haggle with the abbot of great Rievaulx.

✳ 29

Keldacross
April 1343

"Maudlin!" Gervase bellowed into the kitchen. "I've brought you home your son!"

Dame Magdalen had been baking vigil cakes for Nicholas. (Not that he would eat anything during his knightly vigil, but at Keldacross they had a custom of making these tasteless little wafers of eggs and flour and water from Godrich's well—the essential ingredient—which the young man would eat before and after the vigil. No one knew when this had begun, or what exactly it was supposed to do, except, of course, add blessing.) Now she came hurrying out through the kitchen door onto the dais, wiping her hands on a damp cloth and smiling from ear to ear, as she never,

ever smiled. Gervase was shocked, and somewhat offended. She leapt off the dais and ran to embrace William. "Welcome home, William," she said, kissing him. Faces poked around the kitchen door, staring and smiling. William trembled. The smell, the Keldacross smell! Damp, old, gamey, smoky, rushy, and spicy all at once. Rievaulx never smelt like that. Rievaulx smelt clean, and stony.

"Sweet William," Dame Magdalen said. "Dear son." William looked over her shoulder and saw a tall, freckle faced young woman smiling behind her hand.

"Katharine?"

"Who else?"

Everybody laughed.

Then Nicholas came in. "God's Breath!" he cried cheerfully. "If it isn't the Pimple!"

That evening, the eve of their going up to Helmsley, Nicholas and William shared their old bed.

"Is it good luck to sleep in bed with a monk?" asked Nicholas.

"I'm not a monk yet," William reminded him. "I haven't taken my vows."

Nicholas shrugged. Then he smiled. "You don't wet the bed still, do you?" He punched William brotherly on the shoulder.

"Only on feastdays and great occasions." William punched back.

Nicholas laughed and edged away ostentatiously. Then, "What's this Oxenford thing you're doing? Going down to mingle with the southrons? I hope you don't come back talking like one."

"I am going down to read a hundred books so that I can return and be a great and learned abbot of Rievaulx."

"Is that it? In that event I shall be forever quarreling with you, since Lord Ros is always quarreling with Abbot Langeton."

"Oh, sheep and wool, sheep and wool." William yawned disgustedly. "Are they really worth quarreling about?"

"Not so far as I care," replied Nicholas. "On that we well agree. Wool!" he spat. "It makes me sick." He rolled over and fell asleep.

The next morning the sun came through the window on long, burnished streaks. William awoke. Nicholas still slept, mouth partly open, snoring slightly. The backs of William's knees itched. His stomach quivered. Why was *he* so queasy? *He* wasn't the one being knighted. He jabbed Nicholas. "Nickless," he said, "morning!"

Nicholas woke with a start. His eyes flashed open at the sun; his breath came short.

"What's amiss?" William jabbed him again.

"O Jesu," said Nicholas, "I'm afraid I shall do something wrong."
William shoved him out of bed. "Rise, Sir Nicholas," he said.

They dressed and went to the great chamber. Two maidservants were making the bed; Sir Gervase and Dame Magdalen were already up and waiting in the solar, with Sir Ralph and Rab of Torbeck, and Katharine and Sir Henry Emberthwaite, and Wilfrid priest and Stephen the novice master, who had come with William from Rievaulx. The brothers came in through the curtain, and Gervase said, "Boy, you go in first and make your breakfast. You must keep your strength."

"Aye," Katharine agreed. "We don't want our brother all feeble for his first show of arms, do we, William?"

William shook his head.

"It wasn't the tourney I was thinking of," said Gervase.

"No, Father?" asked Katharine. "Then what?"

Gervase winked at Ralph. "It's the colee."

Sir Ralph chuckled. "Aye, Nick. When your father was knighted, and it came time for the buffet, your grandfather whacked Gervie so hard he fell flat on his back on the ground, sword, spurs, and all, and we had to pull him up again."

"Well, it's made me remember my oath, that's for certain." Gervase got up and put his arm around Nicholas' shoulders. "And I intend to do you the same favor."

Rab laughed. Nicholas did not. He did not want to fall flat on his back before the lord of Helmsley and all his guests.

After his breakfast, Nicholas went down to St Godrich's to be blessed by Wilfrid priest. He knelt before the altar with his hands folded on the rail. His back was so straight and his face so still that Gervase, kneeling beside him, thought that he would weep for love. Wilfrid recited a psalm, and Father Stephen and William joined in.

Quisnam est deus praeter Dominum?
Aut quae petra praeter Deum nostrum?
For who is God save the Lord?
Who is a rock save our God?
The God who girds me with strength,
Who makes my foot swift like the deer's,
Who trains my hand for war,
My arms to bend the bow of bronze . . .

Then they made ready, and rode down to Wydclif by the low track that ran, between alders and beeches, by the banks of Keldabeck, tumbling down cold and fresh from the high moor.

They joined Sir Geoffrey's party at Wydclif. Edmund came cantering over the drawbridge on his new horse Saladin, whom Nicholas and Robert had not yet met. The great hooves made a ringing rhythm on the wooden planks. "Hoy, Nick, Rab!" Edmund hailed them. "Hey, Mundo!" they replied, and Rab added, "So that's your wicked Saracen horse!" Nicholas whistled through his teeth politely. He did not mention the obvious truth that Dragon was by far the better animal, for a man did not say that kind of thing to a friend.

Young Geoff followed Edmund on a bay palfrey. He saluted Nicholas worshipfully. Nicholas nodded back. But Eleanor sat in saddle behind Geoff with her arms around his waist, wearing a skyblue hood. She caught Nicholas' eye. He looked away quickly.

They crossed the moor to join the road to Helmsley. When they came under the shadow of a lichened outcropping, Nicholas fell back to trot beside William, who was jogging behind the rest of the company on a black fell pony. Nicholas glanced down at William, leaned forward and scratched Dragon's forelock, and glanced at William again. He seemed ill at ease. William beamed up at him, but the silence went on too long for comfort. Finally Nicholas said in a strained voice, "Do me a favor, will you?"

"Petite, et dabitur vobis," William joked. "Ask and you shall receive."

"What?" said Nicholas.

"I'll do any favor you like."

"Say a prayer for me, is all."

It was awkward for both of them, so William said lightly, "I'm rotten at praying, you know. Ask Father Stephen if you doubt me."

"It doesn't matter if you pray rottenly. Just pray."

"Should I pray for anything in particular?"

Nicholas frowned. He looked puzzled, as if he didn't know what was troubling him.

"Nickless!" William blurted. "Of course I will pray for you. I love you, Nickless."

Nicholas stiffened, taken aback. William flushed. Why had he uttered something so stupid and babyish?

But then Nicholas looked down from Dragon's heights and muttered, "Thanks, Will." He spurred Dragon to catch up with Mun and Rab, and left William elated. To be called "Will" by Nicholas! To be asked to do him favors, even monkish ones like praying!

The company rounded the shoulder of the ridge and looked down on the wooded valley of Rye and the strong brown towers of Helmsley.

Helmsely Castle
April 1343

"This is my son that Abbot Langeton is sending to Rewley in Ox-enford," Dame Magdalen told everyone at the castle, and all the ladies said vaguely and uncomprehendingly, "Oh! What a fine thing." William turned red and smiled at the floor. All these brightly colored ladies with their loops of braided hair and their heavy scents. He kept close to his mother and to Father Stephen.

There were other clerics there, of course. One of them was his Uncle Roger de Wherne, canon of York Minster and Nicholas' godfather. An-other was Bonaventure Thaxby, a greyfriar sojourning in the same city. This Bonaventure had a wry and amusing face, which he used aptly to ape various persons about the castle hall, including Lord Ros, who had a ner-vous twitch. Lord Ros' chaplain was saying a tediously long and sonorous grace.

After the knightings came the tournament, but William would not go to that. "It would not be seemly," he told Katharine, who had pro-tested, and his mother smiled approvingly.

"That's so, my William. You stay by Father Stephen and pray that your brother conducts himself with strength and honor."

"How should Nicholas not?" said Katharine. "Pray, rather, that *we* won't have our purses slit."

William could not tell them that the real reason he would not go is that he hated the sight of blood. He knew they all took solemn vows before the fray to fight only in the exercise of arms and not to satisfy any quarrel. But he also knew that there was always blood and trampling, and he could not stomach it. It was bad enough at pig sticking time. So when the ladies went off to watch the sport, he stayed with Father Stephen, strolling up and down the great hall (so much longer and higher than Keldacross'), peering into the buzzing kitchens, climbing up flights of winding stairs to look out from high archers' slits, and then climbing down again to look at where they'd been. Servants scurried all over the place. The noise of the tournament swelled over the walls and ramparts.

"This is fine, isn't it, Father Stephen?" William leaned over the bat-tlements of the great keep, making himself dizzy.

"It does no harm, I think, to leave our house once in a great while for some such occasion. One appreciates Rievaulx all the more for having missed it."

"Aye," said William absently. He was not missing the abbey.

Suddenly Father Stephen muttered something, sharp, under his breath. "Miserere!"

William turned to look at him. "What is it?"

Father Stephen's face was ghastly pale; he leaned heavily against the wall, slightly bent, sweat breaking out on his forehead.

"Father Stephen! What is it?"

"Cramps," Stephen gasped. "I'm caught short. All that rich meat."

"That's *my* infirmity," William joked stupidly. "I'm the one who's sick all the time."

"Fool! Quick! Go ask someone where is their privy or garderobe or whatever. Quick, I say! Run!"

William ran.

When they had found Father Stephen his necessities, William hung about and said, "Shall I stay with you, sir?"

"No!" Stephen barked. "Go somewhere. Do what you like."

So William wandered out into the inner bailey, where two jugglers were passing daggers and a pair of burning sticks. William gaped. After they had done, one of the jugglers went around holding out his hood and saying,

Som there are that plough the soil,

That knicht in battyl he may toil,

But this is how we fil our purse,

So pitye, frend, be non the worse.

When he came to William, William shook his head and stretched out his empty hands.

"Hah!" the juggler sneered, and gestured rudely. "These white monks. These holy woolgrowers. They've got enough in their coffers to gild their choirs and spread their beds with ermine, but nary enough to drop to a poor juggler. Oh, no."

All the maids and men standing around jeered harshly, making ugly faces.

William retreated. "Lies!" he shouted. "We've got no ermine furs on our beds or any other kind, and if Father Stephen were here with me he'd have a farthing for you, you . . . villein! And I hope he'd cram it up your nose." He stumbled off.

"Whoa ho!" the bystanders jeered after him. "Did ye hear, juggler? Did ye *hear* what he called you? Holy Rood, juggler, you're *flattened*. Whoa, juggler, did ye hear?"

William skulked into a doorway. He stood there, chewing his nails, wishing he could think of something to devastate those lousy churls. Now he wished he'd gone to the tourney, though probably Father Stephen would not have let him anyhow.

"Hey there, little Cistercian Bernard," called a voice behind him. William turned around, glowering. But it was only the Franciscan friar Bonaventure, and he was friendly. "What's amiss? You look as though you've just been dunked."

"Those scurvy rotten churls," said William. "I hope they all go to hell."

The friar whistled. "That's a nice benediction from a holy brother of Cîteaux. What did they do to deserve it?"

Something in the friar's tone made William not want to tell him. "I am going to see how Father Stephen is faring. He is taken ill."

"Oh? Nothing grave, I trust, or you would not be loitering about, bandying words with jugglers."

So he had overheard. William glared, and pushed past him.

"Hey, little brother, not so fast!" Bonaventure caught him by the sleeve. "I meant no harm, only a jest. Truly, I am grieved about your Father Stephen. What ails him?"

"Cramps," William replied, still surly. Then he added, "He is not used to rich foods."

"Then he shouldn't be in a Cistercian house." William flushed hotly as the friar winked. "Nay, I wish him speedy recovery. Now then. How would you like to go up on the battlements of the topmost tower? That's where I'm bound, to see what I can see."

"I've been there."

"Well, come again. I am in need of company. My own brother who was with me is also, shall we say, unwell. In other words, he is under the table."

"I think that's gross behavior for a friar."

"You do? So do I. But enough of him. Let's go on up the tower. I want to see the look out."

So they went up. "Our house is just over those hills." William pointed.

"Yes, I know. I've stayed in your hospital. A noble guesthouse, and so kind to visitors that the hospitaler brought out a fine copy of Cassian for me to look at."

"It's the oldest house of Cîteaux in England."

"No, little brother. I am afraid that credit belongs to the south-rons. The first Cistercian house was Waverley, in Surrey. I've been there, too."

"Oh well, that." William scowled again. "You've been everywhere, haven't you? And you know everything, don't you?"

"Well," said Bonaventure, leaning on his elbow, "I wouldn't say that. But I have traveled much, seen much, and studied much. I am a scholar of Oxford and of Paris." He named the latter with special pride, but William did not notice it, for the name of Oxford blotted Paris from his mind.

"Oxford?" he exclaimed. "I'm going to Oxford!"

"You are, little brother? How is that?"

William lifted his chin. "Abbot William Langeton is sending me there. In the year of Our Lord 1335 Pope Benedict, who was of our order, you know, sent the *Fulgens sicut stella*, which encouraged—nay required—that each . . . "

"Oh," the friar interrupted in a dry voice. "Rewley."

"Yes, Rewley." William bridled. "Why do you pronounce the name in such a way?"

"Oh, soft. I meant no injury. But you might as well hear now as later that Rewley is not the most illustrious of the colleges."

"Who says so?"

"Nobody says so; everybody knows so. With all reverence to the order of Cîteaux, my friend, you must know that the white monks have never been great patrons of learning."

"We have St Bernard and St Aelred; we have . . . "

"Aye, I know all that," Bonaventure interrupted. "The point is that book learning has never been among the highest Cistercian aspirations."

"And rightly so. St Stephen Harding says . . . "

"Aye, I *know* all that. Yet the point remains."

William compressed his lips and stared out over the countryside. The corn grew tender in the brown strips; the greening slopes faded gently into a mild blue sky. And fattening on the slopes and pastures all around was England's wealth, the precious sheep.

"Look, little brother." The friar laid his hand on William's arm. William shook it off. "I did not mean to prick your spleen. I only say what I know, so that you may be prepared. Rewley's library is feeble; its masters are inadequate. I tell you truly, friend. If you want deep Oxford scholarship you will have to seek it outside Rewley, and that will be difficult, since you will of course be regulated by the house, and by the Hours, et cetera, et cetera. What I am telling you, friend, is that Rewley is going to be little more than Rievaulx transplanted south. If you are happy with that, good! There is nothing wrong with it. But if you are looking for high theology and deep learning, you will be disappointed."

112

William glowered, angry, humiliated, and troubled. He said, "And why are you telling me all this, Mr Friar? What can I do about it?"

"Oh, nothing, I suppose. Perhaps if you are brilliant you might improve the quality of the school."

"Well, I thank you, Mr Friar. I thank you very much. You have exalted my spirits excellently. Thank you. Good day." William swung away from the wall, stubbed his toe on a stone, and headed toward the stair door.

"Wait, little brother!" Bonaventure called again. "Your words touch my conscience. My own words sprang out of a certain pride, I admit, and a bit of rancor. You white monks have no love of *us*, I believe."

"Nor you of us. Wherefore I think you have spoken untruths, just to chafe me, who know little of such matters." William pulled on the door. It stuck. "Damn!" he cursed, tugging. "This shitten thing."

"Listen now." Bonaventure came over and leaned his shoulder against the door. "You rightly reprimand me, but I have spoken no untruth. Listen. Tell me. When are you to make your profession?"

"At the end of next month, before I go up to Oxford. Why do you ask?" William yanked at the door again.

"How old are you?"

"How is that your business. I am sixteen."

"Aye, I thought thereabouts. They mean to ensure your return."

"And why not? They are sending me down there that I may come back and benefit the house. Of course they want to ensure my return." William grew angrier and angrier. "And so do I."

"You need not shout, little brother. Of course you are right. But vows too young taken are often vows best not taken."

"Many take vows at sixteen or seventeen."

"And many wither in the life. Look, friend. I am telling you this out of what I know, in my own order as well as in yours. It is better to be a good secular cleric—it is better even to be a good layman—than a bad religious. And there are other ways of getting to Oxford than Rewley. Here, let me try that." The friar gave the door a slight tug. It opened easily. William looked at him with fury, and hurtled down the stairs two at a time.

Bonaventure went back to the battlements and stared into space. "Oh, Jesu," he said at last. "What did I do *that* for?"

Meanwhile, there was a lull in the tournament, and many of the ladies went back into the castle hall to get out of the sun and to take some refreshment. "Eleanor? An Eleanor Wydclif?" A hoarse, throaty voice called across from the castle solar. A very young noblewoman, blonde, slender, and elegant, put her head around a set of carven screens. She had arched, plucked brows, and she stared indifferently while Eleanor came up to the screens. "Eleanor Wydclif? You're wanted."

Noblemen and gentlemen met constantly in the affairs of the castle, but their wives and daughters mingled less often and therefore less easily. So Eleanor, called from her circle of gentlewomen, was a little guarded when she went behind the screens. The lady who had called her name, Isabel Neville, turned her back and leaned out a window with a Percy relation, conversing languidly in bastard Yorkshire-Norman French. "Harry Dacre?" the Percy was saying, "He's muckle beau, and plus bête."

Eleanor looked about self-consciously. "It's I who summoned you," said Ursula de Ros, the lord's eldest daughter. She sat on a bench across from one of her sisters, casting dice on the floor between them. "It's about this new harvest of knights. We want to lay wagers on who'll do the best in melee, and we're talking about the Tewisdale crop. Your brother's one of them. What would you say were his chances of conquering the lists?"

"Lady Ursula, you've seen Edmund fight more often than I. I think you'd judge him better."

"Modest about your brother. Sweet, but it doesn't help any. How about new mounts and equipage? You can tell us about that."

"Well," said Eleanor, "they've all had their mail and gear made by the same armorer in York."

"Those three always have to do everything just the same," Ursula's sister remarked, "ever since they were pages. It was always tiresome."

"And what about mounts?"

Eleanor considered. "Edmund's Saladin's a good charger, and Rab's Satan isn't a bad one."

"But your cousin Nicholas has the best horse by far."

"I believe so." Why ask, if they already knew?

"Sans doute a gorgeous piece of horseflesh," said Isabel Neville from the window.

"Under a gorgeous arse," observed the Percy.

"Coarse, common, base and low," said Ursula. She leaned over and smacked the Percy on the rear. "But what about skill at arms, Eleanor? Don't you have an opinion?"

"No, Lady Ursula."

"Oh, it's an autre espece de prowesse that interests her," said the Neville, and the Percy laughed loudly.

Eleanor frowned. She brushed a strand of hair from her forehead. What did they want from her?

Ursula turned to her friends in the window. "Right, then. I'll tell you my judgment on the matter." She rapped the bench with her knuckles. "Oyez, oyez. I'm about to give judgment."

"We hear, we hear."

"This is my judgment on the men of Tewisdale. Edmund Wydclif is the quickest wit of the three and the slipperiest in a scramble, but sometimes he is gentlemanly to the point of faiblesse. He needs to unlearn some manners. Now, for brawn and brute strength I name Robert Torbeck, but his horse is inferior and he's never had speed. Now Nicholas of Kelda . . . "

The Percy broke in. "This Nicholas she'll judge for steed, speed, and the best pair of hocks and withers this side of Humber."

"Matilda, you are too base. I never look below a man's belt, let alone some callow boy's I grew up with."

The Neville snorted. "We'll let you pass with that lie—if you promise each of us a turn with him tonight."

Eleanor stood horrified. They couldn't mean it. Nicholas was hers. Still, did they mean it? Well, what matter, he had no honor.

"Isabel Neville, you have shocked this poor gentlewoman."

Isabel gave a pretty, throaty laugh and turned back to the window.

Ursula regarded Eleanor. "Never mind. She talks filthy, but the Earl'd hack her into gobbets if she carried out any of her notions. Besides, I've no thought of defiling your coz. All that I've done is to promise to dance before supper with the one who does best in the melee. So. You don't have to worry about anyone's chastity but your own, cherie."

Eleanor returned to her friends. Her heart was tight in her chest, and her skin felt hot. She did not want them to dance with Nicholas, not one of them. It was a rare honor for a plain knight to dance with a nobleman's daughter. Why should Nicholas have that honor? An honorable man should have that privilege, not Nicholas.

As it happened, Nicholas was the best of the young Tewisdale knights that day. Gervase was so proud that he stood for a while at the railing with tears on his cheeks. This would have humiliated Nicholas had he known of it, but he had neither the time nor the opportunity to see it, for he went about with his friends in a kind of exalted stupor. The fact that he had been awake in vigil the whole previous night made things seem even more hazed and dreamlike. He had not fallen over his sword when it was given him; he had not tripped on his spurs; he hadn't even flinched when Gervase struck him hard at the colee. He had done nothing to embarrass himself, his lord, or his family, and he had done far better in his first show of arms than he had ever expected.

Drums started up in the gallery, announcing the dance before supper. Lord Ros led his daughter onto the floor. "What?" said Nicholas. Rab was shoving him in the back.

"Well, go up and claim her, you jackass! Do you think Ursula de Ros is going to come round and beg you for a dance?"

"What? Oh," said Nicholas, and he went across the hall.

Mun and Rab laughed at him, and then Mun said, "I bet Hugh Cliderhou's grinding his teeth. Remember how he used to go around panting after her? But he won no dance from her when he was knighted."

"And he was damn good in his tourney, too," Rab observed. "Where is that bastard anyway? Let's find him and rub it in."

"Well, Nicko," Ursula said as they were finishing their dance. "You did right well today. Your sire's happy with you and so's mine."

Nicholas thanked her. "Mun and Rab did just as well."

"Not *just* as well. But not badly, either. Who would have thought that you three knaves would ever amount to anything?"

The dance ended, and Nicholas walked her back to the dais. "Well," she said, "that was the first and the last dance you'll ever have with me. I'm marrying that Dacre way out in Cumberland. I may not see you again. But my thanks for all those horses you helped break for me. And for getting my hawk for me all those times. And most especially, my thanks for being a prudhomme and not a sweaty bull calf like half your cronies. You're a true gentleman, Sir Nicholas. God bless you." She kissed him on the forehead in front of everybody. Watching from a corner, Eleanor saw, and sickened.

Nicholas went back across the hall where Rab and Mun had been. He did not feel the rushes under his feet. Vaguely, he perceived his mother in the room, smiling approval with her eyes, and his brother, too, with a shining face.

✳ 31

The road
April 1343

The festivities over, Sir Nicholas's guests took their leave. It was a blustery, chilly day, but between the clouds the sun reached down to the spring grass, drawing it up from the earth.

The party came to the place where William and Stephen must ride west to Rievaulx, Katharine and Sir Henry east to Farndale, and those of Wydclif, Keldacross, and Torbeck northward over the moor. Katharine kissed Nicholas on both cheeks, flicked him in the shoulder, and wiped her nose. She gave William a nudge in the ribs and said, "Pray hard and study hard, brother. Come back a learned old scholar."

"Not too old, I hope! I shall be back this next summer, God willing."

"God willing," said Dame Magdalen.

They all sat on their horses by the side of the muddy road, until Sir Gervase and Sir Henry said at the same time, "Ahem. Aye. Well." Everyone laughed sadly, and went their different ways.

As they rode over the old ridge track above Tewisdale, the young knights joked and sang and cast their eyes back at the girls, except Nicholas, who would have none of it.

"What's amiss with our friend Nicholas?" Rab bellowed. "Why is he so gloomy?"

"Don't ask," said Mundo. "He unhorses two knights in his first melee and has half the noblewomen of the North Riding lusting after him, and all he does is look like fish on Friday. Who can understand the humors of Moody Nick?"

"Aye, Moody Nick it is," Rab yelled. "Except his humors are always one shade or other of black!"

Nicholas had been riding ahead a little. He spurred his horse and increased the distance.

After a little, Rab caught up with him. "What's amiss, Nick? I'm sorry if I offended you."

Nicholas stared ahead of him. "Now *that's* done, Rab, what's left to do?"

Rab gawked. "What's *left?*"

Nicholas looked at him.

"Why, man, everything's left. Everything. What are you talking about?"

Nicholas wound his left hand in Dragon's reins and looked out on the moor, frowning.

Rab sat his own horse, solid, beefy, and bewildered. Like Sir Ralph, he was of blunt and cheerful disposition. He loved Nicholas dearer than any man save his father, but he could not follow the darker turnings of his friend's mind. "What is it, man? Another evil dream?"

"I don't know," said Nicholas. "Leave me alone, Rab."

Rab fell back. "As you like. Moody Nick." He turned his horse to rejoin Edmund. "I know one thing that's left," he called back over his shoulder. "We can beat the guts out of Hugh Cliderhou."

At Rievaulx they decided that William should wait and make his profession when he returned from his first term at Oxford next summer, so that he might do it with Gilbert and the others who had been reared up with him.

"We'll do this together, won't we, Will, just as we've always done?" said Gilbert, freckle faced and earnest.

"Aye, Gib, we'll do that," said William abstractedly. His mind was already on the road to Oxford.

Part Three

Than longen folk to goon on pilgrimages
And palmeres for to seken straunge strondes
THE CANTERBURY TALES

✳ 32

The road
June 1343

Williiam traveled to Oxford in the care of two older monks of Byland—and a great, stout yeoman with a longbow. William rode upon the black pony his father had given him (at Dame Magdalen's request) for his travels. The pony he had named "Arrow," so that he might fly like an arrow to university—or rather, William would fly like an arrow to university; the pony preferred to plod. And so, it seemed, did the monks of Byland. They meandered along the highway, chatting lazily with whatever friendly traveler joined them on their road. They stopped for the night any time they came to a town or an inn or an abbey that pleased them, even if they had only set out from their last hostelry three or four hours before. They said, blandly, "Why should we rise hours before dawn if we need not? We're traveling." "Why should we not stop now? This is a pleasant place." "Why should we ride faster? We are in no haste."

It made William want to kill them. Yes we *are* in haste. *I* am in haste. "I want to *get* there," William muttered into Arrow's twitching ear. "I want to *get* there."

Well into the third week of their travels (they were only as far south as Nottingham), William could not stand it any longer. He jumped off the pony and ran down the road, furiously, as fast as he could, rushed back, turned around, and repeated the circuit. "There!" he shouted. "I could run all the way to Leicester and back before you ever achieved that stump up there! Mother of God!"

They reproved him, but mildly. They felt pleasant and lax. The great grey beeches and elms and twisted oaks raised their boughs above them; the road was a great green nave of mossy trunks and high leaves. They were not afraid of the forest because the sun burned bright and birds sang. They were not afraid of robbers because coming out of Lincoln they had fallen in with a nobleman and his sons and their four burly retainers. The nobleman was on his way to London. He was in no hurry either.

William stamped on ahead, jerking Arrow by the bridle, whipping the air savagely with a birch switch. "DIC NOBIS MARI-A, QUID VI-DISTI IN VIA?" He made the hymn sound like some sort of bloody battle chant. He whacked the heads off a clump of tall grass standing in a pool of light by the side of the road.

✳ 33

York and Keldacross
June 1343

Marion stood in a wooden tub in the kitchen, while Mistress Alison poured water over her head from a kettle. Alice was heating more water over the fire.

"How bonny you are, sweetheart," said Alison, rubbing Marion's scalp vigorously. "How beautiful you'll look with your hair all loose and shining. I could never make my hair grow past my shoulders without looking ragged. But look at yours! Down to your waist, and thick as heather."

"Cut it off," said Marion. "Cut it off with a knife."

"Don't be foolish," Alison replied impatiently. "You are a very fortunate girl."

The next morning Marion crouched in her room on her stripped bed. All the sheets and coverlets and curtains had been packed in rolls and trunks that lay before the door. The walls were bare.

"If he's comely, it's fine," Agnes was saying. "If he's ugly and you hate him, it's worse than you think. St William, I should know. Just thank God that your father didn't marry you off to some crabbed old pinch-penny." She was pregnant with her second child.

"Don't talk like that, Agnes," Cecily cried. "Of course she won't hate him. I wish *I* could marry a handsome knight. Remember how we used to play we were great ladies?"

Agnes sat back against the wall. A wry smile twisted her mouth. "How do you know he's handsome?"

"Marion's father said so."

"He might just be saying that to make her feel better. I'll bet the man's got a huge wart on his nose, and no chin. My husband looks like a rat's behind."

"Oh, be quiet, Agnes. You're a great comfort at weddings." Cis turned back to Marion. "I'm sure Sir Nicholas is a very nice man."

Alice went down, jaw set, to fetch Mistress Alison.

"Sweetheart," said Alison, coming through the door, "you must dry your tears and come down. Everyone is waiting. Your father's growing angry."

"I will not go," said Marion. "I will not leave York."

"You will and you must." Suddenly hard and stern, Alison yanked Marion up and made her stand before her. She turned up Marion's face in her hands. "Now look at you. Is that the way to go to your wedding?"

"I can't," said Marion. "Oh please, I won't; I can't."

They rode out of York through Monk Bar with their neighbors the Noyes and the Whewells, except for Agnes, whose husband would not let her go. Monk Bar was the tallest gate in the city; stone men on the battlements kept sombre watch. Marion twisted round in the saddle to look back. The bar towered dark behind them, and the stone men looked at her going, and did not care.

"Do not look back, Daughter," said her father, riding beside her. "Young Sir Nicholas won't want to marry a pillar of salt." He chuckled merrily.

Alice rode behind Adam Scawe on a mule. She kept her head turned back toward York until her neck turned stiff. Long after they passed out of sight of the city, she kept turning round, craning her neck, and straining her eyes, as if to catch a bit of wall or a minster tower in the mist.

Rab gestured impatiently with his arm. They were up in Old Keep, in the sickroom, for that room had the best view of the courtyard. Rab and Edmund crammed at the lancet window, peering and whistling. "Come here by the window, Nick. Have a look. Come on, Nick, you ass. Before they go in."

"Jesu Christ, she's a sweetheart!" Mun exclaimed encouragingly. "You're a lucky one, Nick."

"No need to be glum, Nicko. Just come and *look*."

"That's her, isn't it?" Edmund asked Rab.

"Plainly."

"Plain she is not."

"And we thought she'd look like a ploughgirl!"

"She must have gentle blood."

Geoff Wydclif, now Nicholas' squire, stood in a corner of the room. He worshiped Nicholas. Jealousy consumed him at the very thought of Marion. Besides, he was against her on his sister's behalf. If Nicholas had to marry anyone, it ought at least to be Eleanor.

Nicholas came to the window sideways and looked out with one eye.

"See her?" Rab nudged. "That's her in red. Look how little she is. What a darling!"

"She looked up just a while ago, before you came over. Here, whistle; maybe she'll look up again. Damn it! She's going in. Lord, Nick, she's a sweetheart."

"A little red weasel," said Geoff nastily. "That's what she is."

Rab turned around quick and clouted him.

Now she had to look at him. She had to look at him because they were married. She tore her eyes from the white lamb on the priest's green velvet cope. But she could not raise them any higher than Nicholas' collarbone. So he bent down and gave her a peck.

Laughter. "Oh come now, children. You'll have to do better than *that!*"

Then it was time to go down the steps from the sanctuary. She did not want to. She wanted to creep under the altar and stay there forever, behind the embroidered cloth. Holy Mother of God, help me.

Her father came to her and said, "Look, sweetheart, you're wed now! A married lady!" Lady. He rolled it over his tongue.

She saw his brown beard, his twinkling eyes, the rich broad folds of his mulberry gown, and thought, Take me home, father. Take me with you, home. Mistress Alison came up, smiling through tears. "You'll be having another mother now." Why didn't they stop?

"Daughter," said a cold, strong voice. It was her husband's mother, tall, thin, pale eyed and red haired. "Come to your feast." Sir Gervase was there too, and he gave her a squeeze around the waist, thin mouth smiling under hawk nose, yellow hair beneath green hat. Fathers don't have yellow hair. "Aye, Daughter, come to table. Your first feast at Keldacross— the first of many, God willing." Why did God will that she come here?

"The bride cup!" someone shouted. "Where's the bride cup?"

"Where's the bride*groom?*"

"Ah, he's cut out already, the coward. Never mind, we'll fetch him."

Marion realized that Nicholas was gone, and had been ever since they left the altar. Girls were pulling at her, girls she did not know. "Come on! We must dance you up the hill. Hey, Edward, you little monkey! Come back here with that scarf. If you don't watch these pages, they'll strip you naked. Come on! Oh, Eleanor, look at her face! It's like ashes!"

A very fair girl with violet eyes was shaking a tambourine over her head. Its blue and yellow ribbons danced and shivered with the sound of the bells. "Come, maidens, dance!" the fair girl cried. She sounded wild.

124

"You lead us, Eleanor," they answered. "Come, bride, you must dance with us."

"I don't know it; I can't." Where was Alice? Where *was* she?

"Grab onto my waist and Syb will hold yours," said a girl with long, dull hair like Cis', but it was not Cis. "Don't they dance in York?" Yes. Yes. Different dances. Better dances. She could not cry here before all these people. They danced up the hill through the manor house gate, through the strewn court, and through the hall all hung with summer boughs, into the solar. While the bridal party was in the solar, Nicholas and his groomsmen gathered in the hall.

When the girls had gone through, Gervase jumped up on a table and stamped his foot on the board for silence. He raised a cup. "Yorkisfolk and Tewisfolk!" he shouted. "Bransdale and Farndale, Coverdale and Helmsley!" He bowed toward the great hearth. "Now I know we've just sat through a long mass and a long wedding—no slight to the sacraments intended (Laughter from below)—and so! We're all hungrier than wolves. So let us begin on the *real* stuff of a wedding. What did you come here for?"

"The charivari! That's what I came for! The shivaree!"

"Well, for that, Ralph, you'll have to wait until you're drunk enough to do it properly. So let's begin the feast! Wife, call the maidens in. Squire! Fetch in the groomsmen!"

"First!" boomed someone by the fire. "First we must drink to our host. To Gervase of Kelda, the founder of this feast, which by the looks of it will match the boards of the Nevilles at Middleham! To Gervase!" Sir Godfrey de Ros, honoring Kelda on behalf of Helmsley, raised the gilt cup a page had frantically refilled for him.

"Sir Gervase!"

"Aye, old Gervie!"

Gervase bowed low in the direction of the fireplace. "An honor undeserved, but gratefully accepted. I thank you, Sir Godfrey," he said respectfully. "I thank you all. Now I have a toast to make myself."

"Hell, Gervie! We want to eat!"

"Toast first, then table. I drink to Andrew Comyn, great Stapler of noble York and getter of the delicious maid Marion." He paused. "Soon to be maid no more." Laughter and applause. After drinking, he pulled the stumbling, blushing Andrew onto the table with him. Andrew bowed jerkily, his face all red and beefy.

"To Andrew Comyn, woolmaster, hail! To York and to Flanders; to wool and to gold!"

"Thanks, thanks," Andrew mumbled, smiling into his beard. Mistress Alison thought excruciatingly: He's standing on the hem of his gown.

Nicholas and Marion sat at the dais table, looking out over the swarming hall. A rich green hunting scene (a gift of Lord Ros) hung behind their carven chairs. The gentlefolk came up, dressed in their crimsons, blues, and yellows, and joined them.

Alice sat down below at the bailiff's table, jammed between Adam Scawe and the falconer, with the reeve and the constable and their wives. Joan Faulkoner tried to talk with her, but for the first time in her life, Alice had nothing to say to anybody. She had never been so far from York, and had never been so miserable. She looked at Marion at the high table and thought, See how wretched she looks, my poor curdie pie.

"Would you have some salt?" Nicholas asked Marion in a cracked voice, for Geoff had forgotten to offer her any when he served her meat. She shook her head at the tablecloth.

The feast went on and on, one dish after another: venison, capons, cheeses, spiced stews, boiled chicken in ginger, stuffed geese, herring pies, fruit purees, pears in honey, on and on and on, until Marion thought she would be sick. She went on eating so as not to have to look at faces. Every time her hand bumped into Nicholas' (they shared a trencher), she gagged.

"Don't eat so fast, my girl." Dame Magdalen laid a long freckled hand on Marion's arm. "It's not good for your digestion."

So she was deprived even of that distraction.

An apple flew through the air and struck her shoulder.

"Oh no! Sorry, sweetheart; that was meant for Nicholas!"

"You oaf, Rabbo, can't you throw straight?"

"Sweet fruit for sweet fruit!"

"I can guess which one's the sweeter!" Edmund exclaimed.

"Whoa ho, so can I!"

Her face turned pasty. She studied her meat until her eyes burnt with staring at it.

Then something even worse happened. The food stopped coming. Dame Magdalen touched her arm again. "Time to drink the loving cup," she said.

The young squire stood behind, and Cis was there too, blushing. She and the squire were each holding a handle of the great cup, the mazer. Everyone was looking at Marion now. Men and women had come up from the hall and were standing all around the table, chuckling, grinning, and making coarse jokes.

Sir Gervase stood up again, banging his cup on the table. "Wedding guests! The hour's come! The hour that one of us, I'm certain, has been hankering after all this long while." He winked at Nicholas. Nicholas stared into space. Everyone laughed.

"Charivari! Shivaree!" bellowed Sir Ralph, pounding the table with his monstrous fist.

"That isn't what I had in mind, friend, though you're welcome to it, surely. But let's to the business at hand. The Loving Cup!"

Everyone cheered or hooted.

"Now," Geoff muttered to Cis, and they leaned forward to put the cup on the table between Nicholas and Marion. Cis knocked her elbow on Marion's shoulder and sloshed a little wine onto the cloth. Marion choked. Dame Magdalen closed Marion's hand around the handle of the cup. Nicholas lifted his side before she did, and more wine sloshed out. Then their heads were close together at the rim. Nicholas barely touched his lip to the wine, but Marion took a big gulp.

Someone yelled, "That's right, darling! Nothing better for love than wine from the Loving Cup!"

"Bedding dance!" cried someone else.

Dame Magdalen joined Nicholas' hand to Marion's and made them stand up. The young knights took the torches from the sconces on the walls; the others wound strings of bells around their wrists. All this was solemn and quiet, except for the sound of the bells, and of flame catching the air. But when everyone had what they needed, there was a great noise and waving of torches. "Upstairs, now," said Dame Magdalen, and up they went, followed by all who cared to come. They left the rest below, dancing a long dance. The bagpipes skirled in the hall all night.

Sir Henry Emberthwaite went upstairs with the crowd, shaking his bells with the rest. Gervase and Ralph slapped him on the back and guffawed at him. Henry guffawed back politely and rubbed his pink nose and joined feebly in the refrain of the lewd song they were singing. Ralph bellowed in his ear, tunelessly, but with relish. Henry stayed to see the bride and bridegroom bedded, but the looks on their faces were so agonized that as soon as he could the kindly man pushed his way out. He smiled apologetically as he squeezed past the bed, but they did not notice him.

He stood disconsolately outside the chamber door. Then he decided on Old Keep. He would go to the top for fresh air. He went down through the dancers in the hall, outside to the outer keep door. It was dark in there. On the first flight of steps he bumped into something. "What's this?" he said. A young woman was crouching there. He bent down and peered at her. The moon showed through a slit window, but he did not have good eyes and he did not recognize the face. "Has someone done you amiss?"

She looked up at him. Her wet eyes gleamed in the pale light. "God has done me amiss," she said.

It was Eleanor Wydclif.

"May I help you in any way?"

"No. Leave me alone."

Sir Henry did not know what to do, so he went on up the stairs. At the top he found another woman: his wife Katharine.

She swung around from the battlements like a sentry.

"Only me," he said.

"Ah. Good." She waited for him to come up next to her. Then, unexpectedly, she took his hand and pressed it.

They stood silent, looking over the battlements, down the hill, over St Godrich's squat black tower. Woodenbeck gleamed under dark leaves and shadow branches; they could hear Keldabeck rushing down over the rim of the fell. The cottages huddled around the smudgy fields; the pond shone, moon silvered, in the common. The moon shone over the dark haunch of Kelda and over the wild moor beyond.

"Poor wee thing," said Sir Henry, thinking of Marion.

Katharine looked at him. "Eh?" she said. She had no sympathy to waste on Marion. For nothing could be happier to her than to be at Keldacross. If this York girl didn't learn to appreciate her good fortune in being here, that would be her loss.

Nicholas and Marion sat under the sheets like sticks. Nicholas' nostrils were white; his fingers picked at the nubs in the topmost coverlet. He returned his companions' leers with tight, furious little grimaces. Marion felt that she was floating above the bed and that the faces and voices all swelled in and out. Before she was bedded, one of the older ladies had made her drink a bowl of mulled wine. "It'll be better that way," she'd said, and the other ladies had laughed wickedly. While they were undressing her, she kept clutching onto Alice, thinking she would fall over. Now she thought she was going to throw up.

"Geoffrey! Young Geoff Wydclif!" someone was calling.

"Get Geoff!"

"Here, Geoff, step up and give 'em a song."

"Aye, Geoff, give 'em one of your throbbers, to send 'em off before we go."

"Looks like Nicholas isn't going to need much help. Ooooo! He's wroth. He wants *us* to get the *hell* out."

"We'll give him a song before we go, just to show our goodwill. Come on, Geoff, show your new lady your stuff."

"Shame, Mundo! That's Nicholas' task!"

"And what a task!"

"Give me such a task tonight and I'll be happy for a week!" said Hugh Cliderhou.

"You're not thinking of cuckolding our companion on his very wedding night, are you, Hugh?"

"Nay, but another night will do as well." Hugh licked his lips.

"Whoa-ho." Laughter. But Rab looked at Hugh narrowly. There was something in Hugh's tone that he didn't like. Something uncomradely. Proud, strutting bastard. Didn't even know how to act comradely at Nick-o's wedding. But then, he'd always been that way. Not an ounce of courtesy in him.

Edmund didn't notice. "Step up, Geoff, and sing us out, before old Nick gets up and strews our guts in the rushes."

Out of the swaying torchlit forest stepped Geoffrey, fair, pimply, and sullen. He carried a rebec at his hip. The bow dangled from his other hand. He stationed himself at the foot of the bed and drew the bow back and forth across the strings, cocking his head to hear the tuning until the room quieted down into occasional muted hoots and chuckles.

Geoff began singing, very low. His voice had changed not long since, and it cracked a little.

"Allë nicht . . . " he began, pausing to catch Marion's eye and glare at her.

Her head was thick. She hardly heard the music, but anything was better than the snickering and licking of chops she met when she looked at anything else but her knees—or her husband, but the thought of that turned her stomach.

Allë nicht by the rosë, rosë
Allë nicht by the rose I lay . . . "

The rebec droned, and Geoff began to step up the beat, tapping his foot in the rushes and looking at Marion hatefully the whole time. The others yipped and stamped their feet, linking arms or beating on one another's backs with their empty cups. The stink of wine breath mingled with the strewn herbs and the heavy musk and scent from the ladies' dresses. Nicholas picked at his fingernails. The song went faster and faster, until Marion thought her head would come off. Cold sweat broke out on her forehead. No, please, she prayed, please not now. The song ended on a wild, high note. Marion threw up all over the coverlet.

There was a brief silence. Then someone said, chortling, "Too much excitement."

Marion put her head on her knees, shaking. Nicholas sat staring straight ahead, cracking his knuckles. Finally he said, "Well, don't just stand there, you bastards. Go fetch my mother."

Geoff disappeared. Nicholas cracked more knuckles. The others cracked feeble jokes. Dame Magdalen came in with Mistress Alison and the woman who had given Marion the wine. They drove the men out of the room, except Nicholas, of course, and Dame Magdalen lifted off the insulted coverlet.

"All over that beautiful embroidery," Mistress Alison lamented.

"Poor little thing," said the wine lady, "the passion's too much for her."

Alison dipped a handkerchief into a bowl of rosewater on the great chest under the window. She washed Marion's face with it, patting her hair and saying, "There, there." Marion pressed her face into Alison's shoulder. "I want to go home. I want Alice."

"Your serving girl?" said Dame Magdalen. "You'll see her in the morning."

Alison got up, brushing off her skirts. "Yes, sweetheart, you'll see Alice in the morning."

"Now, son," Dame Magdalen commanded. "Come after me and bolt the door. At least we can spare her any more howling wolves tonight." She threw him the new blanket she'd brought in. He wrapped himself in it, got up, and did as he was told.

In the morning, when Nicholas awakened, Marion was still crying. Could she have been crying all night long? What was wrong with her? The night had been too miserable, so he had left her alone. Or rather, they had left each other alone, huddling stiffly at the opposite sides of the bed. Once in the night, Nicholas had rolled off and bashed his knee on the floor. She had been crying then, too.

Oh God, he thought now. They'll never leave off me when they find that nothing happened last night. They'll be pounding on the door soon. Jesu. He couldn't stand it. He listened to her for a while, then he leaned over awkwardly and tapped her shoulder. She froze up like a corpse. He sat back again, red faced, stupid, angry. Why did this have to happen to him?

"Listen," he said. His voice came out all froglike. He cleared his throat. "Listen. Stop crying. I have something to say to you."

She went on crying.

"I said, stop crying."

She could not stop crying.

"Look," he said desperately. "You have to do what I tell you. I have something to say to you." He tried to make his voice stern and commanding. It had no effect.

So he jumped out of bed and stamped around the room, dragging the blanket in the rushes. Then he came and stood by her side of the bed. "Will you sit up? I want to talk with you."

She sat up, heaving and hiccoughing. She covered her face in her hair. Her eyes were swollen nearly shut.

"Look," he said. "Listen. I don't think either of us much wanted to marry the other."

She shook her head.

"But now that we are married, we might as well make the best of it. Do you know what I'm saying?"

She shrugged.

"So," he said. Then he did not know what else to do, so he thrust out his hand at her. Friend, not foe?

She looked at the hand from behind her hair. He was about to withdraw it angrily, when suddenly she reached out and took it. His throat closed up. "I think," he croaked, "I think you're very fair."

"I'm not," she mumbled. "I'm dark."

Then the rattlings and poundings began. Richard of Tunnersgil, one of the Helmsley pages, had somehow managed to climb the outside wall and was pressing his face against the window. Another blond head appeared. They made pig noses against the glass. Their voices came through, muffled. "Oooo, Sir Nicholas!" Then they dropped out of sight.

"Oh Nicholas!" called other voices at the door. "Sorry, Nick, but morning's here. Time to rise up and see your guests."

"Time to come down, he means!"

Rude, suggestive laughter.

Nicholas turned to Marion. "Pay these churls no heed. They're a herd of bastards."

✴ 34

Keldacross
July 1343

Nicholas found Marion in the bedchamber window. Her father and the Yorkisfolk had ridden away that morning, and Nicholas had gone out hunting with his friends. Why hadn't the women stayed by her? He thought it hard-hearted of them to leave her alone. She saw him and hid her face.

"Hoa," he said.

She laid her head in her arms and wept.

"There," he muttered, "don't cry." He sat down beside her and patted her elbow.

"I want to go home," she sobbed.

He put one arm around her shoulders, and wiped his nose on the back of his free hand.

Dame Magdalen came and stood in the doorway, watching. "Son," she said, "I think it would be a good thing if you took your wife out riding. The day is fine. Let her ride Gillyflour."

Nicholas nodded.

Geoff was in the stable, currying Dragon. Marion hung back, so Geoff said, "Are you afraid of horses, or what?" Nicholas glared at him, and Geoff added hastily, "Lady?"

Marion stared at the beast confronting her on the other side of the thin stall door. She twisted her fingers and whispered, "No."

Geoff said snidely, "A knight's lady must not fear horses."

Nicholas prodded Marion forward. "There," he said, "just pat Dragon on the nose. I know he looks fierce, but he's a snowflake inside. Old Maccabeus is a snowflake too, isn't he, Geoff?"

"Trampled that stablegroom damn good at Helmsley, sir."

Nicholas frowned. "That man was a fool. Anyone who'd . . . Anyhow," he turned to Marion, "you needn't worry about the warhorses. You won't be riding them."

Rab and Edmund sauntered in, munching pears. Rab said, "Remember how your sister Katharine stole Maccabeus and rode him all over Kelda village, howling like a she wolf?"

"Lucky she wasn't killed."

"Dame Katharine's a madcap," said Edmund. "She should have been a man."

"Don't talk like that about my sister." Nicholas led Marion to the next stall. "This here is my father's riding horse. Now he's the one to look out for, is Hellfire."

"His coat is near as red," said Marion.

"And see his eyes," said Geoffrey. "He'd as soon kill you as look at you." He gleamed with malice.

"And here is my palfrey, Wutherwind. He's a good fellow, aren't you, Wuther? Look! He's giving you a kiss." Nicholas bent, and kissed her too. Marion pushed him away. Geoff rolled his eyes at Dragon. Edmund raised his brows, and Rab grinned meaningfully.

"And here is my mother's mare, Greywinter. She's a beauty. Give her an apple and she'll love you forever. Geoff, go get an apple for my lady to give Greywinter."

Geoff stood there glowering. Nicholas looked round, "Well?"

Geoff stamped out. "Not a foot lackey," he muttered, loudly.

"And here's Rab's horse, Satan. Nowt to fear from old Satan, eh, Rab?"

"Nay," Rab replied. "Nowt to fear from Satan or Dragon or Edmund's Saladin, but I'd take care of old Gillyflour over there. She's a demon."

Marion looked puzzled, so Nicholas said, "He's teasing you. Gilly's the one all the babies ride on. She's yours until we find you a real horse. And there's good old Bear. You're a good fellow, aren't you?"

The pony whickered.

"Ne-e-igh? What say you?" Nicholas nudged Marion in the ribs. "The old liar."

Edmund gaped. He had seen Nicholas make an ass of himself over any number of birds and beasts, but never before over a woman. Behind Nicholas' back, he contorted his face at Rab. Rab twisted his mouth and bit his lip to keep from laughing. Geoff came back with the apple and tossed it sullenly at Nicholas. Nicholas caught it and handed it to Marion. He narrowed his eyes forbodingly at Geoff, who pretended not to see and went back to currying Dragon.

"So. Do you want to ride out?" Nicholas watched Marion feed Greywinter her apple. Marion hesitated. The horses stamped and snorted, and suddenly Hellfire tossed up his head and let forth a savage, piercing sound. Marion jumped. She had never ridden in York, except on gentle horses, in the saddle before her father. "I—I think I shall stay in today," she said.

Rab laughed. Geoff sneered.

"Hey," said Nicholas. "You mustn't let Hellfire talk you out of it. I told you he was a devil, didn't I? You'll ride Gilly. Watkin!"

He told Watkin to see Gillyflour and Wutherwind saddled, and then he and Marion walked back across the yard to get cloaks. "What else do you like to do? We could play backgammon some time, if you like. You don't know it? But it's easy; I'll show you. Or sing. Do you like to sing? I can play the harp a little." They went into the hall.

Edmund and Rab leered at each other. Geoffrey threw down his currycomb and did a little dance around the stable, hugging himself and singing passionately, "Marion m'aime, Marion m'a. Oh, puke."

Edmund stared at him. "Rabbo, this brother of mine is an insolent churl. Were we this insolent when we were squires?"

"Na, Never," Rab replied. "But then, we were in love with Lord Ros' *daughter*, not his *son*." And the two of them burst into rude guffaws.

The day was brisk and bright and clear. Nicholas and Marion rode to the top of Kelda fell and looked all around: east over the high moor ("Over there is Bransdale," said Nicholas) and west over shallow Tewisdale with its two gleaming becks and its woods of oak and ash and haw-thorne. To the northwest rose a bare, strange hill. "That's Drumm Tor," said Nicholas, pointing, "and beneath it is the manor of Torbeck. Sir Ralph holds that, Rab's father. You know which one is Rab, don't you? The big, broad fellow. He's a bit rough sometimes, but I hope you'll come to like him. Of all my friends, Rab's the best. In a pinch he's beside me in a second. And on the other side of the tor is Tunnersgil, my father's other manor. Gilbert the falconer is from Tunnersgil."

"What are those stones on the tor?"

"Obstrush. Goblin house. It has its twin over east in Farndale."

She looked at him skeptically.

"So they say. But I've been up there more times than I can count, and never saw a sign of any bones not left by fox or weasel." He smiled at her. "Just an old pile of rocks. If you look down the dale a way you can see the top of Wydclif keep, easterly side, above the trees."

"Where Eleanor Wydclif lives," said Marion.

"Sir Geoffrey Wydclif's house," Nicholas said hastily. "That's where Mundo comes from, and Geoff."

She gazed at the wisp of blue smoke curling up into the sky, and the line of grey stone above the trees.

"Whenever I see smoke like that from here, rising at Wydclif," said Nicholas, "I think of Eadred the Young."

"Who?"

"Eadred the Young. He saw the black smoke at Wydclif. The North-men had set it afire."

She looked at him expectantly. He fumbled. "Na. I'm no storyteller. You should hear Cuth the constable. He's the one who can tell it."

She looked disappointed, so he gave in. "What happened was that Eadred saved all the folk of Kelda by hiding them in the woods. But the Northmen caught him, and staked him down on the ground, and slit him down the middle."

Marion covered her ears.

"He called on Christ and on Our Lady and on St Wilfrid."

Marion uncovered her ears. "And what happened?"

"Nothing. He died."

"Oh no!"

"Aye, but it ends well, because Raedwulf his father came back from fighting by the North Sea, and when he saw that the Dane was in his house and his son slaughtered, he said to his brothers, 'I shall be avenged on this heathen if it is the last thing I do. I shall dig his eyes from his sockets with my own dagger; I shall slit his belly with my own sword . . .' "

134

Then he saw that she was sick faced and ghastly. "That was in old days," he assured her. "Cuth Constable tells it better."

"Where does your sister Katharine live?"

"Emberthwaite. That's over in Farndale. You will see it. They have a fine windmill."

"And where is this abbey where your brother lives?"

"Rievaulx. South, and easterly again. Not far west of Helmsley. But he's in Oxenford now, or on his way."

Neither of them knew what else to say.

"Look . . . " said he.

"When . . . " said she, at the same time.

They looked at each other and laughed.

"You say," said he.

"You say," said she.

"I don't know. I was thinking. Well, I was thinking: whenever you get a longing for York you may tell me, and if I am not about to do service, or if it isn't dead winter, or what . . . It's not that far. We could get there in a day, riding hard."

She put her hand to her mouth to keep from smiling.

That offended him. "What are you laughing about?"

"I don't know," she said. "Thank you." The way he had said it, she had a picture of them both, "riding hard" for York, with fierce expressions and long lances.

"Aye well," he said. "We might as well go down for dinner."

"Aye," she agreed. And they turned their horses homeward.

He was kind to her. But how could he think that she would not always be longing for York, every hour of every day?

Curlews wheeled and called in the air, high above Kelda.

✳ 35

Keldacross
August 1343

Joan Faulkoner and Martha Reeve and Alice were tidying up Nicholas' and Marion's chamber. Martha and Joan struggled with the bed. Alice dusted the window panes. Martha was going on and on about the bailley.

"I was up here on the hill doing my weekwork, see, and vexed I was to be sure, for it was my sister's wedding down at Wydclif, and I wasn't there. 'John Bailley,' I say, 'John Bailley, give me a day's liberty to go see my only sister wed down at Wydclif.' Oh no, he'd have none of that. I say, 'But John Bailley, Hawisa says she'll take my work if I take hers next day.' 'Oh, no,' says he. 'That will put things all off,' says he. 'Soon you'll have everyone chopping and changing and twiddling about, and soon nobody'll be doing their service.' 'My only sister, John Bailley,' say I. But does that move him? Nay. Owd bastard, I say to myself. 'What?' says he. 'Nowt,' say I. And of course we all have to take days out of our own field-work to come shine up his precious house for *this* great wedding. And somehow Thomas the reeve (that's my husband you know), Thomas Reeve gets blamed that everything's late, so *I* get blamed about the head and shoulders by Thomas Reeve."

"Oh, grumble, grumble, grumble, Martha," said Joan, brightly.

Alice came over. "Why, look at that shitten sheet!" she cried. "What? Was he too hot and bothered even to pull off his boots?"

"Sssh!" hissed Joan.

"Ss-ss-ss," Martha sniggered.

"Well, we'll have to change the sheet. We can't leave an old rucked up muddy one like that—or is that how you do things out here on the moors?"

Martha scowled. Joan went to fetch another sheet.

"Now look at that!" Alice exclaimed when they got the new sheet. "If that sheet had been folded properly you wouldn't be so tried and troubled to lay it out."

Martha and Joan stood by sullenly and watched her fold the sheet up again. "Now watch close," she said with an air of patient instruction. "See? Fold in halves, and halves, and thirds, and halves again. And smooth it down. See how well that looks. It doesn't take much wit to learn *that*. Now watch." She took hold of a corner and snapped the sheet over the bed. "See how easy that opens up?"

"It looks just as rumpled as before," said Martha. But it didn't.

"My mistress in York is particular about such things."

"Well," said Joan, "Dame Magdalen doesn't much care."

"Well," Alice rejoined, "Dame Marion does, and these are *her* sheets."

"I don't see her grumbling," Martha muttered.

"Of course not, clodstamper. She's timid. But I know. She likes things the way she's used to them home at York."

"This is home to her now," said Joan, "and she'd best get used to our ways."

"Humph," said Alice, and snapped out another sheet.

Martha went on. "That bailley had so many of us working up here for that great wedding, I don't know how we got anything done in t'fields, St Godrich I do not. I don't know what he thought we'd eat this winter."

"Snow," said Alice. "He's a mean old stoat, isn't he?"

"Sssh!" Martha glanced over her shoulder.

Alice sneered. "What have I to fear from that old wheezer?"

"Well, _I_ have plenty to fear from him," said Martha, "so if you don't mind . . ."

Alice laughed, and flicked a rag over Nicholas' hawk perch. Then she went back to the window and began rubbing glass again. "Old stoat," she said, loud as you please, just as they heard his keys jangling at the door.

Martha caught her breath. Joan sank behind the bed, tucking earnestly. Alice did not even look around.

Joan could not tell whether he had heard or not. One could never tell by his face, which was ever all lined and creased with frowning. He watched Alice's back for a long time.

"Ye've got to rub those windows _hard_," he said at last.

Alice paid him no heed.

John Bailley said, "Sir Gervase paid a pretty penny for that glass. It has to look its best."

Still she paid him no heed.

"Ye've got to rub _hard_." He stepped further into the room, jangling his keys.

Alice, without turning round, spat out her words like sour berries. "I know it. My master's house in York has many such windows."

John stopped, and chewed on the insides of his cheeks, as was his habit when dangerous, and said, "I've heard you townswomen have sharp tongues, and I see it's true."

She said, "I've heard that countrymen have thick skulls, and I see _that's_ true."

Then John said, "Woman, I pity you. No man wants a shrew for a wife."

Slowly she turned around, looking him up and down. "Well, goodman," she said, "no woman wants a fish for a husband." And she turned her back again and scratched at a spot with her fingernail.

Martha stood rigid, with a fixed smile. Joan crouched lower behind the bed.

The bailley strode over to the window and set his hand hard on Alice's shoulder. "Do you know who it is you're scolding, wasp?"

She shook him off.

"It's Sir Gervase's bailiff you're chiding," he said.

She sat back on her haunches and looked him full in the face. "Oh!" she exclaimed. "So *that's* what you are! I was wondering what an old ploughboy was doing trampling through my mistress' chamber."

Joan gagged on the blanket she had stuffed into her mouth.

John swung round to glare at her and then stormed out of the room, jangle, jangle.

"Oh! oh! oh!" gasped Joan into the blanket.

Martha, glued to the rushes, peered at Alice, who was shining up her last pane and smiling grimly to herself.

"He can't do nowt to me," Alice said at last. "I'm my mistress' own maidservant, a free woman, and no serf."

Then she turned on them sharply.

"And I can go home to York any day I like."

✳ **36**

Oxford
September 1343

Wednesday at Vigils. The great psalter book was open on its stand. The tapers glowed; the big pointed notes on their four-lined staves, the text with its red capitals, showed dark against the stiff leaves of vellum. William did not need to read the text, and he had the music by heart. There were some old monks at Rievaulx who had the whole psalter by heart, but William did not think he would ever have that—only the psalms he loved best stayed with him. He would have to work at the rest, and he was not about to do that. His mind was on other things now.

"Caeli enarrant gloriam Dei, et opus manuum eius annuntiat firmamentum, The heavens are telling the glory of God, the sky proclaiming the works of his hands."

William wondered if he could persuade Thomas of Waverley to lend him his book of *The Categories.*

"Dies diei effundit verbum, et nox nocti tradit notitiam, Day speaks word unto day; night makes it known unto night."

He would promise not to eat over it, or to take it out of college.

"Non est verbum et non sunt sermones; quorum vox non percipiatur, It is not speech, not human thought, not a voice that cries aloud."

Well, he would take it out just once to show that ass of Balliol just where he was in error, but it would come to no harm. The ass of Balliol was a scholar William had met in the street and who had argued William down with his fast tongue and slippery dialectic. But he was wrong, wrong!

"In omnem terram exit sonus eorum; et usque ad fines orbis eloquia eorum, But their sound goes out all over the world, and their tidings to the end of the earth."

That ass of Balliol didn't have to take up his time with Office. He had all the time in the world to polish his slick arguments. Why was Thomas of Waverley so close with his book, anyhow? It was not very brotherly of him. He oughtn't even to have his own book, according to the Rule.

"Ibi posuit soli tabernaculum suum, qui procedit ut sponsus de thalamo suo, exultat ut gigas percurrens viam, There He sets up a tent for the sun, who comes forth from his chamber like a bridegroom, exulting like a champion to his course."

At Gloucester College the black monks had their own rooms.

"A termino caeli fit egressus eius, et circuitus eius usque ad terminum caeli. Nec quidquam subtrahitur ardori eius, He enters at one end of the heavens, to the further end is his circuit. And nothing can hide from his heat."

William wished *he* had his own room.

Next afternoon, William was loitering at Merton College gate, watching a tall, brilliant red haired fellow browbeating a blackfriar. It was late in the day, and William was not supposed to be wandering around Oxford by himself, but he had lost Thomas of Waverley in a market crush in the high street a few hours ago, and, somehow, he had managed not to find him again.

"Well, sir," the redhaired fellow was saying in a superior tone, "the hour grows late, and my belly grumbles for its supper. Therefore I will take my leave of you. But I do hope that our argument has proved instructive."

"Instructive?" the blackfriar exploded. "You arrogant young drake! You not even a bachelor of arts, and you think to instruct *me?*" He turned to his companion. "Have you ever known such presumption? The boy has scarcely mastered rhetoric, and he thinks he may 'instruct' me in metaphysics!"

"Now, sir," said Redtop soothingly. "Be calm. I love St Thomas as much as you do, but I am afraid, and you shall admit it soon enough, that in certain essential matters he has been, shall we say, surpassed. Now if you will read in Duns' commentary the question I have mentioned—"

"Damn Duns."

"That," Redtop replied earnestly. "I am unable to do. I believe it is in God's province."

Redtop's cohorts laughed.

"I will hear no more impertinence!" cried the blackfriar. "Come speak with me again, boy, when you have grasped dialectic." He huffed off with his companion, and caught William's eye as they shoved past him. "You, Monkling!" he barked. "What are you smirking at? Ought you not to be in your choir stall? I think I hear a bell."

"It's ringing you to hell," said Redtop pleasantly. He pulled a solemn face at William. "Even out of the mouths of monklings will come words wiser than that fool's."

William stood there, absurdly gratified.

One of the scholars motioned to Redtop. "Come on, Agrestis, let's get some ale."

"Aye, a disquisition that arid needs a lake of ale to wash it down." "Agrestis" winked at William. "Better run, you poor sod; Rewley's calling."

William ran, but he was late.

✳ 37

Keldacross
July 1344

William returned to Yorkshire in the middle of July, accompanied as before by the same monks of Byland. He should have gone directly to Rievaulx, but shortly before leaving Oxford, he had received a dour, doomful letter from Wilfrid priest, so when they came to the crossroads, he said, "Come with me to my father's house." The Byland monks were weary of travel and wanted to go straight home. They argued about it at the crossroads for nearly an hour. Finally William said, "Then I shall go alone."

The Byland monks shook their heads. "Very well, but don't expect nothing to be said of it at Rievaulx."

"Tell them my old tutor is ill and that I want to see him before he dies."

"You tell them," they said. "If we're not taking you to Rievaulx, there's no reason for us to go out of our way there."

"Well, then," William replied. "They do not need to know that I stopped at Keldacross first. It will be only a day or two."

"It's one with us," said the Byland monks, and they bade him farewell. "We shall see you at harvestime," they said.

For the first mile along the old, rutted track, William was alone on the rough empty moorside. On one hand he looked down into green Bransdale, on the east, into the thick trees that flanked Woodenbeck up as far as Wydclif. He was afraid. He remembered the two wretched black monks they had found—naked, bleeding, and swollen—on the road out of Towcester. One of them was half senseless. The other insisted that it was clercs who had done it, Oxford clercs with clubs and long knives. Aelred of Byland had said, "Nonsense, man, your mind is jarred. Or perhaps your attackers had beaten some clercs and taken their clothes. That must be it." "No, no," the man had insisted, "I heard one of them speak Latin." The Byland monks wrapped the battered men in their cloaks, and William gave up Arrow, until they came to a priory of nuns, where they left them, giving the sisters as much as they could for their care. William had laughed nervously: "That's time off purgatory for us." But all the rest of the afternoon they had traveled anxiously, glancing behind them and peering ahead into the woods. They had been glad to meet up with a crowd of Canterbury pilgrims making their way home to Leicester.

Now William's heart leapt, because he saw dust and a cart up ahead. He kicked Arrow, and yelled.

The carter looked around and pulled up his ox. William rode up. "God give you grace! I'm glad as Gabriel to see you! Where are you bound?"

"To Keldacross, Master William," the carter replied. "We're hauling logs for Keldacross' great hearth."

"Marry! It's Tom Bradback!"

The fellow next to Tom leaned out and touched his forehead.

"And Win the Rabbit! What a grace! Win, tie my pony behind the cart. I'll sit up with Tom."

Win jumped down, and William took his seat. Win tethered Arrow, then climbed up in back to sit atop the logs.

"What were you doing riding lonesome, sir?" Tom whipped up the ox. "It isn't safe."

"The churls I was traveling with would go with me no farther. But I only had a little way alone."

141

"A little way is too long." Tom shook his head. "There's been evil doings in Tewisdale. The joiner of Wydclif was murdered not too far from here. They bashed in his head with something right cruel; folks said you could scarce tell who he was when they found him."

William crossed himself, and changed the subject. "Is all well in Kelda? Is my mother well? Is my brother married now?"

"He is, sir, and to a right bonny little bride. They're none of them here now though, except the Lady. They're up at Middleham Castle for the great tournament."

"You've heard of it, sir?" asked Win from behind. "The great tournament? St Godrich, I wish I could go. They'll be having archery matches too."

"You're an ass, Rabbit," said Tom. "They don't hear of Middleham tourneys down at Oxenford."

"You say my mother is home at Kelda, Tom? And Wilfrid priest?"

"Owd Wilfrid's wick as a weasel. His heart went thump one night and gave him a fright, but he's wick enough now to put the fear of God in us again."

"Aye, sir," Win agreed. "You know Garth the tyler's son and Maddy Fowler? Well, sir, they were making the beast, you know, in the very nave of St Godrich's, around Compline time. Well, old Wilfrid's prowling about, and he hears 'em, so he starts beating on 'em with a candlestick."

"So you see," said Tom, "he's as good as ever."

"Deo gratias," said William, and he meant it. He must talk to Wilfrid priest. He wished he did not have to see his mother first. Because of what was in his mind, he dreaded her. But she did not yet know what he was thinking, so when he came into the hall, she embraced him, and stood back and looked at him, and embraced him again. After dinner he went down the hill to see Wilfrid.

Wilfrid sat in Godrich's churchyard, under the yew by the well, wearing a straw hat and shelling peas. He looked up as William came in through the gate. "What's this?" He did not look half so deathly as his letter had led William to believe.

William knelt to receive his blessing. "Wilfrid priest, I need to talk with you. About Oxford."

Wilfrid raised his brows. "Well, help me up, and we'll go into my house." William stood, and Wilfrid took his arm. They went slowly across the yard, Wilfrid pointing out new graves. "There's old Winfrith-atte-Beck. Died last harvest. There's Wat Cottar's eldest boy. Froze to death last winter on the moorside. Lost in the mist."

They entered the cottage. Wilfrid seated William in his old place at the oaken table and went to fetch a jug of beer. "Have some cheese?"

"No, sir, don't take the trouble."

"Good," said Wilfrid. He set the pitcher before William with a cup, sat down, and folded his arms on the table. "So. The wandering scholar returns. Ought he not be at Rievaulx?"

"That is why I need to speak with you." William hid his nose in his cup. After a long time he said, "Wilfrid priest, Bonaventure was right."

Wilfrid lifted his brows again. "Bonaventure?"

William had thought about the greyfriar so often that he forgot that Wilfrid had never heard of him. "Bonaventure. At Helmsley. He disparaged Rewley."

"What?" Wilfrid thrust his head forward. "Come, boy. St Bonaventure, the philosopher whom you mention, visited Helmsley castle? St Augustine and Plato accompanied him, did they? Now, begin at the beginning and make yourself clear. Is rhetoric no longer taught among the seven liberal arts?"

They talked for many hours. Finally Wilfrid said, "Well, lad, in one thing I agree with your greyfriar. It is better not to be a religious at all than to be a bad religious. Is that what you would be if you remained at Rievaulx?"

William laid his head in his arms. "I don't know."

"What do you mean, you don't know? In what way are you unsure?"

"I don't know."

"Indeed, no one knows anything. But tell me what you *think*."

"I don't know. I was walking by Merton College gate; do you remember it?"

"Of course I remember it, what do you think?"

"Well, I was walking there, and I saw two fellows standing on the steps, and they were going at it hammer and tongs—a splendid argument. A redhaired Yorkshireman not much older than I, but brilliant—and free. He goes where he pleases and challenges whom he pleases and demolishes them all." William dropped his head back into his arms. Outside they heard the voice of Garth Shepherd as he urged lambs into the sheepfold.

"So you want to be brilliant and free. Are you telling me you've grown ashamed of your habit?"

"I don't know. Those men in their halls and colleges—they do whatever they like."

"On the contrary. They are bound by the rules of their houses and by the statutes of the university."

"No, but—"

"But?"

William blurted: "Father, I am discontented at Rewley. I am—I am *bored*. O God, forgive me." He rolled his head on the table.

Wilfrid sighed, gazing out the window at the sheepfold. He said, drily, "Son, you know not the meaning of boredom." He waited for William to finish sobbing. Then he said, "My question is this: How long has it been this way with you? Is it perhaps a passing humor?"

William looked up, tearstained. "Wilfrid priest, I don't know. Now that I have this feeling, I feel I have always had it. I don't want to go back to the abbey."

"Then perhaps you had better not. There are too many halfhearted monks slouching about in the world nowadays. There is no need to add to their numbers."

William kicked a table leg. "What am I going to do? What?"

"First you must kneel and thank God for showing you this before you made your solemn vows. The vilest thing in the world is to be forsworn to God."

"I can't. Father Stephen! Abbot William! They sent me up to Rewley. How can I leave. Jesu! What would my mother do?"

"Your mother would be sorely offended. You know why you were given to Rievaulx, don't you? You, one of but two sons?"

"Something about a vow, and dead children."

"After your sister Katharine there were three stillborn sons, one after another. Finally, your mother came down to St Godrich's well and swore to God and the saint that if she might have live sons, the second would go to the white monks." Wilfrid coughed deeply and spat into a handkerchief. "So you see."

William writhed on his bench. "O Jesu."

"Nonetheless, such is not sufficient cause for you to make your profession against your inclination. Again, there was truth in the words of that careless friar."

"But if I don't go back," William shuddered, "what shall I do?"

"Son," rejoined Wilfrid sternly, "you will certainly go back to Rievaulx and tell the brothers what you have decided. You shall be no base runaway."

"Oh, no, no, no," William moaned. "You do it for me."

Wilfrid laughed hoarsely. "Aye. Me, so old I can hardly get from here to Godrich porch. Aside from that, lad, you know that's vain foolishness. Nobody can do it for you."

"I can't. I'll wait. I'll think."

"As you say," said Wilfrid. "This is no step to be taken lightly."

✳ 38

Middleham Castle
July 1344

When Dame Emma heard that her granddaughter and the party from Tewisdale had arrived at Middleham for the tournament, she went to meet them in the outer bailey, where they were refreshing themselves. "Holy Nails!" Her voice rang off the stones of the courtyard. "There you are. I had wondered whether ye'd all fallen into a shitpit or summat. Where's my grandson Nicholas? Where's my daughter Magdalen?"

Katharine answered. "Nicholas and my father are riding up from Helmsley. My mother has stayed to watch the manor."

"That fool girl. What are bailiffs for?"

"Cheating folks and tramping on 'em," Alice muttered from the watertrough, sluicing the dust off her face.

"Where did you stay last night?"

"Jervaulx; and the night before at Fountains."

"Fall into any trouble on the road?"

"No, Grandmother. One of the horses threw a shoe, but our men fixed that soon enough."

"No thieves? Murderers?"

"None, as you see, Grandmother."

"What men did you have with you?"

"Young Geoff Wydclif, Sir Ingram Tarn, Gib Faulkoner, and a few others."

"I suppose that's enough, though I doubt young Geoff's of much account against anybody."

Eleanor made a face. Geoff was her favorite brother. And he had, after all, been of some use. He had dropped his surly ways and actually behaved courteously, even to Marion. He had sung like a lark all the long way, which had cheered the journey considerably, for it was not pleasant riding roads that two week's drought had turned into rivers of dust.

"Let us go into the great hall when you are ready," said Dame Emma. "You will want to see your uncles and cousins. They are all watching the foolery in there."

Actors and acrobats were attempting to keep the guests entertained until the real action began. After they had been there more than an hour, someone announced that the knights from Helmsley had arrived. Marion wanted to run and meet them, but Katharine restrained her. "They will be here soon enough. Hold your horse."

But they were not in soon enough. Marion fidgeted and stood tiptoe to see seven tumblers form a tower on each other's backs. She plucked at Katharine's elbow. "Why isn't he come in? Why are they so long?"

"He's doubtless settling his horse and gear and changing his clothes. They have had a long, dusty road, as you should know."

Eleanor sneered at Marion. "What did you think? That he'd come into the hall all roadworn? This is Middleham Castle, not some inn in York."

The topmost acrobat juggled four apples, touching each with his tongue as it bounced past his mouth. Eleanor laughed. "Oo, look at that."

Dame Emma trumpeted, "They've come." She pointed.

Nicholas was beautiful in a new suit of clothes. He came up the hall with Sir Gervase and some other knights, surrounding a grey nobleman with a scarred face. "That's Godfrey Scarface," Katharine explained to Marion, "Lord Ros' uncle. He was at your wedding. But look at my brother. I am glad he did not choose the parti-colored fashion. He looks well—a modest knight, not a peacock, like some others."

"It is men's business to look well for us women," Dame Emma pronounced. "Their only good business."

Then Nicholas was doing his business well. His russet surcotte set off his figure to great advantage. An oversleeve fell back as he lifted a hand, and showed the undersleeve of forester green, embroidered by his mother with lilies and sprigs of broom. His belt, traced with red chevrons and clasped in silver, was strapped around his hips most handsomely. Marion could not take her eyes off him.

Scarface squinted nearsightedly in their direction and said something to Nicholas. Nicholas bowed and started toward them across the room.

"Ho, grandson!" Dame Emma blared. "You have the whole distaff side of the hall slavering after you, you young stag!"

People turned around to look. Two ladies sniggered. Nicholas ignored them. "Grandmother," he said. She held out her hands. He took them, saying, "When did you all come here?" He nodded to Katharine and Eleanor, but not to Marion. Alice, standing behind, humphed.

"Which?" Dame Emma demanded. "I arrived last night with your uncles. Tewisdale and Emberthwaite arrived not two hours ago."

Then Nicholas turned to Marion. "How goes it? Do you like it here?"

She nodded. He seemed different here, remote, conscious of his bearing, of his place here in the world of men and war. Words jammed in her throat.

"You look very well," he said.

Her hair hung in heavy, ribbon-plaited loops over her ears (Alice had striven over it, cursing, for an hour) and over her gown she wore the marten pelisse that Mistress Alison had bought her, so thriftlessly, from the woman's tailor's cousin last spring in York. She gulped. "You also."

"Did you see Godfrey Scarface?"

"Yes. I remember him from the wedding. He looks right grim."

"He's not grim. He's merry."

"Oh. But he looks—" Marion faded out.

"Have you seen the earl?"

"Not yet."

"What think you of Middleham?"

"It's big. It's as high as York Minster, this hall." Marion gazed upward.

"Aye. Well. There's Rab and Mundo over there." Nicholas began abruptly to walk away. Marion grabbed at him. "No! Don't leave!"

He was prevented, in any event. They all pressed against the wall as a fellow pushed by with a malodorous dancing bear.

"You have Katharine and Eleanor and my grandmother. Why do you need me?"

Marion hung on his arm.

Nicholas looked at her, and capitulated. "Very well. For a while."

Katharine and Eleanor exchanged disgusted glances. Dame Emma, spying an old acquaintance, stood up straight and boomed, "Philippa! How are you? By God, you've waxed fat!"

An elderly lady who had been advancing cheerfully dropped her smile and suddenly changed her course.

"What ails her?" Dame Emma complained. "All these folks. So full of humors."

Rab and Edmund strolled up.

"Nick!" Rab shouted. "Aren't you going to survey the lists?"

"Get off, brother," Katharine commanded. "Folks will think you feeble if you stay with us women all day."

"Aye." Nicholas detached himself. "I'll see you shortly." As he walked away with his friends he looked back at Marion. "I'll send Geoff to look after you."

"We look after ourselves well enough," Dame Emma called after him. "We don't need no bumpy faced boy who thinks he's a girl."

Nicholas could not find Geoff anyway, for Geoff was hanging about the minstrels' gallery, irritating the musicians, wanting to try their instruments, and pestering them to teach him courtly songs in French.

Sweet beautiful lady
For God's sake don't think
That anyone has my allegiance
But you alone.

The rest of that day passed in music and dancing and games, as parties arrived from all over the North. Marion did not much enjoy it. She wished Nicholas would come back shortly, as he'd said, but he never did. Dame Emma went stumping off to blare at a dowager lady. Eleanor spied some girls she had met at the last tournament at Helmsley and went off to chat with them. Katharine sent Alice away, and then stood about stonily, nodding curtly at anyone who greeted her. She was always more at ease in a saddle than at a party, and she could never think of anything to say to Marion.

A knight approached them—a young man, sandy haired, powerfully built. He wore the parti-colored fashion in green and yellow, and Katharine nodded at him as if she did not think much of him. He stopped before them, put his yellow leg forward, and greeted Marion as if she should know him. When she looked uncertain, he said, "I was at your wedding."

"Oh yes, I remember." She did, vaguely, and it made her uncomfortable. She did not like to be confronted with guests from her wedding night. And this man seemed to expect her to know his name. He tucked his thumbs in his belt and looked amused, studying her. "I doubt Nicholas is used to women puking at the prospect of him. You liking Kelda better now?"

Marion turned the color of beetroot, and Katharine broke in brusquely. "Were you looking for my brother?"

"Scarface wants him."

"He's not here."

Plainly, Katharine's distaste for the man was rendering her even more taciturn than usual, so Marion added, "He went to see the lists."

"Went to see the lists and left you all alone, did he?"

Marion glanced at Katharine, who just stood there stonyfaced.

"Well," said the knight. "If Nicko's at the lists, my lord'll have to make do with me. I'm not chasing your brother all over Middleham." So saying, he strode away down the hall.

"Who was he?" Marion was taken aback.

"Hugh Cliderhou. His family live at Eskmere, to the east of Kelda."

At that moment Katharine's husband joined them, mild, red nosed, and pleased to see them. He kissed Katharine respectfully and spoke kindly to Marion. "How do you?"

"Well, thank you, Sir Henry."

"You look so. Vraiment une belle dame."

Marion smiled at him. She was ignorant of French, but it was clear Sir Henry was trying to make her feel less out of place.

They all three went over and stood with Nicholas' Coverdale uncles, who were rambling on about the sport tomorrow, tossing words back and forth that Marion did not understand. She craned her neck, looking all over the hall for Nicholas. He was nowhere. She was weary. She wondered where they were going to sleep.

Katharine pointed upward. "Whose arms?" They all tilted their heads to examine the great scutcheons hanging overhead. They discussed heraldry for half an hour. Marion's mind reeled with all their "crosses crosslet" and "cinquefoils" and "lions rampant regardant." But she gazed upward with everybody else, and remarked vaguely that the roofbeams were pretty.

"What?" Katharine barked.

"The roofbeams, all painted with vines. My stepmother planted such a vine, with grapes, in York, but the winter killed it."

They all looked at her for a moment and then went on arguing about "crosses potent," "metals," "bends," and "lions rampant tails nowed."

That night, Marion shared a bed with Eleanor, Katharine, and two of the cousins of Coverdale. Her whole body ached to sleep, but she could not, and so tossed and turned and shifted for an hour after they crawled in. "I wish Dame Marion would lie still," one of the cousins complained, and so, with great effort, she did. "Alice," she whispered after a while. Alice was sleeping on a mat beside the bed. She did not answer. Marion thumped her head back against the bolster. The sound of sleep breathing came from all over the partitioned room. A lancet window at the far end showed nightblue sky, the rim of the moon, and stars: the Eagle and the Dragon. Nicholas was outside sleeping in a tent. She wished she had remembered to bring her beads; then she could have prayed herself to sleep.

She need not have worried over tomorrow, for Nicholas was not riding the first day. Sir Henry rode against a young knight from Lancashire, and won a good yellow horse. He sold back the armor, which was of no particular value. But Nicholas and the younger Helmsley knights were waiting for the melee on the second day. Sir Gervase rode the seventh joust against a Dacre of Cumberland, and each of them shattered four lances before Gervase finally dealt the Dacre a blow that sent him lurching backward off his saddle. Katharine was far happier over that than she was over her husband's victory—not only because it was a noble Dacre that Gervase had unhorsed, but because Gervase was her father, blood kin, and because she thought little of her husband as a fighter, and of the Lancashire knight even less. "When my father fights," she boasted, "he is a wolf. He is never unhorsed."

Marion squeaked, lurching forward on her bench. "I can see Geoffrey!" She waved. Geoff, who was waiting at the near end of the lists with fresh lances, saw her and saluted gravely. "He saw us!" Marion shrieked excitedly, waving again. "He saw me wave!" Katharine pulled her arm down, muttering, "Aye, aye." The Coverdale cousins snickered. Eleanor rolled her eyes. Marion sat back, oblivious. The shouting of the heralds, the thundering of the marshals, the clangor of the tournament all astounded her. Her eyes hurt from the brightness. She cheered wildly when Sir Gervase unhorsed his Dacre and booed lustily with the others when the Dacre, enraged, untangled himself and rose cursing, drawing his sword. Gervase wheeled his horse around, and the marshals had to ride out. "I remember a time," Dame Emma declared over the noise, "when I was a lass. A knight was angry at being unhorsed, so he stood up and hacked the other's leg off." "Ugh!" said Eleanor. "What did they do to him?" "Stripped him of his gear and made him ride on the list-rails, shield reversed." "Rood," said Katharine, "I wish I'd seen that." Marion pointed, giggling. "Look, see the poor boy."

A little page was struggling up their row, trying desperately not to step on anyone's toes. "Pardon, lady. Oh, sir, pardon! Pardon, lady." His face was pained and harried. Marion giggled again.

Then, to her amazement, he stopped, sweating, directly in front of them. "A gentleman," he quavered, "craves a token of the lady of Keldacross."

Marion looked around distractedly.

Katharine poked her in the ribs. "He's talking to you."

Marion said, "But . . ."

"It's plainly Nicholas asking a token from his own wife. How stupid." Katharine briskly unwound a ribbon from Marion's hair and threw it at the boy. "Take that."

The boy caught it. He screwed up his face with the effort of remembering his lines. "The gentleman thanks the lady with all his soul and promises to wear it close to his heart, like a holy relic."

Marion wanted to sink under the bench.

Eleanor looked at the page intently. "Are you sure he said the lady of *Keldacross?*"

Katharine glared at Eleanor and snapped at Marion, "Say something, goose."

Marion opened her mouth. Nothing came out.

Katharine shifted impatiently. "Tell the knight," she rapped, "that the lady bids him wear her token in all valor and prowess. And bids him also keep himself from harm, for the merest scratch to him will be, for her, a mortal wound."

Marion blushed. The page bowed awkwardly, half to Marion, half to Katharine, and made his way over the toes again. "Pardon, lady. Oh! Sir! Pardon."

Eleanor sat rigidly staring at the field, her mouth set.

Katharine snorted. "Does he have to be so doting? Who asks a token of his own wife?"

Dame Emma agreed. "Damn foolery. And calling her 'lady of Keldacross,' as if my poor Magdalen were in her grave."

Marion was utterly confused. Faces all up the row craned out to see who had caused their feet so much discomfort. She hunched down and lowered her eyes. The noise of the sport and the talk of the gentlewomen around her blended into a blurred clamor. The sun beat down on her head. When she put up her hand to touch her hair, it was hot under her fingers.

The best thing that happened that day was when the sport was over, and they left the galleries for the table. For Nicholas met them down below and offered to take Marion walking through Middleham courts and outside Middleham walls.

"We can eat later," he said, and she agreed. Eleanor cut in. "I too." She linked her arm through Nicholas' free one, which annoyed Marion no end, as she wanted to talk with him alone, but Nicholas did not object. And so the three of them roamed among the pavilions and the stables and the smithies, where armorers pounded dents out of helmets and mended riven mail, and blacksmiths labored over great, twitching hooves. Men at arms stood about at ease, munching apples, and everywhere squires and pages and servants raced to and fro, shouting at each other to bring this or that or to get their arses here or there. The earth was all pressed down flat, imprinted with hundreds of overlapping horseshoes and boot soles. They picked their way between piles of fresh droppings and puddles of muck. Marion and Eleanor lifted their skirts as high as they dared. Nicholas squeezed Marion's arm. His face was the happiest she had ever seen it, all flushed and smiling. He loosed his left arm from Eleanor and made great sweeps, pointing out tents and noblemen. When an old serving fellow passed them saying, "*Two* bonny damsels on your hands, eh, young knight?" Nicholas did not glower, as he usually would, but laughed, and took back Eleanor's arm.

The day was hot and bright and still. It made Marion feel weak-headed, so that when they stopped in a lane behind a green tent, and Nicholas bent down and kissed her, she kissed back, winding her arms around his neck and not caring about Eleanor, or about anyone who came strolling by. Eleanor caught her breath. Involuntarily, she jerked on Nicholas' arm.

Nicholas ignored her and said to Marion, "I will be riding in the melee tomorrow."

"I know," said Marion.

"I will make you proud of me, you shall see."

"I am already proud of you," she said, and they kissed again. Then they went back, without Eleanor, for dancing.

Later that day they quarreled. They sat in an arched window in a long room, looking down into the inner bailey hung with branches and bright, floating pennants. Nicholas was trying to teach her to recognize the arms of various marcher lords, but her mind hazed over. She complained that they were all the same and why didn't he leave her alone?

"Don't be a fool," he replied. "At least tell me *our* arms rightly, in the manner that I taught you."

"I wish yours were the golden apples, like Sir Geoffrey's."

"Not 'golden apples!' Wydclif is vert, chevron argent twixt three pommes slipped, d'or."

"Well, I like it better."

"I don't care what you like. Tell me Keldacross arms."

Marion scowled and stuck out her lip. "Two white stars and a red hatchet on a black shield."

"God damn it! They're mullets, I told you, spur rowels, not stars. Keldacross arms: sable, two mullets argent pierced sable; broadaxe gules. You will make me look like a fool if you don't even know your own arms."

"You're a dimwit," she retorted, "with nothing in your head but arms and beasts."

He was so enraged that he sprang from his seat in the window, pulling his elbow back. She shrank away, and that both shamed and offended him. "I wasn't going to hit you," he said coldly. "If you think so, it shows again that you are an ignorant town girl." Since the first day of their marriage he had never been so discourteous as to mention what he felt must be an embarrassment to her.

Marion's chest heaved. "Who is ignorant? Do you think I am ashamed to be Yorkisfolk? I wish I were there now instead of here with your mullets and broadaxes for chopping people up. I care nothing for them. I wish they were dead," she concluded absurdly. Tearful, she picked up her skirts and ran away to find Alice.

He thrust his hands into his belt and faced the window. His face felt hot; he could not admit to himself that a moment ago he might have struck her. It was said that old Sir Walter Cliderhou used to strike Hugh's mother regularly, and once indeed she had come to Helmsley with a swollen eye. This had appalled all decent men who saw it. It was the kind of thing that villeins did, debased and brutish, unworthy of a knight.

In the galleries the second day, Eleanor and the Coverdale cousins talked above the heralds, who were shouting, at great length, the rules for the melee. "Sssh!" hissed people all around them, but Eleanor shrugged her shoulders, "So?" and they went on talking. "*Look* at that destrier over there!" "No, look at that *knight!* That's what I like. Isn't that Ingram Tarn?" "How does he afford such trappings? I hear Upthwaite's almost in ruins." "He wins 'em. He always takes at least three prisoners."

Marion leaned forward, shading her eyes. "Where is Nicholas? Do you see Nicholas?" She felt terrible that she had quarreled with him yesterday, and worse that she had not been able to find him to tell him she was sorry.

"Look, there's Isabel Neville. No. The one in the blue gown. Yes. The one with the painted eyebrows. I hear that she's deceiving her lord with one of his stewards." "Idle rumor; I never listen to it; which steward?" "Did you hear what she did last tournament here?" "No, what?" "You haven't *heard?*" "Well, *what?*" "She rode in, before the first joust, with a band of women, all seated astride warhorses, gorgeously arrayed like men and all armed and trapped to the teeth. And they said they would send their champion—that was her—into the lists against any knight there, and have the victory." "For shame! for *shame!*"

"That's a shame," said Dame Emma, "worth two hundred *aves* and a trip to Jerusalem. I wish they'd done that when I was a girl."

"Ssssh!"

"What are they saying?" Marion could not understand the heralds.

"Is it to be à outrance?"

"No, à plaisance."

"I didn't hear."

An old knight in a furred gown turned around and glared at them.

"Perhaps if you dames and damsels damped your noise a moment you might catch a word or two."

Dame Emma stared him down. He puffed angrily into his beard and turned around again, muttering.

Marion leapt up. "I see him! I see Nicholas! Behind those fence things, I see him!" Katharine yanked on her. "I see the white stars and the red hatchet! I see Edmund too, with the golden apples, and Rab and the castle-stripes!"

"Bars embattled," gritted Katharine. "Sit down."

Marion obeyed. But she leaned forward on the rail in front of her and peered. There he sat on Dragon, head tipped back, visor up, laughing at something. She knew by his face that he was laughing the way he laughed with his friends. It was not the way he laughed with her. But then he began to scan the galleries, and she knew he was looking for her. She wanted to stand up and shout, "Here I am," but she knew he would kill her for it afterward, if Katharine did not kill her for it here and now. She squirmed. She saw Geoff ride up and hand Nicholas his sword.

Eleanor exclaimed, "They're going to ride in."

"Jesu, it's beautiful."

"There's nowt more beautiful. See! I told you it was à outrance."

"Good," said Dame Emma. "Now we'll see some blood."

Marion turned to Katharine. "Dame Katharine, what's . . ."

"À plaisance: arms of courtesy, blunt weapons. À outrance: no restraint."

"Oh."

The sides were drawing up in double ranks on either end of the lists. "There's my brother in the first file," said Katharine. "Just wait till you see him fight. He unhorsed two knights his first show of arms at Helmsley and drove another one against the pale."

"That was before he married *you*," Eleanor told Marion gratuitously.

"Do men often die, ou . . . ou . . ."

"À outrance. If they don't risk aught, where's the honor?"

"Damn!" someone cursed. "It's going to rain."

A drop plunked on Marion's head. They all looked up at the sky and rummaged for their cloaks.

"Of course," grumbled Eleanor, pulling up her hood. "Two weeks of drought until now, when we don't *want* rain."

Katharine bit her thumbnail. "It'll make the field slippery."

"Maybe it will stop," Marion suggested.

"Hush!" snapped the old knight, turning round again. For the high marshal was raising his great sword. Everyone fell silent, waiting. The combatants lowered their lances. "Now," Katharine whispered, sitting forward. Marion pressed against her. She wished Alice were here, instead of down with the commons.

The marshal roared: "Laissez aller!"

Marion shut her eyes. She waited for the clash, and jumped when it came. When she opened her eyes again, Katharine was sitting at the edge of the bench, peering piercingly into a great cloud of dust. "There he is! There he is, my good brother! St Mary! Good sword!"

"My brother Edmund had better watch himself," said Eleanor. "He moves too near the edge."

Marion watched through her fingers.

"Rood!" Dame Emma trumpeted. "No one swings a mace like old Ralph of Torbeck." Sir Ralph was almost twenty years younger than she.

"Rab is no woman with his. Look at him."

"I can't see any of them," Marion said.

"Well, if you'll take your hand away from your face."

"Oh, that dog!" cried Eleanor. "Mundo's got himself planted against the rails. I told him so! Well, he can kiss Saladin goodbye. Stupid villein!" She stamped her foot on the boards. "Stupid boor of a brother. Can't you stay in any longer than that!"

They watched Edmund ride off the field, shrugging and pretending not to care.

All of a sudden Katharine leapt up, hissing. Marion saw Nicholas on the ground. She crammed her face into her lap.

"What?" Dame Emma bellowed. "Was that my grandson just got himself unhorsed? Yes? Well what did he do that for?"

"That was *foul!*" Katharine sat down again, hard. "That was *foul!*"

"He's not getting up!" Eleanor screamed. "Oh, St Mary, he'll be trampled!"

"He'll get up," said Katharine grimly. "He'll fight on foot."

"No! He's not! Oh pull him out! He'll be trampled!" Eleanor cried.

Dame Emma leaned over and smacked Marion across the head. "Sit up, girl. Don't behave like a puling milkmaid."

Katharine hissed, "That was foul! Why don't they call it foul?"

"Sit up, lass, they've taken him away."

Katharine stood up. "Come, sister," she said. "We will go and see what's happened."

Marion wept into her knees. "I can't."

"Dame Marion," said Eleanor, "ought you not stay here? Geoff said to stay here until he came. Katharine and I can go."

"You can't do anything for him, Granddaughter," Dame Emma pointed out to Katharine. "Leave him to the men."

"I can't just sit here, Grandmother. You stay. If Geoffrey comes, tell him where we've gone. Come, sister, it's your place and mine to be there." She dragged Marion up by the arm. Yanking her along, she pushed their way past the faces that now stared at them for a new reason: "They're of the knight who just got himself unhorsed." Katharine gritted her teeth. Alice met them down below with an eagerly horrified face. "Oh my little lady," she wailed. Marion reached for her. Katharine accosted a knight. "Where have they taken Sir Nicholas of Keldacross?"

"Over there, lady." He gestured with a boar-crested heaume. "That yellow tent. But I don't know if you'd do well to go in there."

Katharine ignored him and hurried onward, tugging Marion by the wrist. They had nearly made it to the tent flaps when two men at arms moved in front of them, saying, "What's your business, ladies?"

Katharine replied, taking charge. "We are the sister and the wife of Nicholas of Kelda."

The men looked at each other. "Ladies, your love is well noted, but it would be best if you went back and waited till you were called for. Things are—not pleasant in there."

"I assure you I am well used to unpleasant things. I am a daughter of warriors."

"Certainly, lady, but . . . " The men looked at each other again. Then the one who had spoken ducked back through the flaps and bawled, "Will Sir Nicholas' squire come out at once?"

Geoff emerged, looking drawn. He looked worse when he saw the women. "What are they doing here?" he demanded.

The man at arms shrugged. "They are ladies of Keldacross. You take care of them."

Geoff frowned at them. "You were to stay in the galleries until I came for you."

"Talk like that to me again, Geoffrey, and I'll knock your head off. You imagine we could sit there enjoying the sport when we don't know whether my brother is alive or dead?"

Geoff shook his head. "He is not dead, Dame Katharine. But we are setting a badly broken ankle—and some other things—and I don't think he wants you—or anyone, Dame Katharine—with him at present. There are other wounded in there as well, and it would be discourteous to them if you came through."

Katharine said nothing.

"Dame Katharine, I must go back. Why don't you go up to castle hall and wait? I'll come when we've patched him up."

"We shall do so," Katharine replied, with dignity. One of the men at arms offered to escort them to the hall, and Geoff disappeared into the tent again.

The castle servants were not unkind, but they were distracted and had no time. They were preparing the hall for the great feast that was to crown the tournament. The minstrels were tuning in their loft, and the sound echoed discordantly in the vaulting. Eventually a butler took note of them and led them to a little room with a deep window and a small fire. A number of women sat there, drinking sweetened wine. Marion would not take any wine, but sat hunched on a chest in the corner of the room. Katharine sat by her, straight as a lance. Alice stayed outside the door, holding their cloaks. The other ladies sat near the fire, two of them astride a bench, playing backgammon.

It seemed long hours before Geoffrey came. He had bloodstains on his surcotte, but he bowed handsomely to everyone and said, "Come now, Dame Katharine, Dame Marion." They took their leave and hurried after him. At the door, Alice got up; she had been sitting on the floor.

"You stay," said Katharine.

"No!" Marion seized Alice by the elbow. "I want her to come too."

They went up and down endless stairs until they came to a round room with five or six pallets laid out in it.

Nicholas was lying on one of them, cursing to Rab about Dragon. "That bastard will never sell him back, never. My father will kill me."

"Well, Mundo's lost Saladin too. We none of us did nobly today, friend."

"With my brother," Katharine announced, coming through the door, "it was foul. The knight who did it ought to be expelled from the lists."

Nicholas turned his head toward them. Marion caught her breath. "Oh! His face!"

The entire left side was black and swollen. He quickly turned away again, and kept his back to them.

Alice gawked. He lay, doubled up, under a woolen blanket. She could not believe her eyes that he looked so little.

Katharine strode across the room. "Brother. Do not be ashamed. It was foul. I saw it."

"No," Nicholas replied, muffled. "It was not foul. It was faiblesse on my part. I wish I were dead."

Katharine flicked him on the shoulder. He winced. "Brother, that's no Nicholas-talk. Now what of these wounds of yours?"

157

Rab answered. "Shoulder popped out, but Geoff and I popped it right back in, eh, Geoff? A few cracked ribs, cuts, bruises, and a broken ankle."

"I'll kill myself," said Nicholas.

"His face," said Marion again.

"Na, sweetheart, that's just cuts and swelling where his helm got crushed in," Rab reassured her. "You'll be able to kiss him again soon enough. It's the ankle that's the sore matter."

"It's my fault," said a voice behind them. Hunkering miserably on the edge of a cot at the far side of the room sat Sir Ralph, still in full armor except his helm and gauntlets. The cot sagged under him, and the man on it, a poor wretch wrapped like a corpse in bloody bandages, rolled against Sir Ralph's broad back. Sir Ralph's face was crumpled with remorse; streaks like snail paths glistened on his cheeks. "It was Magog that trampled him. I couldn't turn him away quick enough."

They did not mean to, but they all stared. Sir Ralph rubbed his face in his hands. "Mother of God. What will Gervie say?"

Nicholas groaned and threw his arm over his eyes. Marion stood aside, by the door, with Alice. She did not know what to do or say. Then they all heard a noise that turned their innards cold: an uneven, jangling step on the stairs, and a hoarse voice demanding, "Is he in there?"

Nicholas' back stiffened. Marion drew back, clutching Alice. Katharine set her jaw.

But when Gervase came in, his face was suffused with paternal grief. He rushed to the bedside, shoving Geoff out of the way, and flung himself on his knees. "Oh my son, my son! I thought you had been dead."

Tears sprang to Nicholas' eyes. He could not wipe them away, because his hands were prisoned, so he rubbed his face against the sheet. "O God. Father, I'm sorry for it."

"Sorry! In God's name I'm sorry too. Your ankle's smashed? You won't be able to walk for God knows how long!"

Sir Ralph moaned. "It's my fault."

Gervase turned on him. "You great oaf! Call yourself a horseman?"

Sir Ralph made a noise.

"Who was your mother, villein, an elephant? Don't you know how to turn a goddam horse by now? What did you learn to ride on, ploughman? An ox?"

Sir Ralph rose up, lumbering. "See now, Gervie, I won't . . . "

Gervase jumped up, clapping his hand to his hilt.

"No! Father!" Nicholas sat up hastily, painfully. "It was no one's fault but mine. And besides"—he sank back and made a feeble little joke—"a knight doesn't need to walk, anyhow."

"That's old Nick," said Rab.

Gervase grunted.

"Father, it was foul," Katharine insisted.

Gervase did not look at her. His eyes narrowed. All of them saw, and braced themselves. One never knew with Gervase what humor would seize him next. Abruptly his voice compressed in cold, iron rage. "Shut your muzzle, woman. It was not foul, but damn bêtise and faiblesse. I am shamed before all my friends." He stared down at Nicholas as if he were a disgusting slug. Nicholas shut his eyes. "Shamed." Gervase repeated it, low and cold. He glared hawkishly around the room, then strode out, jangling ferociously.

Rab released a long whistle. Katharine unwound her fingers from the folds of her gown.

"God," Nicholas moaned. "I'll never have Dragon back."

Katharine jerked her head at Marion. "Go comfort your husband."

Alice gave her a nudge. She crept across the room and stood at the foot of the pallet. "I am sorry," she said.

He opened his eyes. "*You* sorry? Why are *you* sorry?"

"That token I gave you. It brought you no luck."

"Token? What token?"

"That ribbon you got from me yesterday." Marion's voice trailed off under the blankness of his look. "Yesterday, in the galleries."

"What?" Sharp as damask steel.

Katharine blanched.

Marion said, "You sent a boy."

"Why would I do that?" Nicholas' face, the unbruised part, turned white and furious.

Marion's throat hurt. She turned desperately to Katharine. "Your sister said . . . "

"If my sister told you to jump off the Wydclif, would you do it? Christ! If I find out who the bastard is, I'll cut *him* into ribbons!"

"Soft now, Nicholas," Rab mumbled. "Lie down."

Nicholas shouted. "She's a fool! Why would I ask a favor from my wife?"

Rab pushed him back. "Soft now, Nick. She doesn't know anything."

Marion screwed up her chin and covered her mouth. Her eyes began to leak. She tried to stop, but her voice came weak and wobbling. "It's not my fault!"

Nicholas breathed hard through his nose.

"Sir!" Marion cried. "Why are you angry with me over *this?* You might have died!"

He stared at the ceiling.

Katharine beckoned for Marion to come away, and they left the room, Geoff and Alice following after. When they came back to the room where they had waited with the other ladies, Geoff made Marion sit by the fire, and ran to fetch a cup of cider. She was crying so hard that she did not notice his unaccustomed kindness. "Here then, lady," he said gently, proffering the cider. "Drink this."

That night Nicholas took a corruption in one of the wounds in his side, and by morning he was raving. "Bring me Dragon! Bring Dragon! I will ride home!"

Gervase rushed out and found the knight who had unhorsed his son, and bought Dragon back for double his worth. Gervase said also, "I don't hold with doctors," and he made his own sword red hot over the fire and set it to the puss-swollen wound. Marion, standing by with a bowl and linens, shut her eyes.

But the next day Nicholas was himself again.

"Ha!" said Dame Emma. "That's the blood of Wherne telling. We never die."

Katharine said, "It's the hot blood of Kelda."

Nicholas sat up. "I will not stay here any longer to be laughed at. I will go home."

"And how will you ride," Gervase demanded, "with that ankle of yours?"

"I can do it."

"I know!" Marion stepped forward. "We can get a wagon, and make a bed in it, and he can go home in that."

They all looked at her as if she were insane. At times like this, her ignorance of chivalry was too much to be borne.

"I will not," said Nicholas in a flat, dry voice, "go home in a cart."

✳ 39

William passed two days with his mother, telling her at length about his travels and his masters and the brothers at Rewley. She listened attentively, inclining her ear to him over the clacking shuttle of the loom. All the while he felt like scum, but he talked the harder for it, because he could not tell her what he was really thinking about.

On the third day he went down to St Godrich's and found Wilfrid in the sanctuary replacing old candle stubs with new tapers. He ignored William. William cleared his throat, and made much noise coming down the aisle.

The three burning Watchers watched him.

"Father Wilfrid."

Wilfrid turned round, crossly. "Yes, I hear you. What do you want?"

"To talk with you. About Oxford. Don't you remember?"

"Of course I remember. I'm not that much of a dotard. A moment. Let me put these stubs away." He disappeared through the sacristy door. William could hear him bumbling around in there, muttering to himself.

"Father Wilfrid, I have made my choice. I will take my vows and go back to Rewley."

Wilfrid came out. "Have you prayed about it?"

William stared at him. "No," he answered. Why hadn't he? "But I have debated it with myself until I thought I would go mad."

Wilfrid raised his eyes to the roof. He gestured at William. "This holy monk might benefit from debating less and praying more," he said, and disappeared again into the sacristy.

William stood there dumbly. Wilfrid emerged again, carrying an old velvet cope over his arm. "I am taking this up to your mother. She says that it is worn in spots. I cannot say that I noticed it. Pray. And when you have done that, come back and talk with me." He walked out of the church and left William to himself.

William went self-consciously to the altar rail. He knelt there for a long while. His cheek got wedded to the altar rail, and his back ached. From outside drifted the noise of squirrels chattering and the sound of someone digging with a spade. He tried to pray and forced himself to ask for guidance. But pictures of Oxford and Bonaventure and Redtop kept invading his mind. He asked for a sign, and knew that he wanted no sign but the sign that he was to be a scholar. Finally he straightened up and looked behind him, because there was a pattering sound at the porch. Someone came in.

"Who's that?" asked a startled voice. A woman.

William got up. Her eyes opened to the darkness; she saw his habit and said, "Oh, pardon. I'll come back." And she made to go out.

"Nay," he said. "I'm finished."

She said, "You must be my husband's brother."

"Oh," he replied, "then you must be my brother's wife." And he laughed awkwardly, because that was such a stupid thing to say. "When did you get here from Middleham?"

"Not an hour ago. Didn't you hear us ride by?"

"I heard something. I wasn't noticing."

"Oh." She put her fingers to her mouth and looked at him with great eyes. She must think him very holy and undistracted.

"We stayed last night at Rievaulx," she ventured. "It is a beautiful house."

"Yes."

Marion took a step backward.

William said, "I shall speak with you again. I—I must go talk with Father Wilfrid."

"I like your priest," she said. "I like this church. And I like them." She pointed at the seraphim.

The still, winged faces with their open mouths and fire eyes. William had never thought of "liking" them. "The Watchers," he said.

"Do they watch over this place and keep it from harm?"

"They just watch."

She looked at him strangely, so he ducked his head and shuffled out. "I must see Father Wilfrid." He ran across the courtyard to Wilfrid's door. The priest opened it.

"I have met my brother's wife."

Wilfrid nodded. "Come in."

William went in.

"Sit."

William sat. Wilfrid came and stood by the table. "So?"

William met his eyes. "I must get back to Oxford."

Wilfrid said, "So."

William said, "If I don't go back to the abbey, how shall I ever get back to Oxford?"

"So," said Wilfrid. "We will think of a way."

162

When they came up to the hall, everyone was scurrying about because Sir Gervase was home and because Nicholas was ailing again. Geoff was racing out the door shouting, "Fetch Cuth Constable!" For Cuth had skill as a bonesetter. Nicholas, dismounting Wutherwind, had gone dizzy and fallen, breaking the splints they had made at Middleham.

"Cuth's out exercising Cockatrice," said Gib Faulkoner, so Geoff grabbed a horse and went after him.

William was glad that everything was harried, because it saved him from speaking to his mother. She would see his heart if she looked at him, he knew it. He could feel his treason glistening on his face like grease.

"Sir," Wilfrid told Gervase at supper on the dais, "I will accompany young William to Rievaulx, if that is well with you."

"Do what you like," said Gervase.

"I will wait until Sir Nicholas is recovered, in the event . . . I would not like you to have to send to Wydclif for a priest."

"Nicholas will need no priest."

"Father Wilfrid," said Dame Magdalen, "should you make that long journey? Are you strong enough?"

The care in her voice made William's throat ache, but Wilfrid said smoothly, "Ai, I am an old man. It will be good for my soul to stay with the white monks. It will be no more than a week. Sir Gervase, I would you had a chaplain." (This was an old bone between them.)

"God damn it!" Gervase glared at him. "It's only a broken ankle."

And indeed, by the next afternoon Nicholas was sitting up again, calling for Marion to come play draughts with him. So Wilfrid and William departed the next day, shortly after dawn. Dame Magdalen kissed William on the forehead, saying, "Godspeed, my son."

They set off, Win Thornrigg coming behind them with his bow. When they should have gone west on the road to Rievaulx, they turned south instead.

Surprised, Win protested. "But the abbey, sir—"

Wilfrid said, "Do as you are bid, Edwin. We are going to York." He turned to William. "Unless you will change your mind."

William shook his head.

"Good." Wilfrid kicked up his pony with a sense of purpose. He did not look at all sickly now. "Yes," he said, "your uncle Roger de Wherne will be able to help us when we get to York. It's a pity he's not your godfather instead of Nicholas'. But still. For my sake, perhaps, if not for yours. It was I who got him into Merton. He was always a good natured man, well liked among his fellows—which is more than can be said for some others."

William looked at him sharply. "Wilfrid priest . . . "

"Do not call me by that baby name. You sound like an ignorant villein."

"Father Wilfrid, why did you not remain at Merton?"

"Most men leave Oxenford at some time or other."

"But not for Keldacross-on-the-moor. Why, sir? I have wondered for a long while."

"I was an arrogant fool," Wilfrid replied, "with a taste for arguments that led to bloodshed. I made all my friends my enemies. And I, a senior fellow of Merton, stole from the college treasury to buy books for myself. Are you satisfied?"

William gawked.

"So you see. I doubt that many are left at Merton from my day, but if there are, a letter from me would do you more harm than good. But a letter from your mother's brother, a canon of York: that would do you very well in Oxford."

They arrived at York the next afternoon and stayed in an inn near the minster close. In the morning they went in search of Canon Roger de Wherne.

He met them pleasantly, on the south porch. He looked like Dame Magdalen: tall, rusty, and gaunt, but his eyes were brown and his mouth humorous. He said, "Cousin! Nephew! This is most welcome." And he took them to his rooms and fed them bread and honey. But when he heard what Wilfrid had to say, his face turned grave. He asked William many questions. Then he offered to take them through the minster, without saying whether he would help them or not.

William gaped up into the minster vaulting. "Jesu-mercy!"

Roger smiled. "It's a good little church."

Wilfrid said, "It is a very great church. Now, cousin, what say you . . . "

"Of course," said Roger, "we are always building. The nave here was only finished a few years ago now. It was Archbishop Grey who began the work—you can see his tomb over there. It was just a piddling dark old place then. That was in the reign of the third Henry, so you see how long it takes us to complete anything. But it is a labor of love. And St Peter looks over the work with a watchful eye. We have not lost near so many laborers as you might think, when you consider how high that roof is. Let me tell you, kinsmen, it freezes my blood to see those poor wretches clambering about up there on those rickety scaffolds. I have a horror of heights, but *they* seem not to mind it. And as I say, St Peter watches over us. I was coming out of chapter house one day, and these men were repairing something on the roof. Well, all of a sudden it was as if a great hand thrust me backward through the door. And at that moment came tumbling out of the sky a piece of lead as long as your forearm. These fellows leaned over and cried down, 'Holy Mary, Canon, art safe?' And I replied, 'Only by the hand of her you name, and good St Peter.' St Peter is the patron of this cathedral, as you know, and he loves those who care for his church."

"God be thanked!" said William.

"Aye, aye, God be thanked," said Wilfrid impatiently. Will we never get to the point?

They strolled over to the north transept to admire a great window of five lancets and glass of intricate grey and green. "That looks like something my own mother might have woven," said William.

"Yes, some of us call it the tapestry window. This and the south transept are the oldest parts of the new cathedral. Walter Grey built it himself. But we have antiquity too, if you like that. Down in the old crypt we have the Doomstone, and also the very font where King Edwin of Northumbria was baptized."

They went out onto the west porch. "See, here he is," said Roger. "Here's great St Peter." He laid his hand reverently on a foot of the tall figure between the two great doors. William shaded his eyes. The stern face looked down and through him. William looked away again.

"Which brings us to the matter at hand," Wilfrid insisted.

Roger said, "Good cousin, what do you want me to do? The boy is promising, I agree, and I think it would be a shame if he were to cloister himself against his inclination. But I do not like this creeping about. And I have no wish to harm my sister Magdalen."

Wilfrid sighed. "I know. But don't you see? If the boy leaves the abbey—and so he intends—it is necessary that he have something else already in hand to reassure and please her. After all, she knows that great men are made at Merton."

"Like you and me, cousin?"

"You have not done badly."

"Cousin, what can I say? You know as well as I that the college will not take undergraduates. The boy has barely begun his course in arts. Let him attach himself to some hall."

Wilfrid stamped his foot. "We cannot send him to Oxford to wander the streets looking for a hall. You said it yourself—his mother and father! St Mary! If Abbot Langeton doesn't kill him, his father will—unless we have something respectable to offer him."

"Be calm, cousin. I don't know what you want me to do."

"You could write a letter to his mother and father. You could write to Warden Wantyng and recommend the lad to him. He could live in one of the nearby halls, perhaps, under Wantyng's eye."

"Robert de Treng is warden now," said Roger gently.

"Treng is it? Treng then. Ask him to find the boy a good master, a good hall. We cannot send him alone into the forest of the streets when he has lived under the wing of Cîteaux all these years! The boy's already chosen to leave the abbey; it's no fault of yours; you will not be hurting Dame Magdalen by helping him get a good place in Oxford. You have made your choice, William, is that not so?"

William had been standing between them, biting his lips. Suddenly Oxford seemed ugly and dangerous. The thought of the abbey was unbearably sweet: the bell, the orchard, and the shallow river running over rocks, under the stone bridge, out of the hills, down through the forest to Helmsley. He said, "I will go back to Rievaulx."

Wilfrid exploded. "Then out of my sight, craven! I'll have nothing more to do with you!" His face turned a terrible red; his eyes blazed under his grey brows. He was trembling.

"Cousin, what is this?" Roger exclaimed. "What ails you? One would think that you were the one at stake here, not the boy." He looked at William with concern. "What is it that you really want, nephew?"

"I want to be at Oxford. But I can be safe at Oxford as Rewley. And then I will come back to benefit Rievaulx."

"Holy St Peter!" Wilfrid cried. "The boy belongs at Merton! He will pass his course in the liberal arts and enter the college. All this talk has made him fearful, but he will take courage again. I know him. I taught him. I raised him. He *will* make good at Merton."

Roger wiped his brow. "Lord Jesu," he said, "this is a heavy matter. And here I was, thinking myself fortunate to have a visit from my kinsmen. Now I almost wish I had not been here to receive you." To William he said, "Listen, nephew. Why don't you come back and meet me later today, after None. I have business to attend to. Cousin Wilfrid, you stay at the inn and rest." He laid his arm solicitously on Wilfrid's shoulders. "You are weary, sir. I will talk to the lad alone and put him to the test." He smiled at William. "I would not like to find that I send Warden Treng an ignoramus."

"You do stand well with Treng, don't you?"

Roger sighed. "Yes, cousin. Go to The Keys and rest. I will see you later."

Wilfrid recollected himself. "We thank you, sir, for all your trouble," he said stiffly.

"Oh, say not. Blood helps blood. After all, you helped me at Merton long ago, Cousin Wilfrid. I am glad to do the same for you."

"For William," said Wilfrid.

"For William? Are you sure?" Roger looked at Wilfrid long, but not unkindly. He shook his head and hurried back into the minster.

"Well," said Wilfrid in a subdued voice. "Let us go an have an ale, shall we?"

Two days later they traveled west again. William had two letters in his saddlebags, one for his parents and one for Abbot Langeton. They weighed in the bags like lead. He knew neither of them would do any good. He had convinced Uncle Roger to write a third letter—to Robert Treng, which he said he would send with the next trusty man that went south.

When they came to the crossroads, Wilfrid said, "No, I will not go with you to Rievaulx after all. At my age and in my health, I have no desire to be bludgeoned by angry monks whose treasure I am stealing. But be not so timid, boy. You are doing what is right. Where is the great valor of Keldacross?"

"It all went into Nicholas."

"Nonsense. You take Win Thornrigg. I hope to see you before the summer's out. Courage." And Wilfrid blessed William and set off northward over the lonely ridge road banked with gorse and heather. William sat on his pony and watched him go. Then he looked guiltily at Win. "What are you staring at, villein? I go where I choose."

Win looked down and fingered his bowstring.

"Come on," said William. "Let's go and get it done with."

After Vespers, William and Gilbert Kirby slipped out the precinct gate and went down to the river. There they hung over the arched stone bridge, watching the earth-colored water of summer come tumbling round the rocks and roots of the Rye. Layered leaves and branches dappled the bridge with shadow.

A mild breeze rushed through, scattering alder cones on the water. "The breath of God," Gilbert said. "Veni, Sancte Spiritus."

William bent down, picked up a twig, and tossed it into the water. Then he went over to the other side to watch it float out from under the bridge.

"It's good to have you here, Will. I missed you."

William leaned on his elbows and shaded his eyes with his hands. "Monks ought not to have such attachments."

"What?"

"I wonder what we will have for supper tonight."

Gilbert rested his back against the bridge wall. He laughed. "Even after Oxenford, all you think about is food."

"Gib," said William. "If I speak to you about something, will you hear me?"

"Of course I will hear you, you fool. You are my special friend."

"And not hate me?"

"What did you do, murder somebody?"

"Gib, I want to go back to Oxford."

Gilbert shrugged. He looked hurt. "And so you shall, when summer's up."

"But not to Rewley."

Gilbert frowned. "What do you mean?"

"Not to Rewley. To some other school. There's a college called Merton. My old tutor went there. A bishop founded it." William swallowed.

Gilbert stared at him. Then he bent and picked up his own twig. He did not throw it, though, but rolled it between his palms. "I don't understand Oxford," he said. "Merton isn't a religious house, is it?"

William evaded him. "Great men are made there. If I can pass my course in good repute, they might take me." The words tumbled out hastily. He looked away from Gib, down into the river that was rushing away from Rievaulx.

Gilbert asked, "Are you going to make your vows this month?" Foreknowledge flattened his words.

William forced his eyes up to Gib's face. "No."

Gilbert broke his twig in two and dropped the pieces. He turned on his heel and walked off the bridge, back toward the abbey gate.

William hesitated, then ran after. He caught Gilbert by the sleeve. "Gib! It's a hard thing!"

"Talk to Father Abbot about it. Not me," said Gib roughly, and shook him off.

William broke the news to the abbot and to Father Stephen in the same parlor where they had given him the gift of Oxford.

Father Stephen said acidly, "What? Did life with us prove too lax for you? Perhaps you saw the table the black monks set at Gloucester College and decided to sample their seven course dishes of self-denial?"

"No, Father Stephen, it is not so. I have told you why."

"What have you told me? That you admire the way the secular scholars may run about town, seducing any housecarpenter's wife they take a liking to? Is that what you're hankering for?"

"No, Father Stephen, please."

Stephen put his chin in his hand and stared into space. "Whatever happened to the days when men of learning came to *us* to be our abbots?" The world seemed to be moving beyond his grasp. Forty years ago people had done things right. Why did God make things right and then change them? A wave of irritation flooded him. From long habit, he willed himself to look past this anger into peace, and asked for trust to rest quiet. He was silent for a few moments while William shifted from foot to foot.

"Lord Abbot," William said, "I will do any penance."

"Penance?" replied Abbot Langeton. "Penance is poor payment for all the kindness this house has heaped on you since you were a child."

"I will do any penance," William repeated; no other idea would come to him.

The subprior, red faced, puffed out his cheeks. "We'll give you penance all right, you little wretch. We'll truss you up in the cellars until you come to your senses." Abbot Langeton waved him silent, but his spleen carried him on. He addressed the abbot. "I knew you should never have sent him down there. I knew he was too young, too weak. He saw some wench slink by in the street one day and lost his heart."

The abbot rapped on the table. "Order."

"No!" William cried, outraged. "It is not that. It isn't wenches or the world. I have told Father Abbot what I want . . . " What *was* the real reason? "God wants me to . . . "

"Silence!" said the abbot in a grim, quiet voice. "Can *you* say what God wants?"

"What we *can* say," the subprior interjected, "is that what God wants is conveyed to you through your abbot. Do you call your behavior obedience?"

For a moment the room was still. They could hear Rye rushing over the fish dam above the bridge, and the faint chiming of sheepbells. Then the abbot asked, "Does your mother know of this? Your father?"

William shook his head.

"I thought not. And do you imagine they will support you in this?"

William shook his head.

The subprior demanded, "Then how do you think to get back to Oxford? Will you beg your way like a friar?" He spoke the word "friar" with contempt.

If they try to stop me, William thought suddenly, I will run away. "I have a letter from my uncle the canon of York," he said. "He was a fellow of Merton College."

"You little Judas," said the subprior.

Father Stephen regarded William sadly. He had thought the boy had the heart of a monk. He had detected a depth of understanding there that he had seen in few others in his years as novicemaster. But perhaps he had been wrong. He didn't know. For years he had experienced the growing conviction that he didn't know anything anymore.

All men are faithless. Common men are a breath, and great men are a sham. Put them in the balance, and they can only rise, all of them lighter than wind.

So went the psalm for Vespers that evening.

✳ **40**

Keldacross
July 1344

Sir Geoffrey Wydclif, a hawk on his wrist, lounged in Keldacross courtyard with Henry of Emberthwaite. They looked up as William rode in through the gate, wearing clothes that were too big for him and a cloak the color of blackberry juice.

Cuth Constable came out of the stables and stared. Eyes watched from all over the yard. Hens clucked round the pony's feet.

Sir Geoffrey said, "Well damn my soul if it ain't the prodigal monk."

William dismounted, but Cuthbert did not come to take Arrow's reins.

"My mother . . . " said William.

"In the hall," said Sir Henry, looking at William with pity.

William stood there. "My father?"

Sir Geoffrey watched him with cool amusement. "Over at Tunnersgil. Lucky for you."

William stumbled out of their gaze into the hall. Young Geoff Wydclif knocked into him as he came through the door. "Like your cloak, Brother William. Where did you get it, off a whore?" Then: "Your mother's in the solar," he said, and pushed outside.

William walked slowly down the length of the hall. More eyes, staring. Alice, sitting atop a table, bit off a length of thread and observed him, threading the needle by feel. Poor lad. There had been all manner of swearing and carrying on when the priest had broken the news, and Sir Gervase had talked of "dragging him back to the monks on a catchpole."

Marion put her head around the screens of the solar and stammered, "Dame Magdalen, William is here."

"Who," said a grey, distant voice, "is William?"

Alice watched William stop in his tracks.

"Dame Magdalen," said Marion, "your son."

"I have two sons. One is here at Keldacross. The other is at the abbey of Rievaulx. I do not know who you can mean."

Katharine came out and looked at him. "Mother, he's standing right here. Will you not speak to him?"

"What have I to say to him? Let him go down to the priest's house and stay there, since the two of them are so close." Then, except for the clack and rattle of her loom, silence.

William, still standing outside the screens, cried, "Mother, I pray you!"

A voice came from the other side: "Praying is what my son William does for me at Rievaulx."

He thought he would kill himself. The loom shuttle clacked and rattled.

Katharine and Marion stood at the screens, looking at each other. Finally Katharine said, "Mother—"

"Tell him not to think to come to me again. I do not want to see him anymore."

Katharine stepped down and came to him. She put her hand on his shoulder. "Brother, I think it would be best if you were to go stay with Wilfrid tonight, as our mother said."

William hung his head.

"She's banned Wilfrid from the hall. She blames him, you know. It's a low, scabby thing you did, brother. God knows you've thrown this house into a storm the past week. I thought our father was going to spit nails. Never knew he gave a damn for what you do."

"I've shamed him," said William dully.

"Aye. Well, get down to Wilfrid's before he gets back and uses you as a battering ram against Old Keep wall." She smiled, grimly amused.

Gervase did not come home that night, but he was back in time for dinner next day.

William had spent the night in terror and dread. He had dreamed he was climbing a misty cliff with a sense of wild freedom. All at once empty space reached out to swallow him; he could find neither handhold nor

171

footing. He heard his mother's voice calling from below. He knew she reached for him. The touch terrified him. He was going to fall. Panicked, he kicked her away. He heard the sound of her falling.

The next day, he was summoned, with Wilfrid, to the table, not to sit, but to stand before his father like a villein at manor court.

"So it's Oxenford you're after," said Gervase in the hard, compressed voice he used to pick quarrels. Was he not even aware that William had been in Oxford the whole year?

"So its Oxenford. You, who'd have been glad to tend oxen, if you could only stay home with your mother."

William flushed. Magdalen regarded him stillfaced, expressionless.

"So your uncle says you have a 'good intellect.' " (Wilfrid had read out Roger's letter.) "You have a good intellect, boy?"

Words came to William's mind: I am sorry. I'll go back to Rievaulx. I will. But the words did not come out. What he did say surprised him. "Yes, sir, they say so, praise God."

"Praise God, did you say? That's the matter isn't it? Praise God I raised up such a humble son to praise Him up at Oxenford with his marvelous 'good intellect.' " Gervase made it sound like leprosy.

"Please you, sir . . ."

"Please me? What will please me is for you to get your intellect and your arse back to Rievaulx."

"Sir, I could serve you well at Oxford. Wilfrid priest says . . ."

"Curse and spit Wilfrid priest for shoveling such dung into your skull. What good do you think your quibbling about farts in Oxenford is going to do me here in Kelda? Eh? EH?" Gervase leapt up from his chair, toppling it backward, and plunged his knife into the table.

"Husband!" Dame Magdalen warned. "Spare my board."

"Does this jabberer think I am going to pay for him to deliver endless farts at Oxenford? Does he think that I have nothing to do but support his wind? I gave the abbey a great sum of money when he was sent there. Money! Which we will never see again, God knows. Does he think that money comes up in the corn rows of Kelda to support worthless southron booklearning?"

Gervase fell heavily into his chair again, staring around him like a wounded stag. "Why has this thing happened to me, Maudlin? Why do my children persecute me? I am the master of this house, Maudlin, am I not?"

Wilfrid cleared his throat. "Sir. If you will but listen, I think you will not be so dismayed."

"Quit your cawing, you old raven," snapped Gervase. "I've heard enough from you and all your kind. Damn all clercs."

"Sir. Great men are made at Merton."

Gervase wrenched his knife back and forth in the wood of the table. "Oh. Aye. Like Wilfred de Wherne, parson of Keldacross, and thief."

Wilfrid blanched. Dame Magdalen rose and left the room, her back straight and silent.

Gervase said, "The boy has had his inheritance, and he squandered it. He will get nothing more from me. He's worthless. He'll end up selling whelks on Scarborough wharf." He got up and followed his wife out of the hall.

For a long time nobody said anything. Then William said, "Christ, forgive me."

Sir Henry laughed nervously. "Na, that's your father's way. He'll come round, you'll see."

"Nails, he's a demon when he's up," said Sir Geoffrey. "I wouldn't like to be on his bad side in a fray."

"I don't like being on his bad side at table." Nicholas indicated the knife sticking out of Dame Magdalen's table about an inch from his elbow. He looked at William sombrely. "I am going to see the stables," he said, and got up, holding onto the table. Geoff handed him his crutches, and they left the hall. William raised his eyes and saw his brother's wife looking at him. She was pale, and her eyes were dark with compassion.

✳ 41

Keldacross
August 1344

It was decided that William should stay in Wilfrid's house until they decided what they should do about him. And since Marion was often down at St Godrich's, she saw a good deal of him. She liked him when he was pleasant to her. He was a little taller than Nicholas, but he was thin, gangly, and awkward in his step—not like Nicholas with his hard, stiff grace. Nicholas usually smiled with his mouth shut; William's smile, when he smiled, was wide and curving. His teeth were big, and they overlapped in his mouth. And when she laughed at something he said he would turn red up to his hair, and that would make her laugh harder. But when his mood shifted, as it would suddenly, and he was unpleasant to her, she hated it. Sometimes he looked at her warily, as if she were something dangerous, and if he spoke to her it was either short or sermon-like, so that she felt like a fool or something worse.

There was a prayer of St Godrich's that they all knew in the village. Marion had heard Hawisa Thornrigg say it. So she went down and found Wilfrid and William standing alone in the church, and she asked them to tell her more about Godrich, since he was her saint now too.

"He was the holiest kind of man," said Wilfrid. "A hermit. A contemplative. In his lonely prayer he was caught up by love and borne into the presence of God himself. He was given the grace to know what to most people remains hidden in this life."

"Was he like Master Richard, then?"

"What Master Richard?"

"Master Richard, the solitary."

"I do not know who he is."

Marion blushed to know something Wilfrid did not. "He writes books. I have one. My father gave it to me for my wedding."

William turned on her. "Can you actually read it?"

She flushed again. "A little. It's English."

Wilfrid inquired, "Who taught you to read, Dame Marion?"

"My father." She glanced down apologetically. "He did not set out to. He taught me my name, and other things, and he used to set me in his lap and read to me. He ran his fingers over the words when he read, and I watched."

"Well!" said Wilfrid. "I should like to see your book."

She beamed. "I will get it for you." She picked up her skirts and ran out.

William turned to Wilfrid, priggish, offended. "I do not think that women should be bookish."

Wilfrid shrugged.

A little while, and she came in again, clutching the book. It was compact, bound in red with two gilt clasps. She held it out to Wilfrid. "My father had it made for me."

Wilfrid took it from her and undid the clasps. He read aloud from the first page he opened to.

I sit and sing
Of lufe langing
That in my brest is bred.
Jhesu my Kynge and my Joyinge

174

Whan were I to thee led?

Marion laughed. "It opened to my best one! My book knows me now!"

"You have a straw stuck in it is why," said William coldly. "You ought not to do that. Straws moulder and bulge out the pages and so damage the binding."

"Oh! Then I'll take it out." She leaned forward and flicked the straw out onto the floor.

"Nonsense," Wilfrid snapped. "One straw won't damage the book." William scowled. Women should know nothing about books, especially this woman, to whom he would have liked to sit reading in a windowseat. His brother's wife. His scowl settled in, darkly. Wilfrid flipped the pages with his thumb. "This is fine. These are good prayers. It is a good book for you to have." He handed it back.

Marion held it to her, beaming again. "Master Richard Rolle is a Yorkshireman, and he was sent up to Oxenford like you, William, because he was so quick witted." She smiled tentatively at William, and looked away from his scowl. Embarrassed, she rattled on. "The archdeacon of Durham himself was his benefactor, but then, when he was not much older than you or me, Master Richard left Oxenford and fled back to the North Riding to be a solitary. His father and brothers were wroth, but what could they do? He lives in a forest now, near a house of white nuns, and he writes books. He wrote one called *The Fire of Love*—only it is in Latin. Parson John at Holy Trinity had it."

"*Incendium amoris* is the real title," William instructed her.

"Yes? Maybe Master Richard is a saint."

"Maybe." Wilfrid smiled at her.

Encouraged she stepped forward, bright and eager. "Some day I want to visit him, so that I can tell him how much I love his book."

William sneered. "I doubt that the hermit wishes to be swarmed over with women. Why don't you leave the man in peace?"

Marion's face fell.

That made William cruel. "Save your pilgrimages for dead saints, who won't be troubled by you. Now why don't you run along and help my mother? Can't you see that Father Wilfrid and I are having serious talk?"

She left them, angry, hot, and humiliated. She went upstairs to be alone in her and Nicholas' chamber, but Dame Magdalen was there, packing clothes into chests with alder leaves to keep off moths; and Nicholas was at his hawk perch feeding Windiscry; and Geoff and Richard of Tunnersgil were running through, kicking a ball of twine back and forth between them. So she went and sat in the window and bent her head over her book.

Rote it in my hert, the memor of Thy pain
In sekeness and in health Thy love be ever myne
My joy es al of Thee; my sawle, take it as Thine,
My love ay wax and be, sa that it never decline.

Wilfrid rebuked William. "What call had you to speak to her like that? Have you no ounce of courtesy in you? She is no maidservant for you to chide, but your brother's wife."

William shouted. "My brother's this! My brother's that! How glad I'll be to get away from here again, to where nobody has heard of my brother!"

"I see," said Wilfrid dryly. "Your brother and his wife, they're the cause of your difficulties?"

William turned Wilfrid back to theology. "Have you thought, Wilfrid? How can friar Thomas speak of the causes of sin when Anselm says that there can be no cause at all of the action of the free will?"

✳ 42

Keldacross
August 1344

Marion woke Nicholas in the night, because she was laughing out loud.

"What is it?" he grumbled. "Go to sleep."

"Don't you want to hear it? Here's how it goes. A burgher was away in Flanders. And when he came home from there he found his wife in bed with the archbishop." Marion giggled. Nicholas said, "Go to sleep."

"And so this burgher, he goes to the window and throws open the casement. And he stands there and goes like this. Nicholas, you have to look. He goes like this, making the sign of the cross over the people in the street, and then he goes to the other window and does the same thing. And the archbishop sits up and says, 'My son! What in God's name are you doing?' And the burgher replies, 'My lord archbishop, only my duty. You are taking on my work, so I am doing you the same favor.'"

Nicholas looked at her blearily. "You woke me up to tell me this?"

"You don't think it's funny?"

"I don't think it's a tale for a lady to tell."

Marion put out her tongue and made a rude noise. "I've heard your mother tell worse."

"You have not."

"Oh yes! The one about the priest with the burning breechcloth."

Nicholas cleared his throat. "That story had a moral to it."

Marion kicked him. "Nicholas is so chaste hearted, he should have been the monk, not his brother."

"Go to sleep."

She tossed and turned. "Nicholas. I had a thought."

"Will you never sleep?"

"Please. I had this thought. Your brother will be going to Oxenford soon."

"Yes, he will."

"Well, poor soul, he'll be traveling all alone."

"It's his choice, Besides, he won't be alone."

"Menservants don't count, even if your father will lend him one. I mean he'll have no friends. I was thinking: what if we were to go with him?"

"What are you talking about?"

"We could go on pilgrimage to Canterbury."

Nicholas groaned. "No." He pulled the bolster over his head.

"Yes, Nicholas, yes! It would be good! We'd be doing two good things at once!" She sat up straight.

"Go—to—sleep."

"But Nicholas, think of all the grace! Don't you have any sins to repent?"

"None I can't repent right here in St Godrich's. Go to sleep."

She pulled the bolster off his face and hung over him. Her hair tickled his nose. He rolled over. "It would be an adventure."

"I have enough adventures."

"But this would be an adventure for God."

"Holy Rood! Won't you ever let me sleep?" He tugged the blankets over his ears and settled himself angrily into the bed.

The next morning Marion found William skulking around the courtyard and furtively drew him into the solar to tell him what she had been thinking of.

He broke out into his curved smile. "Oh, sister, that's kind. I don't deserve it when I've been rude to you."

She smiled forgiveness. "But there's a knot in it. Your brother. He's afraid."

Nicholas walked in. "What?"

"I was telling William about how you are afraid to go to Canterbury."

He glowered at her. "How should I be afraid?"

"I don't know, but you are."

"Afraid? Well, if I'm afraid, it's for your sake, not for mine. The highway is no place for a lady."

"Tripe. Ladies go all the time."

"No lady from Tewisdale has done it."

"You think that Tewisdale and Helmsley are the whole world."

The two of them glared at each other. William shifted his feet. "I would be happy for the protection, brother, and the company."

Nicholas swung on him. "Damn you for putting such thoughts into her head. Must you cause endless trouble?"

"William did not put them into my head. He did not need to put them into my head. I have my own thoughts."

William jeered. "Not to be traveling with a great armed host is what Nicholas fears. Afraid he won't be able to defend us by himself."

Dame Magdalen came in just as Nicholas knocked William onto the floor. She ignored William but said icily to Nicholas, "I will have no fighting in my house."

William got up, rubbing his lip. Marion cried, "Oh, brother! I'm sorry." She reached for his hand.

He pulled away. "Why are *you* sorry? He did it, not you. Who wants to ride a whole month with a fool like him anyhow? He's got no more brains than a plough horse. What do I care?" He glanced round at his mother. She averted her eyes, returned silently to her loom, and began to work the shuttle. He fled back down to Wilfrid's.

Later that afternoon Nicholas rode down the hill and tethered Wutherwind at the churchyard gate. He found William under the yew, by the well.

"What are you doing?" he asked in a stiff voice.

"Looking," said William.

Nicholas came and looked too. They stared at the faces in the well, and the faces in the well stared back, until Nicholas' neck felt crawly and he looked away. "I will go on the pilgrimage." William was still staring into the well. Nicholas did not know what made him say, "You spoke truly when you said I was afraid. I fear to travel to strange places."

He looked back into the well. In its depths he met William's eyes.

William said, "We are brothers!" as if that were something new.

The night before the pilgrimage, William was allowed to sleep up at the hall. Before he left Wilfrid's, the priest gave him some things. "Here," he said, "I have no more use for them."

William went over and looked at the little pile on Wilfrid's bed. His throat closed up. "No, Wilfrid priest," he said.

"Yes. I am old. What good will they do anyone here? I will keep my Bede. But the Boethius is yours, and the *Metaphysica* and The *Categoriae*. Also the Priscian, in remembrance of all the beatings you had at my knee over grammar."

"Oh God, Father Wilfrid, I can't take these."

"Certainly you can take them. Books are dear. As a scholar you must never refuse a gift of books. And the psaltery: you might as well have that. My fingers are too stiff for it nowadays, and my voice sounds like an old corbie's. You'll be glad of the joyous sound on winter nights, let me tell you, when the wind comes whistling through the shutters and your lamp is spluttering down and your eyes are dead from reading." Wilfrid ran his thumb across the strings. They made a high, sweet, discordant sound.

"I won't take it."

"I shall have it put into your saddlebags. If you do not take it with you, I shall be angry."

"Wilfrid priest!" William covered his eyes. "Wilfrid priest, my father."

"Ai, get you up to bed," said Wilfrid. "I'll come and see you off in the morning."

In the night, Marion went into the Long Chamber, off hers and Nicholas', and stood there in her shift. William sat up, startled, pulling the covers over his chest. "What is it?" He glanced round to where Cuth and Gib Faulkoner and John Bailley were snoring.

"I couldn't sleep. I sleep, and then I wake again. It's on account of the pilgrimage. The crooks of my elbows are itching like fleabites. Do you ever feel that way? The crooks of my knees sting like nettles, and my head is going round and round with thinking, but your brother won't talk to me except to say, 'Go to sleep.' But I can't. So if you are awake, I would talk with you."

"Well." He pulled the covers to his chin. "I am awake now." He wished she were not standing there at night in her shift.

"I'm sorry. I'll go back. We must all rise early tomorrow."

"No," he said. "No, it's well. I'm fitful tonight also."

"Good." The floor was cold under her feet, and she hopped from one to another of them. "May I sit?"

"No. Well. Yes."

She came and perched on the foot of his cot, with her knees up to her chin and her arms wrapped around her shins. "I can't bear it, I'm so happy to be going, and yet so frightened. Are you frightened?"

"Sorely."

"But you've been down there before. You're a traveler."

"But not to London or Canterbury. And this time is all different."

"Your brother is anxious about traveling, but he won't talk about it to me. He says so little. In York there was always talking. Here, not so much. I sit a whole morning with your mother in the solar, and no words pass between us except 'Hand me that red thread,' or, 'Where is the other carding comb?' Your mother makes even Alice quiet."

"My father talks plenty."

"But he's never here. And when he is, it's all shouting about hawks and such, or gentlemen he hates, or how much his family torment him and why doesn't he just set off some day for Jerusalem and never come back."

"It's Sir Job he is," said William. " 'What has he done to merit this? Why has God done this to him?' And all over a dish with too much ginger."

"Or a fire too cold."

"Or too hot."

"Or a dog with worm in its belly."

They laughed under their breaths. It was good. Nicholas would never let her say anything against anyone at Keldacross, even if it were only a joke.

William was saying, "I wonder what my father would do if a real ill befell him? What would he do if he lost a leg, or a hand? Or what would he do if Nicholas were killed? I have often wondered that. What would he do if Nicholas died?"

"No. Don't say those things."

That made him feel angry, and he said, "I say it's not good for my father to be so fond. For any month of service might be the last for old Nicholas. An unlucky arrow, a well-swung mace, a knife between the joints, a kick in the head. And what about illness? Any day he might take cold and die, like Sir Geoffrey's brother Thomas, who died in a week, just from hunting in the rain."

She swung her legs off the side of the cot. "I don't want to hear you say this. Don't you love your brother? I'm going back to bed."

"Now, if I died on this pilgrimage, it would be nothing to my father. But if Nicholas died, well, that would be doomsday."

"Stop it! Nobody is going to die on pilgrimage. We're only going to

Canterbury, not on crusade. Why are you acting like this? I'm going to bed."

"So you said. Am I stopping you? It is not seemly for you to be here."

She screwed up her mouth. "Foul thoughts for foul minds." She jumped off the bed and stamped out of the room.

She climbed back into her own bed and stared at the ceiling. She was cold. Her feet ached from the coldness of the floor, and her elbows were not tickling any longer. Now she wished they were not going. She wished she had never thought of it. She watched Nicholas. None of what William had said would happen to him. She was embroidering a shirt for him to wear under his mail. Wilfrid had traced out the words for her: Clipeus mihi est Deus, Qui salvat rectos corde, God is a shield before me, He who saves the righteous of heart.

The next morning, Dame Magdalen stood in the muddy court with her cloak pulled round her, her damp hood shadowing her face. The rain fell mistily, insistently, into the yard. Everything was grey and soggy. "Soft weather," Magdalen called it. "Mucky weather," said Alice. "Bad omen." Thunder and lightning would at least have sent them off with a certain glory. This was simply drear. Sir Gervase was not there to see them off. He and the other Tewisdale knights had been summoned to Helmsley. Nicholas had been granted leave from service for the pilgrimage.

Before departing for Helmsley, Gervase had handed Nicholas a small purse. "Give it to your brother once you're on the road. Let not your mother see." He looked aside. "He may as well not look the fool he is. Let him get some decent clothes along the way."

"You will stop at Emberthwaite tonight?" Dame Magdalen asked Nicholas now.

Nicholas nodded. "We think to."

"And after that, York?"

"That is our plan."

"And after that, I won't know where you are. But I will pray for you daily. Do the same for me. Remember me when you come to the holy martyr."

"Of course we will, Dame Magdalen!" Marion exclaimed. "How could we forget you?"

"Young folks," Magdalen replied, "think of no one but themselves." Her eyes, steadily averted from William, were grey, cool, without tears, full of pain.

Wilfrid, standing by William, nudged him forward. William lurched a little. "Mother," he said.

181

"Don't be foolish, Nicholas," she continued, ignoring William, "and try not to travel after dark. Stop well before nightfall, no matter how little progress you've made that day."

"Certainly, Mother."

Wilfrid took hold of William's elbow. "Dame Magdalen. You may not see this son again for a long while. Will you not at least give him fare-well?"

"I will give him farewell," she said, looking away. "And I will tell him that he need not come home again, for I do not want to see him anymore."

Nicholas helped Marion onto her mare; Geoff mounted Cockatrice. Tom Bradback took leave of his father. Hawisa Thornrigg said to Win, "Pray so hard when you meet the Martyr that I can feel it up here in Kelda." And she covered her mouth with the tail of her hood. Alice sat astride a saddled mule and said to John Bailley, "Aren't you glad, bailley? You'll be rid of me at last."

"Good riddance to a bad shrew," he agreed. "Don't come back."

"Never fear. I'll go with my mistress to Canterbury, and then it's the freedom of York for me."

"I pity York," said the bailley.

After Wilfrid had blessed them, they took their leave of all who had assembled in the court.

"Godspeed, Sir Nicholas," said Gib Faulkoner. "Godspeed, lady." And everyone said the same.

Nicholas leaned down for his mother's kiss. She kissed Marion too, and patted Geoff's boot, and nodded to Alice, to Tom, and to Win. "Bring back blessing," she said, and went into the house.

William climbed onto Arrow. Wilfrid pulled his hood down over his face as the rain came down harder. Win Thornrigg slung his quiver onto his back.

Then they rode out the gate. Folks followed them down the road, children scampering along behind the horses.

Dame Magdalen went into the solar and picked up her embroidery. For some time she sat over it, her fingers unmoving upon the green heather and purple blossoms on the linen in her lap.

The road opened before them as morning spread over the fells. Win Thornrigg shifted his quiver on his back. He feared that Harry atte-Beck would not see that his mother was looked after and that Simon would not repair the leaking thatch. Tom Bradback whistled through his teeth, glad to be going, for he was sick of working the mill under his father's thumb.

He held on a leather strap Sir Nicholas' two dogs, Magog the mastiff and Tooth the mongrel hound. Geoff sat his horse somberly. Somewhere on the road to Middleham tournament his adoration of Nicholas had turned into passion for Marion. Now she was his All. Nicholas, he was sure, was cruel to her.

"Well!" Alice complained loudly. "This is a right merry company!"

✳ 43

York
August 1344

At the first glimpse of York walls Marion, usually so timid on a horse, stood up suddenly in her stirrups, startling her mare.

"Careful!" warned Nicholas. "We'll be there soon enough."

"Not soon enough for her or me," Alice said aside to Tom Bradback, who strode beside her mule with the dogs. "St Peter, my heart's full. For a while I feared I'd never see the end of your cloddy vill."

"It's a dull place, true enough," Tom replied agreeably. "I've thought more'n once of trying my luck in York. I could do it easy, too, since I'm free." He winked at Win amicably. "Not like Win there."

This chafed Win. "Now why should a man want to leave his folks? I don't want to live in no stinking owd town." He rubbed his thumb along the curve of his bow and scowled at the grey city walls. A jam of carts crowded the tall gate that loomed ahead of them. Strange stone men with boulders in their arms threatened from the crenellated heights. Alice cried, "Thank God, it's dear old Monk Bar!"

Once in the hallowed lanes off Goodramgate Alice went directly to the kitchen and ranted to a captive audience about the evils of John Bailley. In the hall Marion flew back and forth between her father and stepmother, hugging them and kissing them on the cheeks until Andrew laughed, "Peace, nestling, you're wetting my beard!" Alison said, "Come, come, my dear. You're behaving like a child." But she patted Marion's cheek all the same. "I've had Nan bake you your favorite curdie pie, with cinnamon, clove, and currant jam."

Meanwhile Nicholas and William stood awkwardly by the hooded hearth. Adam Scawe brought them wine, but before Andrew had a chance to greet them properly Marion rushed to Nicholas and hauled on his arm.

"Come see my father's house! We'll look at it from top to bottom. We'll go down to the cellars and see if you can guess which sacks are Keldacross wool."

"Daughter!" Andrew reproved her. "Let your husband sit and drink a while."

But Nicholas shook his head. "I'll go with her." Otherwise he would have to sit and talk to Marion's father, and he had not the slightest idea what to say to such a man.

"Well then," said Andrew, a little hurt, but genial. "It's not Middleham Castle, Sir Nicholas, but it's a good, snug house. Daughter, be sure to show Sir Nicholas the silver mazer your uncle brought back from Florence. A beautiful cup, Sir Nicholas."

Nicholas looked stiff, and William sneered inwardly at Master Comyn. One did not display one's wealth. One had it; one used it; one did not talk about it. He felt superior and resentful until Marion took hold of his hand and said, "Come, brother! I'll show you the St William tapestry in my father's counting room, if he says yes."

"Yes, go," Andrew chuckled. He unfastened his belt and slipped off his ring of keys.

Marion thanked him and led the brothers out of the hall. She as good as danced as she went, walking between them on their arms. Her cheeks glowed, her eyes shone, and she chattered like a little sweet brown wren. Andrew was pleased to see her so happy. "I knew she'd soon be glad of the marriage I made for her," he told Alison.

"I hope she does not misplace your keys," Alison worried. "She was always such a child to lose things."

"Ah, but she's grown up now," Andrew replied. "She's a true gentlewoman."

After dinner with the Comyns William hurried out to the minster to find his uncle Roger de Wherne. Thick dark clouds were gathering over the city this afternoon; it was close and heavy, threatening storm. Several large, warm drops hit William's face as he made his way across town. When he came to the canons' lodge, Roger greeted William cordially at the door and suggested that they go confer together at a good inn nearby. "I believe you and Cousin Wilfrid lodged at the Keys when you were here. Shall we go there?"

"Yes sir," said William. He was embarrassed to stay at the minster, where the distinguished canons might look at him and think, "There's the fellow who has betrayed his good abbot at Rievaulx."

When they were established at the Keys with a flagon of wine, Uncle Roger leaned back on his bench and looked kindly at William. "Well, nephew? I think it's all for the best. A quick mind like yours should not be wasted on the white monks. Not that I bear any grudge against the good fathers. But the cloister is best suited to slow, simple minds—either that, or to contemplative saints, and you appear to be neither."

"No, sir."

The Keys was a noisy sort of place, but Roger showed no fear of drawing out his purse and emptying the pockets ringingly on the table. He pushed his forefinger around in the silver until he uncovered something yellow. He picked it out and slid it along the table to William.

William gaped down at it.

"Pick it up; it's yours."

William handled it gingerly. It was beautiful, stamped with a ship on a curving sea, and in the ship a king with a blazoned shield.

Roger said, "Do you know what that is? It's a gold noble. Few see one; fewer possess one. I put it into my purse especially for you. So cherish it. I have decided to become your benefactor, even though I may estrange my sister by it. You are too promising a fellow not to go up to Oxford for lack of funds. But I expect you to shine there, like this coin. I expect to hear reports of your brilliance."

"I am not brilliant."

"You are bright, and that's all that's needed. Only polish that brightness, and don't dull it with women and drink." At which Roger summoned the taverner's girl for more wine.

"Uncle, how may I ever thank you for all you are doing for me?"

Roger drummed the table, waiting for his cup. "Pray for me and do me credit."

They spoke of Oxford and Merton, of Cambridge and its inferiority, of philosophy, and (which seemed dull to William) of the opportunities stemming from the study of canon law. After they had eaten their fill, Roger called for one last drink. When he had finished it, he leaned on his elbows over the empty cup and gazed at William with swimmy eyes. He sighed. "Ah, youth." He began to sing under his breath:

Whan I did com to Oxenford toun
There I sawe maidens plentye . . .

William ducked his head, embarrassed. Roger crooned on pensively, sadly.

I seyd, ma dere, be of gude cheere!
I shall ne naver go away fram here!
Com thu up to ma chaumber for a gude cuppe bere,
And be merye with a lovesome scrivener.

He smiled mistily.

185

And if yow felawes wolde have ma name,
Ma name it is yonge Will-i-am

He broke off. "But if I hear any such of *this* young William, I shall cut off my charity straightaway."

"Uncle," William replied stiffly, "I hope never to be unchaste."

Roger put his hand out and ruffled William's hair. "Sed 'quomodo puram servabit adolescens viam suam? How may a young man go his way unstained?' "

William drew back. "Custodiendo verba Domini," he replied huffily. "By treasuring the words of the Lord."

Roger chuckled. "Don't worry, nephew. Pay me no heed. I will be my sober self in an hour or so." He raised his empty cup. "Yours to increase," he said, and stood up, carefully.

"Don't mistake me, nephew, in my silliness," Roger warned when they were out in the rain again. "It is a grave and serious thing, seeking God through books and learning."

"Sir, I know it."

"Good. Then let us wend our way home, you to your lodging, I to mine. Meet me on the minster great-porch tomorrow. Then we shall speak at greater length of our arrangements. And let me see your brother tomorrow too. It is most discourteous of him not to stop by and greet his godfather."

When he returned to Goodramgate William found Nicholas and Master Comyn sitting across from one another in the hall by the fire, looking uncomfortable.

"Foul weather," Andrew was saying awkwardly. "Hope it's not so foul the whole time you're traveling."

Nicholas replied, "It had better not."

They both looked relieved when William came in. "Adam!" Andrew commanded, "take Master William's cloak. Come sir, change your clothes. You're sodden."

William obliged. When he returned to the hall, Nicholas moved over to make room on the bench. "How's my godfather?"

"Well. He would be pleased at a visit from you tomorrow."

The women came in, bustling and shaking themselves and throwing off their cloaks. "Brrrrr!" Marion hurried to steam herself by the fire.

"Sop, sop, sop," Mistress Alison complained. "We *must* be caught coming out of Holy Trinity in the greatest downpour of the day."

"What were you praying for, sweetheart?" Andrew held out his hand. Marion took it, laughing. "A break in this weather is what we prayed for."

The next day was stormier still. William and Nicholas went to see Roger; Marion visited Agnes and Cecily. Alice ranted to her kitchen audience about the further evils of John Bailley. The day after that was Sunday, and they went to hear mass at the minster. On Monday the sun came out, and on Tuesday they set off south on the Great North Road from London.

✳ 44

Lincoln
August 1344

Marion chattered her teeth. Her bare toes curled up from the icy floor. "Anyone would think it was January. Hurry!"

Nicholas was turning back the sheets suspiciously with the point of his knife. It was he whose toes had met a dead rat at the foot of the bed in that hole of an inn two nights before in Hull.

Geoff, making his own pallet of cloaks and rolled up clothes, smiled at Nicholas' search for the putative rat. Alice was already tucked into her cot, sore and aching and wishing they would blow out the candle and shut their mouths. She could not get used to all this riding. Her mule's bony spine pierced her backsides through the saddle.

"Very well," said Nicholas at last. "Wife, you get in first." Last night's inn had afforded three stubblefaced Lincolnshire men at arms who had howled raucously all night long and who had ended the night in a brawl that left one of them sprawled over a table, bleeding from the scalp. Nicholas had lain tense all night, reaching over William for his sword every time he heard a creak or a footstep. So tonight he wanted Marion to sleep on the middle, between him and William. For some reason William refused. "I'd rather sleep on the floor."

Nicholas was surprised. "What ails you? All right, I'll go in the middle as before."

Stupid ass, William thought. Does he think I'm not a man, to lie by his wife all night and feel nothing at all?

Marion, oblivious, sank into the soft bed. Nicholas had insisted on going round and round this stinking old town, looking for the perfect lodging, even though they were all so weary they would as soon have slept in the city ditches as in a palace. He had dismissed four or five of the hostelries before he came to this one, which, the host assured him, was made especially for gentlefolk and sober traveling merchants. Sure enough, the place was clean, the board good, and the company well mannered and jolly. Two of the company, a wax chandler and his nephew of Scarborough, were going to Canterbury too. "Good," Nicholas said. "The bigger the party the better."

Now Nicholas climbed into bed next to Marion and waited for William to get in after them. He told Geoffrey to snuff out the candle. "Good night, all," he said, and settled himself. Alice was already snoring.

✳ 45

Hertfordshire
August 1344

They were riding through Hertfordshire, and after days of flat, gray marshes, the road had turned lovely. Now they came to a bend in the way that invited travelers to stop and rest by its verges. On the west side of the road a green slope rose gently toward a huge single beech casting shade over the top, but there were no other trees or thickets for criminals to crouch in. Win and Tom went around the beech just to make sure, looking up into its great branches, but there was nothing but peace in that place—peace, and a running stream, and blackberries, some in flower, some hard and rosy, some fat and loose, shining black, the kind that fall apart from ripeness in your fingers. Across the road was a treeless hayfield, mown, but the stubble of the grass was green and growing. Divided from the meadow by a ditch was a wheatfield in strips (about twelve acres, Win reckoned). Green-gold, it was close to ripe, full and fat with fruitfulness. A little, cool wind moved among the heads of grain, and they bowed like so many saints and angels praising in the high host of heaven. The rustling was good to Win's ears. He wondered how the fields were doing at Kelda and who was helping his mam.

Beyond the meadow and field they could see a cluster of wattle cottages and a squat church tower, but no manor house. "Maybe their lord lives in another manor," said Win to Tom, and Tom replied, "Lucky folks!" but did not mean it. Stewards and bailiffs were usually worse than lords, and Sir Gervase was no bad master.

Tom untied a blanket roll from the mule, and Alice spread the blanket under the beech tree. Nicholas sprang off Wutherwind and lifted Marion from her mare. They smiled at each other. Geoff saw, and he felt: My soul is riven in twain, and I shall die. He took the reins of both horses in his hand and turned his back.

William rummaged in his saddlebags. "I'm hungry. Who's hungry? What? There's nothing in here but a stale heel. Tom Bradback, where's the pie you packed?"

"St Godrich, sir! I must have left it on the table back at the inn!"

"Well," said Alice, "there's good money down the privy hole."

"Perhaps some poor soul will find it and have a good dinner today," said Marion.

Alice said, "More likely the innkeeper will sell it again at double profit to the next bumpkin pilgrim who comes along."

"Sir Nicholas." Tom approached Nicholas where he sat next to Marion with his back against the beech.

"Forget it," said Nicholas. He was not a man to shout at villeins over piddling sums of money. Marion suggested, "Maybe you can get something from the village over yonder. A loaf or two and some cheese, maybe."

"And some beer and apples," said the Scarborough waxchandler, pulling out his purse.

Nicholas nodded at William. "Send Win."

William dug into their purse for a few pence. Win groaned inwardly. Now he must go and haggle with southrons for bread. Win feared and detested southrons, because, he said, they talked so that a decent man couldn't understand them.

"Here, Win, take this and bring us what you can."

"Aye," said Win. He turned away from the company and trudged across the road and into the mown meadow in the direction of the village. He grumbled to himself. It was Tom who'd left the dinner behind, like a great lout.

On the beech knoll, Geoffrey secured the horses and then went morosely to the blackberry bushes. It was villainous work with the thorns, but that did not matter, for the berries were for Her. Geoff's heart swelled with the beauty of his sacrifice and self-abasement. He brought the berries to Marion in cupped hands.

"Thank you, Geoff." She took them in a handkerchief and offered them all around: to the Scarborough chandlers and to Tom and to Alice and to Geoff, of course, and then to Nicholas, who had pulled his hat down over his eyes and stretched his legs out in the dappled shade.

189

"Eh?" said Nicholas, and Marion popped a berry into his mouth.

Oh, God! Geoff stood stricken, then stumbled back to the horses. Strains he remembered from the galleries at Middleham rose to his lips. "Trop est jolie la mort," he whispered. Truly Death looked beautiful to him now—dangerously beautiful. The nobility and hopelessness of his love pricked his eyes with tears. He laid his face against the warm flank of Marion's mare and thoroughly enjoyed his misery.

Meanwhile, Win struggled to make himself understood to a stubborn southron granddam who refused to comprehend his speech. She was the first person he saw when he came to the village; she was working before her cottage, feeding hens, and she reminded him a little of his mother, so he'd asked her plain as plain. "Can you spare some bread?"

But she looked at him puzzled like and said, "What?" Half a dozen grandchildren came out from in and around the cottage and stared at him with hanging mouths and snotty noses. A ploughman came stumping down the village street with goad and ox. He saw Win and stopped in his tracks. He chewed a stem of grass and looked at him with a flat, suspicious expression.

Had this man come to Kelda a stranger, Win would have halted his ox, chewed grass, and looked at him with the same expression, but today Win took the man's silence as one more sign of southron stubbornness and stinginess. He raised his voice. "I'm a pilgrim for Canterbury. My knight and my folks are sitting yonder across the road. They're hungry. Can you spare some bread?" (He mentioned the knight just in case these folk meant mischief to strangers.)

"Ow, som *breyda*," said the granddam, suddenly nodding and smiling toothlessly.

It took Win a moment to interpret what she'd said. "Aye, some *brad*," he said. He would not bray like a donkey to say the word. "Two loaves if you can spare it."

"Ich will sparwhathucanstpie," the gammer said cheerfully.

"What?" said Win.

One of the grandchildren giggled. "Brad, brad," she chanted.

"Wha cansthu pie?" the gammer repeated patiently.

The ploughman in the street spat and switched a fly away from his face.

"Ah doan't want no pie; ah want brad only," said Win, angrier by the moment.

"Two rye loaves or barley loaves a farthing," offered the old woman.

"Oh, aye. Two rye loaves then." It seemed a high price to Win, but then it wasn't his money, was it, so why haggle?

When the granddam went into the house to get the loaves, the little giggling girl spoke up. "Thu hast a pink eye like an hare," she said. Win,

190

who understood that all too well, replied crossly, "Tha'st snot on thy face, lass, why dosta not rub it off?"

The gammer came out with the loaves and told Win where he might find the beer and cheese.

"Go with the pilgrim, 'Wina, and asket for him," said the gammer to the giggler. Well! That was a kindness. Win smiled at the old grandmother. "What's her name did you say?" He jerked his thumb at the giggler.

"Edwina's her name."

"St Godrich! My name's Edwin." Then Edwin allowed himself to be led by Edwina to the brewer and the cheesemaker. The ploughman pricked his ox and went down the street toward the common, satisfied that Win was neither a felon nor a long-lost relation come to claim his seven acres of strips.

When Win came back with the food, all the pilgrims cheered, except, of course, Nicholas. He was still dozing with his hat over his eyes. Small Edwina had come along to help carry the beer and take back the keg when they had done. She shrank behind Win when she saw Tooth and Magog panting together happily in the shade.

"Win's brought us a little lass with our dinner," said Marion. She made the child sit down in the shade and told Alice to cut her a slice of bread. The little girl stared mutely at Marion, Nicholas, and the waxchandlers as if she'd never seen gentlefolk or burghers before in her life. When Alice gave her the bread, Edwina stuffed it into her mouth almost whole. She chewed it slowly, her nose running into the bit that was still sticking out.

Nicholas threw his hat off and saw the child. "Someone wipe her nose," he said, and then, "Geoff, where's our cup?"

Geoff pulled the cup from Wutherwind's saddlebags and brought it to the chandler, who tapped the beer.

"Serve the lady first," said Nicholas. Geoff's heart leaped, then sank in despair as Marion shook her head, saying, "I'll drink when I've eaten something."

"Ah," said the chandler's nephew, chomping on an apple, then a hunk of cheese, and mushing them together deliciously in his mouth. "Good food!" Tooth lumbered up from his haunches and shambled over to drool in Nicholas' face.

William lay on his back, a little apart from the others, in the long, warm grass. He'd thrown off his gown and kicked off his boots, rolled his hosen up above his knees and his sleeves above his elbows so as to feel the sun and the grass. He looked at the company sitting and laughing under the great tree: his brother scratching Tooth's ears, Marion plying the little girl with cheese, wiry Win and burly Tom, scolding Alice, and Geoff with a pimple on his nose making a fool of himself mooning over Marion. William was filled with lovingkindness for them all.

"Ecce quam bonum et jucundum habitare fratres in unum," he said aloud.

"What say, scholar?" inquired the chandler's nephew.

"Psalm," said William. "How good it is for brothers to live together as one."

"A pilgrimage is a grand thing," the nephew agreed, speaking with his mouth full.

William wished they could remain in this state, forever fondly together, on a knoll by a tree and a brook, all fears and troubles far away, and small fowls chittering in the shifting leaves above:

Hic, nunc, hodie,

Here, now, today.

William dozed, full of the warm, sweet smell of grass.

Now, the same and forever.

It was time to move on. Small Edwina took the empty keg and went back to her grandmother. Geoff jingled around readying the horses, and Tom and Win and Alice gathered what needed gathering and tied it to the mules. William sat up and rubbed his eyes.

Nicholas was helping Marion to mount, and she was saying, "I wish we never had to leave this place!" Seated astride her mare, she tied the strings of her broadbrimmed hat tightly beneath her chin. Nicholas swung up on Wutherwind. He trotted over and smiled down at William. "Have a good snooze?"

"Aye." William beamed back, and stretched. His heart overflowed. He pulled on his boots, stood up, brushed the grass from his clothes, and picked up his gown from the ground where it lay. Ecce quam bonum et jucundum! Now, the same and forever.

Geoff sang langorously in French as they rode away. "Cure me, sweet friend, of this great longing, lest love itself soon vanquish me."

"Noa, squire, noa. No more Frenchie songs," Tom pleaded under his breath. Win, thinking himself unseen by any but Tom, pretended to fit an arrow to his bow and let it fly at Geoff's back.

"I saw that, Win Thornrigg," said Alice, looking round over her shoulder. She winked. "But I'm not telling." They all three laughed.

Quam jucundum!

46

London
September 1344

"So that's London," said Alice, wrinkling her nose. "I knew it would be a scabby place."

The waxchandler's nephew agreed. "You can smell it three miles off."

"Three? I could smell it ten miles back."

They were waiting by the side of the highway for Tom Bradback to do something about Sir Nicholas' palfrey. Win shaded his eyes. He turned his thin face to Alice and said, "Can't we stay somewhere outside?"

Alice rolled her eyes. "Clodhoppers." She nudged the nephew.

Geoff sauntered over, peered, and whistled. He could see crowds thronging at the gates. Spires and towers bristled threateningly above the city walls. Smoke smudged the sky. Even this far away, the bells were tumultuous. "Ma—rry," he said. "Do we have to go in there? Can't we stay somewhere outside?" Win threw Alice an exonerated look and went over to where Tom was struggling swearingly with Wutherwind's right foreleg. Sir Nicholas was slapping his gloves against his thigh. "Goddamn it, Tom, pry it out. Pry it *out*, is all."

Tom set his teeth. "I'm doing the best I can, sir. I'm no smith." If he'd wanted a shitten smith, why hadn't he brought a shitten smith?

"Do you need to be a shitten smith to pry out a goddamn pebble? Here, churl, if you can't do it, let me. Hell!"

"It's coming, Sir Nicholas. I'm getting it."

"Hell!" said Nicholas.

When they were underway again, William rode ahead with a lawyer they had met on the road a few miles back.

"Is London as much bigger than York as they say?"

"Well, Mr Oxford clerc, that depends on what 'they' say."

"I don't know. Twice as big?"

The lawyer chuckled. "At least three or four times bigger."

"Well, I don't know. York is a great city."

"Scholar, London is as great as Paris or Rome or Jerusalem. You shall see."

"Have you been there often?"

"Certainly. I read law there."

"Oh. Well, then, perhaps you can tell us the best place to stay. We know nothing about it."

"You're going to Canterbury? Well, most people going in your direction stop in Southwark."

Geoff rode up and joined them. "We don't have to go into the city, then?" he exclaimed hopefully.

The lawyer shook his head. "No, I fear you'll have to go right through. Southwark is on the other side of town, as its name should tell you, on the south end of the great bridge. You'll take the Dover road from there."

"Will it be hard to find?"

"Southwark hard to find? It's the only thing there at the bridge end, except for wet meadows. There are a number of inns there. You can take your pick."

"But we have to go through town?" Geoff was downcast.

"Either that, or go around the walls and swim the Thames." The lawyer took pity on Geoffrey's worried face. "Look, I have nothing I must do this day. Why don't you let me lead you and your people in and so save you some toil and trouble? Marry, I'll do more. I'll show you the City, if you like. Or would you like to see Westminster, where the king sometimes sits in Parliament?"

"Rood," said William, turning bright, "I would like to see it all."

"Young scholar, that would take a year and a day."

"You are a kindly man. I thank you from my heart. Let me ride back and tell my brother the good news. It will lift his spirits. I will be frank with you, Lawyer: he is unused to cities, is my brother. A simple country knight, you know."

The lawyer smiled behind his glove as William sallied back, crying, "Brother! Sister! Good news!"

"We go down through the Hollow Way through Islington," the lawyer told Nicholas. "A shame it's not fair-time. Islington's a merry place then."

"We can do without fairs," said Nicholas.

"We'll enter the city by Aldersgate instead of by way of Smithfield. It's more to the point."

"Eh?" asked Nicholas.

"Of getting to Southwark, I mean. You should see the smithfield on a feast day, Lady." He nodded at Marion. "The games are a wonder to behold—football, jumping, wrestling, cockfighting, games without end. And often the knights of St John's in Clerkenwell come out and ride jousts. It's a splendid sight."

"How should that amaze her?" Nicholas asked belligerently. "She has seen the jousts at Middleham."

"Middleham?" the lawyer replied vacantly. "What's that? Here's Islington. You fool woman! Watch your brat! She lets her whelps run underfoot, but she'd be squealing if we trod on one of 'em."

They made it through the city, but by the time they were halfway across the bridge, Win Thornrigg was ready to throw up. His mind reeled with the shrieking and shouting, bustling and shoving, and the twenty different smells and sights and sounds coming at him all at once and from all different directions. Once he got rammed into a narrow side lane and lost the party for a minute or two. He had almost fainted. He would never be afraid of York again.

Their inn at Southwark was called the Buckler, and William and Marion liked it so much that they begged Nicholas to let them stay another day. The lawyer's description of the law courts at Westminster had made William eager to see them, and Alice hoped they would go to Chepeside so that she could test her mettle against the London stallmen and pick up some bargains for her mistress. Marion was agreeable to seeing anything, just so long as she got out and did not sit in the inn all day, as Nicholas seemed to wish.

The lawyer pressed Nicholas. "Don't you want to see Westminster, Sir Nicholas?"

"No." Nicholas stood by the commonroom chimney, his elbow planted stubbornly on the mantle hood.

"We might see some great baron," Marion suggested, but Nicholas shook his head. "I won't go. But you may go, wife, with this lawyer and my brother. Take Win and Alice. You'll be well enough."

William concluded that Nicholas must really hate the city if he'd admit that Marion would be "well enough" under the protection of a clerc, a lawyer, and a ploughman.

Nicholas looked at Marion's disappointed face. A miracle occurred: to cheer her, he made a joke against himself. "That city was the worst melee I ever was in. I'm not going back into it until I get my guts up to it. You're braver than I when it comes to these places."

When he smiled, everyone relaxed and laughed. Two of the other guests were middle aged nuns, sitting coyly together by the fireside wall. They tittered behind their sleeves. One of them giggled. "Oh, no, sir, we're sure you're the bravest of men, aren't we, Cellaress?" The cellaress rolled her eyes idiotically. Nicholas raised his brows, but William understood. They'd come out of their priory for this pilgrimage and were intoxicated with their freedom. They were undoubtedly perfectly good religious at home, but here, abroad, they had to act like fools.

Geoff came in from the innyard, followed by Win and Tom, who had been seeing to the dogs and horses. "Win," Nicholas told him, "Dame Marion is going back into the city. You'll ride the mule with Alice and keep the horses for them."

Win's face turned ghastly, but nobody except Tom noticed. They were all too busy gabbing about how much they could see in one afternoon.

"If the lady is going," Geoff inquired of Nicholas, "shouldn't I accompany her?"

"No," said Nicholas dryly, and without explanation. The lawyer caught his wry look and grinned.

"Hard luck, pilgrim," Tom said to Win.

Win groaned. "You great barleybag! Why don't you offer to go sometime? Like now?"

"Me?" said Tom blandly. "I'm just sitting down to a beer."

"Aye, y'owd milldust." Win felt distressed and beleaguered. He'd been looking forward to settling in a quiet corner with Tom, sipping beer and recovering from the terrors of the morning.

"Ee, Rabbit, you'll live."

Alice came over and said, "Well, go on, Win. You've got to saddle up Bray."

Win gave Tom a mournful look. "Enjoy your ale."

"I will, Rabbit, I will."

When they came out of the inn, they saw that a fog had come up the river. "Too bad," said the lawyer, but William and Marion were too excited to care. They rode together on Marion's horse because the lawyer said, "The fewer beasts the better in a London crush." Alice and Win trotted behind on Bray.

The lawyer led them back over London Bridge—"It makes Ousebridge in York look like Mucklebridge in Kelda," William remarked, infuriating Alice—and through the Ropery and the Vintry down the crowded thoroughfare toward the smelly regions of Ludgate. The lawyer pointed over the foggy rooftops to their right. "See that great square tower over there? That's St Paul's." Alice compared it unfavorably with York Minster. "And what's that stink?" she demanded, holding her nose and glaring.

The lawyer chuckled. "That's the Fleet," he told them, half shouting over the Thames Street clamor. "A pretty stream turned sewer. It's the tanneries that make it so bad. Every few years the city fathers mount a crusade against the Fleet and tax everybody to clear it out."

"Smells as if they're due for another campaign," William shouted back. "Deus vult! God wills it!"

Marion looked over her shoulder to laugh at him. Her cheeks were flushed; her brown eyes danced. William flushed too and did not know what to do with his hands.

"Ah now," the lawyer exclaimed when they had crossed Fleetbridge. "We've come into my domain. This highway's the Strand: it'll take us to Westminster." For a good mile between the cities stone walls and leafy gardens of bishops' inns stretched on their right; on their left, wet meadows sloped down to the river. There was a good amount of going and coming both on road and on river, but it was neither crowded nor maddening. The fog lifted and left a faint mist; all was mild and bright. The lawyer chatted pleasantly.

"Did I point out that house back there near Fleetbridge? That's Whitefriars, praying Carmelites, though it's a mystery how they manage to contemplate God in that Ludgate racket." He addressed William specially. "They've a redoubtable school, you know, famous for learning."

"Aye, I've heard of it," said William, but he hadn't.

"See that field ahead of us, Lady? The Templars held tournaments in it before they were put down. Knights Hospitalers hold the Temple now, but there's some talk of their letting it out to sergeants at law like myself, and I hope it goes through, for there's scarcely enough room for us in town these litigious days."

When they came to Westminster the lawyer took them straight to the royal palace, because William had no interest in the Abbey—or any other monastery. They left Win holding the horses in a little paved court by an arch that looked down some steps to the river. The lawyer led them down a winding lane bustling with important looking officials and pointed out St Stephen's, "where the king held parliament for nearly a month last spring." They went around a corner and through a stone gate into a wide, paved court, and up a flight of broad steps where a small crowd of brightly dressed characters were shoving papers at a beaten looking law clerk. The clerk kept holding out his hands for silence, but had parchments thrust into them instead.

"What do those people want?" Marion whispered. She felt sorry for the clerk.

"Suppliants. They all want something different." He approached the harried clerk and spoke to him briefly. The clerk nodded, and the lawyer announced, "We're in luck. The King's Bench and the Court of Common Pleas are both in session at this moment, and we shall have some fun."

"Fun?" said the harried clerk, "in that mess? It's only my little love affairs that give me any fun." A suppliant shook a parchment under his nose.

The court was fascinating to William but unintelligible to Marion and Alice. The proceedings were conducted in French, and there seemed to be several different cases going on at once. The lawyer gestured to a spot across the great vaulted chamber. "Over there the Lord Chancellor sometimes conducts his business. You should see the hustlebustle then!"

By listening intently, William discerned that one of the cases concerned two outraged wool merchants, one of whom felt he had been outdone of profit by unlawful trickery by the other. The accused man's advocate was bickering shamelessly with the judge. William informed Marion, "It's about the Staple."

Marion exclaimed, "Did you hear, Alice? Just wait till I tell my father we heard them talking about the Staple in Westminster Palace!"

"Don't they know all fleece is grass?" William punned snidely to the lawyer. "Why act as if life and death hang on selling a bit of wool?"

Alice snorted agreement. With due respect to her old master, she was impatient to get to Chepeside before the marketmen closed their stalls. But Marion felt defensive of her father. "If you were a wool merchant, you'd think differently."

"I reckon so," said William, coolly, offhand. Then, ashamed, he added, "No offense to your good and generous father."

"He is that," she replied testily.

The lawyer interposed genially. "We'd better retrieve your man Win if we're to get to Westchepe before curfew."

So they left the palace and found Win standing where they had left him by the arch above the river.

✳ 47

Southwark
September 1344

They were all glad to sit down to supper at the Buckler. Almost all there were going their way or coming back from there, and everyone was talking about it at the top of his lungs, in all different manners of speech. There was even a black haired Irishman who spoke in a way that no one could understand and who became unreasonably angry when William asked him, courteously, to repeat himself. A cook from Derbyshire blared over all of them, talking of the road ahead in loud, familiar tones. He had been there; he knew all about it.

"If you ride steady," he told Tom and Win, "and don't fiddle and gab too much, you can make it in two days. Tell your knight, fellows. Withouten fiddling, withouten gabbling, Canterbury in two days."

Marion must tell Nicholas about their adventure. "And then we went into St Paul's church. Remember, we saw it when we were riding in?"

"Sir Nicholas, it was bad," said Alice. "Never in York have I seen . . ."

"Alice! I'm speaking. We came to St Paul's, and they had shops built right up against the very walls! And when we went in there were shops inside the very church, with people selling bread and meat and pastries right there in the aisles! And your brother said, 'I expect to see Our Lord come in any moment with a whip of cords.' "

Then spoke up a sour faced clerc in a frayed black gown. "If St Paul's offended you," he told William, "Canterbury will shock you. At least they sell honest bread at Paul's. At Canterbury it's hairs from Becket's nostrils." But William dismissed him as a crank.

After supper the lawyer announced that they were such good company that he had decided to spend the night with them, and he put it to them that they should take turns at singing. This was well received. Geoff sang something languid; Alice sang something lewd, with much hip twitching and eyebrow wiggling, which made everybody laugh. But when it came to the lawyer, he said, smiling, "No, I'm no singer."

"Ho," said Nicholas, sitting forward. "You can't refuse."

"Sir, serve me a writ says I can't. But I will tell you a story instead, if that will please you."

"Good enough," said Nicholas.

The lawyer wiped his mouth and sat back against the wall. "I will tell you a tale of two wily monks—and a knight." He smiled at Nicholas. "Once," he began, "there was a knight errant. He's riding from God-knowswhere, and he stops to spend the night at some old abbey, for the weather has dropped down cold, and the wilderness is howling with winds from the north. So he rides into this old abbey and is given a bed and hot victuals, and in the morning the hospitaler says to him, 'Good Sir Knight, I will let you in on a great secret. You must promise not to spread it abroad, for we would not have this place a teeming hostelry for rude pilgrims, disturbing our life of holy prayer.' "

" 'Oh, aye, indeed,' " the pilgrims chorused ironically.

"So the knight swears—on the Rood he swears, and on the wimple of Our Lady. So the hospitaler beckons, sly and soft, and they creep down into the crypt. There, this hospitaler lights him a lamp and says to the knight, 'We have here the holiest treasure in England. I must ask you again, Sir Knight, to give me your solemn vow that nothing you see here will pass your lips once you have left this place.' And the knight swears again, up and down, by the Rood, by the Nails, by his honor as a knight, that he would never tell what he would see in this place, not on pain of torment. So the hospitaler nods solemnly and says, 'I show you only because you are a man of honor and devotion.' And he takes a little key from around his neck and opens a cupboard in the wall. 'This,' says he, 'is the head of St John the Baptist.' And sure enough, in that cupboard sits an old, grinning skull. And the knight, awestruck, kneels in reverence, saying, 'Brother, how may I ever thank you? Here! I will leave with this holy saint my golden ring, so that he may remember this poor knight and pray for him always.' And so he pulls off his ring and hands it to the hospitaler, who bows and gives him blessing. And the knight goes away in joyful tears.

"Now the next evening this good knight stops at another abbey nearby and is just about to settle himself to sleep, when the hospitaler of this new abbey comes and says, 'Traveler, I would have you know a great secret, for your face is both pious and frank'—by which he meant both credulous and rich. 'It is a mystery,' says this new hospitaler, 'that is revealed to few, for we have no wish to make our abbey a teeming innyard for noisy pilgrims as the black monks so often do.' And the knight, amazed at his good fortune, follows the hospitaler into the deepest and darkest corner of the abbey crypt. 'There,' says the hospitaler, unlocking with a great brass key a carven chest, 'there sits the very skull of St John the Baptist.' Now at this, the knight waxes wroth.

" 'Whoa ho,' the company cheered. 'Whoa ho, brother hospitaler, you're caught!'

"Now this knight waxes wroth, and his rage is fearsome. 'Now hear me, monk!' he cries. 'Just last night I lay at your sister house of God-knowswhere and there was I shown the head of the very same John the Baptist. Tell me, Brother, how can this be?' "

"Aye, tell us, brother," said the Scarborough waxchandler.

"Well, the wily hospitaler looks at the knight most humbly and says, smooth as glass, 'Why, good Sir Knight! It is quite plain. Our brothers at Godknowswhere are blessed to have the head of the saint when he was young. We are happier still, for ours is the head of the saint when he had grown in years and wisdom.' And so the knight says, 'Aaaah, God be praised,' and leaves his gilt spurs with the monk and goes away happy."

They slapped their knees with laughter. For an instant Marion looked blank. Then she laughed harder and harder, until she could not sit up straight any longer.

The lawyer grinned. "The lady likes that."

Nicholas frowned and poked her with his foot.

She raised her head. "Oh!" she gasped, wiping her eyes. "For a moment, just for a moment, I thought: 'So? What's wrong with that?' " She went into fits again. They all bellowed. Even William, who had sat rigidly silent through the whole story, chuckled. " 'Aah,' says the knight," he repeated in a low, stupid voice, "and he goes away happy. What an ass." Inadvertently he glanced at Nicholas.

Nicholas caught the glance. "What's wrong with you, brother?" he queried. "Is that the sort of thing you do at Rievaulx?"

The lawyer pounced. Bright eyed, he demanded, "Rievaulx?"

William scowled. "No they do not. Nor nothing like it."

"Rievaulx Abbey, do you mean?" the lawyer persisted. "Are you a lapsed monk, then?"

The company fell silent. Everyone gazed at William with gleeful and expectant malice.

"No. I never was a monk. I never took my vows."

"Ho, ho, he's a lapsed monk," roared the Derbyshire cook.

"I never was a monk, I told you!"

"Which vow couldn't you keep, brother? Poverty, chastity, or obedience?"

"I'd wager my virginity," tittered one of the nuns sitting by, "that it was chastity. Look at that angel face!"

William stood up. "God damn it!" he shouted. "I said I never was a goddamn monk. I told you, I never took the goddamn vows!"

The cellaress said, "Marry! What's sitting on *his* shoulders?"

"A nasty old smarting conscience, I reckon," said the cook. He winked at Marion. She pretended not to notice. An awkward silence stiffened in the room. Then the lawyer pointed at Tom Bradback and said, "We can't make Sir Nicholas sing for us, lady, nor his brother. But what of your two men here? They don't get off free."

Tom said, "Na, I can ne sing."

"You, then." The lawyer jabbed his finger at Win.

Win looked pleadingly at Marion.

"Go on, Edwin. Sing your forster's song. He made it himself," she told the company.

"Must I, Lady?"

"Sing it. It's good."

It was a low, brisk song with a rhythm like riding, like hunting. Win had a good, rough voice, which grew stronger as he saw them all beaming and tapping their feet.

I shot both hart and hind, sir,
I shot both hart and hind.
A brawer, better bow, sir, never shaltha find.
The fenyl and the ferne, sir,
They grow upon the fell, BUT—
A sweter, sherper arrow was naver shot so well.

"Whoop!" shouted the company. "Sing it, man!" Win blushed. He stood up and beat on his thigh.

The drak-e and the duck, sir,
They wallow in the mere,
But I can prick a boar, sir,
And make him fele affeared.
I can bring in the cu, sir,
I can bring in the corn, BUT—
A better, brawer bowman naver was there born!

He finished, blushing redder when everyone cheered. He sat down again in his place between Tom and the Derbyshire cook. The cook thumped him on the back. "Modest, your man," he said to Nicholas.

"I'll not deny what he says," Nicholas replied shortly. "He has cause to boast."

Tom kicked Win in the ankle. "Doan't you wish your mam was here to see this?" Win beamed back at all of them. Suddenly a pilgrimage was a fine, brave thing.

Nicholas rose and stretched. He made a gesture at Marion with his head. Upstairs.

The lawyer said, "Lady, before you retire, we pray that you too will favor us with a song."

She looked around at them. Nicholas did not want her to do it. Well, a fig for Nicholas. She was annoyed at him for embarrassing William. "Very well," she said, "I will give you a song."

Geoff shook his head, disapproving. She looked through him. "I will sing you a holy song, to remind us that this is a pilgrimage."

"That would be a good thing," said the cellaress, suddenly pious.

Marion folded her hands in her lap, looked over their heads, and sang in a clear, true voice.

Man is dethis underling
Man is gest in his dwelling
Man is pilgrym in his passying.

202

They shuffled and coughed as Marion went up with Nicholas. Then they all went to their beds.

∗ 48

Canterbury
September 1344

The nearer to the martyr they came, the more miserable was William.

They had had their breakfast, and now they sat on a bench in the busy innyard, waiting for Geoff to come down so that they could make their way over to 'the minster,' as Marion and Alice insisted on calling it.

"They don't call this a minster," said William for the third time. "I told you. Stop calling it that."

"I heard the minster bell strike, didn't you, Alice?" Marion went on stubbornly. "Where is that Geoffrey? We'll never get to the minster."

"Cathedral. *Cathedral.*"

"He'd better have my boots," said Nicholas. He was cross because in the crowds and confusion of their arrival last night, with everybody running every whichway and cramming their things wherever they could find a cranny, Geoff had misplaced Nicholas' boots.

"Brother," said William in a preaching voice. "I see no need for you to go stamping about Canterbury in spurs. It would behoove you to go as a pilgrim, like the rest of us."

"I don't notice any stones in your shoes, Pimple."

"I'm sick of you calling me that. Call me that again, and I'll thrash you."

Nicholas leaned back against the wall with a self-satisfied expression. "I'd like to see that."

Geoff came rushing out into the yard, brandishing Nicholas' boots. "Found them, sir," he bellowed. He nodded to William, bowed to Marion.

"Geoff, why did it take you so long?" Marion snapped. "It must be way past Prime by now, and . . ."

But Geoff looked so stricken and penitent that Marion stopped, vexed, and looked away.

"But now I can't find my own boots, sir. Do you know where they are?"

"No, I do not."

Geoff swore. "Damn! Damn! Some bastard must have stolen them! Damn this stinking hole of a hostelry! It's an armpit of fleabitten . . . " Then he remembered Marion. "Lady, pardon!" He made cow eyes.

"Again I say," said William, "I see no need for stamping around in . . . "

"Shut your mouth, Pimple. Let's go see the Martyr. Isn't that what we came for?"

Win Thornrigg and Tom, waiting against the inn wall, shrugged at each other. "Think we'll get there by noonday?" Tom asked behind his hand.

"I feel muckle holy," William sneered. Muckle wretched is what he felt. He would as soon go back to Yorkshire without ever seeing the shrine. Who would know the difference?

"A merry company of pilgrims we are," humphed Alice.

Marion turned pink. "If you brothers are going to behave yourselves so, perhaps you had better not go see the Martyr. Alice and I will go alone."

"Not on your life," said Nicholas.

"Why not forget the whole thing?" said William. "Abandon the whole business. Go back up to Keldacross and *say* we've been. Who would know the difference?"

Win stared at William in horror. These gentlemen were crazy. All this way for nothing? And he knew, most certainly, who would know the difference.

"Why do you talk of going back to Keldacross, Pimple? You're bound for Oxford, remember?"

"Go to hell then!" William jumped up. "I'm not going any farther with you!" He burst into tears.

"What in God's name?" Nicholas shouted. "You blubbering clerc!"

"Oh, this is *good*," said Alice.

"So what are we going to do?" asked Geoff.

"Go without him if that's what he wants," Nicholas grunted. "It's one with me."

"No!" Marion cried. "I hate you both!" And she rushed back into the inn.

Alice glared round at them scathingly. Then she ran after her mistress.

Nicholas and Geoff went out to stamp around town in their boots. (Geoff's had turned up under Alice's cloak.) Nicholas ordered Tom and Win to stay at the door of the inn where Marion lay, snuffling and red eyed, on the bed. Alice left her and went down to the common room to scold and gab against Sir Nicholas and Master William and Keldacross in general.

"You know not how blessed you are to live in Scarborough," she told the waxchandler's nephew. "Mark my words. Never leave there again. Country folks are clodheads, even the gentlefolks. Especially the gentlefolks."

But the waxchandler's nephew was somewhere else in his soul. "Just wait till you see the Martyr," he said. "I had such a feeling . . . "

William skulked through the door. Alice caught sight of him. "Dame Marion is in the room, but she wants to see nobody." Her face said, especially not you. So William stood about by the fireside feeling sick with himself. Soon afterward Nicholas and Geoff came in. The brothers avoided each other's eyes. Finally Nicholas asked Alice, "Where's your mistress?"

"In the room, but she doesn't want to see . . . "

Nicholas turned to William. Stiffly, he said, "I am sorry for it."

"I'm sorry, too," William replied readily. "It was stupid and knavish of me."

Nicholas said to Alice, "Tell your mistress we've forgotten it, and we'll go to the church whenever she's ready."

"I'll tell her," said Geoff.

"No, squire," said Alice dryly, "that's my office." She went upstairs, leaving Geoff affronted.

So they went together to holy Thomas' church. They entered through a stone gateway into the cathedral close, where there were stalls and shops and unctuous hawkers of ecclesiastical trinkets (just as the disgruntled Southwark cleric had reported) and a woman, apparently mad, who stood in the middle of the close yelling at the top of her lungs.

A solemn, middle-aged cleric made his way through the crowd, saw the Keldacross party gaping up at the great church, and offered to Nicholas to show them the site of the martyr's death.

"Do you want him?" Nicholas asked Marion.

Marion considered. "Yes, I think. We can come later by ourselves at some quieter time."

"The best time for that, Lady, would be about evensong, when most folks are taking their supper," said the clerc, very obliging, and Marion said, "Thank you. We will go with you now."

So they followed him across the court up the great porch steps. They were not prepared for what they saw within. They had heard, and believed, but now, seeing it, they were struck dumb. Even Nicholas stood rooted, gaping up at the heights. The light pouring through the rich windows made garnets, sapphires, and rubies on the smooth, stone floor. In the dim places of the side aisles and in the depths of the distant transepts, banks of candles glowed and wavered and there was no pillar or door or chair or arch not carven with some wonderful figure or foliage. A great soaring of beasts and leaves rose up above them on the supporting pillars. Scores of travelsore pilgrims knelt on stone flags, forgetful of self in the amazement of the place.

"Gaw," breathed Tom, and Win rubbed his nose with the back of his hand. Tears pricked his eyes; he wished his mam could see this.

"This is St Thomas' church," explained the cleric kindly, "and would you see his shrine now, or the place where he was so foully murdered?"

"Take us to the place," said Nicholas. So the friar took them, and they knelt sorrowfully. Then they shuffled, awestruck, with crowds of jostlers, into the chapel behind the high altar, where they marveled at the glowing windows, and the gems—real ones here—and they stretched out their fingers to touch the noble stone figure on the rich tomb.

A dirty brat with lousy looking hair whined behind them. "Gammer, I can't see; I can't see." Finally Nicholas turned round, bent, and lifted him above the crush. He set the child on his shoulders so he could see, and the child clutched Nicholas' chin with his skinny, scabby little fingers. Win drew in his breath and stared at Nicholas. Truly a pilgrimage was a very great thing. Alice saw and said, "Well, Mother of God."

William knelt. "Holy St Thomas, please help me to make a place for myself at Oxford, so as not to shame my mother any longer. And pray that through my learning I may seek knowledge of God and not seek my own advancement."

Marion knelt beside him. "Holy blissful martyr, keep us safe," was all she could think of at first; then: "Oh, and my father and my stepmother and Cis and Agnes and Adam Scawe and Dame Magdalen and Sir Gervase, and everybody. The whole world," she added hastily as an impatient penitent struggled to take her place.

Their guide led them next to a quiet place in the north transept and told them the story of the martyrdom in the words of one whose very own grandfather's grandfather had seen the murder with his own eyes. He told them of King Henry raging in Westminster, "Will no one rid me of this meddlesome priest?" And of the knights riding through the dark and violent night, and of the archbishop feeling his doom yet going out as usual to say mass, and then the axe blows crashing upon the cathedral doors and the knights coming down the nave with heavy iron in their hands, and how they shattered the saint's head as he knelt before the sanctuary.

"Those were no knights but a herd of bastards," Nicholas observed. "I hope their guts are spilled for all eternity."

"No, we must pray for them also," said Marion.

Back outside in the cathedral close, Nicholas spent a good sum of money on a ring for Marion. It looked like old work: engraved silver, set with an uncut garnet. Under the stone, said their guide, was a relic, a piece of the bone from the Martyr's skull. One of the monks who had witnessed the deed had gathered it up, and another had set it in this ring. "See?" The man held it up to the sunlight, and sure enough, Nicholas could make out a piece of dark something behind the stone. "What's it say?" He handed the ring to William.

William, turning it about, read the inscription inside. " 'Sum fragmentum Thos. Cantuariae, I am a bit of Thomas of Canterbury.' "

"I'll buy it," said Nicholas.

William nodded knowledgeably. The ring looked old, and the cleric looked honest. "I am only selling it because I must," he told them. "It has been in my family for years. But I will part with it because I see how much the lady loves St Thomas." He held out his thick fingers. "Anyway, it's made for a woman, not for me."

Nicholas put the ring on Marion's finger.

"Oh," she breathed, holding her hand away from her. "This is the best thing in the world!" She kissed the ring and kissed Nicholas. Geoff looked on mournfully. "I'll wear this until I die," she said, "and then my daughter and her daughter, and hers, and hers, and hers. And all of us will remember that St Thomas is here to pray for everybody who comes to him for help, until the end of the world."

Alice said, "I reckon it'll get lost before that," but William drew out the leather pouch from under his gown, for he was the one who kept the pilgrim's purse.

At suppertime Marion, Alice, and William went back to the cathedral, as their guide had suggested. Nicholas told the host to keep their meal warm, but he did not go along. "I'll return tomorrow," he said, and kept Geoff with him to check on the horses. Tom and Win sat together over beer, awestruck and drained.

Once at the church again, Marion and Alice went straight to the Martyr's tomb. William snooped among the side chapels and, in one of them, stood before the sacrament in a mindless, wordless, maundering sort of way. Eventually he returned to the Martyr. He found Marion and

Alice praying under the eye of a smooth looking canon who hovered about with a proprietary attitude, flicking surfaces with a linen handkerchief and coughing as if their presence was inappropriate.

Alice spoke to William out of the corner of her mouth. "Aye, mister, keep an eye on Dame Marion; she's fixing to loot the shrine."

William whispered back, "Will no one rid us of this meddlesome priest?"

Alice choked and spluttered, but Marion did not admonish them. She held her ring to her lips, too full of wonders to notice.

✳ 49

Southwark
September 1344

"Do we have everything?" Nicholas stood in the middle of the room.

Geoff recited his list, pointing at each item in the roll: "Purse, daggers, cloaks, hoods, halters, saddlebags, spurs. Bows, arrows, swords, buckler. Leads, gloves, lantern." He took a breath. "Bodkin, thimble, razor, needle, thread, pumice, shoes, gowns, tunics, hosen, shirts."

"Do the villeins have the dogs?"

"Yes, sir." One morning they had left a particularly bad inn in a hurry. They had traveled three miles before Nicholas had noticed that they were missing Tooth, and he had made Geoff ride the whole way back to fetch him while the rest sat on the grass and ate meat pies.

William had divided his things from the others' the night before. Now he piled them on the bed and looked at them. "Pens, ink, parchment, reedwax, pumice. Books. Tunic, hosen, psaltery, shirts, cloak, hood. Shoes, purse, dagger, penknife, currycomb, needle, thread, cup. Bow, quiver, haircomb."

Marion stood still as Alice fastened her wimple and draped her traveling veil. "Change your mind, brother," she said.

He shook his head.

"Then go with God."

He nodded.

Tom and Win came up and began to lug the baggage away.

"Stay with me a little longer," William begged. "Go home by way of Oxford."

"No," said Nicholas. "It's too far out of the way. I want us to get home before the cold begins."

The cold had already begun.

"Go with God, brother," said Marion again.

He stretched a smile.

Alice said, "It will be a dreary journey without you, Master William."

They stood about for a little. Then Nicholas said, "I reckon we'd best be on the road, if we're to make any distance before dark."

William nodded. "Days draw in."

They all went downstairs. The host came out to wish them a safe journey. "Godspeed, pilgrims. And trust no innkeepers south of Humber, saving me, of course."

Their horses were being held for them in the innyard. William watched them mount.

"Ride with us as far as Aldersgate," said Nicholas.

"No. If you will leave, leave."

"Aye. Well. Farewell." No one knew what to say.

"Farewell, Oxford scholar," said Geoff, friendly.

"Aye, farewell, Master William." Tom and Win.

"God keep you, Master William." Alice.

Marion brushed her eyes with her glove. She tried to smile and could say nothing.

"God keep all of you," said William.

They clattered out of the innyard. William followed them to the street and watched them until they passed out of sight. Just before they rounded a corner, Nicholas turned and saluted him. Then they were gone.

William crossed the yard again and went through the common room. The host said, "Come, sir. Eat and drink on the house. A woeful face like that deserves some charity."

"I thank you, no."

In the empty chamber, William lay on the empty bed. There was a hole in his chest. A darkness seemed to close in around him, heavy with unclear and ominous meaning.

That night he woke in a panic. When will I see them again? When will I ever see them? He could not get to sleep again until daybreak, and by then the whole inn was up and stirring.

Part Four

Alle tyme that is given thee
It schal be askid of thee
How thou hast dispended it.

THE CLOUD OF UNKNOWING

✳ 50

Oxford
September 1344

The porter of Merton came out of his lodge and said, "Quis es?" He looked at William as if he were something unnatural.

William replied, "My name is William, of Keldacross in Yorkshire. My uncle Roger de Wherne wrote a letter for me . . ."

The porter made an odd, flapping motion in front of his face.

William stepped back, startled. Then he continued cautiously. "My uncle, canon of York and former fellow of this college, sent a letter to Warden de Treng concerning me, and I have another from him here, on my person."

The porter flapped again. "Yea, yea. Treng's not in college this afternoon. You will have to wait." He turned his back and shuffled away through a doorway. The door slammed. William remounted Arrow, fumbling with the reins.

A huge voice boomed in his ear. "Are you looking for a hall? A master? A pedagogy?" The man was unmounted, but his huge, freckled face, haloed by a frizz of orange hair, was nearly level with William's. He was very tall. Redtop! Redtop, who had browbeaten the blackfriar! His expression was urgent. "Are you looking for lodging?"

"Well, yes."

"Excellent. We are well met. I can lead you home straightaway." The man grabbed Arrow's bridle and tugged. "Come. We'll get your beast stabled, and then on to Chimney."

"What?" asked William distractedly. "No. Thank you. I must first speak with Warden Treng. He will find me lodging. I thank you."

"Forget Treng! You may do what you like, mayn't you? Look. Come hear our master. Hear him for three lectures, no fees, no commitment,

213

and you will see. He's a great master. Brilliant. Excellent. Unsurpassed. Our hall is packed with excellent fellows."

William said, "Thank you, but first I must speak with Warden Treng."

The man grew wild. "Listen, you *must* come with me. You *must!* I owe Claus the bookseller six shillings. I've got to have the money!"

The sun was glaring off the white stone of the porter's lodge and glinting from the glazed windows. The man's breath was oniony and hot. William felt faint. "How would my coming to lectures help you?"

"I get a cut for hauling you in, you fool. What did you think?"

"Well, I thank you very much, but I must wait to speak with Treng."

"I look to see you at Chimney Hall tomorrow morning at six o'clock for the first lecture of the day. If you're not there, I shall come find you and beat you with a stick." Redtop said this wheedlingly, pleasantly. Then he strode off, his grey gown billowing behind him.

William wondered about the quality of this unsurpassed master, if the red top were so hard put to get students for him. He went and found an inn. Next morning he ventured back to Merton, and he met the warden just as he was coming out of Merton gate, flanked by his chaplain and the college bursar.

"Roger de Wherne?" the warden said. "Certainly I know Roger. You are his nephew, you say?"

"Yes, sir. Sir, in July he sent you a letter."

"Letter? From Roger de Wherne? Oh yes. But I have misplaced it; I do not remember the matter." Warden de Treng was an imposing man in his red cappa and furred hood. William's voice cracked, and his face felt stupid.

"Don't look so crestfallen, boy. It is to be expected. I have much work to do, and little time. What was the matter of his missive?"

"Sir, it concerned me."

"That much I gathered."

"Sir, I have a second letter that he sent with me. I have it here."

"Wise Roger. Here, let me have it."

William pulled it from his belt and handed it over, keeping his eyes on the warden's long black shoes.

Treng's reading silence was eternal. Finally he said, "Well. I remember now. Yes, I will see you into a good hall. I like Roger de Wherne—a man of sense and kindness. I'll keep an eye on you for him. If you are as promising as he says, and keep yourself from mischief, we may well find you a place at Merton."

"Sir, this is most kind!"

"Where are you staying now?"

"Sir, at The Angel."

"Good. This afternoon, expect a student from Chimney Hall in Kibald-twychen. Chimney's as good a hall as any, wouldn't you say, John?"

The chaplain nodded. "Assuredly."

"Yes. Alexander is a good principal, and that way you will be close by. Kibald street's just north of this one, behind Oriel over there. Does that suit you?"

Chimney? Where had he heard that name? "Master Warden, I am ever grateful."

"Good," said Robert Treng. "Now run along. I shall send them for you. Master Alexander is a rigorous teacher. Does that sway you?"

"Sir, I am come to study diligently."

Treng and his friends chuckled. "Such becoming earnestness," said the bursar. "May it never wane."

"No, sir," said William.

"Then go," said Treng. "I shall have my eye on you."

William fled.

He hung about The Angel all day, and by suppertime he was angry, because he thought the warden had forgotten him again. He was afraid to go to Chimney Hall by himself, and even more afraid to go back to Merton. So he sulked by the inn fire, watching the door and biting his nails.

It was not until after Compline that a fair, handsome fellow in a green tabard came strolling through the door, announcing languidly that he was looking for a Yorkshireman.

William leapt up from his bench. "That's me, William of Keldacross."

The fellow sauntered over. "I am Stephen Haigh of Melcombe Regis in Dorset. I have come to guide you to Chimney Hall, if you're willing."

"Certainly I am willing. Let me get my things, and my pony."

"Arrow?" said Stephen, after they had stabled the pony. "Did I hear you call that beast 'Arrow?' "

"So?"

"I can scarcely think of anything less like an arrow than that fat, shaggy donkey. He looks like a wintered bear."

"He's a Yorkshire fell pony, and a good, sturdy fellow."

"Doubtless. Nevertheless, I maintain that his resemblance to an arrow is slight. Unless, of course, you mean to argue that his essence is Arrow under the accidents of Fat Beast."

A sandy, beanpole man loped around a corner. He wore a shabby cappa, and the striped hood of a Master of Arts hung down his back.

"Hail, Magister," Stephen called. "Look, here's your new student that Warden Treng sent you. I've just brought him from The Angel."

"Bene, bene," said the magister. He made some vague gesture over William's head and went gangling on past them.

"That's Alexander the Scot," said Stephen, "as you probably guessed. Do not be deceived by his otherworldly manner. He is a hard master and, in particular, a devastating logician. He will begin by saying, 'Ah, I'm but a poor ignorant man from the northern wilds, with but little way with words,' and soon he's got you laid out on the floor. A poor ignorant from the northern wilds. Aye. Like John Duns Scotus."

William laughed nervously. Stephen smiled. "Here we are at Chimney. But wait. Before we go any further." Stephen stopped in his tracks and pulled William up short. "I must warn you. There is a man in there of whom you must at all costs beware. What Master Alexander claims to be, this man *is*—not ignorant, I mean, but wild and savage, and inclined to violent acts. You must never cross him, and if you are engaged in disputation with him, you must make sure you allow him to destroy you. Believe me, it is better that way. However, you must also not yield easily but give him a good argument, or he will crush you like a flea. You will know him directly we enter the hall. I can already hear his voice. We call him the Red Dane, or else Agrestis. He is a Yorkshireman like yourself."

They climbed up the shallow steps to the heavy oaken door. Stephen pulled it open. The voice blasted them as soon as they stepped over the threshold. A tall, ruddy man of eighteen or so presided over the hall. Frizzy orange hair stood out from his head in lumps, except where it was squashed down by the greasy linen cap tied down with a string under his chin. He had one hand on his hip; the other he threw out in great gestures, sweeping and chopping the air at every cutting point in his "utter destruction" of his victim's "noxious insipidities." The victim was trying to sidle away, but the Dane caught him short with a resounding "Stay! Stay, heretic, while I demonstrate once and for all your vile and pernicious error!"

William knew him well enough. Redtop, who had threatened to beat him if he did not get his cut for William's attendance at Master Alexander's lectures. This was indeed the same redhead he had encountered last year the time he had escaped from Brother Thomas of Waverly to loiter around the schools and so had been late for Vespers.

His present victim moaned feebly. "Yes, Agrestis. I see it now. Yes, of course, that is so." Then he cried out, "Oh God, Agrestis, mercy! I agree. You are perfectly right. I agree." His peaked face contorted in terror and despair. He ran his fingers feverishly through his hair.

Redtop, enraged, stamped his foot. "Ass! Fool! I do not want your groveling surrender! You must not only *say* you agree, you must *really* agree in your *mind!* Else fight it to the death!"

Stephen whispered in William's ear. "The only one who will ever stick it out with the Dane is fat Miles Spottiswoode. But he's not here at present."

The wispy victim shook his head and crept off into a corner to recover himself. The Dane flew into a fearsome rage. His broad, high-boned face turned blood red. "God curse you puling little churchmouse! You can *not* make asinine statements without being prepared to defend them!" He glared around the room. The onlookers shrank back. "God!" He switched from Yorkshire Latin into Yorkshire English. "It makes me want to kill!" He clenched his great red fists and shouted at the victim in the dark corner. "Uthred do they call you? Well, henceforward it's Putrid. Putrid the Puler you shall be called!"

Stephen cleared his throat. The Dane looked around. The Puler seized his opportunity and crept away, out of the hall.

"What's *this?*" the Dane demanded.

"This is the fellow Warden Treng sent us to fetch from The Angel, except you wouldn't come, since you were so bent on trampling poor Uthred. His name is William, and the reward is mine."

"You swine!" Redtop glared at William. "You would not come with *me* when I bade you! You come with him instead, emptying my pockets?" He strode up to him. "I'll pay 'Claws' the bookseller with your teeth!"

Stephen stepped in front of William. "Calm yourself, Agrestis. Give the man better greeting than that. He's to be our fellow for God knows how many years."

Agrestis reached around Stephen and pulled William out and examined him. "Yorkshire?"

William nodded, dry mouthed.

"What part?"

"North Riding."

"What part?"

"Hambledon hills. Not far from York."

"I am a dalesman." This was uttered belligerently. "Swaledale." William mumbled, "Keldacross."

"What? Curdlecross did you say? Speak louder."

"Keldacross. Under Kelda Fell, in Tewisdale."

Agrestis shrugged. "Never heard of it. But I live near a place called 'Keld.' My name is Goodram Hawe of Scarra."

William did not know what to say, so he smiled tentatively and chewed a hangnail on his left thumb.

Stephen said, "Well now."

Agrestis interrupted. "What liquid do they use to baptize at Curdle-cross, man? Where'd you get that piss-yellow hair?"

Everyone waited for William to answer.

"I asked you where you got your piss-colored hair?"

William lifted his chin, looked Agrestis in the eye, and said, "From heaven."

Agrestis made a horribly disgusted face.

William continued. "Straight from God. It is because of fair men like me that we worship God in this land and not demons."

"Absurd statement. Defend it."

"I have it on authority."

"Cite it."

"None other than our great Father, Pope Gregory himself."

Agrestis raised a ruddy brow.

William paused. Then, "Non Angli," he said, "sed angeli."

Stephen snorted. Agrestis regarded William speculatively. Then he took William by the shoulders and shook him and kissed him on both cheeks. "Only a Yorkshireman would have the blasphemous guts to twist Bede around like that," he crowed. "God, I love this man." He turned to the others. "Know ye," he pronounced, "that from this hour forward this angel is my friend and brother. Any injury to him will result in speedy vengeance upon the perpetrator." He threw his ropy arm around William's neck. "Good angel," he said, "lend me thy fiery sword, and together we Yorkshiremen will smite this sea of seething southrons till it sinks in supplication at our muddy shoes. What say you, Angel?"

It was decided that William should share a room with Agrestis, Stephen, and the fat, sombre fellow called Miles Spottiswoode, nicknamed "the Ockhamist." This was a great honor, since those three were the senior students in the hall. "Under the magister," said Agrestis, "all owe their allegiance to me."

Stephen and Miles the Ockhamist shared a bed; William would share with Agrestis. There was no fire or grate in the room, but William was used to that at Rievaulx. "When Peter the German was here," said Stephen, "he had a little stove that made good heat safely all winter long. But Peter went off to Paris just before the long vacation."

"I thought of killing him, throwing him in the Cherwell, and saying that the townies did it," said Agrestis, "so that we might keep the stove, but my conscience dissuaded me."

"You mean Peter's huge brawn dissuaded you," said Stephen.

"You lie," said Agrestis. "The man was a dwarf."

218

"You will have Peter's study," Miles told William glumly.

The "studies" were nothing more than screened carrels by the windows, each equipped with a table, a plain joined stool, and an iron candlestick. William had but half a narrow window—the back of his carrel formed the front of Stephen's—but it was all marvelous in his eyes. "My own room," he said, and set Wilfrid's books in a row on the pocked and rickety desk.

"Aha!" Agrestis ran his finger over the black and red bindings. "The poor scholar arrives in Oxenford well provisioned. Where did you steal these?"

"They were a gift," said William.

"Fraus tecum," said Agrestis, "Fraud be with you."

They drove a nail into the wall and hung Wildrid's psaltery on it. "Naturally," said Agrestis, "this seraph has an angelic instrument." He looked at William in mock terror, and began to back, trembling, against the window. "O great power from on high," he supplicated, wide eyed.

Stephen laughed. "Set him at ease, great messenger."

William grinned. "Noli timere. Be not afraid."

For the moment, he forgot all sadness.

✳ 51

Oxford
September 1344

The scholars rose from their beds with the sun, washed their hands and faces in basins of cold water and made a light breakfast of bread and watered wine. Then they went down into the hall to hear the first lecture of the day. It was in logic—Master Alexander reading from Porphyry's *Isagoge*—and it was three hours long. Afterward Alexander took William aside and shot questions at him, one after another, relentless, like an archer on the battlements. Agrestis, Stephen, and Miles stood by listening, Stephen leaning against a roof post, Agrestis standing behind the master, making grotesque faces at William. Sweat broke out on William's forehead as he strove not to laugh. "Well, well," said Alexander at last. "Your grammar is good, you respond quickly, and you seem to possess some degree of the faculty of reason. I welcome you to this hall. I hope you can bear the company of one such as I, a poor rustic of the northern kingdom, unskilled in letters and argument, but nonetheless a lover of learning."

"I desire it, magister," said William.

Alexander nodded benignly. A glazed, distant look came over his face (his eyes up to now had been searing), and he made the same vaguely benedictory gesture he had made yesterday afternoon in Kibald Street. Then he wandered out of the hall.

"The fraud," said Stephen, when he was well out of earshot. "He shams fey purposely, to confuse and destroy us."

"The next lecture is at noon, after dinner," said Agrestis, "but we shall not attend. The arrival of an angel demands a feast. We shall do no more work today. The occasion demands the Puking Prelate."

Stephen explained. "That's The Mitred Head in Northgate Street. Agrestis rechristened it because it's such a hole. But you can get more beer there for your money than anywhere else in this thieving town."

"Are we permitted to go into taverns?"

"Of course not. One doesn't ask; one goes."

"Yes," Miles the Ockhamist spoke up. "And if one is Agrestis, one goes and goes, seeking any excuse to do so."

Agrestis ignored this, but his face turned grim. He shoved it into William's. "Which do you follow, Thomas or Duns? I will not insult you by asking if you follow William of Ockham."

William laughed dazedly. "I scarcely understand Rhetoric yet. I dare not choose theologies."

"Such humility. But do you hold no opinions?"

"I don't know enough to have opinions."

"Well, I do, and I have."

Miles made a noise.

"They are all envious of my brilliance," Agrestis went on, "except Miles here, who has not the sense to be." He drew William's ear to his mouth and whispered stagily, "Yes, my friend. Miles belongs to that vile order of men, that base species, that unfortunate race known as . . . Well. Let us say that on the Ladder of Life he represents a rung slightly below that of the slug, or perhaps the biting flea. He is, in a word, an Ockhamist."

"I do not hate the agrestis," Miles said blandly. "How is it possible to hate nothingness, mere privation, complete absence of being?"

"Many have held," Agrestis explained to William, "that evil is non-existence, the negation of good. But you, Miles Clot, embody your nothingness in all too generous a corporeal substance."

220

"Did you ever consider how you might relieve yourself of the wart that is your brain?" Miles wondered. "I know several excellent charms."

"What deluded fool named you Miles?" Agrestis bellowed. "Look at those pudgy, feeble limbs. 'Miles' signifies 'warrior,' but you couldn't lift a donkey switch let along a broadsword."

"A miles Christi need lift neither switch nor sword."

"You canting hypocrite! I hate you like leprosy!"

"See how brilliantly they dispute," Stephen drawled. "Always on the heights of metaphysics."

Miles bowed to William. "I take my leave. I have much studying to accomplish today. Do not let the Dane poison your mind against me. I assure you, he understands nothing of the New Logic." Miles went heavily up the stairs.

Agrestis watched him go, pushing up his nose to make a porcine face. Then he said, "To The Prelate!"

They rambled around town a bit, then turned up Northgate Street. "There it is," said Agrestis, "the sign of the Puking Prelate. Look how the artist has rendered him. Does he not look distressed? Nauseated? Or perhaps it is simple flatulence."

"Agrestis is obsessed by flatulence," said Stephen.

"Yes. I am composing a treatise on the subject: *De generatione et corruptione flatuum Oxoniensium.*" Agrestis grinned. "I myself can deliberately evoke flatus—an invaluable skill for the purposes of disputation. A good krumhorner will disarm an opponent faster than anything I know. When we enter the tavern I shall point out to you, if you are attentive, the near infinity of loudness, scent, and musical quality to be encountered there."

"I thank you, no," said William.

"No? Have you no intellectual curiosity? Why have you come to university?"

"My father did say he feared it was for wind," William smiled.

They went in. The place was low and dark and crowded, mostly with students, though a clutch of angry looking artisans huddled at the corner of one table. Agrestis chose a place near the door "so we won't die of the stench."

They settled themselves on benches. Eventually the taverner came over. She was a burly woman with a surly face and curt speech. She folded her arms underneath her bosom as Agrestis said, "Good day, good Bet. God sending you good sale? He might, if you improved your ale. You water it down so much of late I'm afraid we'll have to drink a whole keg to get the benefit of it."

"You don't like my brews, there's the door." She jerked her head in that direction.

"Na. 'Tis well enough. Just bring us quantities in careless abundance."

"Have the silver for it?" Bet gazed at him impassively.

"We'll all throw our shavings into a hat, eh, friends?"

After they had each drunk five or six large tankards, William found himself gurgling into his ale over some stupid joke he himself had made, and then standing on the table singing a lewd song with a somewhat irreverent refrain. Agrestis had taught it to him patiently. "You must sing it," he had told him. "It is required that you sing it through publicly, three times without error, or you must pay for this whole celebration."

William did not need much persuasion. He could feel a wild, careless blood coursing through his veins. He sang the song through without error and then, because faces below were laughing and cheering, he sang it again with gestures. The third time through, his eyes focused and fixed on the blue stare of a dark, wiry little man in the white rochet of an Austin friar. This man turned his head and said something to another short, dark Austin. William, in his drunkenness, could not tell whether it was English he spoke, or villainous Latin, or some other tongue altogether. Then the first Austin addressed William in clear Latin. "Is it wise to sing such a song? I would tremble to sing it. Are you a Christian?"

"Nay, he's a Saracen," said Stephen, "and worships Mahound. Therefore he cannot help but utter blasphemies."

"Go away, Pharisee," said Agrestis. "Go trumpet your piety on the streetcorner."

The man ignored them, never removing his gaze from William. "I doubt this is the behavior they taught at Rewley Abbey."

William's throat closed up. He tried to get down from the table, but it lurched, so he sat on it, and wiped his mouth.

"You used to live with the white monks, did you not?" the cold, high voice continued. "No wonder you saw fit to leave them, since your talents lie with raucousness and blasphemy."

"Good Lyra," said Agrestis, "you are as drunk as we, else you would see that this is no white monk, but simply a sotted secular. What are *you* doing in here, anyhow, mingling with tax collectors and sinners? Gawd!" He nudged Stephen. "First Miles Clottiswoode and now the Welshman. It's too much."

The tapster, filling the artisans' cups, smelt trouble and bawled across the room, "Take your quarrels outside!"

The Welshman shook his head. He treated William to another icy blue stare. Then he and his friend left the tavern.

"It's me the Welshman hates," said Agrestis. "His name is Iago ap Rhys. I call him Lyra because he has a voice like a strangled goose. And their kind are supposed to be great singers! Here, Angel, don't fall on me. Pugh! Smell I brimstone?"

✳ 52

Keldacross
October 1344

Three weeks after William came to Chimney Hall, Marion and the others returned to Keldacross from pilgrimage. Alice came back with them, though she longed to stay in York. To see the tower of the minster rising above the town in the mist, to bask in the warm kitchen in Goodramgate, and then to depart yet again for the wilds of Keldacross—the thought almost killed her. But Marion had whispered to her that she had had no blood for three months—didn't that mean she was with child? So Alice had groaned and said, "Aye, well, I'll stay with you until you're brought to bed." "Alice," Marion had replied, "you may stay in Goodramgate if you like. You are really my father's servant, not mine." Alice said, "Your father'll be pleased as punch that you're giving him a grandchild. Nay, I'll stay with you till the bairn is born."

In the great bedchamber at Kelda Marion was standing in a steaming wooden tub while Dame Magdalen poured water over her head from a kettle.

"Ow! Hot!" she cried.

"Sorry, my love," said Alice. "I shan't keep it on the fire so long."

"Oh, but it feels so good to be clean again," Marion sighed.

"I envy you your hair," said Magdalen, "but it takes so long to dry it. You must sit by the fire when we've done, and not go rushing about the house like a madcap, catching all the drafts."

Sir Gervase blundered into the room. Marion sank into the tub. "Husband!" Dame Magdalen stepped in front of her. Gervase retreated, slamming the door.

"God damn it, Maudlin!" he shouted through the oak. "How did I know she was in there? Hell! May a man not enter his own bedchamber?" They heard him stamp away.

Marion put her hand over her mouth and laughed. Then she hung her toes over the edge of the tub. "How good to be home," she said. "How good it will be to sleep in our own bed!"

Nicholas had gone to the stables to see Dragon. Dragon was not there. Another horse, a roan, was in his stall.

"What's this?" he turned to Cuthbert. "Where's my destrier?"

Cuth opened his mouth and said nothing.

"What's happened?" Nicholas rattled the stall door. "Did my father sell him? God curse him if he did!"

"What's this?" Gervase came into the stable. "Cursing your old sire the moment you step over his threshold? Jesus Christ, why do we make children? They only persecute us." But he embraced Nicholas fiercely and kissed him. "Darling son, sweet lad. Did'ye pray for your old father, as he asked you?"

"Where's Dragon?" Nicholas pulled away.

"Er," said Gervase, looking at the constable, who was standing, nervously twisting his hood in his hands, in the stable doorway.

"Sir Nicholas," said Cuth. "It's a sad thing. Dragon took a fire in his belly. He swelled up and died. I am sorry for it, sir."

"What?" Tears sprang to Nicholas' eyes. "How did that happen? You fat fool! You larded ox! You sat the horse and killed him!" Nicholas stepped forward wildly. Gervase checked him with his arm.

"Nay, son, it was no fault of Cuth's. I would slit his gullet if it was, eh, Cuth?"

"Aye, sir, that you would."

"And Cuth felt so sore about it that he asked leave that very day to go out and find you a new horse. Didn't you, Cuth?"

"Aye, sir, that I did."

"And this roan is what he found you. And a finer, nobler beast I never saw under a Percy's arse. Don't you think him fine? As biddable as a lamb, but spirited as a lion. I've ridden him. By St Godrich, Nicholas, he's a nobler horse than ever black Maccabeus was in his prime."

Nicholas went over grudgingly and inspected the roan. He broke down and fed him a bit of hay. "Well," he said stiffly, "I beg your pardon, Cuth. You are a good horsemaster, and you know your horseflesh."

"Think nothing of it, Sir Nicholas."

"Did you keep Dragon's tack? I want it."

"Yes, sir."

"I shall never forget him."

"Never, sir. Of course not."

"Come inside, then, my son." Gervase clapped him on the shoulder. "If those vixen are speaking to me, we may have a merry homecoming feast for our pilgrims. Eh?"

At table Marion asked for Wilfrid priest. Was he ill?

Dame Magdalen set down her cup. "My cousin is dead these three weeks."

Marion choked on her bread and put her hand to her mouth. Gervase crossed himself and helped himself to salt. "Aye. Old Wilfrid croaked his last sermon and fell off the pulpit like an old crow off a winter bough. Preaching good, wasn't he, Maudlin? He was telling us the one about the churl that couldn't pay his debts and went about throttling other varlets for money. Wilfrid says, 'And the king said to that wretched servant, You knave! I forgave you much, and you will not forgive your fellow servant his pittance? And the king said, Drag this scum down to the dungeon and hand 'im over to the torturers till he pays me every last penny.' And then Wilfrid looks amazed and clutches his breast and that's the end of him. Eh, wife? Isn't that how it happened? Godrich! Hope it wasn't a sign of the old thief's present whereabouts." Gervase chuckled.

Marion stood up. "No! Oh, no!"

"Sit down, wife," said Nicholas crossly. "Wilfrid was an old man."

"I loved Wilfrid!"

"Sit down," said Nicholas again. "You hardly knew him."

The new priest was named Oswin, and the village liked him very well. He was big and slow and friendly (Wilfrid had not always been friendly), and he understood their ways. In Wilfrid's day, when they had tried to dance holiday nights in the churchyard, Wilfrid used to charge out of his house with a cudgel, threatening them with excommunication and damnation. But after Oswin priest came, they tried it again, and Oswin just poked his head out the window and watched. And the next morning, when they sat with their bread and beer under the beech in summerfield, he told them a joke.

"I heard tell of this one parson who was kept awake all night by the folks dancing the saint's wakeday. They were singing in the churchyard, 'Sweetheart have pity.' Over and over he heard them: 'Sweetheart have pity.' So what happens next morning is that he rises up to say mass, and instead of 'Dominus vobiscum,' he says 'Sweetheart, have pity.' And oh, if there wasn't a noise then!" Oswin was of Urra, ten miles north, and a good freeman's son.

Marion went down and saw the stone Wilfrid lay under, in the nave

225

of St Godrich's, under the eyes of the angels who watched, and, watching, burned.

✷ 53

Oxford
November 1344

The chapel of St John the Baptist had been an ordinary parish church before the black monks of Reading had granted it to Walter de Merton for the use of his scholars. Henry the Third had confirmed the grant, on the condition that the college provide a chaplain to serve the lay parishioners in perpetuity as they had been served before. Then, so the townsfolk of Oxford saw it, the black tide of scholars had surged into the neighborhood, swarming into their halls and colleges, crowding all decent folk out. But not all hardworking people had been supplanted by the disputatious clercs; baptizing and marrying still went on within St Johns-Within-the-Walls: a woman was waiting on the porch now with her mother and her brothers and an infant in arms.

Agrestis and William and Stephen were coming down St John Street just as the baptismal party was coming out of Merton gate. The babe was in christening clothes, but the mother's face was dour.

"What ails them?" William wondered. "They look as if they'd buried the bairn instead of baptized him."

"Oh, that," said Stephen. "That's the cordwainer's widow, and that's his post mortem whelp. He died a fortnight ago or thereabouts. They're of this parish."

"Poor woman."

"Poor woman; happy us." said Agrestis. "Richard the shoemaker was the bane of my existence. He used to set his journeyman on me every time I ventured into the high street. I'd see Richard lurking in his shop, waiting, holding the journeyman in till I came close; then he'd unleash the man, who'd come out baying like a dog at quarry. It's true; I swear it!"

"He's not lying, Angel. I should beware John Hand the journeyman if I were you. You can't miss him. He's a huge, hulking lout with a face like a mottled pear. If you chance to pass him, try not to look at him. He takes offense at it. If Agrestis fears him, you know he must be something awful."

That afternoon Miles the Ockhamist came into their room, where William was poring over a borrowed *Isagoge*. "There's a man here to see you."

"A man?"

"Austinfriar. I assume he's a man, though I did not lift his gown to prove it. He's in the hall."

William went down. It was the little dark Welshman, standing in the middle of the room, his arms folded and his mouth compressed at the corners. William was perplexed and, for some reason, fearful. He came down the stairs slowly. The Welshman looked up and smiled. Suddenly William felt illumined. He smiled back.

"Do you remember me?" asked the Welshman.

"Yes," said William, with a surge of shame for the drunkenness and the insults and, mostly, for the knowledge that here was someone who knew about Rewley and Rievaulx.

"That is unfortunate, because I fear that I was uncharitable in my speech in the tavern that day. My dislike of Englishmen in general, and of your friend Agrestis in particular, prompted my pharisaical behavior. My conscience has been pricking me ever since, so today I gave in to it and have come to make apology."

"How did you know about Rewley?"

"Someone said, 'See that fellow singing on the table: he was with the white monks.' And I remembered seeing you about."

"Why do people remember me? I didn't think I was so noticeable."

"You have a certain brightness to you," said Lyra, "and perhaps it is rare nowadays to see such brightness in a monk."

"I never took my vows," said William. "I was only a novice."

"Yes," said Lyra. "Well, again, I beg your forgiveness. Good day." He nodded to William and to the others in the room, and left the hall.

In the week following the Welshman's visit, William saw the shoemaker's widow again. She was struggling up St John's Street from her mother's, under a large willow basket heaped with onions, parsnips, collards, apples, and eggs. A child dragged on her free arm, mewling, and ramming a dirty fist into his eye. "Mam! I want sweeties. Mam! Mam! I want sweeties!"

"Ho!" William knocked into her as he bounded around the corner. Her basket lurched and almost fell. He skipped out of the way. "Pardon."

She grunted at him. Her wimple had come loose; it was hanging under her chin. Dark hair straggled from under her kerchief; her face was tired. She made to go past him, but the child stopped dead. "MAM!" he wailed. "I want *sweeties!*"

William smirked at her. "Is this a kinsman of yours?"

She scathed him with a green stare. "Aye, he's my old gaffer." She yanked the child's arm and pushed past.

William bounded onward, past Oriel gate. Lyra had said that he would help him with geometry. William found that he liked the Welshman very well, and if Agrestis didn't like it, Agrestis could go he knew where.

He met Lyra on the sunny steps of St Mary's. But, "Look you, man," Lyra said, "I'm hungry, and I've neither the money nor the wish to eat at The Mitred Head. Why don't you come with me, and I'll forage up something to stave off the wolf—if Cyan the Harp hasn't eaten everything in my secret hoard. The man is as thin as is a rake, but his appetite is unbounded."

Lyra's room was small and bare, in a house of Welsh Austinfriars on the west side of town. The only furniture was a bed, a table, and two stools. The walls were whitewashed and plain, except for red letters painted over the door and over the small, shuttered windows. But the bed was covered with books and all sorts of oddments. Besides several bits of colored glass, there was also an astrolabe and some other strange instruments that William did not recognize. William stooped and peered at a parchment covered with geometric shapes and lines and arrows. His mind rebelled. He would be quite happy never to have a look at a cipher or a compass or an astronomical table.

"What's all this abracadabra?" he joked, as Lyra hung their cloaks on a peg behind the door. "Magic? Let me out of here, Brother Lyra. I'm afraid of necromancers." He read aloud from one of the books on the bed: " 'But is it possible that an infinite sum of number can be related to an infinite sum of number in every numeric ratio and also in every non-numeric ratio?' *What?* I hate it, Lyra; you'll never make me like it. And what's all this strange glass you have lying about? Did you smash a church window in a fit? What is this book, anyway?" He flipped the cover. "*De luce?* Give me enough light to read by in winter, is all I ask."

Lyra frowned. "Fools mock what they do not understand."

That made William anxious. "Don't be angry, Lyra. I'm only joking. I can't understand such things, it's true. But what is all the glass?"

"It's an experiment. Extending the work of Grosseteste and Master Roger Bacon," Lyra answered cryptically.

"Not for the ignorant?"

"You have it."

William read further. " 'But if there are posited the infinite sum of all the doubles continuously from unity and the infinite sum of all the halves, then after subtraction has been made, the ratio of two to one will no longer hold between the first sum and the remainder of the second sum. Nor does the ratio hold any longer . . . It is necessary that what has been subtracted be an aliquot part or the aliquot parts of an aliquot part of an infinite number.' Jesu! Why do you like this? Where can it lead you?"

Lyra cleared a place for him to sit. "Well," he said, "St Augustine would tell you, I think, that those for whom the final purpose of *any* study is pride, or power, or even the mere satisfaction of curiosity, are traveling on the road to hell. For no scientia of any sort that has not God as its heart and its end is of any value—indeed, it leads to man's destruction. But since all creation is of God, we are doing a good thing to love and study it in its proper order—always in its proper order. It is a roundabout way of knowing and loving God." He stopped, annoyed. William was gazing abstractedly at the inscription above the window. It was a saying of St Augustine. Inquietum est cor nostrum donec requiescat in te: Our heart is restless until it rests in You.

"I am not much of a philosopher," Lyra continued. "To love is better than to know."

William read the inscription above the door. Da quod jubes et jubes quod vis, Give what You command, and command what You will.

"Why, Lyra," William said. "You are quite a holy Welshman, aren't you?"

"I did not paint those," said Lyra, frowning again. "And I am by no means holy. Do not speak frivolously, man."

Suddenly they were impatient with one another.

"Do you want me to help you with the Euclid, or not? If not, go now, for I have work of my own to do."

"I don't need to understand it now anyway," said William. "I have years before I need to understand it."

Lyra shrugged and looked at the door.

"I'll come back when I want to sup on sanctified leeks," William mumbled stupidly as he bumped out.

Lyra turned smiling to his astrolabe. "Dduw, Dduw," he said to himself in dry mirth. "Lord, Lord. These English! What's wrong with a good leek, sanctified or otherwise?"

✳ 54

Oxford
December 1344

The last week of Advent. Chimney Hall was hung with boughs of juniper and holly cut from the waste of Brokenhays at the beginning of the season. The wind and the rain beat against the black windows; torchlight flickered on the walls. William brought down Wilfrid's psaltery and tried to strike up "Nowell sing we both all and sum," but nobody would join him, which annoyed Agrestis exceedingly. "Nowell, damn it," he said. "Nowell! Blast you to hell, keep Christmas with cheer!"

"Nowell yourself," said Uthred the Puler, and cringed as Agrestis advanced on him.

William intervened quickly. "There was a lay brother at Rievaulx who thought he could see into days to come. And if you gave him something, he'd look into your palm for you or drop bird bones into a pile and read them, and all manner of such things."

Agrestis spared Uthred. He came over and sat across the table from William. He plucked a raisin out of Stephen's half finished pudding and popped it into his mouth. "And could he really see the future?"

"No. Nothing he said ever came true."

"What did he say for you, Angel? Or did you keep yourself pure of such things, as canon law prescribes?"

"No, I went to him. And it was on account of me and my friend Gilbert that he was found out."

"You Judas."

"I didn't intend it. I was in great terror."

"How so?"

"On account of what Brother Thomas predicted for me. He said that if Gilbert and I saved apples for him in our sleeves and came down into the cellars after Compline, he would prophesy for us. Well, Gib quailed at the last, but I was afire to do it, so I crept down, and there was Thomas with a candle looking so grim that I almost quailed too, and fled back up the stairs. But my curiosity overcame me, and I went back to him. I think he was angry not to get Gilbert's tribute, for he foretold me the direst things."

"Well, what were they?"

Everyone in the hall was listening. William warmed to the story.

"First of all, that within three months the Scots would come down on Rievaulx and burn it to the ground."

"That did happen once before, didn't it?" Agrestis interrupted.

"Yes, the Scots came and burned the abbey because King Edward had stayed there."

"Langshanks?"

"No, the second Edward. Bannockburn Edward."

"Scots should all be tortured and flayed alive," Agrestis suggested calmly.

"Don't let Magister 'Screws' hear you."

"In *any* event . . . " Stephen leaned forward impatiently. "What did he foretell you?"

"He said he saw me running from fire, with my clothes burning. He made a smoke and saw things in it. He saw them chop off Abbot Langeton's head and skewer Father Stephen. He said the blood was terrible."

"No wonder you were shaken," said Stephen. "You can hardly bear the sight of red meat."

"Then he made a ghastly face and shuddered like a leaf. My blood curdled. He said he saw me burnt to cinders and ashes, lying in the mud, with holes for eyes, and a book in my hand."

"A *book?*"

"He was probably reading it on the privy when the fire started."

"Aye, like Peter Ymer at Oriel. Runs out with his hosen about his ankles, clutching *Sic et non.*"

"Well," William continued, "I tore up those stairs like the wind, ran back to the dorter, and fell on my bed weeping."

"Poor little fellow."

"And Gilbert heard me, and I told him, and he fell to weeping too and said, 'We must tell Father Stephen.' "

"And so you did."

"So we did. I remember begging Father Stephen to make Abbot Langeton ask Lord Ros for a garrison of knights to protect us until that time was past."

"What happened to the necromancer Brother Thomas?"

"He got a flogging, and bread and water, and he had to go about for a week with a paper crown writ round with 'Propheta,' and signs fore and aft saying 'Jeremias' and 'Ezekiel.' "

"I'm sure he loved you for that."

"Was it my fault? I didn't sleep for three months, for fear that what he said was true."

"And weren't you punished?"

"Certainly." But William did not tell them something else that Brother Thomas had seen: a black mist creeping in over the sea from the south and covering all of England. It had struck him with special horror at the time, but now for some reason his memory excluded it from the tale.

Miles the Ockhamist came in. Agrestis cried, "Aha!" and strode across the hall to meet him. "Nowell, you dupe of Satan!" The others drifted after, hoping for a fight.

William stayed behind, picking at the remains of Stephen's pudding. His heart hurt him for Gilbert, and Christmas at Keldacross, and lost Rievaulx.

✴ 55

Keldacross
January 1345

The whole village was up in the great house, which made the hall warmer than it had been for months. It was Twelfth Night. In one corner of the room they were banging their cups on the table, lifting a carol. Across the room Oswin priest was trying to teach the children another song, which he wanted them to sing before the gentlefolk that evening:

Gabriel from heven-king

Sent to the maiden swetë . . .

The carollers drowned him out: "And bring us in gude ale, gude ale, and bring us in gude ale . . . "

"For mannës love," Oswin had to sing again. "For mannës love will man become and takë flesh of thee, maiden bright."

"For our blessed Lady's sake," bellowed the carollers, "bring us in gude ale!"

There was a game of hoodman blind over by the dais. Marion had to stand and watch, because she was pregnant. Dame Magdalen would not let her play. If only Dame Magdalen would go see to something in the kitchen, Marion would play anyway. The baby would not mind.

Dame Magdalen went away. Marion leapt into the game and was made the hoodman. She swung this way and that, hands out, laughing. Then someone shoved her too hard. Nobody but Eleanor would hit so hard. "Ouch! Stop it!"

"Here come the mummers!" someone shouted excitedly.

A herd of men with antlers on their heads charged into the hall, scattering shrieking children before them.

"Caught you, rotten pig!" Marion shouted, pulling off her hood, but it was Thomas Reeve's daughter she'd caught. Eleanor's eyes flashed. "Can't catch me! There's nobody can catch me!" And she whipped Marion across the face with her knotted capuchon. Dame Magdalen returned, and Marion retreated to the dais with her hand to her cheek.

Th'angel went away with that
All out of their sichtë
sang Oswin.

"When do we eat?" bellowed Adam Bradback. "I can smell the feast, and I want it in my belly."

"Sir Gervie'd better have a good one for us, or we'll cook his goose!" bellowed Cuth Constable.

"We'll pound him up for motrewes!" yelled Wat the cottar, carried away. Motrewes was a fancy pudding of spiced sausage. "We'll eat the bailley in herring pies!"

Sir Gervase and Sir Geoffrey Wydclif came in, stamping snow off their boots; Nicholas, Mun, and Hugh Cliderhou followed. Behind them came Mark Fletcher and Win, carrying a pole between them. The pole sagged under the weight of a great grey buck whose head dangled, eyes glazed, throat gashed.

"That our dinner, Sir Gervie?" Cuth shouted. "Better skin and cook him fast—we're ready for him *now!*"

"Nay, Cuth," Gervase roared back. "This is your after dinner tidbit. Take care you don't swallow it whole, you glutton."

"Who killed the buck?" asked Dame Magdalen.

"Win Thornrigg shot him, and Hugh finished him off."

Nicholas and Edmund laughed loudly by the fire. Eleanor ran over to them. "Cousin! Come play hoodman blind!"

"Na," said Nicholas.

"Nick's had enough sport for today, hasta not, Nick?" asked Hugh Cliderhou.

"At least I didn't fall off my horse."

"At least I killed something."

"At least I don't let the huntsmen do the shooting for me."

"Come, coz, play with us. It's dull without men."

"I see your brother Geoff in there."

"He doesn't count for tit, and you know it. Come, cousin."

"Na."

"He's afraid of the hard knocks you'll give him—love," said Hugh. Hugh and Eleanor had been betrothed since All Saints. He reached out to take Eleanor's arm, but she ignored him and instead tugged Nicholas across the room. Hugh watched. Edmund shrugged apologetically. "She's a wild one, is my sister."

"Well," said Hugh, "someone will have to teach her manners."

Before she could drag Nicholas into the game, the herd of antlered villagers came pounding toward them and galloped around Nicholas, butting Eleanor out of the way. Nicholas laughed. "Help! What's this?"

"The revenge of the deer, Sir Nick," the hayward answered. And they began shoving him back and forth. The hayward pinned Nicholas' arms behind his back. "Now lads," he cried, "skin him!"

Nicholas struggled. "Help! Mun! Aren't you going to come to my aid?"

"Not on your life," said Edmund. "I'd rather watch you be flayed."

Eleanor watched Nicholas avidly. Hugh watched Eleanor.

The horned men pulled Nicholas' scalloped mantle over his head and unbuckled his sword belt. They grabbed his legs and yanked off his boots, and tossed everything to Wat Cottar, who had somehow got hold of Sir Gervase's green hat. He had it pulled low over his eyes, the way its owner wore it. He swaggered wildly at Nicholas. "Buckle me up, boy!" he bawled.

"Not on your life, Wat."

"Then we'll have to thwack him, won't we? We can't have varlets not doing their service." Wat gave Nicholas a none too gentle blow across the chest with the flat of his own sword.

"Let me do it, Sir Wat," cried Hog the swineherd. He knelt before Wat. The others shoved Nicholas away and pranced about, lowering their horns at any woman who came over to watch. Wat stamped around the house, dragging Nicholas' sword. Nicholas' boots, loose on Wat's thin legs, sagged around the knees. Wat smacked everyone who came near him with the sword, bellowing, "Dogs! Swine! Out of my way! I am the master of this house, am I not? Maudlin, am I not?"

"Nay," came a rasping falsetto. "You are not. 'Tis I!" Someone minced up in a woman's apron and slapped Wat over the head with a plucked chicken.

"Nay!" yelled a woman. "We'll show you the *real* master of this house." And Mary Reeve and the thatcher's daughters pushed John Bailley into their midst. John Bailley grinned humorlessly, like a badger.

"So it's you, is it?" Wat screamed. "You villein bastard! You jumped up scum! You lying, cheating old fox! You've had the run of this manor too long. Well, I've had enough of you! I've seen through you, I have! And now I'll run you through, this very night!" He lunged at the bailley.

"You watch yourself, Wat!" shrilled a voice—Ragenhilda's, his wife's.

Gervase stood on the dais, chortling, scratching his hatless head. Nicholas came staggering up. Marion laughed at him. "Have they skinned you, poor dear?" Nicholas shook his head, smiling.

"Give 'em their head tonight, eh, Gervie?" said Sir Geoffrey.

"I hate to think how this hall will look tomorrow," sighed Dame Magdalen.

"Already looks like harrowed hell."

Edmund came up on the dais, nodded to Marion, and drew Nicholas aside. "You'd best watch out for Hugh."

Nicholas scowled. "What do I care for that bastard?"

"He says he doesn't like the way my sister's 'cozening up' to you. *I'm* offended at that, if you want the truth. The foul minded son of a . . . "

"Let him go to hell."

"Praise God, they're bringing on the fare!" Sir Geoffrey exulted.

Gervase ribbed him. "You'll run to fat, like Ralph. You'd best forgo the feast."

Dame Magdalen led the party to table.

After an hour or more of eating rich dishes, Marion felt crammed and queasy. Dame Magdalen took note. "By all means, girl, call Alice and go to bed."

Marion looked down the hall and spied Alice sitting at one of the long trestles with an arm around Win Thornrigg, rocking her bench with laughter at some practical joke. She looked flushed and rowdy, the happiest she'd been since she'd last come from York. Marion did not want to ruin her Twelfth Night. "I will go by myself," she told Dame Magdalen.

"Your room will be cold. You mustn't take chill."

"Alice has laid the fire. I have only to light it and to warm my bed."

"Nonsense," Dame Magdalen began, but Nicholas interrupted. "I'll go with her."

Magdalen raised her brow at him. "As you like."

Marion protested. "You needn't miss the feast."

"No, I'll go with you. I've eaten my fill."

"But the company . . . "

"I've scarcely seen you since pilgrimage." He stood, and held out his hand to help her up. They told Dame Magdalen and such company as was near them goodnight, and went down the hall to the door of Old Keep. They were sleeping in the sickroom there, because they had given up their own chamber to the Wydclifs.

They climbed the short, cold flight of stairs to the low door, which they found shut. Nicholas pushed it, and grunted in surprise.

"What is it?"

"Barred from within!" Nicholas stepped back and saw a faint line of firelight glimmering under the door. They looked at each other questioningly. He rapped at the door. Nobody answered. He pounded with his fist. "Whoever's there, open the door!"

They heard a murmur of voices then, and the bolt being drawn back. The door opened slowly, revealing Hugh standing there in the firelight. Behind him, sitting on the bed in disarray, was Eleanor.

Marion blushed and looked at the floor. Nicholas inquired, "What the hell are you doing here?"

"Seems I might ask you the same." Hugh aimed a lopsided grin at them, enraging Nicholas further.

"This is my shitten bedchamber," Nicholas uttered in a tight, formal voice. "My lady would like to retire."

"Oh aye? Well, how was I to know?" Hugh turned and frowned at Eleanor; turned again to shrug at Marion. "Sorry. I didn't know it was your chamber."

Marion mumbled, "It doesn't matter." She kept her eyes on the floor.

"Well?" said Nicholas in the same tight voice. "Leave my shitten bedchamber." Marion pressed his arm; he was only making it worse. She peered anxiously at Hugh, who still blocked the doorway, dark against the hearthlight, broader and taller than Nicholas, and looking down on both of them.

"I have said I didn't know it was your chamber, Nicko." He turned back to Eleanor. "You and I will go elsewhere."

Nicholas twitched. He snapped, "Do you think the lady's father will approve?"

Eleanor, who had not moved or spoken, now laughed sharply. "I'm going back to the hall," she announced. She stood up, straightening her gown.

"No," said Hugh testily. "I said we'll go elsewhere."

But Eleanor pushed past all three of them and went running down the stairs. Hugh glared at Nicholas before he shoved out after her.

As soon as he was gone, Nicholas pulled Marion into the room and yanked the door shut. He shot the bolt violently and stood still, breathing with white nostrils.

"Nicholas! You only made it worse."

"That bastard has no goddam courtesy!"

"He said he didn't know . . ."

"The devil he didn't."

"That's ridiculous! You make him out to be a monster, when he's just a rude man."

Nicholas turned his back to poke the fire. He answered curtly. "You don't know him. He's always got to prove some goddam thing."

And Eleanor too, it seemed, had to prove some goddam thing, though he could not explain that to Marion. He cracked his knuckles and glowered at the flames. Jesu-Mary, it had only been that once, and her fault at that. What right did she think she had to hold it against him? Mother of God!

Downstairs in the hall, Cuthbert-priest's children were singing before the gentlefolk:

From her was born our Christ anon
Sooth God, sooth man, in flesh and bone . . .

Next morning before breakfast the family and their guests went down to St Godrich's. After mass, Hugh caught Nicholas by the shoulder, detaining him and Marion on the porch while the others went by chatting.

Nicholas stiffened under Hugh's touch, but neither the touch nor Hugh's look were unfriendly. He said in an open manner, "I'd like to speak with you, Nick."

"About what?"

"Jesu-Christ, man, I'm your father's Christmas guest. Can you not be comradely for once?"

Hugh seemed in earnest, and Nicholas did not know what to do. Hospitality obliged him to be generous. He shrugged irritably.

"A few words in private, Nicholas." Hugh smiled at Marion. "I'll keep him but a moment."

Marion smiled back uncertainly until Nicholas nodded her in the direction of his mother. She went, all bundled in wool and furs, crunching on the old, brown snow. Nicholas watched her until she caught up with Dame Magdalen, whose crisp voice cut the winter air: "Girl, in your state it were wiser not to hurry."

Hugh spoke. "Despite her sire and dam, you've got a good little brood mare, Nicholas. Does your bidding right quick."

Nicholas scowled. Comparing his lady to a beast, as if she were some villein! And what business had Hugh to mention her parentage?

A freezing gust blew over the icy fell and shook Godrich's yew. The tree creaked; wet snow fell from black branches to bleak earth. The icy gust mounted up, the tree groaned, and the two young men retreated wordlessly into the interior of the church.

For a moment they stood mute in the nave with their arms folded. The sanctuary light flickered red and dim behind them; the seraphim flamed on the walls unnoticed. At last Hugh said, "What say you and I go hawking?"

"Hawking?" Nicholas asked incredulously. "It'll storm within the hour."

Hugh answered acidly, "I meant another day. After my wedding, in August, when you and I are cousins by law."

"Aye, well, perhaps." Nicholas felt mildly chagrined at having misunderstood Hugh. But why in God's name mention an August hunt in January?

Hugh cleared his throat. "I'll be frank with you. I want to ask you about your cousin Eleanor."

"What about her?"

"It galled me last night that you disbelieved me when I said I had not known it was your chamber. It was your cousin's thought to go there; I'd no knowledge of it, and no wish to offend you."

Hugh not wishing to offend? This was new.

"You'll take my word?"

Nicholas supposed he must. He shrugged, nodded. Did Hugh expect *him* to apologize?

"She's an odd little partridge, your cousin. First she's hot, then she's cold. I'd no plan to dally with her; it was she who began it. But then she makes me look the fool."

Hugh waited expectantly for a response. Nicholas shifted his weight so that his shoulderblades rested against a pillar. What was he supposed to say? Could he help what Eleanor did or said?

A silence. Then Hugh remarked, coldly, "I'm betrothed to the woman, remember?"

Nicholas bristled. "What do you mean by reminding me?"

"I just don't want a wife who'll trouble me."

"No man does."

"Well, she's a teaser, would you not say? She cozens up to *you* right well."

Nicholas thought, I'll be damned if I'll discuss this with Hugh of Eskmere. What the hell's that woman been hinting at? It's her business, not mine, if she wants to soil her family's name. Best she safely marry Hugh and forget the whole thing, forever. "Perhaps she has a few wild ways," he mumbled. "They mean little."

Hugh seemed easier at that. He relaxed his back against the pillar opposite Nicholas. "Well, she's a fair thing despite her 'wild ways.' Fair enough to make me overlook 'em now for the sake of same in my bed later. Eh?"

By God, we're in *church*. The man really has no courtesy. Nicholas looked briefly toward the sanctuary.

Hugh caught the glance and thought, Chaste, perfect, bastard. But thinking of Nicholas' prudery reassured him again, and he was in a mood to forgive. He joked affably. "Coldest place on earth is always God's good house. What say we go back to the fire?"

On the ice-slick track before the well, Hugh stopped and made a motion as if to clasp Nicholas' arm. He was going to say something friendly, he knew not what; but Nicholas seemed not to notice the gesture and kept on walking on through the churchyard gate.

Hugh, a pace behind him, could not be certain that Nicholas had meant to ignore his hand, and he was damned if he'd extend it again to find out. Cold, righteous bastard, always better than everyone else.

✳ 56

Keldacross
February 1345

Alice brought a steaming cup of mulled cider to the kitchen inglenook, where John Bailley was studying his ledger. She stood over him with the cup and peered down at the open pages on his lap.

He looked up, scowling, and covered the writing with his arm.

"Aye?" he said impatiently.

"I'm just bringing you your cup, as you asked me."

He slammed his book and laid it to one side.

"If you're cheating Sir Gervase in there, you needn't fear me," she said. "*I* can't read."

He snorted. "Never feared *that*."

"My mistress can read. Her father taught her. She can write a little too."

"Good for her." He drummed his fingers on the book cover.

"Well, aren't you going to say 'Christ preserve us from women who can scold with pen as well as tongue?' or aught like that?"

"I'd like ma nog," he said.

"Take it, then. I was just trying to be friendly. But then, you're not a friendly man, are you?"

He took a swallow of his drink. He gulped, bug eyed. "Jesu Christ, woman, you might have cooled it a little!"

Hope it scalds your guts out, you old stoat. "You could have let it cool a bit yourself before you began swilling."

He warmed his hands on the cup.

"That's how we make it in York," she said.

He made her no answer.

"That's how my mistress likes it, but I can't get these cows to do it that way. They heed me not at all, though I'm Dame Marion's own maid-servant since she was a baby. But I'm not of Keldacross, so I don't count for nowt among *them*."

"Got to be stronger tongued with 'em," he said.

"Well, Mary and the Rood! Never did I think to hear you say *that*, Master Bailley."

"Na, you're *rattle* tongued. Don't rattle at 'em, just *tell* 'em."

"They'd pay me no mind no matter what I did. It's on account I'm not of Keldacross."

"Dung," he said. "It's because you rattle."

"I 'rattled' no less in York, and folks did what I told them."

He chewed the insides of his cheeks.

She shrugged and went back to cleaning a goose for supper.

He sipped at his drink until it was cool enough to swig down, and then he swigged. "That was good," he said, grudgingly.

"Why, thank you, John Bailley. I think that's the first kind word you've ever said in this kitchen."

"Bring me some more."

"In my own good time. I've other things to do than scurry at your beck and call."

He opened his book again. After a while he said, "I think I'll ask four brown hens of you, Wisa Thornrigg."

Hawisa looked up from her fish-cleaning and wiped stray brown hairs from her forehead. "Candlemastide again, John Bailley?" she said hopelessly.

"Aye. Three times make custom." He sat back and smiled, foxlike, letting his eyes dart over to Alice. "And since that's so, I'll have that noggin now, and by right."

Alice threw down her bird. "You're a rat, do you know that, John Bailley? A scrounging old gutter rat."

He lifted his lip at her, showing his teeth. If he'd had whiskers, he would have twitched them.

✳ 57

Keldacross
April 1345

"Oh my poor little mistress, my sweet dear darling, my poor little maiden," Alice wailed.

"Maiden no longer," said Dame Magdalen, "as we can plainly see." Marion began to blubber.

"Collect yourself, daughter. Tell me how long you've had the pains."

"I don't know. Hours and hours."

"What? Fool girl! You lay there like that? Why did you not call?"

"I heard it's false sometimes. I thought it would go away."

"Mother of God," said Magdalen, exasperated. "We'll up to the sick-chamber. Joan, you help. Alice, run and fetch Wisa Thornrigg."

In the sickroom Dame Magdalen told Joan to settle Marion on the bed and light the fire. She went down for blankets.

While she was away, Alice came bustling in with Hawisa.

"I want Nicholas," said Marion.

"He's at Helmsley, as you know." Dame Magdalen came in again. "We'll send for him if there's need."

"Drink this, lady." Hawisa held a bowl, and the stuff in the bowl was as slow and thick and bitter as Wisa herself. Marion choked in it, but Dame Magdalen said, "Drink!" so she drank.

After she had little Magdalen, Marion lay in pain and fever for a week. When that was over, she was thin as sticks and whey colored, and her hair was tangled and sticky. Her lids and lips were gray and peeling, but Geoff, who came up to see her, thought he had never seen anything so beautiful in all his life.

"Oh lady," he sighed, "you are narrow and pale as a birch."

Alice, tending mutton broth over the fire, barely restrained herself from spitting. She contented herself with banging the spoon against the sides of the broth pot. Holy Mary. A woman could not even retch and puke without some man making it into something to please his fancy.

"Where's Nicholas?" Marion demanded crankily.

Geoff made his face completely neutral, therefore utterly condemnatory. "Sir Nicholas has gone deer hunting with Sir Gervase. You know, lady, that he hates to see you ill."

"Well," said Marion, "I am sorry that it offends him, truly." She turned her face to the bolster and rubbed her hand under her nose.

Geoffrey took his advantage. "Lady, it's true that a sickroom always turns his stomach, and I think it a shame, for I do not know how many hours you spent over that stinking yellow wound he got in his thigh last summer."

Alice would not bear it. She swung round, waving her spoon. "We want no talk of pus here! If this is how you cheer my mistress, you can go away, for she wants none of it."

Geoff tried to stare her down, but she withered him first. He slunk out, mumbling something about coming back later with his rebec.

"Aye," Alice sneered, when he was gone. "All we need is him whining over his fiddle for hours on end."

Marion kept her face turned.

"Do you know what I think, love? What would rid you of yon grease face for good? I'll tell you. Some day, when you're well again, get him alone and give him a great juicy buss right on the mouth. That will scare the fool straight into the North Sea, faster than you can blink."

Dame Magdalen came in with her mother and overheard. Dame Emma was twice a great-grandmother now, but young enough to ride the four days from Coverdale for the christening. She still had most of her teeth. ("St Godrich," Gervase had protested when he heard she was coming. "You daleswomen never die!" And Magdalen had answered, "God forbid.")

"Alice," Magdalen warned now, "there is the danger that the squire might prove braver than you think."

"In that event, Dame Magdalen—and I'd wager my maidenhead otherwise—in that case she can scream bloody murder, raise the hue and cry, and *that* would scare him into Scotland. Either way, she's rid of him."

Dame Magdalen laughed. "I confess I do not know why men think that we like all this mewling and sopping over us."

"Men," Dame Emma declared, "do not know nor care what women like." She stamped over to the bed and laid her hand on Marion's cheek.

"Poor lass, you've had your troubles, haven't you? God, I hated childbed. By His Mother I swear I pass my days happiest as a gnarled old crone. Pray, lass, that you will outlive your husband by many years. Then you may do what you please."

Alice said, "*I'll* never marry, I can tell you."

Dame Emma sat on the bed. "I reckon it's true that some folks like it—the mewling and slopping I mean. But never I. Once I had an amoureux—so he called himself, as if putting it French made it any less asinine, and all the melting looks he gave me made me feel I was having pears in honey poured over my head. Not a happy feeling. You want to scrape it off."

Marion smiled.

"There's a lass. You brave it out. If you live through it all you'll have a merry old dotage to make up for it. No men nor bairns to plague you."

Down in the hall Geoff sat on the dais, oiling Nicholas' best boots. He sang as he did so, raising his eyes to the rafters. "Blou, northerne wind! Send thou me my sweting. Blou, northerne wind, blou, blou, blou!" Sir Ralph, who felt too fat (too meaty, he said) to go hunting, sat in Gervie's chair by the fire and wept, because the song was so beautiful.

With lovesome eyen grete and gode,
With browen blisful under hode,
May he that reste on the Rode
Her lovely lyf honoure.
Blou, northerne wind.

The hunters had killed a doe, and when they returned, and Nicholas had washed his hands and face, he went upstairs to see Marion. He stood in the doorway. "You look better," he said.

Marion nodded.

"You've taken your time in coming," Dame Magdalen reproved him.

"We shot a doe, so we'll have fresh venison tonight." He asked Marion, "Can you eat any?"

She shook her head.

"Shame."

She nodded.

"The babe is looking bonny. I saw it in the hall."

Alice made muttering noises into her brew. All swaddled up at Hild atte-Beck's breast. Don't see how he could see her looking bonny or any other way.

"Look," he said in a strained voice. He glanced furtively at the other women. His mother turned away politely. Dame Emma stared balefully. He averted his eyes and ventured into the room. "Look, I've brought you." He pulled a crumpled grey sprig of something out of his sleeve and offered it to Marion.

She took it. "I thank you."

He looked up. His grandmother gazed at him unblinkingly.

"Look." He shifted his weight. "I'm right glad you're better." He *was* glad. He had been sore afraid when she took fever. He had spent half the night praying his beads over it. Why were they looking at him like that?

'Listen!" he blurted. "When you're well, I'll take you to York. For Easter if you like."

Alice's head jerked up. Dame Magdalen bent over the broth with a ladle. Dame Emma observed.

Marion raised her eyes. "That's kind. I thank you."

Nicholas bent, pecked her, and departed speedily, taking leave of neither mother nor grandmother.

"Rude boy," Dame Emma remarked. "Has no more courtesy than a dung carter."

"I love him." Marion examined the crushed, mangled plant he had brought her. It might have been fennel or thyme; it smelt more of Nicholas.

"Ah." Dame Emma patted her hand. "But you can do without him."

Little Magdalen was baptized when the air was soft and warm under the springtime sun. When Oswin priest bade Satan leave the child, she squalled, and everyone laughed.

In the midst of the feast that followed, Dame Emma decided to retire to her chamber, or rather to Nicholas' and Marion's chamber, which always went to guests. She called Magdalen to her.

"I thought you'd like some rest from all those belching men in there," she said, "and I have a question for you."

"A question, Mother?"

"Old Wilfrid's not being here to do the dousing reminded me. Have you any news of my grandson?"

Magdalen closed her mouth.

"The lapsed monk. The Oxenford scholar. The will-o-the-wisp. Have you any news of him?"

"I have not."

"Well, I have."

Magdalen sat down on a chest.

"He thanks me for my largesse. I sent him some money. Or I sent it to your brother Roger, who sent it down with some of his own."

Magdalen pressed her hands between her knees.

"He says that he does well in whatever they do down there. Most of all, he begs me to plead for him with you. So I do. Daughter, remember your son. Forgive him and grant him your blessing."

"He shamed me, and cheated Rievaulx. He made me forsworn to God."

A spring shower had blown up. Rain beat on the window. A quivering shadow of diamonds and drops and liquid streaks lay across the room, across Magdalen and her mother.

"Show some mercy, woman. After all, he didn't make you 'forsworn to God,' as you say. You gave him to the white monks, just as you promised, and when he was older, he chose otherwise. And that is through no fault of yours."

"I do not want him to be a secular clerc, running about all worldly."

"Your brother Roger reminds you that not all secular clergy are worldly, and also that great and holy men have lived in Oxenford."

"Roger!" Magdalen rose and looked out the window. The gusty wind was pulling some of the Maybuds from the fruit trees. "I must go back to my guests, Mother. Will you rest now?"

"Aye. I will lie down."

"I'll send a maid to you. Rest well, Mother." She went out.

Dame Emma sat on the bed, fumbling stiffly with her wimple and veil. "Send in the maid, girl," she muttered. "Where's the shitten maid?" She gave up and lay down clothed, regardless.

✳ 58

Oxford
May 1345

William went home from visiting Lyra by way of the high street, which meant that he went through the cordwainery, which touched the draper's quarter on the west side of Cornmarket. He saw the widow in her stall. Her wimple was fastened; her kerchief was straight; her face was full of quick shrewdness. She was speedily persuading a sallow faced ironmonger to buy a pair of shoes. William approached. The ironmonger glanced at him with hostility; the widow ignored him. "Now look, good-man, feel this heavy stuff. Look at the stitching. These are shoes we're making for Master Fenn the spicer, but we wouldn't make them any less careful for you. Look. I may be a woman, but I know my stuffs and stitch-ing as well as my husband did; you needn't fear that because he's gone we'll start shoeing you shoddy. I know my cloth and I know my leather. Now if it's leather you want . . . "

William interrupted. "I was thinking of a new pair of shoes." He hadn't been, but suddenly he felt a great desire for them.

She gave him her green look and said, "Wait your turn." She smiled at the ironmonger. "If it's leather shoes you're after, I have a right sturdy Cordova leather that will last you a lifetime of cobblewalking. Marry, I made myself a pair out of it a full two winters since, and I'm still wearing them. Have a look." She bent and pulled off one of her shoes, saying, over her shoulder, "John, bring us out that new skin that Paul Tanner brought us yesterday." A huge journeyman rose hulking from where he had been seated on a bench, trimming a length of red cloth. He had a face like a mottled pear.

William decided to go. He wasn't going to wait around for an iron-monger. Shopkeepers acted with respect in York. He sent the widow a haughty look and stopped purposefully at the next shoemaker's stall, to admire his wares loudly.

"By Our Lady," said the ironmonger, "these clercs think they're god-almighty, don't they?"

"I reckon they do," the widow agreed. "Here's John. Good. Now feel of this. See what I mean? Soft but sturdy."

"Marry," said William at supper. "These townsfolk are too much. I was about to buy a pair of shoes today, but she acted as if she were some-body and I a low fellow."

"She?" asked Stephen. "You must mean the widow Judith. Didn't I tell you what that family thinks of scholars? In her eyes you are unclean. Pass the cheese."

Before William could oblige, Agrestis lunged forward and grabbed the last hunk. He popped it into his mouth. "Why the townies hate us so much is one of the eternal mysteries. They began persecuting the scholars long ago, when there were hardly any of us to take up their filthy streets. Remember The Three Hanged Men." He spoke with his mouth full.

"What?" said William.

"Remember The Three Hanged Men. Lord, they did keep you clois-tered at Rewley, didn't they? What *did* they teach you?"

"Just tell me."

"Very well." Agrestis reached across the table and pulled Uthred's grease soaked trencher from under his nose. Uthred protested. Agrestis tore off the crust and handed the rest back. He chewed thoughtfully. "It was in ancient days, when men first gathered to hear the wandering doctors who lectured on the church porches and in the gateways of the town. Students had no place to stay but in whatever freezing, cheerless hovel they could let from some townsman for a huge sum of money."

"Pardon, Agrestis," Miles broke in, "but you are, as usual, misstating the case. You say rightly that in early days there were no colleges, but the three hanged men were long after those days. As I recall, it happened in the reign of John only a few years before the chancellorship of Grosseteste."

Agrestis bared his teeth. "Clot the Chronicler," he said, "we thank you once again for your unquenchable ability to bury substance under useless facts."

Miles narrowed his eyes and bit into an apple.

"As I was saying. The townies hated us then as they hate us now. And so one night they descended on the miserable cell that four poor clercs were sharing in a ruined lodging, with no light but the door and no fire but their sputtering candles. The fourth man had run away, but they found three of them and dragged them off. A few days later they hanged them outside the town, in defiance of all justice and in contempt of ecclesiastical liberty."

Miles blew a sigh through his nostrils. "You forget, Agrestis, that one of them had just murdered a townswoman, which is why the burghers 'descended' in the first place."

"It is not known that he killed the woman, and whether he did or not is not justification for the townsmen's crime. Or perhaps murder justifies murder, Clot? Are you a lawyer as well as a chronicler? In the pay of the townies perhaps. One wonders why you are forever eager to defend them."

"I only prefer that things be related as they happened, not wildly and carelessly. It's men like you, Agrestis, who cause riots by spreading false rumors."

"Next riot I cause, Clot, I shall make sure that your head is cracked by an accidental brick."

"Might not a substantial brick better achieve your purposes?"

"Clever, Miles. But you must remember that as an Ockhamist you refuse to make the distinction between substantia and accidens. And so I think that one brick will do as well as the other."

Miles spat out two apple seeds, vigorously, one after the other. "The dark well of your ignorance, Agrestis, is unplumbable."

Agrestis explained to William, "Miles is a brave fellow. He has ventured a long way down the via moderna, and he thinks that he cannot keep Reason and Faith in the same purse. And since we see that he is still a very prayerful fellow, we must assume that he has abandoned Reason somewhere along the road. Therefore we must take care not to use a great number of philosophical terms in his presence. It is discourteous to remind him of his loss. Let us choose simple words so that he may not be confused, and chide him not, for blessed are the simple of heart. Our Miles is indeed a natural man."

William smiled sheepishly at nobody and bit his nails.

"I shall not argue with you, Agrestis." Miles spat out another seed. "You think in terms as broad and uncouth as the moors you hail from."

"I chance to have been born in a rather deep and narrow dale," Agrestis replied smoothly. "Holy Virgin. At the moment I think there is a single question at this table: Can the Clot truly be conceived? Does a Simplicity exist greater than which no simplicity can be conceived? If so, the Clot's existence is self-evident, like his belly."

"Before you venture into the domain of high theology, Agrestis, perhaps you had better master the Trivium. You might try a course in logic."

"Indeed, Clot, your own mastery of the trivial is perfect."

Miles shook his head sadly and reached for another apple, which he took upstairs.

"Fructus ignorantiae," Agrestis shouted after him.

William said, "You never finished about The Three Hanged Men."

"Oh aye. Well, what happened is that King John would do nothing about it, so all the clercs, both masters and scholars, up and deserted the town. Not one was left in the entire university. Oxford was desolate."

"But not the townsfolk, I wager."

"No, but their merriment did not last long. Soon they were begging us back. The fools don't realize it, but we are two thirds of their living. Without us to milk of our groats and pence, what would they do for sustenance?" Agrestis pounded the table. "Curse the Clot. May he die a horrible death."

"Bite your tongue," said William. "Such words are better not spoken."

"Why?"

"My mother says that curses fly back at the curser like spit on the wind."

"Your mother." Agrestis gestured at the hall at large. "Holy St Wilfrid. The Clot cites himself as an authority; this man cites his mother. I don't know which is more ludicrous."

✳ 59

Keldacross
July 1345

Marion sat in the walled orchard behind the manor house with little Magdalen in her lap. She was doing some light mending on the baby's cap and listening to Eleanor go on and on about how she and Nicholas used to play Pinch Me and Bob Apple at Christmas when they were children. Marion was more uncomfortable than bored, for Eleanor seemed to be using these long-gone games as some odd weapon against her. She was almost glad when Geoff came stooping through the little door in the wall. He sat himself across from them on the low bough of the apple tree.

"Hoy, brother," said Eleanor. "What are you loitering here for?"

"Sir Nicholas and Sir Gervase have gone hunting. I asked leave to stay."

"What? Geoff not hunting? What can be amiss?"

"Nothing's amiss, sister."

"No? Good then. I think I shall go back to the house and see if Dame Magdalen could use my help with that altar cloth. Besides, all this sun is making my head swim." Eleanor got up and went in, looking back over her shoulder at Marion before she slipped through the door.

Marion finished her darning and pulled the cap over the baby's head. Geoffrey watched her worshipfully. God, she was beautiful. She was wearing her broad brimmed pilgrim's hat, and it cast a lovely shade over her face. She looked up at him with a set mouth (why was she so cold to him?) and said, "You should have gone hunting, Geoffrey. It isn't often we have such a fine day."

"Too fine for hunting," he breathed. "Too hot."

"It is muckle warm." She looked down at little Magdalen. "Oh buh buh buh buh. Is that all you can say?"

"Would you have me fetch you something to drink, lady? Shall I bring you cider from the cellar?"

"No. I'm not thirsty."

"Shall I sing for you?"

"No. I'm tired of singing."

"Aye," he sighed. "So am I."

"I think I'll go in now. The bairn is wet."

Geoffrey leapt off his bough. "Let me carry her!" Yes. He would do even this, to save her discomfort.

"No. You don't know how to hold her." She stood up.

He flushed. "Lady, have I offended you?"

"Why do you say that?"

"Nothing. I only—"

"You only what?"

"Lady!" he cried. "You are the most beautiful thing God ever made. Why did God ever make anything so beautiful?"

Marion turned on her heel and made for the gate. Geoff reached it before she did. He stood before it with a desperate, pleading look on his face which made her want to slap it.

"O lady, do not be angry with me! I cannot help myself! But I mean nothing base, I swear it, by the Rood I swear it, and by the robe of the Virgin."

"You have been listening to too many silly romances. My husband would be angry if he heard you talking like this. Now let me through."

He remained, trembling with contrition. "Say that you pardon me, lady! I beg you!"

She stamped her foot. "Pardon you for what? For acting like a half-wit? Very well. I suppose you think you are Lancelot or Tristan or somebody. Well, stop thinking it. It makes me feel like a fool."

"Oh, never Lancelot, lady. I never think of anything base. I will make you a vow of chastity and never look at another woman."

She laughed in his face. "Now that is the silliest thing I ever heard of. I don't notice the other squires acting like such babies. And speaking of babies, look what you've done. She's wet through to my gown, and now I'll have to wash it."

He moved aside and let her pass. She stepped quietly over the mossy flagstones. He watched her until she rounded the corner of the wall; then he fell back against the door, clutching the shoulder she had brushed in passing.

At night in their chamber Marion said to Nicholas, "I think I should tell you that Geoffrey thinks himself in love with me."

Nicholas fixed a collar around Tooth's thick neck.

"I think he was the one who got the token from me at Middleham."

"I know it."

"He told you?"

"No, I saw it. He has it sewn to the inside of his yellow surcotte."

"And you're not angry?" He smiled at her. "You're not going to knock him down?"

"Do you want me to?"

"Oh. No."

"I know I have nothing to fear from you or Geoff," he said smugly.

That annoyed her. "Well I am happy you are so certain." Nicholas scratched Magog's ears. The mastiff drooled. "Isn't it strange?" she said. "The brother loves me, and the sister loves you. Of course she doesn't say so, but it's plain."

"Eleanor?" said Nicholas. "Eleanor's getting fat."

Eleanor was to marry Hugh Cliderhou of Eskmere on the feast of St Peter ad vincula, that is, the first of August.

"I am glad for it, Hugh," said Edmund politely, at Helmsley. "Do you love her?"

"Love her?" said Hugh. "I don't know that, but I sure enough would have her." He smiled wolfishly. Nicholas twitched his shoulders; Rab frowned; Edmund turned away glowering. Christ! That was no way to talk to a man about his sister.

Marion went with Dame Magdalen to visit at Wydclif. Eleanor and Marion and Eleanor's youngest sister Meg clambered down the steep path leading down the side of the cliff away from the village. Meg carried a big straw basket, and they all wore thick gloves for berrying and broad hats to keep off the sun. It was a heavy, humid day.

"There ought to be a good crop of blackberries," said Eleanor, "if the village brats haven't gone and stolen them."

"If there isn't, you can call manor court and check teeth," said Marion: " 'For having purple teeth let John and Wat and Joan be fined fifty shillings each and let them eat nothing but gooseturds and turnips for the rest of their days.' "

"There it is," said Eleanor. "See that great patch beyond the beck there? Pull off your shoes, ladies. We must wade."

They splashed around in the cool water for longer than necessary. Marion pulled a hollow reed from the bank and sucked water through it, which she then blew at Eleanor's face. "Wash your face, lass," she said, like Mistress Alison. "Always keep it clean and scrubbed."

But Eleanor grabbed the straw and broke it and threw it in Marion's face. "Do I need *you* to tell me that, shopgirl?" Meg, who had been tit-

251

tering, stopped and put her fingers in her mouth. "Oooo," she said, eyes shining hopefully, "that was a bad one."

Marion, lips screwed shut, shook her head. Then she said, "Eleanor is ignorant. My father is a great staple merchant and alderman of York. He does not keep a shop."

"Woolseller, shoeseller, pisspot maker, what's the difference?" Eleanor climbed the opposite bank and headed for the blackberries, pulling on her gloves again. "Come, sister, with the basket."

Marion stood in the water with her gown tucked up around her waist, ripples reflecting facets on her white legs. She thought of turning back up the hill but decided that she would not allow them to snigger against her behind her back. She climbed the bank and went after them.

Eleanor was tearing berries off the vines and throwing them violently into the basket, so that most of them squashed. Meg protested. Eleanor plunged deeper into the bush and snatched for more. A long, cruel tendril caught her around the ankles. "Ow! Ow!" She stooped to yank it away. Another tendril caught her across the face. She began to weep. "God damn you! I hate you! I hate you!"

Meg laughed, but Marion went over and unwound Eleanor. "They're wicked things," she said. "Look! Now it's caught my ankle too. Ouch!"

Eleanor rammed her out of the way and ran splashing into the beck without removing her shoes or even lifting her skirts. She stumbled up the bank and ran across the meadow to the cliff path. They watched her clamber up the hill and disappear through the wicket gate at the top.

"She doesn't want to marry Hugh Cliderhou," said Meg.

"I don't care," Marion shouted, pushing Meg aside. "Let her marry the Devil!"

✳ 60

Oxford
August 1345

For some reason William went back to the cordwainer's shop. This time only the journeyman was there, looming over the counter, wielding his long scissors and whistling tunelessly through his yellow teeth. William saw this too late. The journeyman had already bawled, "What d'ye want, clerc? Speak up!" William tried to act like Nicholas. He strode up and looked past the man's ear. "Let me see the cordwainer," he said.

"Can't do it, clerc. The cordwainer's dead."

"I mean let me see his wife."

"Look, clerc." The journeyman leaned his blotchy face forward. "If you want a pair of shoes, I'm the one to get 'em from. Otherwise, make scarce." He straightened, and snapped the scissors in the air.

Somehow it was the scissors that put William out of countenance. His Nicholas persona vanished, leaving only William. He mumbled, "Aye, then. Measure my foot."

The journeyman jerked his head. "Well, then, come behind here. How can I measure when you're standing out there?"

William stumbled into the stall. He did as he was bid, and put his foot up on the bench.

"Why, lookathat!" the journeyman bellowed. "Look at that dainty little foot! Why, you're blessed, Master Scholar. You'll have to pay but a woman's price in cloth or leather."

William went crimson with feeble rage. His neck prickled at the leers he felt from the street. He could not stop himself. "If my brother Sir Nicholas were here you'd behave yourself, churl."

The journeyman scratched his chin. "I'm sorry, sir. I didn't hear you. What was that you called me?"

William blanched. "Ch—ch—ch . . ."

"Ch—ch—ch—" the journeyman jeered. "That's right strange. I've heard a bird that sounds like that, but I can't mind me of his name. But then I'm no learned clerc, am I, sir?" He took hold of William's foot so that William could not stalk out, as he had been about to do. Why, why had this happened to him? Why had he come in here? Why had he ever left Rievaulx?

The widow came out of her house and stood in the doorway with her hands on her hips. William turned his face away, but not before she saw how miserable it was.

"How may we serve you, sir?" Her voice sounded friendly.

"Shoes," he muttered. "I want shoes."

She advanced. "Here. John, get back to work. Why did you not call me out before? Can't you see this is a gentleman?" There was a hint of mockery in her tone, but she approached solicitously, so he collected himself. "Yes," he answered, almost steadily, "I want a pair of new shoes. Red."

She smiled. "Would you have Powlis windows carven in them? It is in great favor among the young noblemen." (It was an elegant pattern

253

traced after the rose window of St Paul's in London.) "Aye," said William, "I'll have that."

"Ah." She nodded earnestly. "And how shall we cut the toe? I hear that noblemen at court are some of them wearing their toes tied up to their knees. And we can make them piebald, if that's your pleasure, sir. What of scarlet and yellow, sir? Or perhaps green and violet?"

He reddened.

"I'd take care, mistress," said John Hand, looking up from his cutting. "If we make him angry he may get his brother the knight to come and run us through. He near scared the soul from my body with that, before you came out."

The widow waved him away. "Hush, John." She smiled at William again.

"Brown," he said, defeated. "Plain brown."

"Good then, sir. We should have them done by Thursday, I should think. John's taken your measure? Have you chosen the stuff?"

Thursday afternoon William walked up and down the row for an hour until he saw John Hand go thundering down the street with five or six other journeymen, kicking viciously at a pig bladder. Then he went to get his shoes.

The widow came out. "Pray you wait, while Andrew fetches them." The prentice scurried into the house. They waited. She tapped her foot. He picked his nails. Suddenly she said, "If it's not too bold, sir, where's your home? I can tell a Welshman straightaway, and a Scot, and a Londoner, and a Cornishman. You're of the North, that much I can tell."

"I'm of Yorkshire."

"Hm," she mused. " 'Hasta. Hasta go-ot ma shoon?' " He glared. What right had she to mock his speech? He would go off and leave her with the rotten shoes. That would teach her. She was not even looking at him, but at something beyond, in the street. The journeymen were charging by again, in the opposite direction. "They'd better not knock anything down," she warned, and swung around. "Drew! Andrew! What's keeping you?"

The prentice emerged. "Here they are, mistress."

She looked the shoes over a last time before she handed them to William. They were of a soft leather, redder than the one he had chosen. They had Paul's window cut in them.

"But these aren't mine," he said. "I ordered plain."

"What?" She looked surprised. "But you said you wanted the window."

"But I changed my mind."

Now she looked offended. "I can take them back if you don't like them. I'll find somebody for them."

"No, no. I like them. I shall have them. Only—"

She waited.

"Only doesn't it cost more? I've only brought what you said for the plain."

"That's good enough."

"No, but . . . "

"That's to pay you for the rudeness of my journeyman. Now try the fit."

"Oh," he said, all confused. "Oh, aye."

"Now how do they feel? Wide? Narrow? Short?"

"No. They are very good."

She nodded. "They look well too, even if I say so." She took his money. "Now get you home to your books." And she stepped back into her house. As if she were Dame Magdalen, telling him what to do and when to do it. He went down the high street, watching his shoes. He wished he had yellow hosen, to shine through Paul's window like the sun.

✷ 61

Eskmere
November 1345

In August all the gentle families of Tewisdale had gone northeast to Eskmere to see Eleanor Wydclif marry Hugh Cliderhou. The wedding festivities were not pleasant for Marion. They reminded her of her own wedding, which was not a day she liked to think of, even though she now loved Nicholas well. If Eleanor had looked happy, Marion could have enjoyed the feast better, but Eleanor was not happy, and this was plain to everyone.

Eleanor laughed often, but too loudly and always about the wrong thing. The whole time the ladies were helping her dress to go to church, she kept making nasty jokes about Eskmere, how it was "so rough and ugly it might as well be in some such place as Cumberland or Scotland."

"Daughter!" Dame Edith, her mother, exclaimed, "you must not speak so."

"At least I'm glad to see they've got glass in their windows instead of stretched oiled rags. I shall have a view of their scummy moat and the gray puddle yonder. Is that the Eskmere? Full of salamanders I don't doubt."

Whenever anyone tried to say something good about Hugh, how handsome he was or what a good horseman, Eleanor would shrug. "I suppose it was the best my father could do for me, once he botched a better match." At that Dame Magdalen looked up sharply and said, "Hush, woman. Be wiser!"

"You aren't my mother, Dame Magdalen, are you?" Eleanor replied bitterly, and some of the other ladies whispered, "Such insolence!" But Dame Edith put it down to wedding nerves and chose to ignore it.

But now the wedding was three months past. It was cold November in the season of All Saints and Souls. Lord Ros was calling all his men to Helmsley because of a rumor that the Scots were mustering. "God's death," grunted old Sir Walter Cliderhou, when he had the news from Helmsley. He was sitting at table with his sons and Eleanor, eating midday dinner. "That knockkneed fool calls us to do service whenever he hears an ewe lamb bleat. Some day he'll call me on one of these false alarms and I'll tell him to stick his sword up his arse."

By this time Eleanor should have been used to Cliderhou manners, but she could not overcome her disgust at Sir Walter's speech. Her father would never have spoken of Lord Ros in such a manner, nor would Sir Gervase or any other knight in Tewisdale.

Sir Walter went on. "But men like that lickshit Gervase will go on kissing arse till kingdom come." Sir Walter addressed Eleanor. "That's how your cousin Nicholas got to be Lord Ros' squire, by his father kissing Helmsley arse. By rights, Hugh should have had that service, by God he should." That issue had been settled years ago when Lady Ros requested her husband to dismiss Hugh from his body service, and Sir Walter still boiled over it.

"Well," said Hugh, "since we're going to Helmsley I think I'll keep you by me, wife. I'll not leave my plump partridge as fair game for any passing Scot or tinker who strolls this way while I'm gone." Sir Walter chortled approvingly.

Eleanor swallowed her pride and said, "Since I am going to Helmsley perhaps I might also go see my mother at Wydclif? If you'll give me leave?"

"Maybe, maybe not. We'll see how good you are to me twixt now and then." It was at table, in front of all his kinsmen and servants that her husband addressed her so. There was no lady there to reprove them, for Hugh's mother was two years dead, and his living sisters had been married

256

into other houses. Aside from rare visits from the nearest sister, Eleanor was the only woman of her station in that house.

Eleanor could not read or write, nor could any of her kin at Wydclif, and somehow it never occurred to any of them to send letters through their parsons. Wydclif was too far for easy visiting, and the weather had been foul since October, so Eleanor was utterly alone. Actually there had been one letter, delivered by a man riding to the coast at Whitby. It had been a letter from Marion—Eleanor knew that much by looking at it. She was so desperate that as soon as she got it she crammed it into her sleeve and almost ran with it to the church to have the parson read it for her. But then, pulling it out and looking at it, she was shaken by a sudden fury. Of all the people who could have written, it had to be Marion! She would have none of it. She hurled it down among the rushes by the hearth and walked away.

"Your letter from Kelda," Hugh asked that evening. "What news was there?"

"Nothing. Just my younger brother Geoffrey wishing me well."

Next morning Hugh noticed the letter on the floor. He picked it up and saw that Eleanor had never unsealed it. What the hell? he thought, and then shrugged. "Well, if she doesn't want it, nor do I." And he tossed it into the fire.

After that there were no more letters.

✳ 62

Oxford
January 1346

Agrestis' lamp guttered out. He came out of his study cursing and rubbing his neck. He was wearing his green tabard over his hose, and over that, his red tunic, and over that, his thick grey gown, and over that a woolen cloak. His fingers stuck out of frayed gloves, and he had a scarf wrapped around his head.

"Why do we do this?" he demanded. In the heavy winter cold that lay like a frozen cloak over the city, so that to draw breath was to cough, they had been studying late into the night.

"Be quiet," said Stephen. "Angel, read that again." William and Stephen were huddled under Stephen's blanket. William was reading from the *Sex principia*. Stephen was holding the candle on his knees. From Miles' study came the sound of endless droning mutterings.

"Tell me why we do this? This is the most senseless form of self-torment conceivable. I refuse to participate in it one moment longer." They ignored him, so Agrestis took his lamp downstairs and refilled it. He came back up, refilled it, and crouched again over the *Posteriora analytica*.

After a while he emerged once more and announced, "We'll get our new proctors this Lent."

"Read that again, Angel."

"I hope the election will be tumultuous. We shall see how well or ill Chancellor Northwode can control convocation. I'd bet my life on William Ingestre for junior proctor. What do you think, Clot?" He intruded his head into Miles' sanctuary. The droning continued unbroken.

Agrestis stamped around the room, chafing his hands. "Reflect, my friends, reflect. *Why* are we doing this? Why?"

"I, for one, would prefer not to make a fool of myself at the exercitia tomorrow." Stephen cupped his hand around the candleflame.

"But why *do* exercitia? Why do any of this?" Agrestis ceased stamping and raised a finger toward the ceiling. "What is the life of a student? For four years have I thumbed greasy parchments. For four years have I bruised my arse on splintery benches, listening to pompous doctors rant on and on about dead philosophers. For four years I engage in questions and disputations with pustule covered youths whose very breath reeks of ignorance and stupidity. For what? So that I can in due time present my supplicat to Chancellor Jack and bribe a collection of masters to testify that I have done something these four years other than drink beer. So that I can be called a 'bachelor' and lord it over those same pustule covered youths, as I embark on the even more tortuous quest of my licentiate. And wherefore?"

"Oh, hush, Agrestis. You know you love it."

"And wherefore? So that one day I might make some northern prelate a secretary, inherit his see, march about with a crozier, and eventually sit on the throne of Peter. Wait. I just answered my question."

"I thought we were doing this because we seek Truth," William protested, half jovially.

"Utterly secondary, my friend. The scopos and telos of all academic effort is Personal Ambition."

"That's not so," William insisted. "Look at Master Alexander. Look at Lyra the Welshman. They don't care if they never leave here."

Agrestis went back to his carrel, but before he went he turned and said quietly, "To tell you the truth, Angel, neither do I. I don't care if I never leave Oxford." Purged, he sat down to commune with Aristotle.

But William was troubled in his spirit, and he kept stammering the words he was reading, until Stephen, with an oath, grabbed the book from him. Miles' voice droned on. A wind rattled at the shutters, demanding in, in. Some of it seeped through a crack in the wood and rushed across the room, blowing out Stephen's candle. "Jesus," said William. "I give up." And he went to his own bed, pulled the coverlet over his head, and shivered in the dark.

✳ 63

Oxford
February 1346

The weaver's wife observed her friend Judith from under her brows. That yellow-haired clerc was there again, perching his skinny backside on the kitchen table (as if the shoemaker's widow had room on it to spare), swinging his gangly legs, knocking his heels against the trestle, and talking, talking, talking, until she thought that Judith (by the look of her) was going to brain him with her churnstaff. She could not fathom why Judith did not have John Hand throw the fellow out.

"Do I talk too much?" Finally, he felt the air in the room. Judith was thumping the churn angrily, her back stiffer and pricklier by the second. "Nay, I know I talk too much. That's why I was thrown out of Rievaulx. Nay, that's not so: I was not thrown out; I asked to leave; but it's because of my talking I was sent up to Oxenford at first, to talk as much as I pleased. So you'll pardon me, won't you? It's all those years of being corked up in cloister—waters will flow—so—make me shut my mouth if I talk too much. I'm well used to that. It's my life's tale, is that. But they say all Yorkshiremen talk too much, though I know a good many who—. Aye. Well. Very well. I'll depart. I'm a gabbler, it's true, but I'm no thickwit. I'll be off." He slid down from the table and landed with a thud. He turned surly. What right had this ignorant shopwidow to give him such looks? As if she were Dame Magdalen or somebody.

"Well, farewell then. I'll leave you to your drudgery." He sauntered out, but spoiled it by tripping over nothing at the door.

Judith glared at him, breathing hard. She turned to the weaver's wife with a frenzied grimace and pounded her staff till the churn rattled on the floor.

The weaver's wife burst out laughing.

After his encounter with the widow, William felt ravenously hungry; at dinner he wolfed his meat, dripping the juice down his front and sucking loudly on his fingers. Agrestis and Miles were arguing as usual. William did not hear them. His mind was on the widow and what he would say to her when next they met, to instruct her in the seemly behavior of a low woman toward a man who was a scholar and a gentleman. But then he heard Miles change his voice and say, with a nauseated look, "The way William of Keldacross eats disgusts me."

William looked up, stuffing one side of his mouth with blankmanger.

"William of Keldacross, son of an ancient house, do you know who was my great-grandfather?"

"No, Miles, and I care not."

"My great-grandfather was a miller."

"Good for you, Miles. That is truly blood to boast of."

"Do you know who is my father?"

"The Sire of Coucy? The Duke of Burgundy?"

"No, William. He is a common, if well landed, franklin. Yet unlike you, William of Keldacross, son of an ancient house, I and my brothers and sisters were taught to eat in such a way as not to disgust others. We were taught to wash our hands before the meal, so as not to begrime our bread with blackened fingers. We were taught not to let gobbets of flesh fall into our laps, and not to slurp swinishly into our beer. We were taught to wipe our mouths of grease so as not to sit about glistening like sides of fatted pork. We were taught all these things, William, and my great-grandfather was a miller. I am amazed that such things were not taught at Keldacross. You must have been a sore trial to the brothers at Rievaulx frater. Were they able to hear the holy readings while you were eating?"

William wiped his mouth, glaring. "I was hungry."

Miles shook his head pityingly and turned back to Agrestis. "Your angel, Goodram, has the manners of the barnyard. But perhaps that is simply Yorkshire table custom?"

"Oh, aye," Agrestis replied. "And whenever we see fat pigs like you, we long for Yorkshire bacon!" He rocked back on his bench, guffawing.

For some reason this set everyone off, and the whole table turned uproarious. Uthred the Puler tried to squash Miles' face into the trencher they were sharing, uttering, "Oink, oink, piggy, find thy trough."

Master Alexander had to come and stop the fight.

Helmsley
March 1346

By chance Eleanor and Marion came to visit Helmsley in the same week. Marion came a few days earlier under Dame Magdalen's orders; Eleanor came along with Hugh because he was still taking her with him wherever he went. The night Eleanor arrived, she and Marion shared a bed in one of the castle's odd, small rooms off the twisting stair that climbed the castle keep.

"Marry, I was happy to see you, Eleanor," said Marion ingenuously. They lay in the dark with their noses sticking into the cold air above heavy blankets. "All the ladies here were old, and it was dull before you came. And to think that I came up because it was so dull at Kelda! Dame Magdalen said, 'My girl, you're as cross as a crab. Time for you to take a change of air.' Is it as dull at Eskmere? In York it was never dull. At the minster they used to have plays . . . "

"I know nothing of the minster," Eleanor cut in coldly. "But at Eskmere life is good enough."

"Indeed I'm glad to hear it. I wish I could say the same of . . . "

Eleanor interrupted again. "I think I am with child. Of course I hope to have a son first, and not a daughter, as you did, because a son would please Hugh and put him in better humor."

"Nicholas was never in bad humor over little Magdalen. Sir Gervase was, a little, but Nicholas said it mattered not to him which came first."

"That's my coz for you. Never a man to give a fig for any creature sans feathers or four legs."

"Oh, he likes Maddie well. He doesn't make much over her, but it's plain he cares."

Eleanor lay silent for some time. Eventually Marion judged that she had gone to sleep, so she rolled over to settle herself, tucking the blankets around her.

But then Eleanor murmured in a confidential tone, "Marion, how well do you like my cousin Nicholas?"

Immediately Marion felt uneasy. She pretended to be half asleep. "Mmmm?" she said.

Eleanor jabbed her ribs. "Do you like my coz?"

"Yes, of course I like him."

Eleanor's voice got strangely breathy. "You know what I mean," she wheedled. "Do you *like* him?" She paused. "Need I say more?"

Marion muttered, "Why do you ask me such a question?"

"Heavens, if young married ladies who are friends may not speak their hearts in such matters, who may?"

Marion did not answer. The tension in Eleanor's voice frightened her. Eleanor felt a hot, bitter rage bubble up inside her, but she restrained it because she was so hungry with the desire to *know*.

"It's just that I grew up with my coz," she explained, "and he was always a great boor, caring only about beasts and such. But perhaps he's different now. Tenderer. You know. Do you please him well, do you think?"

Still Marion said nothing, so Eleanor added, "Maybe he's more courteous now that he's lived so long with a great York lady of such gentle breeding."

Marion felt the sting. She grew hot with anger and confusion. Eleanor had always made her uncomfortable, and her jealousy had been plain almost from the outset. But now there was something Marion had not sensed before. She wished she could get out of that bed and go somewhere else to sleep. She said, "I don't know what you want me to say."

"My husband Hugh," said Eleanor. "I have to imagine he is someone else at certain times. Can you guess what I mean?"

"No!" cried Marion. "And I do not want to talk about this. At all. Please, Eleanor."

"Oh, you Yorkisfolk are too delicate for us countrywomen. But who am I to talk to if not you? Do you know *who* I imagine Hugh to be at those times?" Eleanor's whisper sounded frantic.

"I don't want to know!" Marion was equally desperate. "If you need to talk to somebody, talk to your mother! Please! Tell it to your mother!"

After that they both slept fitfully. When Marion awakened, stiff and aching, Eleanor had already risen and gone in search of her brothers Mun and Geoff. She called for Alice to dress her and made her way down the long stair toward the great hall. At the foot of the steps two elderly ladies said, "God bless you this morning, my dear." They were the kindly old aunts of Lord Ros with whom she had spent the last two days. After Eleanor, their company would be refreshing.

But first she wanted to see Nicholas, so she curtsied to the ladies and went on into the hall. She spied Nicholas right away, standing with some other men halfway down the hall by the old central hearth. (This hearth was disused, for Lord Ros had built a fine chimney in the wall, but for some reason the knights liked to stand by it anyway.) Nicholas saw her and beckoned to her, moving a little apart from his friends.

"How dosta?" he said when she reached him.

"Not well. It was dull until Eleanor came, and then when she came it was—stupid."

"Hard to please you these days," Nicholas joked. He took her arm and smiled down into her face. She smiled back faintly. "How was the hunting yesterday?"

"Well enough. We didn't shoot overmuch game, but it was sport anyhow."

"Your cousin Eleanor said stupid things last night."

An odd, uncomfortable look crossed Nicholas' face. Marion frowned at him, and he said, "Eh? What was it? What? What did she say?"

"Asked stupid questions of me, said stupid things."

"Well, pay no heed. She's always been a bit queer."

"She said embarrassing, shameful things about her and Hugh."

"About Hugh? She'd better watch how she blabs."

"I feel sorry for her. She is plainly so unhappy."

"Aye, well." Nicholas detached himself hurriedly. "I'll see you about."

"Won't you stay with me a little while?"

"Na, I've things to do." And he went back to stand about with his friends.

Marion walked away disconsolate. She didn't expect she would see him again all day. She was thrown again upon the company of the dear old dames and their embroidery. She remembered that she had left her needlework bag up in the little bedchamber, so she ran back up to fetch it.

On her way back down the stairs, she encountered Hugh Cliderhou.

"Dame Eleanor up there?" he asked.

"No, sir. She's out riding with her brothers, I think."

"And you not with them?"

"No, they didn't ask me."

"Well, that's lousy."

"I don't mind. I have other company."

Hugh was blocking her way on the stairs, and she did not want to squeeze past him.

"You and Eleanor have a nice gossip? She's been missing her friends of Tewisdale?"

"It was good to see Eleanor." Marion made a motion to show that she wanted to go down. Hugh held out his hand to help her step around him. She did not want the help, but she did not know how to refuse it without giving offense. As she passed, he squeezed against her unnecessarily.

At that moment a door crashed open on a level above them, and Lord Ros himself came striding down the stair, followed by a panting steward and two huge dogs. Hugh and Marion stood against the wall to make room for him, but he took them in with a sharp glance and stopped on the step above them.

He addressed Marion. "This man bothering you?" The lord asked the question in a light tone and a wink at Hugh, but one could not be too watchful when it came to the reputations of the wives and wards of vassals. Blood feuds had erupted at his own table over matters as small as one knight touching another man's wife alone in a stairwell. Besides, he noticed that Marion looked uncomfortable.

"Just passing a word with the lady," said Hugh.

Lord Ros looked at him sharply. Hugh had grown up under Helmsley roof and had never been known for his courtesy with women. The lord offered Marion his arm and said, "Come down to the hall with us." Hugh remained on the stair.

Reaching the hall, Lord Ros took her directly to her husband. He barked, "When you bring your lady to Helmsley, Nicholas, you make good and certain that she's properly attended. And explain to her what could happen if she isn't." With that, Lord Ros strode away down the hall, his steward and his dogs still panting behind him.

Nicholas stood among his friends, pale and mortified. The other knights looked away politely and began to talk loudly among themselves.

Nicholas gripped Marion's elbow and steered her behind one of the screens beside the great chimney.

"What's the lord talking about? What in hell were you doing?"

"Nothing! Hugh of Eskmere was talking to me on the stair, that's all."

"Alone? Just him and you?"

"I had gone up to get my embroidery bag, and he was coming up to look for Eleanor."

"God's Death!" Nicholas exploded. "Holy Rood!" He was so violent that Marion jumped. He folded his arms, looking away from her and breathing loudly through his nose.

"Jesus Mary! What terrible thing have I done that you should speak so angrily with me?"

"Look," he answered. "Just do as I say. If you want something, tell a maid to fetch it for you. And never go loitering about this place by yourself, chattering to men."

"I did not 'loiter' and I did not 'chatter' to Hugh Cliderhou or any other man. You make it sound like a case for the York Assizes!"

"Do as I say. Stay with the women, and you will not create these problems."

"Problems?" Marion was incensed. "I want to go home."

"Do it. Have Alice pack you up and ride back to Kelda. You serve no purpose here."

Marion's chin shook with anger more than hurt. She glared at him.

"Oh, Holy Rood, Mother of God," he muttered.

Marion said nothing.

"Listen, I am only looking after your honor."

"You do not care for my stupid honor," she said, too loudly. Some of the knights looked toward the screen.

"For God's sake!" Nicholas whispered.

Marion lowered her voice. "All you care about is how you look in front of your friends. I don't want to go 'home' to Keldacross. I want to go home, to York. You said more than once you'd take me there if I asked you."

"You know I can't take you anywhere now. I'm with Lord Ros."

"Well, then, will you send me there? I want to stay until after Easter."

Nicholas was quiet for a moment. He unfolded his arms, clasped his right hand over his left, and cracked a knuckle. Then he said in a stiff voice, "Easter?"

"Yes. I want to spend Lent and Easter with my father."

It was plain that he did not want her away for that long, but he would die before he would say so.

"If by chance you want to see me, who am so useless and troublesome and without sense, then you can come to York—if it would not dishonor you to walk on city cobbles."

"Do what you like," said Nicholas. He walked away from her, without a nod, back to his friends.

Next morning early Marion set off for York with a borrowed manservant and Alice exulting loudly under the sun.

From the first moment in Goodramgate their visit was perfect bliss. Good Adam Scawe saw them first as they clattered into the close, and he ran out, wreathed in smiles.

"Master, master!" he called back over his shoulder, up into the house. "Look who's here!"

Andrew put his head out the window, and so did half the other people in the close.

"My daughter!" Andrew cried, flustered and delighted. "My nestling, my daughter!" And Mistress Alison came hurrying out the door with hands outstretched.

✳ 65

Oxford
March 1346

On the morning of the second Friday in Lent Agrestis said, "I have read all the books for my course. I have shone in every exercise I ever took part in, and I have heard more lectures than I care to think of." So he went to Chancellor Jack (as he alone called John Northwode) and presented himself for determination as a bachelor of arts. He did not need to "bribe" the necessary four masters to stand up with him. They did it most willingly, for they agreed with Master Alexander that if he was a loud, arrogant, and occasionally violent youth, he was a brilliant one and devoted to learning.

"The man spends half his time at the Prelate, choosing quarrels and consuming rivers of beer." Stephen shook his head at William. "How could he have passed anything but water?"

"I do not need," Agrestis told him, "to labor over a page for hours on end in order to comprehend it, as do the rest of you. That is the answer. I am not like Miles the Ockhamist, who squints at three lines of English as if it were some subtlety of Averroës."

Miles responded, "Through many hours of study, Agrestis, I have weakened my eyes. That is why I squint. But you, of course, never needed to study. You read something once, and immediately it is illumined for you. The Holy Ghost, I'm sure, is your obedient servant."

"No. Just a *dulcis hospes animae*, a sweet guest of the soul."

Miles chanted, "*Sine tuo nomine nihil est in homine; nihil est innoxium*, Without you, there is nothing harmless in man." Well, Agrestis, you are certainly noxious to me and to many others. So perhaps you ought to make a greater effort to discern between good and evil spirits."

"My spirits are too high today to allow me to dispute with you, Miles." Agrestis grabbed Wilfrid's Boethius out of William's arms and set it on his head. He did some sort of bounding harvest dance all around the hall. The book remained balanced for an amazingly long time. Then it crashed to the floor. William ran to get it before Agrestis could desecrate it again.

"Is that the proper behavior of one on whom has been conferred the right to teach any book in the faculty of arts?" Stephen inquired, "and who now seeks admittance at Merton college gate?"

Agrestis replied, "Let us go and debauch ourselves."

"How shall we accomplish this?"

"In gluttony and strong drink, of course, at the Puking Prelate."

William said, "I have no wish to partake of the masses of decayed matter that the Puking Prelate calls food."

Agrestis rushed over and throttled him. "No! No! How many times must I tell you? Quality is of no account. It is Quantity we desire. Great, vast, unlimited Quantity. Quantity abundant, unbounded, infinite, over-flowing."

"Perhaps so." William freed himself. "But Alexander is lecturing on the *Topics* in half an hour, and I wish to hear him."

"Disregard Alexander. I will teach you all you need to know."

Since the statutes of Merton declared that no one who was not "chaste, well conducted, peaceable, or humble" should be admitted to a scholarship there, no one could conceive how Agrestis had managed it. But on the Wednesday before Maundy Thursday Agrestis had the news.

"I'm chaste," he maintained, when Miles confronted him with this contradiction. "Have you ever known me to be unchaste? As for the rest, I have a year's trial, as do all the others, to temper my faults. For the sake of Merton, even I can do that."

But he was sad to leave Chimney Hall. On the morning he left it he embraced all of them, even Miles. He kissed William and said, "Hurry and be determined, Angel. If I don't see you at Merton Easter after next I shall come and beat you with a stick." He rubbed his eyes on his sleeve. "And if I find you've let Miles take my carrel I'll kill you with a mace." He slung his bag of books over his shoulder and tucked his roll of clothes under his arm. William carried his lamp and his little coffer, and Stephen his iron candlestick, and they went over with him to Merton.

They met Warden Treng in the Mob quadrangle. He welcomed Agrestis and greeted William. "Henry Wyly's nephew, yes?"

"No, sir, Roger de Wherne's."

"Ah yes. I've kept my eye on you," said the warden. He had not.

A week later, Agrestis was back to visit Chimney, complaining humorously about Merton. He sat himself at one of the trestle tables in the hall and gorged himself on Uthred's trencher as if he had never abandoned them.

"We have these horrifying 'scrutinies' three times a year. Scrutinies. Mother of God. Everyone rises up and condemns everyone else. You ought to see these two fellows in particular: solemn doctors of divinity. They have some terrible quarrel that John Wyliot tells me has thrived for seven years. He said it began as an argument in philosophy but quickly degenerated from discordia into rancor. I swear to you, friends, these two masters of Merton make Miles and me look like David and Jonathan. Roll your eyes if you like, Angel, it's true. An example. Last scrutiny, one accused the other of theft; the other countered with a charge of sodomy. It's not to be believed!"

"Were you accused?"

"Oh yes. Of 'making a tumult in the chambers.' Rood! If a man cannot lift his voice in the fervor of an argument once in a while, why live? Besides, I could accuse Master John Wyliot of 'making a tumult in the chambers' with his loud snorings, if I chose, but I chose not. These senior fellows are so petty it's *not* to be believed."

"What punishment did they mete out to you for your tumults?"

"I was sconced for a keg of beer. I swear, these seniors convene at night to plot trivial accusations against the rest of us, so that they can make us pay for their bibulosity. Was this the school that fostered Duns Scotus? I am sore disappointed in it."

"Perhaps," said Miles sarcastically, "you can infuse it with new greatness."

Agrestis sighed. "I hope so."

✳ 66

Kelda; York; Oxford
April 1346

Holy Thursday

St Godrich's church was naked, the altar stripped and God's house bare, His Body taken from its place, the image upon the roodscreen shrouded in black linen.

Oswin spoke to the villeins simply and without eloquence. "Tonight he has washed his friends' feet and shared with them his body and his blood. But then he's been taken away to be beaten worse than any man here would think to beat his ox. And his friends they have all run away. And in the morning he will bear a splintered log upon his back like an ass withouten cover nor blanket for his poor raw back. Tomorrow they will spit in his face and drive iron through his feet and his hands. And all this he has suffered for love of you. In nomine Patris et Filii et Spiritus Sancti, amen."

Godrich's well must be covered tonight, for tomorrow God does not show his face. Oswin stumped out under the yew, and Win helped him roll the heavy lid on its side and lift it over the well's mouth. Deep are the waters below the earth. What mortal flesh has seen their foundation?

Good Friday

At Holy Trinity in Goodramgate an itinerant Franciscan friar preached to the assembled wool merchants and their households. He stood in a rough patched gown and bare feet. He was determined to shake the complacency of the wealthy burghers, and he preached in a loud voice designed to stir them into wakefulness at least for a moment.

"Rich masters! See the gorgeous glass you have bought to honor the house of the King of Bliss? See your windows cast their colors on the floor. Just so, you cast your garlands on the ground when Christ rode through this goodly city Palm Sunday last. But tell me, rich masters, where now is your King of Bliss? Run to your minister and see if he is there, enthroned at the high altar, robed in riches and offering sacrifice with your great archbishop. What? You do not see him there? Then where will you find the King who rode among your waving palm branches?

"Masters, I will tell you where to look. Take yourself over to Pavement, where you whip your petty miscreants. Go down Ousegate to Ousebridge End. Do you see the prisonhouse where your felons sit in darkness and in the shadow of death?"

Andrew Comyn played with his sleeves and looked sideways at Matthew Whewell, annoyed by the friar's tone. Mistress Alison dabbed her nose with her handkerchief. Marion, her knuckles white, kept her eyes fixed on the preacher.

"Hasten to Micklegate Bar," the friar continued, "and go outside the city walls, pious masters. See there, on the crossroads? A gibbet."

The preacher continued after a silence. "See how the Scapegoat hangs between heaven and earth in the extremity of pain and in the coldest reaches of darkness and abandonment. Oh, no, you say, that cannot be the King of Bliss. But how should you know his face when *you* have so sorely disfigured it?"

Over their cold turnip soup that evening, Andrew agreed with Alison that the friar had preached "well enough." "But," he said, "I disliked that he addressed us as if we were a pack of hypocrites. Because a man is rich does not mean he is to blame for all the ill done in the world."

Marion did not understand exactly how she was guilty, but she knew it was so. The image of the man twisting on the gibbet stuck in her mind, and she could not swallow her soup. The low sun gleamed in at her father's windows and shone on the bowls and mazers ranged upon his chests, but to her the room seemed dim, as if a mist had settled there, blotting out the light. Horror and grief engulfed her. "Father, will you excuse me?" she asked. "I am weary and would like to lie down."

"Of course, my dear," Andrew replied. He watched her tenderly as she rose. She gathered her skirts about her and turned her face to hide that she was crying. "She's a good child, my nestling," Andrew remarked to Alison when Marion had gone upstairs. "She's become a great lady."

Privately Alison thought the girl lacked the commonsense necessary to be the "great lady" of any household, but she said from her heart, "She's a good girl. She has a loving soul."

"God reward her," said Andrew. His mind wandered to little Magdalen and to the grandsons who would be born at Keldacross. They would come to visit him, and he would walk supported on their knightly arms before all the merchants of the Staple.

Holy Saturday

Stephen, Miles, and Uthred had gone to Tenebrae prayers at Merton chapel with Master Alexander, but William had not chosen to join them. He found himself wandering aimlessly around Oxford. He felt an emptiness inside him and wanted to be alone. The sounds in the streets seemed muted today; students and shopkeepers moved about quietly as if some silent doom brooded in the air.

In the shadow of Balliol gate an ugly man was squatting. His clothes were caked with months of filth; his eyes were yellowed, mad. William had seen him often enough; he was one of Oxford's Beggars Regular, as Agrestis called them. Some said he was a scholar who had driven himself crazy with theology, because he was always muttering what sounded like angry profanities in Latin. But when you listened closely you heard it was only gibberish, mere imitation of sounds he had heard on the steps of the churches and colleges where he crouched, ate, and slept. William walked

270

a little arch out onto the street in order to avoid him. The man stuck out thick, blackened hands. The fingernails were brown and cracked, broken from top to bottom. He looked up sideways. William said, "I have nothing to give you" and quickened his pace. Tenebrae, thought William unaccountably. Shadows.

He found himself in front of the Welsh Austinfriars' house. He noticed for the first time that the iron hinges on the door were shaped like dragons. Just then the door opened and Cyan the Harp came out in his white rochet. He was carrying what looked like wrapped loaves under his arms. He smiled at William and said, "Benedicite."

"Benedicite," William repeated vaguely.

"You look forlorn. Do you want to come in? I'm about to go out, but I'll ask our prior if you may join us for prayer. Your friend Brother Iago is addressing us in sermone."

William hesitated. He was reluctant to relinquish his solitude but curious to hear how Lyra would preach.

"Come wait in the hall. No, on second thought, go right into the chapel. I'm sure you'll be welcome." Hoisting his loaves more securely in his arms, Cyan smiled again and went out the dragon door into the street.

As William entered the little, dim chapel, Lyra was just standing up to be blessed by his prior. The Austinfriars sat in plain stalls across from one another, their heads inclined attentively. William took the backmost empty place. He tried to be inconspicuous, but he knocked into the misericorde seat as he entered the stall, and it came down with a noise. Except for the man nearest, no one turned his head. Lyra was looking into himself, collecting his words, and took no notice.

He spoke in his quiet, Welsh-touched Latin, but the familiar asperity was absent. A true Augustinian, he preached in the manner of the saint they loved. He began by considering the words of the prophet Isaias:

"Qui credidit auditui nostro? Et brachium Domini cui revelatum est? Who can believe what we have heard; and to whom has your power been revealed? Help me, Lord, for I do not understand. Infinity encased in finite flesh and conquered? Unquenchable Light consigned to Uttermost Darkness. It is of this day that we affirm, 'He descended into hell.' How may this be explained to the satisfaction of a questioning mind?

"Yet Augustine says, 'What good would our life have been to us had you not come as our Redeemer?' And he says, 'It availed us nothing to be born unless we are to be redeemed.' Remembering that we are dust, Lord, you became dust that you might share our finitude. But how could you share our condition more completely than you have shared it from before the beginning, since before the beginning you are 'closer to us than we are to ourselves'? Who can believe what we have heard? And how can this mystery be explained?"

As William was walking back to Chimney he saw the ugly beggar again, chewing on one of Cyan's loaves. As William passed, the man held out a torn, grimy chunk in William's direction. He made mumblings with his lips. William flinched away. "No," he told the man. "No, I thank you." He as good as ran from there, hitching up his scholar's gown so as not to stumble on it.

✳ 67

York
April 1346

At midnight in York the changes of Easter were ringing. Marion heard the first bells far away from a church in another street: St Denys' perhaps, or St Margaret's in Walmgate across town. Next the deep voice of St Mary's Abbey without-the-walls, and then, close by in Goodramgate, an answer from Holy Trinity itself.

This is the night.
This is the night when first you saved our fathers.
You freed the children of Israel from their slavery
And led them dryshod through the sea.

Now finally the Minster boomed its exultation to the clamoring air, and the great city shook in its foundations. Alison and Master Comyn awoke, sleepily wished each other the joy of Easter, then slept again. Marion, alone in her childhood room, lay sleepless on her bed.

Easter in York! The bells boomed like the deeps calling to the deeps, and the high bells like the stars who sang together when first the world was made.

This is the night
When the pillar of fire
Destroyed the darkness of sin.

In the darkness of the abbeys they had lit the Easter fires, and in the firelight they had blessed the fires and the candles and the waters, and they had proclaimed the great Exultet:

O happy fault,
O necessary sin of Adam,
Which gained for us such and so great a Redeemer.

Marion pulled the covers over her head and pressed her face down into her pillow in profundity of joy. "I will die!" she thought. "I will die!"

This is the night
Of which Scripture says,
"The Night will be as clear as Day."

Shortly after dawn Marion bundled up and took Alice to meet Cis at her husband's house so that they could go together to see the great Easter candle at the minster. A small, cold wind was playing about the houses, but the three young women did not feel the chill. They hurried along, clutching one another's elbows.

"BEEF WITH MY ONIONS TONIGHT!" somebody bellowed from a casement above them. They could not see who it was, for they were under the overhanging gable, but Alice shouted back: "NO MORE COD, FOR GOD IS RISEN!" And whoever it was howled with laughter: "AMEN!"

Behind them in the street some artisans of St Saviourgate emerged from around the corner, making a procession toward the cathedral and singing *Dic nobis Maria* through their noses.

"Let's hurry!" said Marion. She wanted to have time in the minster before it filled with people.

The minster was a solemn place this early morning. The new paschal candle burned palely under the grey heights, and the cathedral canons glided about noiselessly. But it was a different silence from the terrible one that had reigned during the last three days. As the women stood together in the south aisle, one of the canons stepped out from a little door near them, carrying over his left arm a thickness of black and purple velvets. It was Roger de Wherne. He did not know them, but he smiled cordially and said, "Christ is risen, young women!" "He is indeed," they replied, smiling back, and Roger went away to put aside the minster's mourning clothes, until the season of dust and ashes should roll round again.

"Cis," said Marion, "what was that old rhyme we used to say when we were little, that Parson John taught us, about the hall in the forest all covered in pall?"

"I don't know, Marion."

"You must remember, Cis; we sang it all the time."

Cecily smiled wistfully. "Our maidenhood seems so long ago now."

"Not to me, Cis, when I'm here in York," Marion poked Cis in the stomach, "even if you are an old doe rabbit with three bairns already."

The artisans from Saviourgate came in. They had collected several more worshipers, and all of them were singing tunelessly and loudly, "Tell us, Mary, what did you see on the road?"

"She saw our Savior," joked Alice, "running away from your godawful noise."

On Easter Wednesday Marion went to see Cis again. She would soon have to leave York for Keldacross.

"I wish I were you, Cis," she said, her lips trembling. Here was Cis, married to a middling prosperous young stapler with bad teeth but a kindly disposition. Cis bustled, perfectly happy, about her house and back and forth to her mother's and up and down the lanes doing kindnesses for old people. Her domain was peaceable, small, manageable. And it was in York.

"Don't be silly, Marion!" Cis sounded practical, like Mistress Alison. "Just count your blessings. Why, from what you say Sir Nicholas is a courteous man, and he certainly *looks* well (I remember him from your wedding—*don't* think I didn't notice). What if you were Agnes, married to that gruel-slurping old stick in Petergate who'll hardly let her out of his sight for fear that she'll betray him? Come, let's go back to your stepmother's. I want to return a dish I borrowed from her."

Before they reached the close, Adam Scawe met them in Goodramgate, a silly smile on his face. "I was just sent to fetch you at Mistress Cecily's, lady," he told Marion. "There's a visitor for you."

"Who, Adam?" She had a sinking feeling.

"Dame Marion, come and see."

Marion and Cis entered the little close and then the big front room of Andrew's house. Andrew was sitting in the high backed inglenook bench facing them. The visitor sat on the opposite bench, concealed. "Ah, daughter!" Andrew rose to his feet, jovial. "Here's a gentleman suing for your hand! I don't know. Should I let him have it?" Of course it was Nicholas. He stood up to greet her, smiling, but she was so distressed that she did not notice how he looked.

"Oh, sir! Please will you let me stay a few more days, for I am not yet ready to go back to Kelda."

Nicholas' smile faded. Andrew intervened. "Sir Nicholas and I have just agreed that it would be pleasant for him to stay with us a day or two."

Andrew had been worrying about Marion's coming to them so suddenly and staying with them so long, and he was relieved to see the good will his son-in-law bore his daughter. He was also relieved that Marion's entrance had unburdened him of the task of trying to make conversation with Nicholas by himself. When asked about his father, mother, and Keldacross flocks, Nicholas had replied only, "They're well," and looked at the fire and cracked his knuckles. At last Andrew had asked in consternation, "Is there anything wrong, Sir Nicholas?" "No," Nicholas had replied, and gone on cracking his knuckles.

Now, looking at Marion's face, Andrew's fears revived. "A little honey-eyed wine by the fire will do them good," he thought to himself, and Alison went upstairs to direct the servants in making up the master chamber with the finest linens and cushions. Cis stayed as long as was decent, and then returned Mistress Alison's dish and took her leave. Andrew bade Adam Scawe to set the wine by the fire, and then he too left the room. But still Marion and Nicholas had nothing to say to each other.

"Well," said Nicholas to Marion after an unbearable silence. "Your mare has missed you."

"My mare!"

"Aye, Geoff's taken on all her exercising."

The silence grew heavy again. Marion did not know what to say. Her mare?

Desperate, Nicholas astonished himself. "Wife," he blurted, "what do you want me to do, moon and warble French songs at you, like Geoff?"

"St Peter and St William!" Marion cried. "God forbid!" And then she began to giggle. She laughed so hard that tears came to her eyes. When she had wiped them and looked again at Nicholas, she saw that he was grinning at her delightedly. She had forgotten how sweet were his rare, wide grins.

"C'est bien," he said, and although she knew no French she could tell by the sound of it that it was very poor. "Because je pense que mon French is even plus mal que Geoff's."

Knowing the cost to him of a joke against himself, Marion came toward him. "Sir Nicholas, I cannot reach you past these long legs you have stretched halfway across the room."

He stood up. "It's been a longish Lent," he confessed.

"Well, be of good cheer," said Marion, reaching up to pat his shoulder. "Beef with your onions for supper tonight."

"What say you?"

"No more cod," she explained, giggling again, "for God is risen."

"Aye," said Nicholas, still puzzled but smiling. "So he is."

"Well then," said Marion, and managed to kiss and hug him twice before Adam Scawe came in with a discreet face, bringing more wine.

275

Those two days in York, Nicholas let Marion lead him around. They went the whole circuit of the city wall and inspected all the bars; afterward he spoke admiringly of the fortifications to Andrew, who was gratified. The next morning he went with Marion to see Agnes, whose churlish husband was barely civil, but Nicholas concealed his distaste, and was cordial.

At the end of their visit in Petergate, Agnes drew Marion not very subtly aside. "You fool!" she hissed. "Never let me hear *you* gripe about husbands again!"

"Agnes!" Marion was ashamed.

Agnes turned and curtseyed, smiling, to Nicholas, keeping her eyes on his face a moment or two longer than necessary. He nodded to her, thinking uncomfortably that she reminded him of Eleanor. She had the same butter colored hair and small, tight mouth, and something, he thought, of the same manner.

But Marion thought, It is lovely having him here in York. She wished they could stay here always, and never go back to the moors, nor to Helmsley, that cold, hard place.

✳ 68

Keldacross
July 1346

When Dame Magdalen saw that Gervase was going to talk about Bannockburn again, she got up and went to attend to something in the buttery.

"Aye, I remember," Gervase mused, stretching his legs out to the fire. Marion settled down beside him, to spin. "As if it were yesterday."

"Yesterday," Sir Ralph echoed.

"Ralph and I were squires, younger than young Geoff here. When Scarface joined King Edward's host, we followed him."

"I have heard," said Marion, "that it was the greatest host ever seen in England."

"Jesu! It is so. We were in the hundreds of thousands. There is no earthly way the Scots could have defeated us. They had mustered the forces of hell, I am certain."

Sir Ralph nodded. "No earthly way."

"In front of our lines was a cursed bog; beyond that a hillock, where the Bruce had drawn up his petty force. They dug pits before them and covered 'em with branches and leaves. Traps for the chivalry."

Nicholas came in with Rab and, noting the matter of their talk, strode away to the far corner of the room. He could not understand why his father would dwell on such a shameful defeat. He told Geoff to fetch the backgammon board.

"The signal was given; the king ordered us forward. I'll never forget the terror of it, lass, and you know I'm no shirker. The mount in front of me—I remember watching him sink into the bog, deeper and deeper with every step, weighed down with mail and rider. Mounts and men all around me, sinking, clamoring, clambering, floundering. Banners and shields trodden in the mud, and all under a hornet's hail of arrows and stones and spears. And Bannockburn was my first battle."

"Mine too," said Sir Ralph.

"Ralph made it up the hill. I didn't."

"I wished I hadn't."

"For when they made the charge, they fell into the trap pits and lay there, all jumbled."

"Only God's grace saved me, Gervie."

"And then a wave of Scots crashed down over the hill, cutting left and right with axes and swords. We were slaughtered in the thousands. Edward turned craven and fled. In that one day he undid all Langshank's work in taming the Scots."

"Puling bastard got what he deserved," Sir Ralph growled.

Marion looked up from her spinning. "Why? What did he get?"

The two knights glanced at each other. "Er. You don't want to hear it."

Nicholas called across the room, "No she does not. And don't tell her."

So then she must hear it. "Yes! Tell me."

Rab looked up from the backgammon game. "Surely, Dame Marion, you have heard of Queen Isabella and Roger Mortimer?" The gruesome look on his face made her think she did not want to hear it after all, but it was too late. "They were lovers and hated her husband the king. So they made him prisoner and had him tortured to death with a red hot iron. Know how they did it?"

"Rab," Nicholas warned.

"Stuck it up his . . ."

"Rab!" Nicholas shot up, knocking back his stool. "Shut up!"

"Ho! ho! ho!" Rab slapped his knee.

"Hard to believe," mused Gervase, "that our present Edward is son to that puling bugger and that she-demon from hell."

"Aye, *this* Edward's a true knight. Remember Halidon Hill?"

But Marion heard screams in her head, echoing against stone, and saw a fire burning.

She did not understand how people could even think of doing such things.

"Ah, Halidon's a different story altogether."

So now Nicholas joined them. "Do you remember, son?" smiled Gervase. "How we went down to Helmsley after Halidon Hill? You were a little colt at the time."

Nicholas nodded. The only thing he remembered from that visit was a horrible dwarf with a broad, flat nose and no lips, no taller than he was, leering at him and shaking a bladder in his face. This was apparently intended to amuse him. Nicholas had fled behind Dame Magdalen, weeping. All the ladies had laughed. Nicholas did not relate this.

"Aye, we turned the tables on the Scots then, all right," Gervase went on. "Two hills. Between us, a treacherous fen. Scots charged down into the fen and were picked off by our archers. Not one of 'em ever reached us for hand to hand."

Sir Ralph grumbled. "I was hankering to cleave a Scot."

"Ah, you've done plenty of Scot cleaving in your day, friend." Gervase patted him fondly. "I'll never forget the fight at Drumm Tor. Don't know how many notches you put in your sword that day."

"Drumm Tor?" Marion's lips were dry. "The Scots came all the way to Drumm Tor?"

"They damn well did."

"Did they—come to Keldacross?"

"They would have done, but we stopped 'em, eh, Ralph?" Gervase leapt up and paced around his chair. His hand itched.

Nicholas said, "I remember my mother setting the archers on the wall, preparing the fires, boiling the kettles. I remember her taking me by the hand, and my brother, and Katharine following, and we went up Old Keep and she put us in the sickroom and made Katharine bar the door from within. I remember Katharine and me crowding the window to see, and Katharine was wroth because she wanted to be up on the wall with the archers."

Sir Ralph chortled.

"And what was William doing?" Marion wanted to know.

"Sitting on the floor, singing."

Everybody chuckled.

Then Marion thought, If the Scots come down again and I am lady of Keldacross, I must be like Dame Magdalen. It was impossible.

✳ 69

Oxford
August 1346

The boy sat on her table again, as if she had nothing else to set on it, swinging his legs and gabbling on senselessly like a baby. She wondered how long she could stand it. She wondered what her husband Richard would have done if he had known she was going to allow a scavenger clerc to perch on his table, by his hearth, drinking cider out of his cup. She cleaned a lyngfish, savagely.

"Holy Mary it's warm, isn't it, widow? I was just coming down Kibald twychen when I met my friend Agrestis, and he was cursing like a ship-man. 'What's amiss, good Agrestis,' say I. 'Wherefore do you increase the stench of the streets with your blasphemies?' Says he, 'It is the weather; I cannot bear it.' 'By the Paraclete,' say I, 'in winter you rail ceaselessly against the cold; in the summer against the sun. It cannot always be May.' And he says, 'If August made not my clothes stick to my body I would not object to it.' So I say, 'Marry, friend, throw off your gown if you are so miserable.' And he says he cannot, because he is already naked under-neath. And sure enough, I look down, and there are bare calves sticking out below, white, with red hairs on them. God, how I laughed. And then we went down to the Puking Prelate and . . . "

But she could stand no more. She threw down the fish. It landed with a cold, greasy flop in the wooden bowl. She wiped her hands roughly, twisting them in her long apron. She fixed him with her green stare.

"And we—we drank beer," William finished lamely, "and then we went back to our rooms and studied." He got down from the table. She turned back to her lyngfish.

He did not go away. He sat on a stool and leaned his elbows on the table, watching her hands. "Those shoes you made me have worn well."

"I am happy for it."

"They are well made."

"Aye. Some thought I couldn't do as well as my dead man, but they

279

didn't know I used to do half his work for him when he was alive. He was sick before he died," she added, "for a long time."

"I think it must be hard for you, being a widow."

She jabbed the fish and said in a hard voice, "What makes you say that?"

"All the work. You must see to the shop, and make your wares, and see to the journeyman and the prentice, and keep your house and your bairns and all that. You must be master and mistress both. It must be hard."

"Tha thinkst so, dostha?" she imitated him.

"Aye, so I do. You ought to marry again soon, for your husband is dead now almost two years. It is not good for women to remain unmarried, unless they be nuns."

She dumped the bowl of fish guts into the swill bucket for her pig. "Tha knowest what's good for me, dostha?"

He glowered. He hated it when she mocked his speech.

She glared back, sea green. "You men are always hopping to tell us what's best for us. Well, let me tell you, lad. Hear it from the horse's mouth. Or the mare's. What's good for me and what's a trouble to me or a joy or a care, you, clerc, know not from Adam or Eve. So say me no more sermons. You know naught about it." His injured expression enraged her. "Get you gone. Go home to your Master Aristotle and vex me no more."

He slouched away, but she called him back. "I have more to say."

He could not fathom why he was standing here in a shoemaker's house, letting himself be chided.

"You men always tell us what to do, and clercs most of all, who know least. Clercs! Running over the whole town babbling about God knows what. Morum snorum quiddidisti sauciae pauciae."

"What?"

"It's all swillum in the pot, isn't it? Tell me, lad, have you ever thought on how God did not make himself into one of your masters of arts or one of your great doctors at the university?"

"There was no university in those days, widow," William instructed her patiently. "That was in olden days, before there was even a town of Oxenford."

"Don't talk to me as if I were a simpleton! Let me mind you of something. It was no scholar, but a lad far humbler than you, standing there in that temple-church, feeding those doctors their meat. And if I remember right, that lad was none too pleased with those same wisebeards when he was grown. Do you know what hell is full of, Master Clerc? It's full of tonsures and chasubles and mitres and scholars' gowns."

He stood there smarting. It seemed that whatever he did someone must despise him for it. "What you say is doubtless true, woman," he retorted, "but I am certain we shall see plenty of aprons there, too, and spurs and spindles and ploughs."

"Do you reckon on going there to see it?"

William sighed heavily. "Libera me."

"That much Latin I know, clerc. And if you want to be libera'd from me, there's the door. You have only to walk out and go back where you came from."

He did so.

She tossed a fish head to her cat, told her eldest to change the baby's drawers, and went out to help John Hand in the shop.

✳ 70

Keldacross and Durham
October 1346

"Ha HA, ha HA!" Sir Ralph was still gleeful over the news they'd had from France two months before. He drew back the string of an imaginary longbow. "Fffft—thunk! That will teach that slug eating Philip to mess with a real king. Won't it, Gervie? That'll teach frog sucking Philip to mess with us goddams! What say?"

"I wish to hell we could have been there." Gervase shook his head. " 'How did you fare in the French wars, Grandsire? Where is the sword you wielded at Crecy?' 'Grandson, I did not fight at Crecy. I sat on my arse at home, waiting for the shitten Scots.' Christ."

"I think it could not have been so very great a battle," Nicholas brooded. "They let the bowmen do all the work for them. What's noble about that?"

Next week, he and Rab and Edmund rode west with Godfrey Scarface to Ripon, for Scarface had some prayers to make there to St Wilfrid. His sword arm was giving him trouble. Ever since winter the elbow had been stiff; sometimes he could not unbend it for an hour.

Two days later Nicholas and Rab were charging back into Keldacross courtyard, spattering Cuth Constable with brown ooze and sending Thomas Reeve leaping out of the way. Old Tooth ran out barking; chickens scattered. The young men flung off their horses and splashed through the rain into the hall.

"Father! Father!" Nicholas shouted. Rab came after him, bellowing, "Father!"

Gib Faulkoner stood up, tall and reedy, with a Norway hawk on his arm. "What news?"

"You haven't heard? Where's my father?"

"Heard what? Down at St Godrich's. Heard what, Sir?"

Nicholas and Rab rushed out of the hall again and splashed back across the courtyard, through the gate, and down the hill. Their fathers were standing with Dame Magdalen and Marion and Oswin priest on Godrich's porch.

"I daresay we could make the windows five feet higher or more," Gervase was saying, "without lifting the roof. But hell, why not lift the roof? It's too damned low anyway; you feel your prayers don't get up any higher than the crown of your hat. Remember that lierne vaulting we saw down in Lincoln last summer, Ralph? Why the hell not?"

"Why not build you a cathedral and make your Oxenford son a bishop? Hell."

Oswin priest thought, If he raises the roof, where shall mass be heard while they're building? And he wondered too about the fire-eyed seraphs, and if they would suffer being pulled down for lierne ribs. He tried to say something, but he was too afraid of Sir Gervase.

The two young knights crashed into the churchyard. "Father!" Nicholas shouted. "Evil news!" But his face was aglow.

Rab exulted, "Base villainy!" His eyes glittered.

"What's this?"

"You haven't heard? No one's come before us?"

"We rode as fast as we could. You must get to Lord Ros as quick as you can!"

"Scots! King David's marching!"

"The whole chivalry of the north is called! Archbishop Zouche has ridden out of York!"

The falconer and Cuth Constable had run down to hear. The villagers were straggling into the yard, wide eyed, murmuring.

"Cuthbert!" Gervase barked. "Ride over to Tunnersgil. Tell them to make ready."

"Good!" cried Nicholas. "Rab and I will ride back to Helmsley." And the two of them bounded away.

"Have you been by Wydclif?" Gervase shouted after them.

Nicholas nodded over his shoulder, aye, and waved.

The others rushed up to the house. Marion stayed with Oswin priest. Oswin looked at the sky for a moment and scratched his heavy jaw. Then he stumped into the dimness of the church and peered up at the seraphim.

"See them?" he asked Marion. "Maybe now the knight will forget about lifting the roof. They ought not to be pulled down, those angels."

"Nicholas," said Marion. "He said me not a word."

In the panic of being unhorsed and in the terror of lying in the trampled grass, weighed down by mail and tangled in weapons, while huge legs and hooves churned around him and a man approached with a knife, Nicholas had one clear thought and it was very long and calm and loud; he was unsure whether he had spoken it. The thought was, Now they'll think I can't even sit a horse. The man came with the knife. He bent low to peer at Nicholas's face. Nicholas recognized the colors on his sleeve. He croaked, "English!" but the man did not hear, or he did not care. His eyes were greedy. Nicholas realized that his left hand was free. He groped for his dagger. Suddenly there was another hand, coming from behind the long knife; it grasped the knife-arm and wrenched it back. Before Nicholas went black, he thought, What's a bowman doing here? For the arm that saved him was strapped with the leather guard of an archer.

In Durham town, the clerc read aloud what he had written. "Let it be known that we have manumitted and liberated from all yoke of servitude by Edwin the son of Simon-by-Thornrigg, whom previously we have held as our bondsman, with his whole progeny and all his chattels, so that neither we nor our successors shall be able to require or exact any right or claim on the said Edwin . . . ."

"He saved your arse, you know," Gervase growled to Nicholas as they rode homeward. "You might say a friendly word to him."

Nicholas shrugged.

"Well in God's name you ought. He's a hell of a bowman, and he saved you honest to God hand to hand. For a scrawny, sniffle nosed clodhopper he's damn well got guts and strength. God damn it!" Gervase leaned over and gave Nicholas a blow in the face. "If you need goddam villeins to save your skin, you can at least show them some charity."

Nicholas turned his burning cheek and spat on the ground.

Win was the wonder of the village when he came home from the war with his charter of freedom. The first thing he did was go to Thomas Reeve and ask for young Mary. The reeve was jolly and made him sit down at table with a cup of blackberry wine. Martha Reeve stood beaming in the background. She said, "Let me get my daughter, and we'll see what she has to say." Win folded his hands around his cup; the reeve tipped back on his stool and rested his shoulders against the wall. "You'll get a good lass," he smiled, "and I can think of no man in the village I'd sooner have as my son."

Win blushed into his cup. "Thanks, reeve."

"We'll up to the house and talk to old Sir Gervie," said Thomas. "Could be he'll reduce my bride fee for your sake."

"Could be," said Win.

The door stood open; a rectangle of light lay on the floor beyond it; outside they could see a corner of Thomas' pig fence and Martha's bean-poles and pea rows along the path to the village street and, across the street, the wattle wall of Adam Bradback's barn. In front of the barn, a spotted goat was tied to a sapling elm, eating every last leaf and bit of bark off it. Voices came near, young Mary's saying, "Couldn't the soup have waited, Mam? I'd nearly filled the basket." The women were carrying a lug of apples between them.

"Well, Mol," said Thomas Reeve, right off. "How'd you like to be Goodwife Thornrigg, and live with Edwin the bowman come summer next?"

Mary dropped her side of the lug, so that a score of hard green apples went rolling over the floor.

"That mean yea or nay?" asked Thomas, winking at Win.

"Oh!" said Mary, red and flustered. "Yea!"

Thomas Reeve made a party for Win that very afternoon. He invited the freemen and the rich villeins, as well as Win's parents, who were neither rich nor free. They set up trestle tables in the yard in front of the tithing barn, and Tom Bradback's wife Edith (who brewed as her father in law milled; honest, but dear) supplied a six gallon keg at no charge at all. "For you, pilgrim, Edith will spare her sixpence—since I tell her to," Tom explained.

The October air was chill, but the beer warmed them. Women brought baskets of ruddy apples and brown pears to set on the table, and Martha Reeve brought out a great wheel of cheese. The sunlight, gold and mellow, slanted down upon the table and gilded the barn and the russet flanks of the fell. Squirrels and chipmunks with bulging cheeks rushed up and down trunks and branches, and boys with slings tried to hit them so that they could be like Win Thornrigg the Archer. Oswin priest blessed all the food and the company, "and, specially, Lord, the Bradback ale!" They all laughed except Edith, who was still mourning her profit.

Later in the evening they asked Edwin how he happened to be in the thick of the fray at Neville's Cross. His recollection was unclear; things had happened fast. He could only tell them that horsemen had ridden under the trees where they were not expected; the archers' line had been broken, and he'd found himself pushed into the middle of the fighting, where he had lost his bow and had nothing but his knife and his two feet to save him. Win laughed. "I wasn't thinking owt but 'O God, get me out of this. St Godrich. O God, get me out.'"

"And who can blame you?" said Mary Reeve.

"Well, I kept trying to dodge back out and find the archers. But then I saw the Wydclif and Keldacross arms nearby. It was Sir Nicholas and Sir Edmund and they were going at it right brave, hammer and tongs against two great Scots with beards and maces. The horses were sweating and men screaming and swords clanging and axes swinging, and then arrows started whizzing down again in flights. I thought, I'm not staying long in this place. But then I saw Sir Nicholas go down. One of them big toads, them corpse robbers, was standing over him."

Young Mary spoke up again. "You were brave enough to go where he'd fallen?"

"I dunno. I didn't think of owt. I reckon I just didn't want him to die. We were pilgrims together. And there was this toad man squatting over him with a knife, about to strip him of his gear without him even dead."

"An English toad, too," Mark Fletcher added. "This one had Clifford colors."

"Well, there's one less in the world now," said Harry atte-Beck, with satisfaction.

"But how did you get the knight out of there, Rabbit?" Matt Hayward inquired. "A knight's no coney to sling over your shoulder."

"I couldn't tell you," Win admitted. "I think I dragged him for a bit, but it was no good. Then the worst of it moved away from us like, and after a bit one of the Pickering knights saw me, and we got Sir Nick up on his horse. He was still blacked out from that mace blow on the head."

"Ee!" cried Edith Bradback.

"Aye, that's how he was unhorsed. Sir Nick was quick enough to fend so that the blow didn't crush his skull. Anyhow, we got him out beyond the archers' line to this hill where the wounded were, and I sat with him till Sir Gervase came."

"What'd Sir Nicholas say when he came to?" Tom wanted to know.

Mary Reeve looked misty. "He said, 'Brave and stalwart bowman, you have saved my life.' "

Win shook his head and sipped his beer.

Mary guessed again. "He said, 'God save you ever, Edwin Thornrigg, I owe you my deepest thanks.' "

Win laughed. "No, lass. He said summat like 'Who is it? Where's my horse?' A man don't make pretty speeches when he's been conked in t'head."

"Nor when he's as proud as Lucifer and ashamed of losing his mount," said the fletcher, less charitably.

"Well, Win got all the thanks he needs from Sir Gervase," Hawisa pointed out.

The miller turned to Simon, who sat next to Hawisa with his nose in his beer. "Your son's a free man and a champion, man!"

I ain't free, Simon thought. It don't help *me* none. But he said, "Oh, aye, I'll drink to t'lad." His face was blurred and beery. He started to loft his mug, but it wobbled in his hand, and the ale sloshed down his sleeve and over the table.

Hawisa hardened her mouth and looked into her lap. Martha Reeve touched her elbow and said, "It doesn't matter, Wisa. Just look at the *son* you've got. Just *look* at him."

The battle of Neville's Cross in County Durham was a great victory for the English. Young David of Scotland had thought to take advantage of King Edward's absence in France, but he sorely miscalculated the strength of the great marcher lords and the army of the North. His own host was routed. The banner of St Cuthbert shimmered like gold over the field. King David was led in shame to London, and he spent his next eleven years in the Tower.

But none of that moved Kelda village so much as the fact that Edwin Thornrigg was made a free man.

✳ 71

Oxford
December 1346

William came to Lyra's room in the house of Austinfriars and said, "I want to seek counsel and make confession. Will you hear me?"

Lyra said, "I'll be glad to hear you, but don't you have a regular confessor?"

"Yes, but I want to ask your counsel in something particular."

"Well, clear the stool off there and sit down." William did so. "Now, what first?" asked Lyra. "Confession or counsel?"

"Counsel, I think. Then I'll know better what to confess."

Lyra looked at William with friendly interest.

"I don't know exactly how to begin. My mind is fogged even as to the nature of my question."

"Don't fret just now about clarity."

"Then it is this." William felt like a fool, but he must say it somehow. "Will I never be—satisfied?"

"Satisfied in what way?"

"Always I feel my understanding lacks. I know not how to say it— my mind pushes and pushes and pushes, yet my heart is always troubled."

"If you are speaking about knowledge of God, then it must always be so. Any satisfaction would be delusion."

"But will I never reach any degree of ease or satisfaction?"

"Not in this life. Inquietum est cor nostrum . . . "

"No, I mean my reason only. I do not expect my soul to be satisfied."

"Are you asking me whether your intellect may one day comprehend God?"

"I'm not that stupid. But I should like to know enough about him for—my present purposes." William laughed, embarrassed. Lyra did not smile. William stopped laughing.

"What are your 'present purposes'?"

"I'm not sure. To speak of him eloquently, perhaps, in order to illuminate his nature for others."

"So you want to go on and study theology rather than lingering in the less noble sciences. Well, that seems good enough. Why then are you troubled?"

"Because the more theology I read, whether it be Duns or Thomas, Bernard or Abelard, or even just the *Sentences*, the foggier my mind becomes."

"You are young to venture into these intellectual thickets."

"It's not just a natural confusion I'm complaining of. I don't want to boast, but I must tell the truth. I can usually follow a fairly complex argument without much difficulty."

Lyra leaned forward on his elbows and rested his chin on his clasped hands. He cast a glimpse of recognition at William.

"Something is preventing me," said William, "I don't know what. I was wondering whether you think it is some sin in me, pride perhaps, that puts up this barrier. When I come up against it, I feel frantic, like a caged beast. I am embarrassed to tell you all this."

"Look," said Lyra, leaning back in his chair. "Let us lay aside the question of your feelings for a moment and consider a philosophical point. Why do you wish to try to know the unknowable?"

"Is it wrong to want to know what God is?"

"Jesu, man, it is almost too much to know *that* God is; to know *what* he is is sheer impossibility."

"And you an Oxford clerc! What would St Thomas say to that!"

"He would say, friend, that our learning power takes us only so far. Remember, he said it was all 'as straw.' "

"But straw is not without worth."

"Not at all. Use it to make a torch of reason so that you do not go about stumbling into pits of error. But don't think your little light will show you the face of God. Consider Denys the Areopagite."

"Oh, St Denys."

Lyra was amused. "Yes, St Denys. Why do you pronounce his name with disparagement?"

"I see not what that fellow can say to theologians."

"You don't? Thomas the Angelic Doctor evidently saw otherwise, since he was continually citing 'that fellow.' "

"Why are *you* dwelling on Thomas? I thought you were an Augustinian."

Lyra made a noise. "Thomas and Augustine are both saints of the church, just as Aristotle and Plato are each fruitions of the divine Word among the virtuous pagans. Shall I reject one wisdom because I love another? Do not make false dichotomies, man. It is like these new fellows with their via moderna: shall it be Faith, or Reason? As if there were some mutual exclusion."

"But you seem to be making false divisions yourself."

"I make a distinction, not a division. St Denys might help you, if you'd let me return to him."

"Why do you assume I would ever find him helpful? Agrestis would say that Denys is too obscure to be useful to a clear thinking man."

Lyra interrupted. "This is how your friend Agrestis thinks. He thinks: I know not everything there is to know—not yet. One day I will be a great doctor of this university and then I will be able to say, I understood every page I ever read. Except he will not truly have understood, for if he had, he would understand that he has not understood. William, our understanding is always imperfect, and that is not even to be regretted. We are finite beings in a finite world. How can we comprehend God, who is Infinite Existence itself?"

William responded heatedly. "Does your St Denys say that God is existence? As I recall, he denies all God's attributes and says that he cannot even be said to exist."

"To 'have' existence and to 'be' existence are two different propositions. A chair or a stone or a man may *have* existence. Denys says that God does not have existence in this way."

"To deny God's existence seems a strange and dangerous thinking."

Lyra shook his head. "I don't know why this is so difficult for me to express, for at heart the idea is very simple. Let me try again. God does not *have* existence. He cannot come into existence or go out of existence like the chair or the man. God *is* existence itself. The chair and the man only exist because they exist in God. Remember what God said through Moses: I AM WHO AM."

"If God's existence cannot be described, then what's the point of theology, or philosophy, at all?"

"The point is that God gives us reason and we are expected to use it as far as we can take it. It is not that our thoughts have no value, but that God goes so far beyond them."

William left his stool and made a few quick turns around the room. He looked obstinate. "Look, man," Lyra said, "an ant can grasp Aristotle better than we can grasp God. Remember what the Lord said through Isaiah: 'As high as the heavens are above the earth are my ways above your ways and my thoughts above your thoughts.' God is not like us, William. And, seeing what we men are, that is something to be thankful for. Which brings us to your second mission. What do you wish to confess?"

William sat down again, sullen and disgusted. "I think I wish to confess a sin of pride." He elaborated a little for Lyra, who inclined his head to listen and then said, "Remember what St Paul tells the Corinthians, 'If anyone imagines that he knows, he knows not yet as he ought to know.' Remember too that it is good to labor after God as you are laboring, using all the faculties he has given you. Moses himself struggled sweating up the mountain, but it was only when he had come to the end of his powers and stood alone and blind in the mist that he knew the Lord his God."

William's discomfort increased; a peculiar unpleasant tightness clamped his heart.

"God is nearer to us than we are to ourselves," Lyra said, "as our father Augustine teaches us. And in reality there is no distance between us and God, who is our very being. But it sometimes pleases him to withdraw from our highest and holiest notions of him, even our warmest affections. Then we are left alone with God as he Is, instead of our mere ideas of him. God as he Is is impenetrable darkness to us. Of course the darkness is ours, for he is Light. We cannot see the Light, but only the cloud wherein God dwells and speaks. All the intellect can tell us is that the cloud is there. Then the will must take over, impelled by love. Love goes naked into that cloud and gives itself to God as Moses did on the mountain. But this is a hard thing and a gift from God. We must never lust after it."

William could not remember ever having lusted to enter Denys' Darkness of Unknowing, and he said so.

"It is not what you think," said Lyra, and then, abruptly, "Enough. I'm rambling. Forgive me. Do you have other troubles to present for Christ's mercy?"

William had entertained impure thoughts about a certain woman, but he could not admit them now. His sins must be great and worthy of high theology. Cordwainer's widows could not keep company with such majesty.

So he received absolution and came out feeling worse than before. He went down onto the street, where the sun was bright, and people were shouting.

✳ 72

Keldacross
December 1346

Rorate Sunday

It was the last Sunday in Advent, and at St Godrich's Oswin intoned the ancient hymn, "Rorate caeli desuper, et nubes pluant justum, Rain down from above, O heavens; let the clouds rain down the One of Justice." That afternoon the rain poured down from heaven like a flood. Bundling herself up in her cloak, Alice went down to the village into Simon Thornrigg's house, seeking a physic for Marion and also a remedy for one of her boils—this time it was on her elbow and causing her no end of grief. In Simon's house Win squatted by the fire with his sleeves rolled above his elbows, mending the handle of an iron pot. On the floor next to him lay a rake with two teeth missing, a broken flail and a bent harrow. Winter was time for fixing tools, an occupation that Win considered more leisure than work.

"Wisa Thornrigg?" Alice strode in, squinting against the smart of the smoke. "Where's that wretched husband of yours?"

Wisa sat across from Win, sorting with chapped fingers a sack of beans in her lap. She nodded to Alice. "Come in," she said ironically.

Win looked up pleasantly. "Evening."

"Evening, Win. Marry, you're pleased with yourself, aren't you, pilgrim? Now that you're the pride of Kelda. Hawisa, I'll not tell you how when we were in London, your brave son clung to me closer than a crablouse all the while we were in the Chepe. And not out of love for me, neither."

"Now, then. I liked you well enough."

"No doubt I should swoon because the great champion of Kelda village 'liked me well enough.' Wisa, I've come for one of your physics and salve for a boil. This one's beat all its grandsires for soreness."

Hawisa got up onto a stool to pull down some bags from the rafters.

"I saw your father heading toward the threshing barn all on his own yesterday, and I could scarce believe my eyes," Alice observed to Win.

"Aye, it was him. But he broke the thwacker," Win indicated the flail with his elbow, "and we had to borrow another from Thomas Reeve."

"Is he by some miracle of God out threshing again today?"

"Doan't ask." Win drew it out.

"No business of hers, anyroad," Hawisa said shortly, pounding the herbs together in a bowl. Alice considered Win as he bent over his work, and mused that Sir Gervase ought to see his best bowman better fed. Or maybe Win was just made that way. When you looked at him closely you saw that he was wiry over his skinny bones. His forearms below his rolled sleeves were roped and twiny with muscle.

"Our gallant Sir Nicholas hasn't even looked at you sideways since your great battle, has he?"

"Na, it's no matter."

"What's it to Edwin? He's a free man now, isn't he?"

Alice shrugged. "The chivalry are a lot of louts, if you ask me. My old woolmaster in York has more manners than the whole chivalry of the north put together. Here, now, have a look at this."

She offered her elbow to Hawisa, who glanced at the boil and said, "For one as tough as this it's the needle or nothing."

"Mary Mother Matchless!" Alice exclaimed. "You clodhopping herbswomen! In York, a pothecary'd salve me up and cure me in no time." She conveniently forgot all the boils she had had to have lanced in York.

Hawisa spoke sourly. "It's not me stopping you from going back. I'll make you a salve as good as any in York, but I warn you, it'll come to the needle sooner or later."

Alice chose to ignore this. She spoke to Win. "So, you're fixed to marry the reeve's daughter. No doubt she'll bring along a few goods and chattels when she comes."

"Aye, she'll bring summat, even after Thomas Reeve pays his bride fee to Sir Gervase."

"Pay to marry, pay to work, pay to die," said Alice. "I bet the bailley's there with his ledger to make you pay to get into heaven."

Win smiled.

"Well, if ever a clodhopper deserved blessing and good fortune, it's you, Win. Any yokel woman must rejoice to have you for a husband."

"Well, he's my son," said Hawisa, putting the bowl of physic into Alice's hands and showing her the door. "And no one else's." She shut the door behind Alice and went back to the beans.

After a bit Win said, "You know, Mam, I think come summer I'll just make this house bigger by a bit, if you and him don't mind."

She looked up, her eyes brightening. "Oh no, son, I shouldn't mind at all." She had feared that Win would build himself a new house, as he had every right to do, and leave her alone with Simon. But now she saw what a good son he was. Win hummed one of his songs under his breath as he worked, and Hawisa smiled. She was not going to lose him. A wife was well enough, but a boy needed his mother.

They sat quietly listening to the rain come down on the thatch and the fire spit and crackle. Then Win spoke up. "Here's a riddle. Guess it."

Fleeting I fly, fleeing forever.

Shade I make, no shelter take.

Home have I none in sky-helm nor earthen-house.

Great greyness am I, yet green my grandchild.

"Oh, son," said Hawisa, "a baby'd know that one. Raincloud, what else?"

"Well, you top it then."

Hawisa said right off, "Soft hand, hard heart; long leg, loud fart."

"I know *that*," said Edwin. "That's a gentleman." And they both roared, even though it was Simon who had thought up that joke.

Win added a dry cowpat to the fire and rubbed his hands together over the flame. Hawisa scrutinized him and worried about his stuffed nose. She began to plan the ways that young Mary Reeve could help her care for him.

In the dimness of St Godrich's, Oswin read over the ancient hymn by candlelight: "Let the earth open to receive the dew, that she may bear the fruit of salvation, with justice blooming at its side."

292

✳ 73

A dull, dark winter's day. The wind blew high drifts against the manor house walls. Nicholas hung about the hall, bored, ill humored. The sky threatened more snow, and he saw nobody whose face did not annoy him. His father was in bed with a hacking cough and suffering it with bad grace. Nicholas despised this. He was never ill. Even more unpleasant was the fact that Hugh Cliderhou was there with Eleanor. Apparently Eleanor had thrown some kind of screaming fit at Eskmere to make Hugh take her to her mother's in this vile weather, but yesterday's storm had stopped them at Kelda. Nicholas thought it odd that Hugh seemed gulled by Eleanor's show; everyone knew he was anything but a softhearted husband. But Nicholas was too irritable to wonder much about it. He just wished they would pack up and get out.

Hugh had been surly from the outset, and then he had taken Gervase's cold. He sat heavily in the solar, blowing his nose, making muffled curses into his handkerchief, and watching Eleanor out of red eyes. Once he gave Nicholas a narrow look that made Nicholas want to grab an axe and bash his head in.

Every damn thing set his teeth on edge. Geoff was there, crooning endless lovelorn dirges to the ladies. Marion sat uncomfortably on a bench, embroidering something. Her face was crumpled and crabbed. She was with child again. How Geoff could make himself passionate over her when she looked like that Nicholas could not fathom. He leaned angrily against a wall and listened, scowling.

"Fowlës in the frith," Geoff wailed, "the fishes in the flod, and I mon wax wod. Muckle sorrow I walkë with, for best of bon and blod, The birds in the wood, the fish in the stream, and I will go mad! I walk in great sorrow, for best of bone and blood."

Marion said, "Why must you make me miserable with your dark songs? It's dark enough as it is."

"I agree, daughter," said Dame Magdalen. A painful gnawing was at the pit of her belly since Christmas or before; she could not remember when it had begun. She could not stand for long at her loom nowadays; she must rest against a high stool. She complained of it to no one, and no one spoke to her of it, because her face forbade them.

"Get me the harp, and I'll sing you a *very* merry song," said Eleanor.

Geoff went to the window, took the harp from its stand, and unwrapped it. Just then, a low, hacking cough echoed in the hall. Gervase came and stood at the screens, glaring like a wounded hawk. He clutched blankets around his body, his bare, horny toes on the rushes. "Baudlid," he said plaintively, as if it were her fault he was ill. "I am so wretched. Why does God treat me so, Baudlid? Why don't you come and comfort me? Why must I suffer alode?" His head was like a weight, barely supported by his flimsy neck. His eyes were puffed and runny, his nostrils swollen and chafed. Worse than all this was that his anguish went unrecognized. Here they were making merry in the solar while he suffered alone in his bed.

Nicholas twitched. How could a man who laughed at stinking wounds turn into such a mewler over a piddling cold?

Magdalen sighed. "You'll never be well if you wander about the house catching all the draughts. Go back to bed, and I will come up with a hot cup." She rose slowly, bracing herself against the loom frame. Gervase shuffled out of the room.

"Sir Job he is," said Marion. Nicholas froze her with a look.

Eleanor ran her fingers over the harp strings and sang: "When the turf is thy tower, and the pit is thy bower, thy flesh and thy white throat will be food for worms."

"You call that merry?" said Marion.

"What helpeth thee then," Eleanor continued sweetly, "all the world to win?"

A strange note in Eleanor's voice made Nicholas uncomfortable. They were all looking at her, but Hugh said sharply to Nicholas, "What are *you* looking at?"

Nicholas, having had enough, walked out of the solar without replying, and whistled for Tooth as he left the hall for the stables.

✳ 74

Oxford
January 1347

"Three o'clock and dark already." William lit a candle. "How is it possible to accomplish anything?"

Stephen looked out of his carrel. "I am sorry, Angel, that the cycle of seasons displeases you. Why not summon God to Westminster and bring suit for redress of grievances?"

William bent over the book of St Denys that Lyra had lent him. He sat crosslegged on Uthred's bed, squinting at the dimming lines. "What's the use?" he said at last. "This book darkens my mind anyway. Listen. He says, 'These things thou must not disclose to those who cling to the objects of human thought, and imagine that there is no superessential reality beyond, and fancy that they know by human understanding Him that has made Darkness his secret place.' Yes, yes. But this Denys is not above using his intellect to tell us that we can understand nothing by our intellects. Besides, that is not wholly true. God has given us all sorts of things that we may understand him by. Has St Denys never heard of Our Lord Jesus? Not to mention the whole creation, from which we may learn by analogy. And then he goes on to say (St Denys I mean), 'Into this Darkness we pray that we may come.' We do? I don't. I don't want to 'renounce all knowledge and understanding.' "

"You don't want to relinquish gabble."

William, disgruntled, rose and set Lyra's book with the others in his study. "I'm going to catch some sleep."

"Sleep eternally, Angel," said Stephen, "for that is your only quiet state."

"No," Uthred reminded him. "He talks in his sleep."

"And what," said Master Alexander the next morning, standing in the hall before the fire, leaning his sharp elbows on the carven lectern (the lectern had one short leg; it rocked as Alexander shifted his weight), "what mean you by that?"

William's voice faded out. He had been rambling for what seemed like hours while Alexander fixed him with his cold attention, washing him over with the clammy chill of the grey North Sea. William pushed the hair back from his eyes. His forehead was sticky. He raised his eyes to Alexander's chin and dropped them again. He had no idea of what he had been saying. He had only half heard the question; he had forgotten Agrestis' objections; he had not read the prescribed assignment. "Magister," he said, striving to rally his wits, "I meant to say—I know I was imprecise, but I meant—"

Alexander's sighs were icy blasts, his coughs and twitches restless waves slapping angrily against rocks.

"Let me begin again. Let me state it more precisely." William glanced desperately at Agrestis, who was mouthing something that apparently was supposed to help but only made things worse.

"Begin again, certainly," snapped Alexander, "but do better than to put it more precisely. Make some modicum of logical sense."

William flushed. "May I hear again Agrestis'—I mean Goodram's—I mean, may I hear the objection again?"

"Do you remember the original question?" asked Alexander, "or shall that be repeated as well?"

"Yes, magister. I mean, no, I remember."

"Then refresh my memory. It has been so long, I have forgotten it."

William's cheeks grew fat and hot; his tongue thickened. Inside his skull his brain melted into gray custard. "It was—it concerned—well, it concerned . . ."

Agrestis, unable to support the agony any longer, burst out, "Sin! It concerned sin!"

Alexander never shifted his gaze.

"Malice," William spluttered feverishly. "Malice as a cause of sin. Whether one can sin without it. Malice, I mean."

"I thank you," said Alexander dryly. "And what was Goodram's argument?"

"He said—he said—" William had a sudden flash of clarity. "He argued that malice itself is a sin. If, therefore, we were to say that malice is the cause of sin, that would be saying that sin is the cause of sin and so on to infinity. But an infinite regression is pointless and absurd."

"Very well. Now answer that argument, and not some other, mysterious one. Your previous reply seemed an utter non sequitur. But perhaps your apparent lapse of attention was actually a subtlety of logic that my uncouth mind was unable to discern."

"Yes, magister," William babbled. "I mean, no, magister, it was not non sequitur, but I stated it most unclearly."

"Certainly you did," Alexander interrupted. "Kindly clarify."

Stephen got up from where he had been lounging on a bench. "Let me take the question, magister," he said in a yawning, languorous voice.

"No!" Agrestis clenched his fists. "Angel! What's wrong with you?"

"Stephen!" Alexander barked. "Sit! Goodram, silence!"

William pushed his hair back. "Magister, please. Have me excused. I am greatly weary. I did not sleep well last night."

"If you are too weary to draw fresh argument from your own store of brilliance, perhaps you can give us one of St Thomas'. His arguments are usually fairly sound." Alexander drummed the lectern with the first three fingers of his left hand. With his thumb he beat a rhythm on the open pages of his book. He waited.

Agrestis mouthed. William stared at him uncomprehendingly. "Magister, I did not read for this question."

Agrestis cursed under his breath. Alexander slammed his book shut.

His voice was colder than the coldest depth of hell. "You did not read for this question? That is curious. Did I not lend you this book for that very purpose?"

Yes. To Stephen and Uthred and Miles as well. Why not choose one of them to persecute? Yesterday I was prepared. Yesterday I could have shone. But you pick today, you bloody Scot. You bloody, torturing Scot. "Yes, magister. I am sorry. But I had not the time to read it."

Alexander picked up the book and dropped it again. The lectern rocked. "You had not the time? What are you here for? If you are not reading, what are you doing?"

"Sir, when I had time to read it, I was weary. I fell asleep."

"When you *had time* to read? I repeat, if you are not reading, what are you doing?"

"Too much beer at the Prelate," Stephen whispered audibly in Miles' ear. This was friendship? Stephen might at least have whispered "Too much St Denys" to let Alexander know that William had been distracted from St Thomas by high theology.

Agrestis stamped back to Merton. Why should he waste his time coming over to assist Alexander if all his old friends did was to make fools of themselves?

William meanwhile went to the Austinfriars in a state of anxiety and humiliation. Cyan the Harp let him into Lyra's room. Lyra was engrossed in some mathematical problem, and he looked up crossly when Cyan spoke to him.

William held out the *Mystica theologia*. He spoke in a cool, flippant voice. "I am sorry to disturb you, holy learned Welshman. I am come to return your St Denys, whose doctrines are more unintelligible than the Hidden Divinity he seeks to preach."

Lyra looked irritated. "Thank you for returning the book so graciously. Just put it on my bed, for now."

William complied, then stood watching Lyra fiddle with a compass and his astrolabe.

"Well," said William after a while. "How does one go about it?"

"Go about what?"

"Emptying oneself, as Denys says."

"Man," replied Lyra, still squinting at his work, "I cannot answer your question."

"Cannot answer?" William yelled. "You force me to read this book and persecute me with its philosophy, and now you tell me you cannot answer my question?"

Lyra sighed. "Friend, you asked to borrow the book. I was not aware of persecuting you with it. The Emptiness of which Denys speaks is not something one does. It is an act of Divine Love that is sometimes given to people in prayer. It is not something I can explain through syllogism."

"The book is not useful if its doctrines cannot be clearly expounded."

"Well, if it isn't useful to you, forget about it. Perhaps some day you will like it better."

"If you mean to chasten my pride, you have done so."

"I never meant to chasten you. I am sorry if it has seemed so."

For several minutes William watched Lyra making meticulous adjustments in his incomprehensible instruments and his obscure lines and figures. William peered over his shoulder. "What are you doing now? Do those arcs indicate the paths of stars?"

"Dduw!" Lyra exclaimed.

"I am sorry. Have I made you botch something?"

Lyra laid down his instruments and looked at William with controlled resignation.

"I apologize, Lyra. But you know I can't sit quiet for a moment. You don't know how much I wish I could just feel quiet, just for an hour or two. So you see why St Denys is wasted on me. I'm blind to it."

"So you are." Lyra put away his constrained patience and smiled at William with genuine humor and kindness. "But it will be an easier blindness, Saul, when you quit 'kicking against the goads.' Listen, man, do not worry overmuch about the Divine Nothingness until you have filled yourself with God's more daily gifts. How well are you acquainted with the sacraments lately, and with Scripture, and with good works, and common prayer?"

"Why must you always treat me like a child? I will trouble you no further."

"You are no trouble," said Lyra, and, all evidence to the contrary, he meant what he said.

"Do not feel you have to be courteous," said William, and he thanked Lyra for his time and went away.

"I have unwittingly led the Englishman into misunderstanding," Lyra worried to Cyan. "What Denys meant is not merely intellectual humility. No, it shears far closer to the ground than that."

And he returned to the paths of the stars, which God had placed in the sky in direct testimony to the clarity of creation, though human eyes were too darkened to understand.

* 75

Eleanor rode up from Helmsley at dusk one day, pallid and all alone.

They pulled her into the hall and made her sit by the fire, for outside it was stark, bitter cold. Eleanor's teeth rattled, and the snow sloughed off her in chill pools on the floor. For the longest time she would not let them take off her cloak. Marion did not know what to do. Dame Magdalen was lying on her bed with eyes tightly shut (but she would say only that she was weary), and Marion did not want to disturb her. Alice and Joan Faulkoner stood about until Marion said, "Alice, go fetch some of my clothes for Dame Eleanor and bring them into the solar." Women put their noses around the kitchen door behind the dais. Marion frowned at them, but they went on whispering and clucking at one another. Alice came down with the clothes. Joan and Marion helped shivering Eleanor to the fire, where they stripped her and dried her and dressed her in layers of wool. She did not speak a word the whole time. Marion had her brought a cup of mulled wine and watched her drink. She chewed her lip. If only she dared call Dame Magdalen.

"Eleanor," she said finally. "Why are you here? What's happened?"

Eleanor replied. "I will not talk to you. Where is my little brother?"

"Geoff's down at Wydclif with my husband and Sir Gervase."

"Then I will go down to Wydclif."

"Oh no, you must not! Already you look almost dead. Please, Eleanor, tell me what's happened!"

"I will not talk to you."

"Don't then, but you can't ride out again. It is almost dark, and what if another storm comes?"

Eleanor shrugged.

So Marion sent Alice for the bailley. He came in with his brows knit. "Dame Eleanor," he said, gentler than they thought he could. "What's amiss? How came you here all alone?"

Eleanor looked at him with empty eyes.

John Bailley said, "By your leave, Dame Marion, I shall send somebody down to Wydclif."

But Hugh Cliderhou had already come riding through the gate.

"Sir Hugh!" Marion ran across the hall to meet him. "What is the matter with her? What's happened?"

Hugh's face was splotchy with cold and rage. "Happened? All Helmsley scouring the moor for her is what's happened. Except I knew she'd be here. To shame me more." He thrust past Marion and strode into the solar. He yanked Eleanor by the arm. "If you were not in the house of one who is a lady and not a slut," he said, "I would beat you to death here and now." He turned to Marion. "Where is the lady?"

Marion began to cry. "Sir, sir."

"Where is Dame Magdalen, I said?"

"Abed. She is ill."

"Where's my good dear friend Sir Nicholas?"

"At Wydclif. Oh, sir, don't hurt her. She is acting like a madwoman. She was going to ride down to Wydclif like that. In this weather."

"To Wydclif." Hugh looked at Marion oddly. "You said Nicholas was at Wydclif, didn't you?" He twisted Eleanor's arm so that she cried out.

"For Jesus' sake, Sir Hugh," cried Marion, "tell me what is the matter."

"Matter? What matter?" Hugh shoved Eleanor before him out of the solar. "Your little friend just prefers Kelda, or Wydclif, to Helmsley that's all."

"Don't go now, Sir Hugh. It's dark. Stay the night. I'll call Dame Magdalen. She'll make you stay."

Hugh waved her out of the way. "We shall ride to Wydclif to have a chat with my dear friend Nicholas." Marion could see his nails digging into Eleanor's arm. They went out into the gusty, snow driven court, and mounted Hugh's horse and rode out the gate. Marion ran back into the hall, hugging herself and shuddering.

✳ 76

Keldacross, Helmsley, and Eskmere
February 1347

By the time Hugh and Eleanor reached Wydclif, Nicholas and Gervase had already departed for Helmsley. So Hugh sent Eleanor back to Eskmere through the bitter cold while he rode on to the castle alone. There he spent the next two days choosing quarrels with Nicholas over this or that piddling thing, or shoving into him and saying, "Pardon, my good friend," smilingly, with narrow eyes. Once Rab had to pull Nicholas' fist down, saying, "Come on, Nick, you know Hugh's a bastard. Pay no heed."

Nicholas breathed through his nose. "On my honor, Hugh," he began.

But Hugh sneered, "On your honor, Nick? Where's that?"

"What was *that* about?" Nicholas shouted. "What was *that?*"

Mundo said, "Nick, he's always been a swine. Forget it."

But that night Nicholas awakened with a start in the castle hall. A woman's body was beside him.

"See what I brought you, Nick," said a voice in the dark. "Fair and plump, Nick, as you like 'em. A groat a night, and the treat's on me."

Nicholas sat up. "I don't know what in hell you're talking about, Hugh, but I'm sure as hell you mean offense."

"You got it, Nick, you swine!"

Nicholas sprang up. "Shitten villein bastard! I've had enough of you! I'll spill your guts!"

"I'll spill *your* guts if you don't hold your noise," a voice grumbled from somewhere in the dark. Someone else lit a torch. Hugh stood there by Nicholas' pallet, sucking his lower lip under his teeth. His eyes were hard, and his hand was on his sword.

Rab scrambled up. "Come, Hugh, this is a bad joke."

"It's no joke, damn you."

"God damn you stinking bastard!" Nicholas yelled. "You want to quarrel, give me the cause of it, so I'll know what I'm killing you for!"

"Here, what's this?" Another torch was lit. Someone said, "Get Gervase of Kelda." Sir Henry Emberthwaite came over. "Here, young knights," he said mildly. "Let your tempers cool. Speak your mind, Hugh, and perhaps we can end this quarrel tonight. Be frank and honest."

Hugh spat. "Frank. Honest. If a certain man were honest there would be no quarrel."

"I'll kill him!"

"Peace, peace, Nicholas. Hear him out."

"Hear him out? I'll lay him out!"

"Laying folks out, Nick," said Hugh. "Isn't that what you do best? Laying out other men's wives?"

Edmund came up and said, "What in God's name are you talking about?"

"I mean, Mundo, that your dog of a friend and your whore of a sister have been lying out in haystacks or dung holes or wherever swine like that do their business, for God knows how long."

301

"You're a liar, Hugh," said Rab, advancing.

"What? What?" Nicholas struggled out of Sir Henry's grip. "What?"

"What? What?" Hugh mimicked. "Go to hell with your whats. I had it from the woman herself. Just sat up and told me of her own accord. But I want to hear it from the dog first, before I draw his brains out through his nose."

Geoff, his face appearing in the torchlight, shrieked, "You liar!"

"Nothing to say, dear friend Nick? Not much to say when you've been cuckolding a companion in arms, is there? Except, 'I am scum.' Say it, Nicko. Say it now: 'I am scum.' "

Edmund and Rab stepped between them. A crowd gathered. Sir Ralph lumbered into the light, Gervase at his elbow.

Geoff disappeared and came stumbling back with Nicholas' sword. Sir Henry pushed him away. "If this must be fought, let it be fought by daylight, not here like this. Wait until morning when tempers cool."

"Aye. Aye." Gervase, worried, looked from his son to Hugh. "Let tempers cool."

"I say that we ride to Eskmere tomorrow," said Sir Henry, "and see for ourselves what Dame Eleanor has to say."

"I told you what she has to say," Hugh shouted.

They rode east in the morning and came to Eskmere by midafternoon. Nicholas listened in silence while Eleanor murmured, soft and serious as a dove, "Why, yes, I have told you. Three times since Christmas. And long before that. Many times, for long years."

They looked at Nicholas, who was staring at Eleanor. He shook his head. "It is not true."

Gervase looked from Sir Geoffrey, her father, to young Geoff and Edmund, then back to Eleanor. Sir Geoffrey returned his old friend's look, then strode forward and slapped his daughter backward. "Admit it's a lie."

Her face was red, but she said, "No lie." She looked at Nicholas, her eyes shallow.

They all turned again to him.

"Once," said Nicholas. "Once, before she was even betrothed, or I married."

Sir Geoffrey took in his breath. Edmund, cupping his hand over his eyes, stared at the floor and young Geoff stared at Nicholas.

"He swore he would marry me," said Eleanor. "He swore."

"I swore I would try. And I did try. And after that there was no more."

"He tried," Gervase assured Sir Geoffrey. "This is true. The boy tried." Sir Geoffrey grimaced.

"He swore," said Eleanor, "and then he took my maidenhead."

"Did I ask you?" Nicholas shouted. "You made me!"

Geoff ran out of the room.

"But the rest," Gervase insisted. "All the rest is lies."

"No lies," said Eleanor. Her eyes looked strangely bruised.

Hugh looked at her, frowning, and quickly back to Nicholas. "Is it lies?" Nicholas cracked his knuckles. Worse than Sin, he hated Hugh Cliderhou. "Is it lies, Nick?" Doubt entered Hugh's voice. If Eleanor was crazy, that was better than his being a cuckold. He would beat hell out of her either way.

Nicholas said, "I'm not going to say it again. Do you want to fight it out? I will not forgive your words against my honor!"

"Come, come, young men," Sir Henry pleaded. "The poor girl's crazy. You won't fight over the ravings of a madwoman."

"Eat your words," Nicholas said to Hugh.

"Eat dirt," said Hugh.

"I'll kill you," said Nicholas.

They all looked at Eleanor. Her mouth was happy. "Now everybody knows," she said.

Edmund found Geoff down under the bare trees by the reedy fen called Eskmere, leaning hunched with his head against a trunk, shrunk with shame and misery for his sister and bent with bitterness against one whom, when he was young and ignorant, he had worshiped as a perfect knight.

"Come, we're riding back to Helmsley," said Edmund bitterly. "Hugh must know now that our sister is out of her mind. But Nicholas won't forgive his insults, and Hugh won't apologize. So they'll have to fight. Still, nothing they do will mend our sister's reputation, or our shame."

Lord Ros was not there when they got back, and Sir Henry, still hoping that the quarrel could be mended, persuaded them to wait until his return. That night Nicholas came to Keldacross, accompanied by Rab, to spend the night, in the event (but he did not say this) that he should not see Marion or his mother again. However, when he arrived he hardly spoke to them, but went straight to the stables and joked in a loud, harsh voice with Cuth and the stablegrooms. When he finally came into the house he was unusually attentive and courteous to Dame Magdalen. Neither he nor Rab said anything about what troubled them.

After a while Nicholas asked Marion if she would come hawking with him. She did not like hawking, but was afraid to refuse him. She went up and pulled on her black cloak and her thick leather gloves. They went riding over the top of Kelda fell, onto the moor. The moor was icy, the hard, unthawed ground showing through the snow in grey stripes. The sky had cleared; it was a stark, hard blue. The sun burned small and pale and far away. Nicholas, his mouth hard and his eyes flat, flew old Windiscry. When the falcon stooped from a great height, it seemed to Marion that it made a long, thin rent in the sky.

"Got him," Nicholas observed, but without satisfaction.

When they got back to the manor, Nicholas went into the house, but Rab, who was waiting about in the stables, took Marion aside amidst the hanging tack and said, "I need to talk to you on behalf of my friend Nick."

"Will you tell me what's ailing him? Why are you both here? I can't stand this."

"Just know whatever happens and whatever they say, it's all false. I know Nick'd never say a word to you about it, so I'm doing it instead."

"What are you talking about? I don't understand."

"Why, Nick barely looks at another woman, no matter how long we're away in service, no matter where we go. I've been his friend since we were snot-nosed brats, and there's nothing I don't know about old Moody Nick. I'd swear it by St Wilfrid's chair if they asked."

"Swear what? Ask what? Please!"

Rab went blundering on. "We've laughed about it often. 'You should have been the monk,' we tell him, 'not your brother.' Men off on service, you know," Rab coughed, looking at the floor. "We've tried to tease him into it, you know, and all that, but no, it would insult his lady wife. The same damn thing every time: 'I have a good lady at Keldacross; why should I insult her?' I know he'd never say a goddam thing about it to you, because he's soft in the heart about you. There's the truth."

Marion's knees began to weaken. A shadow took shape at the door of her mind.

"It's been that way ever since he married you, I swear it. Even though before that he couldn't stand the thought of a burgher's daughter, you must know."

Actually Marion had not known it for certain, since Nicholas had never been so discourteous as to say it.

"And even before that, he was never as bad as Mundo or me, running about all randy. It's because his father treats his mother with such honor and that's how Nick thinks it must be. So you see what kind of man he is."

Marion sat down on a barrel. "Sir Robert, what has happened? Why are you telling me all this?"

"I've got to go find Nick. We've got to get back to Helmsley before the Cliderhou swine think we've run away." Before he left the stable, he gave Marion a strained look. "Anything ill should happen, my father and I'll take it out of the Cliderhous. My old sire is as sworn to Sir Gervie as I am to Nick, so you're not to worry."

Marion was terrified. She went straight to Dame Magdalen, who stopped her shuttle, sat in the window, laid her hands in her lap, and told Marion how Eleanor had sinned with Nicholas before either of them were married.

Next day Sir Henry rode in from Helmsley, looking grim.

Marion jammed her knuckles into her mouth.

"My son," said Dame Magdalen. "He is unhurt?"

"He is unhurt."

Dame Magdalen put her hands to her belly and sat down. "God protects the just man."

"Hugh was unhorsed. He cried craven, and Nicholas left him to his shame."

"Thank God," Magdalen said. "Mercy reaps mercy."

"Mercy?" said Sir Henry, and his eyes reddened around the rims. He spoke in anger. "Mother of God, the young, stupid dogs! For mercy and pity and peace they have nothing but contempt!"

"What is it?" said Dame Magdalen, for it was plain that he had more to tell them.

"Poor old Ralph of Torbeck is sonless. Rab quarreled with Hugh's young brother Walter on Nicholas' behalf. Walter pulled his dagger, and Rab is dead. Dead. Your son then found Walter and pressed his face into the dirt. Made him eat muck. Would have killed him, if Scarface hadn't stopped him. Mother of God." Sir Henry turned his back abruptly on the women. In the cold winter light passing through the solar windows, he crossed himself and wept openly for the young, stupid dogs and for poor old Ralph Torbeck.

A fortnight passed before Gervase and Nicholas came home. Not long after, Geoffrey came up from Wydclif, where he had been staying since the quarrel, and Nicholas and Gervase stood in the hall to hear him out.

His whole body was shaking with fear and fury. He addressed Nicholas. "Since you have brought shame on my family, I will serve Henry Emberthwaite, soft and old as he is, rather than you. My brother Edmund also sends word that he wants no more of your friendship."

Nicholas stood with a stiff jaw, cracking his knuckles and examining Windiscry on her perch as she stretched a great, speckled wing. She spread her long flight feathers, fanned and preened them with her curved beak, then extended her left leg. Absently, Nicholas unfastened her strap and took her on his arm, without glove. He winced when the talons pierced his sleeve. He did not look at Geoffrey.

Dame Magdalen saw indeed that Geoffrey could not serve Nicholas any longer. Since neither her husband nor her son would speak, she said, "Geoffrey, I am distressed that you should make light of good Sir Henry Emberthwaite in this house, for he is my daughter's husband. But you know that you are at liberty to go wherever you may find service. You are a fine squire and will make a good knight. You have been almost like another son in this house. I am sorry it has come to this."

Geoff bowed stiffly. "Goodbye, Dame Magdalen, and God keep you. You and the other lady (he looked at Marion) have done my family no wrong."

"And meanwhile," Gervase said grimly when Geoff had gone, "I will be crawling to his father to beg forgiveness because *his* daughter's a whore."

Nicholas said. "It was only the once. Jesus God."

Magdalen felt a great weariness of husbands and sons overcome her and settle in her belly with the constant pain. She said, "The once was enough to lose Rab Torbeck his life, lose you your squire, and maybe lose Eleanor her wits. I fear for her now, for Hugh Cliderhou is not a kindly man."

For many nights Marion did not want to touch Nicholas or speak to him except to say once, "How could you have gone about as if nothing had ever been promised between her and you, as if nothing had happened? Look what has come of it."

But neither did Nicholas want to be touched or spoken to. Night after night he lay in bed heavy and cold as iron. Mundo an enemy and Rab dead. Dead. On my behalf. Christ! How was a man to live without his friends?

"That was a truly frightful thing, John Bailley," said Alice, standing with him in St Godrich's yard. She had come down to light a candle for Marion in her last month of pregnancy, and had found him here among the graves, looking anguished. She had never seen him shaken before.

"Aye," John agreed. "Now Sir Ralph has no son for his old age."

"Perhaps he can marry again."

John looked down at the nearest wooden cross. He prodded it with his toe. Here lay old Winfrith atte-Beck. John himself felt old these days.

Alice shook her head. "Poor Sir Ralph."

"Aye." The bailley looked at her from under his bushy brows.

Alice sighed, and shook her head again, and patted the cross.

"Aye," said the bailley, still looking at her. Then, abruptly: "I was thinking I could do with a wife."

She folded her arms and looked him over wryly. "Why, that's a pity, John Bailley. What woman'd want you for a husband?"

"You?" he said.

"Me?" she cried. "*You!* Ha!"

✳ 77

Oxford
March 1347

Agrestis came over from Merton to Chimney to lead the senior students in preparation for one of Master Alexander's grueling exercitia. Miles, saying that he needed no help from Agrestis, holed himself up in his carrel with what Agrestis called "some noxious tract of the moderni."

"If what I just said was self-evidently asinine, Agrestis," Stephen was saying testily, "why do you insist I defend it?"

"You mean you simply spewed forth that train of illogic without prior consideration? If you cannot defend what you say, do not speak."

"If you must know, Agrestis, my mind was temporarily distracted by the image of a girl I saw by Balliol wall this morning."

Agrestis' glowering face suddenly assumed a warm, paternal glow. "Ah, that's different. The lusts of the flesh," he murmured benignly.

William scratched his ankle and craned irritably over the book that lay between them on the table. "Let's get on with it."

"Do I detect an air of superiority on the part of our Angel?" Agrestis wondered. "Has he forgotten his widow? He has no lascivious visions? Perhaps he is in fact a non-corporeal angel. Or if corporeal, we may wonder if something corporeal is missing in him. Has John Hand inflicted the fate of Abelard on him? Or has he done some violence to himself, in the manner of some excessively ascetic heretic?"

Miles thrust his head out of his carrel. "Your conversation is both disgusting and distracting."

"Aha! Notice that the Ockhamist was not distracted by our earlier discussions of Euclid, but only by our present discussion of buxom succubi. Has even the cold modernus Clottiswoode, immersed in his barren syllogisms, felt the lewd lures of lust?"

"Or does the voice of Agrestis become louder and more raucous when discussing the subject that interests him most?"

"Since you are a member of the human genus, Miles, we are entitled to assume that you have at one time or another entertained lustful thoughts and images."

"You may say so probably, but not certainly."

"True. And it is also probable, though not certain, that your brain is encased in your skull rather than in your arse."

William, impatient and disgusted, snatched up the text and stamped toward the door. Uthred made timidly as if to follow William, but Agrestis launched himself in front of the door and blocked their way. He glared at William as if he were Iscariot.

"You support this nominalist?"

"At the moment, I don't give a putrefied fig for your stupid rivalry. I just want to understand this Euclid. Is that too much to ask?"

"Well then." Agrestis looked chastened. "Give me back the book, there's a good fellow." Perhaps wit did war with charity? He pushed the thought aside. But afterward he tried to conciliate by offering to buy everybody, including Miles, beer at the Prelate. Miles declined, saying he had too much to read, and William said no, he felt too irritable.

After Agrestis left with the others, the hall seemed becalmed, expectant.

William flung himself on his bed. The unlooked for stillness reminded him of Rievaulx, and he thought of Father Stephen: the lined, stern, kindly face saying, "Beware the squabbles of the schoolmen."

After a while he got up and went to Miles' cubicle. He coughed diffidently.

Miles looked up from his work grudgingly.

"Miles, I am an ignoramus."

Miles looked less grudging.

"Miles, because Agrestis is my friend I usually follow him against you, but I don't really understand the animosity you bear each other."

"It's more rivalry than animosity," said Miles. "And Agrestis fears that Ockham may be right after all."

William said, "Because I am Agrestis' friend, I am supposed to be a follower of John Duns Scotus, but I confess that I actually have little comprehension of the Subtle Doctor, and certainly no clear and distinct ideas about your William of Ockham and the via moderna."

Miles came close to looking pleased. "Of course you are my junior," he said.

"You surpass me in both reading and experience. At Rewley and Rievaulx they said that the sole desire of the bookman should be the learning of Scripture, with the commentaries of the Fathers."

"Count your blessings," said Miles cordially. "Much better than teaching you to try to cram God and his revelation into a strait philosophical garment never made to fit them." He pushed back his chair. "Look. Soon it will be too dark to read. I have a good raisin tart stowed in my chest. Would you like to share it?"

William smiled. It was good to be friendly with Miles. William watched him draw the knife from his belt and cut the pie precisely and cleanly down the middle, creating no crumbs whatsoever.

"This is a good tart, Miles." William smacked his lips.

"Better than some of our theology, perhaps. These endless efforts to fit God into the mold of our own minds. Remember that Thomas said it was all as straw."

William interrupted. "Thomas did not repent of his intellectual life; he merely saw how little it was in relation to the truth of God. I do not like it when people criticize theology and philosophy. You sound like Lyra the Austinfriar."

"I have no objection to sounding like the good Welshman. His views are not so far from my own."

"Explain your views."

Miles laughed mildly. "I cannot give you the via moderna in half an hour. Soon the barnyard will invade this quiet again. Perhaps sometime we can find a good corner at one of the better (namely, quieter) inns."

William felt some of the same discomfort he always felt at Lyra's. But he wanted to get some grasp of the new logic, so he said, "Yes, thank you, Miles."

Miles nodded, wiped his mouth with his handkerchief, and set about lighting his lamp. "I think I'll do some reading after all."

William burst out suddenly, vehemently. "Lyra's all wrapped up in St Denys' Darkness of Unknowing, which I have read but do not understand."

Miles looked up, blandly surprised. "You've been reading the Areopagite?"

"What if I have?"

"It's more than I expected, that's all."

William ignored the slight. "I still think, against him and your

309

school, that however transcendent God is, we can still reasonably deduce things about him from observing his created universe, which we perceive all around us."

Miles said, "I in no way reject philosophy. It is just that we must understand that whatever categories we humans apply to that created world and its creator, are categories that come from our own minds, and we cannot assume that they correspond with external reality."

"But . . . " But then they heard the others come into the hall downstairs; soon there were clompings on the stairs and the sound of heated, argumentative babbling.

That night in the bed beside poor, uncomplaining Uthred, William tossed and turned and gritted his teeth against what, he did not know. Whatever it was seemed to fill the whole room and demand something of him that he could not possibly give. Finally he could not stand it any more. He swung his legs out of bed, grabbed his gown, and went over to his carrel. A half moon cast faint, silver light through his narrow window. By that light he lit a lamp and hauled out Wilfrid's Boethius. He bent his head over the orange, flickering pages and strained his eyes to read the familiar, reassuring discourses. Christ! he thought, after reading for about an hour. The Holy Spirit works so hard to help us get even a little understanding. Why should these fellows want to take even that little away?

The moon set behind Oriel roofs across Kibald-twychen. At dawn William was asleep with his cheek on Wilfrid's Boethius; his lamp had guttered out.

✴ 78

Keldacross
April 1347

"Hop, Master John!" yelled Cuth Constable, over the sound of bagpipes. "We want to see you dance!"

"Na." The bailiff mopped his face. "I'm not dancing any longer." Sweat was running into his eyebrows.

"Shame, Master John! What will Alice think of your courage?"

"She can think what she likes." John went over to tap one of the kegs they had set up in Godrich's yard. "She'll know it soon enough."

Calls and hoots from the crowd.

"Alice!" leered Joan the falconer's wife. "How do you reckon John Bailley's courage?"

"Marry," Alice called back. "Don't make me think of it. My old sire used to say, 'Maids, when you're young, never wed an old man.' I should have heeded him."

"Oh, come, Alice," Thomas Reeve wound his arm around her waist, "we know you love the bailley. Let's hear you say it."

"I love him. Like fish on Friday, like cold bean broth in January, like six weeks in Lent withouten meat."

Everyone laughed. "Nay, come, Alice, say it. Say you love t'bailley. Nobody forced you to marry him, Alice!"

"If I must live in this cloddy vill," she replied, "God knows I might as well have the upper hand in it."

"Whoa, John Bailley," roared Mark Fletcher. "Did you hear that? She'll have the upper hand of you? How do you like that, John Bailley?"

"Oswin priest, let 'em take back their vows!"

"Maybe if they said 'em backward."

"Bodes ill for you, bailley."

"Hmph." John filled his cup again. "We'll see what bodes ill for who."

Win Thronrigg danced with Mary Reeve. He and Mary had stood up with John and Alice that day before Oswin priest in a double wedding. Mary had apple cheeks and robin's eyes like her father's, and his great, wide smile. Her brown hair came loose and whipped round her face as they danced. She never tired. When Win slowed down, gasping and laughing, she yanked him on and danced harder. Round and round the common they went. She was a strong, hardy young woman, as tireless a worker as she was a dancer. Win knew he had made a good match. And he was fond of her besides.

Hawisa sat at Martha Reeve's side, at the trestles set up in the church-yard, hands clasped in her lap, exultant, too happy to eat. She did not even care that Simon was already drunkenly snoring into his meat. Win was free, and now he would be prosperous as well. If ever John Bailley came by again asking for Wisa's February hens, she would laugh in his face. She had given all her hen house to Win and Mary as her wedding gift, so by rights he couldn't touch them.

"But the eggs and the chickens, Mam," Mary had whispered, when she learned of Wisa's present. "We know they're really yours." And she'd clasped Wisa's hands in a glee of shared shrewdness. Then Wisa knew that there would be no trouble between the two of them at all.

Two days later, John Bailley came running across the court, smiling broadly, as Gervase and Nicholas rode in from hawking. "What say you, Sir Gervase? You have a grandson!"

Nicholas swung hastily down from his horse. "Are they both well, bailley?"

"Right as rain, Sir Nicholas."

"Ha, ha!" In jubilation, Gervase threw off his hawk. The bird ascended with a wide soaring of wings to the top of Old Keep, and they had a hellish time getting her down afterward.

In the sickroom Katharine said, "Our father is right. The child should be named for him." Her mother had asked her to come and help with the birthing and the guests. "I am weary lately," Magdalen had said. Her hair had turned thin, brittle, and gray; only a few strands of russet remained.

"No," said Nicholas. "His name is Robert."

Katharine threw her embroidery into her lap and glared at him. "Why do you go on tormenting yourself and the rest of us with guilt? Calling the child Robert will not bring Rab back. The boy is Gervase."

"I want him to be called Andrew." Marion startled them. They stared at her.

Katharine dismissed it. "There are no Andrews among our kin."

"There are among mine."

"The boy is Robert," said Nicholas.

"Think of what our mother wants, will you? Do you think she wants you to pass over your father just to salve your conscience? Why don't you . . ."

"Not one word more," said Nicholas.

The three Watchers looked down on the baptism. (Gervase had forgotten about lifting the roof for lierne ribs.) The child twisted and kicked in Katharine's arms when the water went over his bald head, and let forth the newborn's strange wail, "Lla, lla, lla, lla!"

"Robert Andrew," said Oswin priest, "I baptize you in the name of the Father and of the Son and of the Holy Spirit."

Old Dame Emma, on whose arm Magdalen was leaning, proclaimed, "Good lusty bawl. He gets it from my blood."

Andrew Comyn beamed at Gervase. Even though his own name should have come first, his flesh and blood would inherit two manors, Keldacross and Tunnersgil. Gervase returned the tightest of tight smiles. His own grandson named after a merchant, and his own name omitted: well, leave it to a burgher to get the better of any transaction. Katharine met her father's eyes, and the two of them communed in wrath.

✳ 79

Kelda
April 1347

It did not take Win long to learn why a man ordinarily left his mother's house to cleave to his wife in his own dwelling. It wasn't that there were quarrels. Mol was such a merry girl, so helpful and tactful that she knew just how to make Hawisa love her, and they got on famously. As for Simon, Mary didn't bother to quarrel with him or even speak to him, except indirectly. "Let him get his own beer," she said right in front of him, the first time she saw Hawisa about to go out in the dusk with an ale-bowl to Edith Bradback's. "You've worked seven times as hard as him today."

Hawisa stood caught between Mary's fervor and her own habit. In the end she succumbed to habit, but she beamed at Mary nonetheless.

No, quarrelsomeness was not the problem. It was privacy. Hanging a blanket from the rafters between the old part of the house and Win's extension simply did not do the trick. It was especially bad now that Wisa seemed to have developed a restlessness at night. It seemed that every time Win and Mary would settle down to get cozy, they'd right off hear Hawisa stirring, no matter how quiet they tried to be. Pretty soon they'd hear her up out of bed, puttering around the house. Check the latches on the shutters; check the bar on the door; check to see that the fire was out; and once, incredibly, sweep the floor and clean the hearth three or four hours before daybreak. This happened almost every night, until finally (the night Hawisa swept the floor), Mary began to shake with silent laughter until she thought her ribs would break. Fat tears squeezed out of her eyes and rolled down her face. "Oh, Win, does she do it on purpose?"

"I doan't know," said Win grimly. But he was going to find out.

"Mam," he said purposefully next morning early when Mary had gone out to do the milking.

"Yes, son?" Wisa looked up from the porridge she was mixing in the clay hearthpot.

"Mam, have you been anxious anights? You're up and down all hours. Mary and me hear you puttering around."

"Well, yes, son, since you ask. Ever since that thief got into Hilda atte-Beck's I've been wakeful. Have I kept you from your sleep, lad? I'll try to be quieter."

Win was irritated. She wasn't no ewe lamb born yesterday. "Mam, it's not sleep we're missing. It's summat else. Mam, I'm a married man!"

"Oh, son! Your mam's an old fool."

But it was no better the following nights. She didn't putter any more, but they could *feel* her wakefulness, her strained and unsuccessful efforts to fall asleep or at least to make them think she had done so. And there was another hazard. Ever since Win's manumission, Simon had taken to keeping later and later hours with the most worthless men in the village. They'd all sit around the fire of Gythie Brewer, a disreputable middle aged widow, and sing, and quarrel, and give one another lumps on the head, and then stumble home by moonlight (if they were lucky), wrecking everybody's sleep as they careened down the street. One of those nights Win and Mary had just settled down nice and comfortable in the sound of Hawisa's sleepbreathing. Suddenly there was a great thumping and crashing at the door, and then huge, sobbing bellows.

"Hawisha! Hawisha! Lemme in! St Gorish hep me! I'm barred fra my own house! Hawisha! God!" Hawisa had barred the door regardless of the fact that Simon was still out. "St Godrich carry me away before I sleep one more night with the house open to burglars," she'd said. Now she leapt from her pallet, threw up the bar, and flung open the door. "You stinking old black boar! Why I don't leave you outside to feed the wolves I don't know!"

Win and Mary heard Simon stumble into the house. Apparently he walked right into the hearth, because there was the sound of crashing, clanking, and breaking earthenware. "Look what you've done! You've broke my best cookpot! St Godrich, what's a woman to do! And those poor bairns! Will they never get a moment's peace?" Simon crumbled onto the floor right outside the blanket partition, where they heard the noise of his blubbering snores.

This time Mary began to laugh out loud. "St Godrich! It's too much."

"Aye, that it is," said Win. "Come on." He pulled Mary out of bed and snatched the heavy blanket from the rafters.

"What are we doing, Win?" She doubled over with mirth as they climbed over Simon's heaped up body.

"We're moving into t'cow-byre, that's what."

"My dear bairns, I'm so sorry." Hawisa stood in her smock with her grey braid down her back.

"Goodnight Mam," Edwin said curtly.

"Doan't worry yourself, Mam," Mary shrieked hilariously, and the two of them disappeared into the cross-passage to the barn.

As soon as he'd been promised Mary, Win had torn down his father's old ramshackle barn. Harry atte-Beck had helped him raise this new, sturdy one, snug with its corncribs and strawticks and cozy stalls for the beautiful calving cows Sir Gervase had given him. It had a stout oaken door and a loft that smelt of herbs and hay and sweet smoked hams. Even so, it was not the place a man would choose to lodge with his bride at night.

"If your dad knew I'd be moving you into a cowbyre, he'd never have let me marry you."

"Oh, Win, I'll kiss you in the corncribs any old day. Come on now, love, let's get comfy."

When dawn broke next morning, the door of the byre was open wide. Sunlight poured in on Mary as she milked the cows. Shizz, shizz, shizz. The milk flowed into the wooden buckets. Mary had the best milking style Win had ever seen: *their* cows would never be teat sore. Mary turned her head against the cow's warm flank to twinkle at Win. "Morning! Look man, now isn't this good? I don't have to move two steps out of bed to do t'morning chores."

A voice was heard outside the door, and Hilda atte-Beck put her face in. "Morning, Mary," she said. Then, surprised, "Morning, Win." She made no comment as he sat up in the straw, pulled on his leggings, and brushed himself off. "Wanted to know if we could borrow your pruning hook."

"Aye, aye," said Win.

Pretty soon Jack Thatcher strolled in. "Win, you going to take Gabe Cottar today, or should I take Wat?"

"Take Wat," said Win, fastening his belt.

"You're late getting up, Win," Jack leered.

Win glowered at the thatcher, but before he could reply, Gabe Cottar was at the door, and crazy old Hereswith the gooseherd screaming about some stolen gander, and then Hawisa with a steaming porringer.

St Godrich! thought Win. There's no peace in this vill. It'll be all over the village before noon that I make my marriage bed in a barn.

80

Oxford
June 1347

Agrestis had come to Chimney before the great ceremony of his induction to see Master Alexander and his friends. Today he was to be accepted into the gild of Masters and granted his licentia docendi by Chancellor Jack himself.

Master Alexander spoke to him with true fondness. "Goodram, I am not ashamed to have claimed you as one of my more brilliant students."

"How long before he gets his Doctor sacrae theologiae, Master?" William asked. "He will go to Paris and astound them all!"

"One step before another," warned Alexander, "and it is time for you to step quickly now so as not to miss the procession."

Agrestis strutted. "Pomps and trumpets! If only my boorish brothers in Swaledale could see me now."

"If they're anything like my brother," William teased him, "they would not be much impressed. If they're like my brother, they'd say, 'What's that pipsqueak think he's doing?' "

Agrestis retorted, "Angel, not even my boorish brothers think me a pipsqueak. And thanks to their generosity, my feast to you all will make the tables groan with stuffed duck and pheasant, capons, and jugged hare and ginger, and wine from Burgundy, herbed cheeses from Languedoc . . . "

Stephen moaned. "Hurry and graduate then. We've been fasting since yesterday in anticipation of the feast."

"Go!" Alexander gestured Agrestis out of the hall. "Get back to the masters at Merton. I shall see you at the induction."

"And we'll be on the street to see the procession," said William.

Having elbowed their way through the crowd into a good place, Stephen, William, Uthred, and a couple of freshmen planned to yell in unison: "HAIL, GREAT MAGISTER FARTIS" when Agrestis paraded by in his hood with the other masters of arts. But when William heard the first note of the approaching horn, his throat closed up, and when he saw the procession come round the corner of Kybald street, his eyes smarted. By the time Agrestis came by them in cappa and hood, solemn for once, with sober jaw, William could hardly choke out an audible noise. Uthred stood with his mouth open, and Stephen kicked one of the freshmen who had begun to bleat, "Hail, great . . . " all by himself.

Agrestis' feast was as good as his word. They had it in combination with the other new masters, and everyone sang rollicking songs and made bad puns in Latin. Warden Treng of Merton went about the tables blandly greeting Alexander and other well-reputed masters, and he nodded genially at William as he went by. Then Agrestis came down from his high place to speak to his old friends. "We'll have you at Merton next term," he told William, "and I shall vilely revile you at Scrutinies so you will be sconced to pay for my bibulosity. But now, since I'm paying for yours, drink up, Angel!"

"To Goodram of Scarra, the Red Dane of Oxenford, we'll drink till we puke," William assured him.

"Speech, Magister Goodram!" Stephen pounded the table. "Astound us with your eloquence!"

"The fullness of my belly has driven out my eloquence. But I will borrow that of an ancient orator known to us all as Ecclesiastes: The light of day is sweet and pleasant to the eye; if a man lives many years he should rejoice in all of them. But remember that the days of darkness will be many. Vanitas vanitatum: everything that is to come will be emptiness. Amen."

They sat silent for a moment, surprised at the seriousness of his tone. Then someone struck up Gaudeamus igitur, and they all sang, beating the table with their palms.

Gaudeamus igitur, juvenes dum sumus.
Post jucundam juventutem,
Post molestam senectutem,
Nos habebit humus;
NOS HABEBIT HUMUS.

Let us therefore rejoice while we are still young, for after happy youth, and the miseries of old age, the grave will have us.

The next day, Stephen and William and Agrestis went to loll in the river meadows outside town. They folded their tunics between their backsides and the knobbly roots and wet grass, and stretched their legs out to the sun. William tipped his head back and watched the Cherwell through half closed eyes and through the green swaying of fresh willow branches. "Ah sun," he breathed. "Ah, sky, blue, with clouds rushing. Ah green grass growing."

"Ah sumer," said Stephen.

"Bulluck sterteth; buckë ferteth," said Agrestis.

"Merry sing cucu," said William.

Stephen stretched and yawned. "You were no coward, Agrestis, answering that Gascon in Greek. That will teach him to put on airs." A master of Balliol, Gilles of Bordeaux, had challenged Agrestis with a quotation of Plato in the original, and Agrestis had replied with a question of his own in Greek, which the Frenchman had failed to understand.

"I know more Greek than you know I know," said Agrestis mysteriously.

Said William, "If I speak in the tongues of men and angels, and have not love, I am a noisy gong or a clanging cymbal."

"Quiet, Angel. You're envious."

"Your wise man, your man of learning, your subtle debater—all they all not limited to this passing age?"

"God, I hope so. I'd hate to find Ockhamists in heaven."

"What if God's a modernus?"

"Nay, the Devil's one and teaches that evil and hell are only flatus vocis."

They sat and watched the river, and the clouds and trees in the river, and the ducks and geese and young fowl quacking along in the watery sky.

After a while, William said, "Marry, Stephen, have you told Agrestis?"

"Told him what?"

"What we found in Miles' clothes press?"

Agrestis sat up eagerly. "What did you find? Prohibited books? Evil tomes of necromancy? I knew the man was a magician." He crossed himself ostentatiously.

"No," said Stephen lazily. "You tell, Angel. It was you who found it."

"Well." William pulled up a strand of grass and shredded it between his fingers. "I was looking for my Boethius that he had borrowed and not returned, and it was nowhere in sight, so I thought I was justified in searching his chest."

"You lend that Ockhamist your *books?*"

"Yes. And there was nothing in the chest but his winter cloak and some hosen and linens and four wrapped meat pies . . . "

"All of which he consumed that day after supper, no doubt."

" . . . and one other thing." William paused. Stephen lay back with his arms behind his head, smiling.

"Well?" demanded Agrestis.

"I put my hand down under the linens and felt something like an animal. But it was animal no more. It was a hairshirt."

"*What?*"

"A hairshirt."

Stephen opened an eye. "Aye, truly. And he'd worn it all Lent."

"A hairshirt! My God! If the man wanted to do penance why did he not begin by refraining from secret meat pies?"

318

They all laughed. William let his lids droop again. He saw the meadow and the willow branches and the muddy bank and Agrestis's red hair through his lashes, rainbow touched. He saw river ripple around reeds, and sunlight broken into quivering sparkles. So he said,

Be you small, be you tall,
I break you into fragments.
The strongest metal I bend
The stoutest oak I rend and mend
Sun, moon, and stars in shivers send.
What am I?

"Reflection in water," said Agrestis. "That's easy."

"I was thinking, 'God,' " said Stephen.

"But that's the answer to every riddle. A particular riddle demands a particular answer, not the universal."

"You begin to sound like an Ockhamist, Agrestis," said Stephen. "Watch yourself."

William got up and went to the riverbank. He looked at his wavering self in water, and the clouds and sky rushing beneath. A pang pierced his chest. Suddenly, an old yearning for some other river, unknown, a hankering for some other meadow, nowhere, or in a dream forgotten. It burst from him: "Where are you?" He blushed, and looked around. But Stephen and Agrestis had not heard. They were discussing the demerits of the proud Gascon.

Hic, nunc, hodie.

"He's no logician," said Stephen. "He has no syntax."

Cucu, cucu. A voice called out of the trees, and laughed across the meadow.

Here, now, today.

✳ 81

Keldacross
June 1347

Shortly before noon Hawisa and her daughter-in-law were crawling on their hands and knees in the black, wet earth of their garden, pulling weeds from among the roots and beans that Hawisa had grown. Simon Thornrigg sat on a wooden bench against the wattle wall of their cottage, snoozing after a dinner of black bread and onions. Hens and chickens pecked and clucked at his feet, but he was oblivious to them.

"His snores stink from this far away," Mary remarked, and Hawisa grunted assent. Win was not in sight this morning. He had gone at sunrise to hack brambles from the outfield Sir Gervase had granted him. Mary would go join him soon with hoe and hook, but right now she enjoyed the ease of garden work under the mild June sky.

The Knee of Kelda rose steep above them, but its shadow had withdrawn under the hill's feet as the sun climbed to midday. The garden bathed in sunlight, and in the thicket hedge of wild blackberries that separated the fell from the garden, small fowls twitted one another. A rabbit hopped from a hole in the thicket and made free with some of Hawisa's turnip greens. He was either a young and innocent, or a stupid rabbit, because he did not budge when Hawisa called, "Shoo!" and Mary picked up a stone. But the shot was long and late, and the rabbit safely reached his brambly hole.

"Win'd've brained that coney," said Mary.

"Aye," Wisa agreed, working with blackened nails at a particularly tough dandelion. She grunted, "Hand me the spade." Then she added, "Best marksman north of Humber, I heard the knight say once."

Contentment overwhelmed Hawisa. Winter was past; there were good things in the earth; and they had at least one good man working under the sun. She began to sing to herself.

The ewe's in the meadow
The cu's in the corn
Tha'rt lang in bed, man,
Rise up with the dawn.

"That's a song tha'lt never have to sing to Edwin," she said after a time.

"Aye," said Mary. "Sometimes I wish he'd stay longer in his bed."

"Tush," Hawisa teased.

"Oh, Mam, that's not what I meant. You old women think we young ones think of nowt else."

"And you don't?"

"He works too hard," said Mary. "He does t'work of two men."

"That's as it's always been."

"No, but he saved the knight in battle. He should be able to sit about the great house and go shooting and the like, as Gib Falconer does. Why should he waste his arm in fieldwork? What's the good of freeing a man if he has to work harder than before?"

"Nay, I don't know what Win'd do all day without his fields and beasts."

320

"Wear soft clothes and play the harp, maybe," said Mary. They both laughed at the absurd picture.

"The sun's above us," said Hawisa. "You'd better take Win his dinner—if Simon hasn't eaten it all."

Mary rose and brushed the clothes from her skirt. Brown stains remained over her knees. She walked up the path to the cottage, singing as she went:

Tha'rt alying all idle
As new sucking bairn
The man will ne work
The man will ne lern.

Simon woke and squinted at her with one sullen, hopeless eye.

Meanwhile Win overheard Hilda atte-Beck gossiping to Edith Bradback while he was pitching hay behind the tithing barn and they didn't know he was there. "That Win Thornrigg's still got poor Mary in his cowbyre, and I don't know why she stands for it."

"I don't know why she stands for old Hawisa! I'd have put my foot down before now, believe me. 'Edwin,' I'd say, 'you build your own house like a proper man, or I'll teach you what wifelessness means.' "

"Think he'd do it even then? Wisa's got that much hold on him."

Hilda snickered. "Think she's given him one of her herbs? A son-stay-at-home-with-mammy herb?"

Win hefted his pitchfork over his shoulder, strode around the corner, and surprised them.

Edith Bradback coughed. "As I was saying, Hilda, the rats in the mill are getting terrible brave. Just last night a fat one scuttled right over Tom's nose."

"Ee, you need a better mouser," said Hilda. Then, sweetly, "Afternoon, Win."

"Having a good chat, Edith, Hilda?" Win replied in an ironic voice.

"We were just saying as how the rats are getting bigger and braver every day in t'mill, Win. You been having trouble with vermin lately?"

Noa, my trouble's with busybodies, Win felt like saying. But there was work to be done, and no time to waste on gossips.

82

Oxford
June 1347

Uthred hurtled into the hall at Chimney. "Miles! William of Ockham is at Oriel!"

Miles did not bother to glance up from the book he was sharing with William and Stephen at the long table. "I doubt it."

"It's true! Peter Ymer says Ockham's in disputation right now over in Oriel quadrangle!"

Miles spoke calmly. "Peter Ymer is playing you for a fool. If the master had returned from exile in Bavaria to the college of his youth, we would have heard of it by now."

"Maybe he came quietly, so as to avoid a stir."

Miles shook his head. "Think logically, Uthred. If he were avoiding a stir, would he be displaying himself in Oriel quad?"

Uthred looked deflated. "Well, *some* great thing is happening at Oriel. You can hear the argument from the other end of Kibald-twychen."

William sat up, straightened his back, and stretched. "I think I'll investigate the true cause of this disturbance. I could benefit from a change of air."

William and Uthred crossed Kibald street and went round to Oriel gate, where they had to bribe the porter to admit them. Once inside, they saw two Franciscans disputing volubly on the steps of the hall. One of them was a distinguished looking man with greying temples and a cool, supercilious manner. The other was stocky, sweating, and fuming. The quad was filled with blundering, disgruntled undergraduates.

William asked Uthred scathingly, "Does anyone here appear to be William of Ockham?"

"Well, Ockham's a Franciscan," Uthred replied lamely.

"So's Friar Tuck. Look, Uthred, at least twenty-five imbeciles like ourselves are milling around in this quad. The porter and Peter Ymer are well supplied with enough coin to last them a fortnight."

Peter Ymer sidled up to them in his cappa. He touched William's elbow and pointed to the urbane friar on the steps. "There he is, the great William d'Ockham."

William shook him off. "Your little joke is past its prime, Peter. I suggest you give it last rites."

Peter grinned. "It was merry whilst it lived. And profitable."

"I've seen that man before," Uthred exclaimed. "He's a conventual Franciscan visiting from some worthless Cambridge college. Hardly William d'Ockham. What kind of gull do you take me for?"

"An eager, sophomoric gull whose ratio vivendi is to be duped by his elders and betters." Peter smiled blandly.

Uthred looked shamefaced and changed the subject. "Who is the stout man with the Londonish speech?"

"The stout man is one of the Spiritual Franciscans, a radical. Note his frayed habit and self-righteous expression. But stay a while and enjoy the dispute." Peter glided off.

They listened to the friars dig at one another's weaknesses. The radical hammered out quotations from Scripture, which the conventual smoothly deflected with quotations from ecclesiastical documents and urbane witticisms.

Two overgrown freshmen blundered their way into the assembly and loutishly stationed themselves in the direct line of William's vision. Callow yokels, William thought, but he did not deign to correct them. The friars' argument was boring anyhow, utterly predictable. Yawning, he said to Uthred, "Pity the radical's so shrill. Actually, he's got the better case."

He was amazed when one of the callow yokels swung round on him with a sharp, moist, zealous face. "He hasn't got the best case. He's got the only possible case."

William stared coldly at the source of insolence. It spoke with a strong Yorkshire accent mixed with an objectionable note of precocious pedantry. William recognized it as one of the new crop of rustics attached to a hall associated with Balliol. Its companion glanced anxiously over its shoulder at William's chilly face. "Jack, why stick your nose into other men's private talk?"

"The purification of the mendicant orders is not a matter for private talk! It is as public as Doomsday, and this is a public quadrangle." The offender pushed sandy hair back from his forehead. He peered at William nearsightedly.

"Distinguo," said William drily. "The quadrangle belongs to Oriel, where you came not by right, my lad, but by bribery. But since you see fit to lecture your seniors, let me point out that if there were but 'one possible case' in this issue, there would be no disputation, would there?"

"There is only one possible case for a Christian!" The youth grew heated and waved his arms. "How can the argument of this luxurious possessioner friar be anything but false? Is it not plain that Francis himself, if living, would support the Spiritual? St Francis obviously preached literal poverty, and well he might, for the Gospels are clear on it."

The youth trod firmly on his friend's foot. "Jack, shut your mouth."

William answered wearily. "If you love the Brothers Spiritual, join them by all means. You can share a billet with Ockham in Bavaria and snarl at the pope from a safe distance." Uthred, listening, mused that William was beginning to sound wonderfully like Agrestis: magisterial, lofty, established.

The youth retorted, "If ever an heir of Peter deserved disapproval, it is now, as he wallows in decay in the thrall of secular men. Or do you approve of this Babylonian arrangement?"

William and Uthred looked at each other and laughed. "The pope does not often ask for our approval," said William. "Your zeal does you credit, lad, but your judgment wants refinement. I suggest you learn some manners before you blunder further around Oxford insulting your betters. You are fortunate that I am not a certain redhaired Merton man, who would have pulverized you at your first insolence."

The zealot's curlyhaired companion looked desperate. "Please don't mind my cousin, sir. He knows not when to hold his peace."

"Obviously."

A few minutes passed while they all listened to the greyfriars. Then the curlyhaired freshman turned around once more. He looked at William with a diffident, ingratiating face.

"Yes?" said William.

"Sir, I couldn't help noticing your speech. May I ask which Riding?"

"North Riding."

"God's truth? John and I are of the north Riding too. What place?"

"I doubt you've heard of it. Keldacross in Tewisdale. Do you know Thornton le Dale? Helmsley? About ten miles south of Helmsley."

"God's truth, not Tewisdale? I do know it. Aren't there some Wyclifs or Wydclifs there?"

"Wydclifs, certainly."

"God's truth! We're a branch of that family, John and I. I think we share a great uncle or summat with those Tewisdale people. Did you hear, Jack? This gentleman's practically neighbors with us in Yorkshire."

"Oh aye?" Cousin Jack looked around with a pleased expression.

William nodded. He hoped that these babes weren't going to try to attach themselves to him as he had to Agrestis years earlier. His studies for the baccalaureate were coming to their climax and he did not have time for new friendships. "How small is our finite world," he said tritely, patronizingly, to maintain distance. But curlyhead nodded eagerly, and Cousin Jack said, "Aye, so it is!" They looked at William brightly, expectantly.

324

The radical Franciscan raised his voice.

"Listen!" said John Wyclif, chewing excitedly on his nails. "He's using Ecclesiastes to great effect."

"Vanity of vanities," William observed casually to Uthred. "Well, I'm going back to Chimney. Boethius awaits." This was a good time to withdraw, while the freshmen were transfixed by the disputation. But curlyhead turned again as they were leaving and said, bravely, "We'll see you about then, sir?"

"Undoubtedly," said William politely, and he and Uthred left the quad.

After that he saw them often in the streets, but he could think of nothing but his baccalaureate and his entrance at Merton. He had no time for the Wyclifs or other insignificant youths.

Vanitas vanitatum et omnia vanitas: All is uselessness and chasing after the wind.

✳ 83

Keldacross
August 1347

It was an evil year for the fields at Keldacross. The harvest was wretched. The ground had not thawed until a week after Easter, and now, in August, it rained all day most every day. The corn had been cut and bound, and stood in stooks in the fields, but whenever they thought it was dry enough to cart, in came another storm and soaked it through. They were terrified that half of it would molder before they could get it stacked, and there was little enough as it was. It was now one of the few fine days since the end of July. And of course they had to waste it bringing in Sir Gervase's oats and barley, while their own lay waiting to be drenched again.

Wat Cottar, in the big wagon, straightened from piling the sheaves Edwin was tossing up to him. "Hold a bit," he said, rubbing his back.

"A bit young for that, aren't you, Wat?" Thomas Reeve shouted from the shade of the oak. "Get moving."

"It will rot," Mary lamented, gazing at the dark clouds building beyond Drumm Tor. "We'll never get it in."

"That's one thing I don't never have to fret about," said the cottar.

"Getting in my own corn." He laughed nastily. "Them as don't have don't worry about losing."

Edwin wielded his pitchfork determinedly. His face was strained. Thomas Reeve shaded his eyes, also watching the clouds. Oswin priest plodded up next to him. "I have prayed and prayed for this rain to stop. I have lit a candle to Our Lady and to St Godrich every night since harvest began."

"I feel the frost coming. I feel it in the soles of my feet. It will come even earlier than last year."

John Bailley strode over to them. "Reeve! Why am I doing your job for you? Make those churls get to work!"

Thomas moved off. "Ragenhilda! Bind up those sheaves again. No! That stook over there. You blind?"

"Whoever bound these here should have her nose cut off," said the bailley, indicating a sloppy stook.

Oswin looked on, shaking his head slowly.

"Eh, priest," John went on. "The laborers are many, but the harvest is scant. Eh? What are we going to do?"

The storm waited until they had got the knight's corn safely in. Then it broke with a vengeance. Their own corn bowed and flattened under the sheeting rain, and, later, rotted.

✳ 84

Keldacross and Oxford
March 1348

March in Kelda this year might still be February, so bleak it was and iron cold. The dung carts plodded slowly up and down the winterfield. The ground was bony with frost; the villagers were manuring it, putting it into good heart. Wat the cottar trudged behind Win's cart, hauling off the dung with a two-pronged drag. The length of the handle left him well clear of the manure as it fell, but still he must walk forward through it. His hands chafed, and his back ached more sorely with every step. "Wait," he told Win, who was driving the beast.

Win looked back. "What's amiss?"

Wat shook his head. "Nowt. Rest." He leaned on the drag.

"Noa, it's too cold to stand about."

A man with all the blessings can never pity a man with none, Wat grumbled to himself. He lifted the drag. "Go on, then." You pink eyed rabbit.

Win liked the smell of fresh manure in the cold of dead winter. Warm it was, live and rich with grass and bracken and good cow smell. But today for some reason it made him feel sick. He was sweating hard, even though it was Wat, not he, doing the heavy work, and even though the wind was so raw it made crystals of his breath on the woolen scarf Mary had wrapped round his chin that morning. There was a lot of stuff in his nose, as usual. He wondered whether his father had got off his arse and done some threshing. If not, he would have to do it himself, for his mother's back would not bear up to that work much longer. And the thatch was rotted over her bed, water leaking through—better get that done too; Simon never would. Mary had better go see if she could beg a hen or two from her father. Weasels or summat—why hadn't the damn dog barked? Useless cur! Do more good served up in a stew. Might come to that too, this hard winter. Win coughed and brooded and wiped his nose on the back of his chapped hand. There was a sore on his thumb that he couldn't get rid of.

Oswin priest came by next day because he had heard that Win was sick abed, and that concerned him. Lying abed was not like Win at all. He felt even less happy when he saw how Win looked, gray and drawn, under a load of blankets his mother had piled on him.

"Ee, lad, you look bad."

"Na," said Edwin. "I'll be right tomorrow." It was plainly hard for him to breathe. Sweat stood on his forehead, and his hair was plastered down like on a hot June haymaking.

"Where's Mary?"

"Out with Wat and Gabe, seeing they do the mucking."

"You've a good lass there, Win."

"Aye. Lucky." Win coughed up some phlegm. He closed his eyes and turned his head on the straw.

"He'll be better in no time," Hawisa said, determined. She stirred some pungent medicinal herb in her iron kettle. The steam of it rose and filled the rafters. More steam rose from the nose of Win's favorite cow, which Mary had brought in to warm and cheer him. The cow was tied to the foot of his bed, a sleek little creature with a rose and cream coat and a tight, firm udder. She had a kindly, sweet expression as she chewed her cud over Win's blanketed toes. Win called her Molly-cow.

"You make this man rest, Wisa," said Oswin.

"Reckon I'd have to tie him down with ropes if he wants to work tomorrow," said Hawisa lightly.

"Stay in bed, lad. I tell you as your parson. Remember, even God rested from his labor."

"Aye," said Win, joking feebly, "but he didn't have no assart field to muck."

Oswin felt too uneasy to let Edwin by with that one. "God sweated muckle when he walked on t'earth," he said sternly.

"I know it. I meant no ill. He was a poorer man than I am."

It was unlike Win to speak so. He was a good enough Christian, but he kept such thoughts to himself. Oswin was troubled. "You make this man rest tomorrow, Hawisa, or I'll count you as a sinner."

When Oswin came rushing back to the cottage that night he was too late, because Hawisa and Mary had refused to believe that Win was anywhere near death. When his breath had come bubbling so you could hear the liquid rumble across the room, Simon had said, "That boy won't last the night." But the women had ignored him. They had gone on bustling about the bed with broths and salves and remedies, and called too late for Oswin priest.

When Oswin came in, Simon went and sat on his three-legged stool by the hearth and spat into the fire. Oswin stood in the doorway with the freezing winter outside. He saw Mary kneeling by Win clutching his gray hand, and Hawisa still bumbling around the bed, wiping Win's mouth with a warm, damp cloth.

Sir Gervase himself went down to see Hawisa when he had the news next morning. He stooped to get through the door. The women who had come to mourn with Wisa and Mary quit their wailing when he came in. They stared at him. Dame Magdalen and Dame Marion came into villeins' houses, but never Sir Gervase. Gervase found Hawisa in the crowded darkness and spoke to her in a harsh, stiff voice. "The best damn bowman I ever had. I do not forget what he did for me. If that husbandman of yours still proves worthless, don't fear you'll starve. Let Dame Magdalen know what you need."

Hawisa stood before the knight with a sort of dazed dignity on her face. Mary, kneeling on the floor, suddenly stuffed her face into Win's blankets. Simon, slumped on his stool by the fire, did not even lift his head.

Gervase saw Molly-cow, still tethered to the bed. He cleared his throat. "You need not worry about paying me any heriot beast," he told

Hawisa. "I'll instruct John Bailley." Then he stooped and went out of that place.

Simon mumbled, "Doan't you know it, Sir? T'owd sow never cared for owt but the runt she farrowed in this sty. But what of me? I'm his dad." He mumbled, slurring so that he was scarcely understood. The women did not ask to hear him better; they resumed their mourning.

Because Edwin had been to Canterbury, Oswin said this psalm over his grave:

They are happy whose home is God
When they set their feet on pilgrim ways.
They lose their way; yet drink they deep from wells of water.
They pass from strength to strength
They win from outer wall to inner
And God shows his face to them in Zion.

Afterward, the villeins looked on Win's passing as an omen.

Fat Tuesday night in Oxford, the scholars, reveling in large drunken numbers, saw fit to tie on animal masks and stay out past curfew, defying the watch with catcalls and hoots. William had no mask, but he chalked his face white and stained his mouth and lips with ink. He caught his reflection in a torchlit window as they went by and startled himself. "Ut hoy, ut hoy, I'm the lilywhite boy," he chanted weirdly, fastening his hands around Agrestis's neck. Agrestis screamed horribly through his pig snout. Stephen knocked William across the back with a quarterstaff. "Off, demon, off! In nomine Patris et Filii et Spiritus Sancti! Off, I say! Begone!" William matched Agrestis' shriek and pretended to writhe against a wall. Something squelched and cracked underfoot—and then he began to scream in earnest. "O Jesu! O God!" He leapt away from the wall and ran, dragging one foot on the cobbles.

"What the devil?" Peter Ymer of Oriel caught him by the hood. "What are you yowling about?"

William scraped his foot against a post. "Uch! Uch! A dead thing! I trod on a dead thing!"

Agrestis went and peered into the dim gutter. "Rat. Mmm. Maybe we should take it home on a pole. Sin to waste good meat, with weeks of meatlessness at hand."

Stephen clouted him with his stick. "Go away, Agrestis, you're a disgusting pig."

Agrestis tapped his snout and made repellent noises.

They proceeded down the street. Someone struck up a song of Paris.

Then they spied a big man in a long furred gown hurrying down the other side of the street, accompanied by a torchbearing manservant.

"Ho!" Agrestis bellowed, "is it not Master John the Vintner?"

"Master Vintner!" The students swarmed across the street to bait him.

The manservant brandished his torch. "Stay back!"

"Alms, Master Vintner! Charity for poor freezing clercs!"

"Will you take us in, Master Vintner? Are your fires warm?"

"Is your wife warm?"

"Go to hell," the manservant snapped. "It's warm down there."

"Hear that, fellows? A layman sending clercs to hell. Is that proper?"

"You don't need anyone to send you there," the vintner retorted. "You'll get there easy enough on your own. Now move on!" He pulled his knife.

They fell back, and followed at a distance. "Why out so late, Master Vintner? It's past the curfew."

"Seeing if his daughter's run off to a tavern with a lusty scholar."

"Nay, he's visiting Master Christopher's pretty wife, I'm bound. Isn't old Christopher in London this week?"

"For shame, Master Vintner!"

"Say, we know a fellow who'll give you an easy penance if you tell him about the sin with enough description."

The vintner hurried on, cursing under his breath. The manservant brandished his torch at them, then followed his master.

"How's your table, vintner?" William shouted. "By the looks of your belly it's bound to be good!"

The vintner reached his house and pounded on the door. A woman opened it, and he swept in. The manservant snuffed his torch and made one last jab at them with the smoldering end. Then he slammed the door.

They gathered around the house, singing up at the gables.

Ou EST porc ET boeuf Et mouTON,
MaLARZ, faiSANZ et VENoiSON,
GRASses geLINES, et CHApons
Et BONS froMAGES en GLAon!

Where there's pork and beef and mutton, duck, pheasant, and venison, fat hens and capons, and good cheeses in baskets.

Throughout most of the country last harvest had been poor, and by now villeins were weak and thin, but in Oxford William gave it no thought. In university one thought less often about such things.

Part Five

An hydeous fire sal sodanly come
That all the world sal wholy burn
And nathyng spare that is tharin.
THE PRICKE OF CONSCIENCE OF MASTER RICHARD ROLLE
THE HERMIT

* 85

Oxford
Ash Wednesday 1348

William collared Agrestis as he came down St John's street. "There's a Padua doctor at the Prelate, and he's got a ghastly tale to tell of that sickness we've heard about abroad."

"Is he still there?"

"Last I saw, and I came straight. Did you hear of the earthquake in Italy?"

"Naturally. They say it swallowed up half the churches in Rome."

"Not quite. But the Padua doctor says it was fumes and gases from the earthquake that are making this sickness."

"Save me from all leeches," said Agrestis irrelevantly. Then, "I expect the earthquake simply let a few more devils out of hell to scourge those greedy Italians."

"As long as it doesn't cross the water, it's one with me. But let's hear that doctor of yours."

By the time they got back to the tavern, a large crowd had gathered, and another man, a foreign sounding blackfriar, was arguing with the Paduan.

"You say it was an earthquake," he said, "but I say it was the cursed Genoese." He turned to the crowd. "Don't you know that the Tartars besieged the Genoese at Feodosia? Well, the pest struck the Tartars in their camps as they lay outside the walls. And then the Tartars used their catapults to hurl the corpses over the walls, so that the Genoese might taste the agony. And those among the Genoese who did not die fled home and brought this horror with them. The plague on them was the punishment of God, for lately they had helped the Saracens slaughter the Christians of Romania. And when they came home to Genoa, they were driven away with blazing arrows. For everyone who has seen this disease knows that it is carried by the breath or touch of the afflicted, and not by floating gases.

That is, except our learned physicians who look at books of Galen instead of at the agony of the dying."

"I do not deny what you say, Fra Giocondo, but your history of the Genoese galleys does not explain how the Tartars were afflicted with the disease in the first place, nor does your theory of divine wrath against the Genoese explain why it should now be equally visited upon the other cities of Italy."

"No. But neither have you explained with your miasmic gases the most terrible of all terrors: the contagion from hand to hand." Giocondo appealed to the audience. His face was pained and angry. "For when anyone stricken with it dies, all who see him or visit him in his sickness, or even carry him to his grave, quickly follow him there. It is a terrible thing. You cannot know. In Florence, thousands die, alone. No priest will come near them."

"The passing of the disease through the afflicted may be explained in this way," the doctor replied. "The atmosphere is corrupted through the means which I have described. Now, the corrupted atmosphere tends to gather around a man or woman in a sort of—shall I say—nimbus cloud. The victim then radiates, as it were, the putrescence to any who come near him. That is my opinion. Those as well versed in medicine as I may put forth their own." He surveyed them cooly.

Agrestis spoke up. "Tell us, Doctor Leech. Will these gases cross the channel?"

"It is quite likely that they will disperse before they arrive this far north."

"What is it like, this disease? We have heard the most terrible descriptions."

The friar answered. "The more terrible the more true. The most hideous swellings in groin or armpit, the smallest the size of almonds, full of stench and pus. I had a friend." The man's face twisted. "It was a boil as big as an apple on his neck, and he screamed so that I fled, and he died alone."

William shuddered. How could a man desert his friend like that?

"Yes," said the Paduan. "Another symptom is the appearance of dark stains or streaks, as from under the skin. I have noted this on many corpses." He paused to let everybody feel the comparison between his courage and the Florentine's. "I have also noticed that the disease kills in four to seven days. If the boil breaks within a week, the victim will most likely survive. But few endure the pain for that long."

"We hear, doctor, of men dying in a few hours, or overnight."

"Rare. Although there seems to be a variant of the pest wherein the afflicted, spitting blood, dies invariably within one or two days."

"Doctor, is it true that people go mad? We hear that people go mad."

"I saw a man," Giocondo answered, "who climbed up on his roof and threw the tiles down into the street."

Someone laughed nervously.

"Very rare," said the doctor, "though in some cases there seems to be a sort of drunkenness or lunacy. I would imagine that it stems from the discomforts of the disease."

"What are you looking so wan for, Angel?" Agrestis demanded, as they walked back to college. "It's not going to happen here."

"How can you know that?"

"Things don't happen in England the way they do abroad. Besides, you heard what our learned friend said about the gases dispersing."

William did not reply.

"And look. The Saracens are infidels. The Italians are corrupt. The French stole the pope and King Edward's lands. But what wrong have we English done?"

"No wrong."

"No wrong. So, friend, don't worry yourself. Gaudeamus igitur."

"Let's rejoice. But first we'd better go to St John's and get our ashes."

There, with Stephen, they heard the first sermon of Lent.

The preacher sucked in his cheeks. He let his breath out slowly, with a hiss. "And the serpent said, 'Eat, and you shall be like gods.' Isn't that the way some students go about nowadays, seducing others?" The preacher gestured dramatically. "I have even found that some lead their friends into taverns."

Stephen nodded devoutly. "Amen," he whispered with a pious expression. William thought he had better look away.

"Who are more malevolent nowadays than students? Who are more obstinate than scholars? Laymen keep from evil at least by fear of punishment. But students fear neither temporal nor eternal excommunication." The preacher scanned his congregation. "Remember. Your friends and parents have worked hard to maintain you in the schools so that you may bring honor to them and to others."

"Such as Widow Judith," Stephen whispered through a slit in his lips.

"And now you waste your money on evil uses."

"Yellow hosen." Stephen nudged William.

"Why do you think the houses of layfolk are forbidden you? Is it for nothing that the proctors patrol the streets with pole axes? Who are more roisterous than clercs?"

"Has he never met John Hand the journeyman?"

"O criminous clercs." The preacher beat his breast. "I tell you, there was a time when the scholars of Oxford were loved for their sweetness and devotion."

"When was that, the days of St Frideswide?"

"Sssh," said William. The preacher had trained his eyes on them. He pointed. "But you, sunk in all manner of violence and lechery, you are known only for your depravity." He paused. When he resumed, his voice had changed its tone. "Do you think that the great God who punishes the French and Italians for their sins with this terrible plague will ignore your own? Repent, I caution you, before the Lord sweeps down upon us as he did upon the cities of the plain. Pray that he may not harden your hearts as he did Pharaoh's, that he may not bring the plague upon England as he brought it upon Egypt."

They came out with ashes smudged on their foreheads.

"Well, vipers," Agrestis said, "shall we repent? Or shall we visit the Prelate for more effective absolution?"

"He spoke too much of sin," William muttered.

"When you're a fine preacher, Angel, you may ignore sin on Ash Wednesday and speak only of beer."

But Stephen rubbed at his ashes with his finger and looked at the blackness of them.

Later that evening William felt he must go to see Lyra. Lyra answered the door with a reserved face, but he bade William come in and be seated. Cyan the Harp sat by the window over a book. He looked up at William's knock, nodded at him when he came in, and went back to his reading.

William told Lyra all that he had heard that day. Then he added, "But I have heard from others that the Paris doctors have ascribed this thing to the stars—an evil conjunction of the planets. Tell me, Lyra, what do you think? You love astronomy."

Lyra leaned his chin on his hand. "It is true that in March three years ago occurred the configuration you name. Saturn and Jupiter and Mars, as you know, are held to be heralds of destruction. The conjunction of all three planets would reputedly not be a happy one. Nonetheless, William, I think the connection between the conjunction and the plague far fetched to say the least. After all, the conjunction occurred three years past."

"But the sickness began three years ago, only it was in strange, far places, so we did not hear of it. The Florentine said he heard from a sailor that it was in Cathay."

Lyra shook his head. "William, I do not know. And if truth be told, I don't think anyone knows. I would say to all these doctors, if I could, that their duty is not to worry over the heavens, or earthquakes, or gases, but to attend to the suffering of the sick and to do what they can to lessen it."

"Don't you want to know why this is happening?"

"None of these explanations tells us why; they only say how. The why is in the mind of God, and that is darkness to us."

"No it isn't. God shows himself in this world! He speaks to us through revelation and the church and the Holy Spirit. He gave us intellect to discover him through creation, no matter what the moderns say! He is not this Dark Being you make him, a dark cloud so utterly other that we cannot even think about him let alone come to any understanding!" William bit his lip, for he felt as if he were going to shout frantically.

"William, you misunderstand. The darkness of which I speak is not God himself, but simply our unknowing of him. As far as the heavens are above the earth are his thoughts above our thoughts. The darkness is ours. But God himself is light."

"But we may come to the Father through the Son! That's the part you omit, Lyra!"

"But how do we come to the Son? By stripping ourselves of self and as it were crawling back into the womb."

William stood up glaring.

Lyra said, "You want God to be some Ultimate Master of Metaphysics, the Subtlest Doctor, the Unsurpassed Logician. You want to make God graspable, so that you may find comfort in thought. But God cannot be thought. He spoke to Job out of the whirlwind, and his answer to him was No Answer. It was I AM."

William stepped backward. "Lyra, stop it. It's not going to happen here."

Lyra leaned forward and grasped William's hand. He looked kindly into William's face, and his voice grew quiet. "William, what St Denys says is true. All my life I have loved astronomy and geometry, and truly I believe that God does speak through propositions and the shining stars. But what is the meaning of these propositions and this shining? All my life I have striven to know, and now I know that I will never know. And I am content." He sat back. "Even if this thing comes, still I am content. God does what he does, and I am content."

William pulled his hand away. "Well, thank you, Brother Lyra. You have certainly set my heart at rest."

Lyra replied, "How should it be at rest?"

William said, "Go to hell," and slammed out. They heard his feet running down the stairs.

Cyan looked up from his book and said in Welsh, " 'Death comes like a black smoke, with no mercy for fair countenance.' "

"The fairest of all," said Lyra, "sweat blood."

✳ 86

Keldacross
April 1348

Alice stood in the kitchen lecturing in the preparation of spiced meat pottage, and they all had to listen to her and do what she said, because she was now the bailley's wife.

"I don't hold with that much ginger," grumbled the cook, "nor do the gentlefolk like it."

Alice was about to reply when Martha Reeve burst in from the hall. "Quick!" she shouted. "Where's John Bailley?"

"Up in the outfields, I think. What's amiss?"

"Wisa Thornrigg's gone and chopped into Simon with a sickle!"

"What! Is he dead?"

"Noa, but he's none too snug, neither."

They all ran out of the kitchen and down the hill, except for the cook, who stayed behind to make the pottage his own way.

"He's a slug," Hawisa was saying, grim as death, still clutching the bloody sickle, which no one had yet dared wrest away from her. "He's better dead than alive."

Simon writhed on his sagging bed. The roof that he'd failed to mend all winter leaked thatchy rain onto his feet. The fire smoked, stinging everyone's eyes. The blood oozed from his split side. "You bitch," he croaked. "You sow."

"Mam, no," Mary was begging. "Mam, please, no."

"Who did the thrashing all winter?" Hawisa demanded, in a low, steadier voice. "Win. Who was up on the roof in the white storm mending the thatch before it all fell in? Win. Who bakes the last bit of wheat flour for us to eat this very evening? Me and Mary. Who eats the whole loaf? You, you worm, you fat nightcrawler. I'll chop you into gobbets before I'm done. I'll reap and thrash you! I'll send you to your Father in hell."

"Mam, no!" Mary screamed. John Bailley ran in with the miller, and they got the sickle away from her.

"Poor Wisa," Alice went on that night, tucked into her bed with the bailley. "It's a cruel shame to jail her. If anybody should be trussed up in the cellars, it's that Simon."

"Women's justice," muttered the bailley. "Praise God we're preserved from it."

"Is that all you can say? Well let me tell you about men's justice. I know of more than one husbandman who feels no gripe of conscience at beating his innocent wife and bairns to pulpmeat once or twice a fortnight, and no judgment falls on him. Yet if Hawisa strikes Simon, whom all know to be a leech and a toad who as good as killed his son with his laziness, Hawisa's trussed up for a felon in the rootcellar. I've no use for man's justice. Give me barnyard justice instead; it's closer to God's than yours." She turned away from him.

John did not know how to answer such bitter disparagement. At last he said, "There are too many mouths to feed in this village."

"Then let's weed out the Simons, not the Hawisas."

"We're not clearing the outland fast enough. We need to plough more land."

In bed in the great chamber Dame Magdalen insisted, "Stop it. Stop keening over these villeins." Marion shared Magdalen's bed while the men were away because nowadays Magdalen was always cold, her hands and feet frigid. She even let the dogs up on the bed, regardless of fleas.

"But what will become of Wisa?" Marion wept.

"I don't know. She had better pray that Simon will live. She may then escape with a whipping and a fine."

"I will go down and comfort her for Edwin's sake. He was pilgrim with us to Canterbury. And he saved Nicholas' life."

"Her daughter-in-law is with her. They do not want you there. Grant me that much knowledge of these people."

Marion went on weeping until Magdalen said wearily, "Child, won't you let me sleep? I am so sick."

Immediately Marion ceased crying. It was the first time Dame Magdalen had said those words.

When at last Dame Magdalen slept, Marion crept out of bed. She lit a taper in the hall and took it down the slimed and mildewed darkness of the cellar steps.

She found Hawisa trussed up against the mouldy wall between two great sacks of garlic. Despite what must be extreme discomfort, she was

339

sunk utterly in sleep. Edwin's widow sat wakeful next to her, huddled under some rough sacking she had wrapped round them both.

"Eh?" said Mary, startled by the lady's presence.

"It's Dame Marion. May I bring you food or drink or blankets or help you in any way?"

"Oh . . . no, thank you, lady. We've got what John Bailley's allowed her."

"If I say she may have more, she may have it."

"Thank you, lady, I think it's better not." Mary added, "But it's good of you to ask. Our Edwin thought much of you."

It was an oddly familiar speech from the widow of a ploughman, but Marion could not take offense. Standing in the darkness, she felt strangely moved, as if the whole world were slowly, invisibly, rolling upside down. Because things were strange and murky in this way, she replied, "I dreamed of Edwin a few nights back."

"Did you, lady?"

"It was a clear dream. He looked . . . " Marion did not know how to say how Win had looked. The dream had been so powerful, she had woken from it trembling.

Mary said simply, "I never dream of Win."

A silence. Then Mary said, "His mam don't dream of him either. Only thing she ever sees is a picture of him rotting in the ground, meat for worms and maggots, right when she's dropping off to sleep. After that she can't close her eyes till morning's come, and then she must up and work." Mary paused, looking around the cellar.

In the darkness, Marion paled. "I will pray that you both may dream happily of Edwin," she offered faintly. "You are certain I cannot bring you any comforts?"

"Dame Marion, it wasn't right what Wisa did, chopping into Win's dad. She knows it, and she doan't expect comforts."

"They say Simon's wound is not so bad as it first seemed."

"That's good, lady."

There was nothing more to say. Marion retreated back up the stairs into Dame Magdalen's chamber. As she climbed into bed, she realized that Dame Magdalen had wakened. "I see you went to the cellar after all."

"I am sorry."

"You meant well."

After a while Magdalen spoke again. "I regret that I have not let you take more on yourself in looking after this household. Soon enough it will rest entirely on your shoulders."

Marion lay under the coverlet and was dumb.

340

"You may call Katharine to help you when she can. But she is to help you, not bully you. Do not let her order you about. It is you, not she, who are lady of Kelda."

Marion thought, I cannot do it.

✳ 87

York and Oxford
June 1348

Andrew Comyn and his wife went down to Holy Trinity in Goodramgate to hear the archbishop's letter read from the pulpit.

" 'Insofar as the life of men on earth is warfare, it is no wonder that those who battle amidst the wickedness of the world are sometimes disturbed by the uncertainty of events, on one occasion favorable, on another adverse.' " Parson John looked up. "And this also says our archbishop: 'For almighty God sometimes allows those whom he loves to be chastened, so that their strength can be made complete by the outpouring of grace in the time of their infirmity.' " The priest went on: " 'Everybody knows, since the news is now widely spread, what infections there are in diverse parts of the world which at this moment are threatening the land of England.' " The priest cleared his throat. " 'This surely must be caused by the sins of men who, made complacent by their prosperity, forget the bounty of the Most High Giver . . .' "

"Tripe," said Andrew as they walked home. "I don't hear that it's killing the rich any faster than it's killing the poor. Nay, in fact I hear the opposite."

"Husband," said Alison, "don't go to London as you have planned."

"Devil I won't, wife. There's no plague in London—and if there were, I'd gamble. If I'm to die, I'd rather die rich than poor. I'll do what business there I need do."

"Aye," said Thomas Noye, "that's what I say."

"It's prayers we need," said Alison, "not business. All the people of York should stay put and say their prayers as the archbishop says. Please don't go, Andrew."

"We're not so wicked as London," added Mistress Noye.

"Perhaps God will spare us if he finds us praying. Please, Andrew," Alison begged. "I pray you."

"The Devil," Andrew retorted. "We've enough monks and women

341

in York to fill the churches and drone litanies all day till kingdom come. I'm to London as I planned."

"Can't stop living," agreed Thomas Noye. "Can't stop working every time there's a danger in the world."

Andrew looked Alison in the face, and softened. "Never fear, my good wife. I'll stay clear of any illness I see. Besides, it's you who always says it: a rumor grows worse with every mile."

"There are plenty of miles between them and us," said Mistress Noye.

Andrew Comyn arrived in London on his business of the Staple. At table in his hostelry he met a well fed Oxford clerc. The clerc was amazed: "Certainly I know William of Kelda! He lives in my very hall. In my very room!"

Andrew replied. "Faith, this is a strange meeting, but a happy one, for I swore that I would see this pouch delivered, and this will save me sending my good servant Adam."

Adam Scawe stuck out his lip. He had looked forward to the trip to Oxenford, looked forward to being on his own for a while. Miles Spottiswoode, on his part, hoped that the merchant might spare a penny for the trouble that Miles was sparing him. Miles had nearly exhausted his traveling purse. But the merchant disappointed him. So he received William's pouch with bad grace, went on to Oxford, and forgot to give it to William for three days. When he remembered, he found the letters crumpled up at the bottom of his saddlebags. He dropped them rudely on William's bed. By that time both letters were nearly two months old.

William picked them up and rubbed the dust off with his sleeve. He recognized his Uncle Roger's hand. The other hand was strange. He decided to save the mystery for last, and broke Roger's seal. He took the letter to the window and held it to the light.

Miles came in. Uthred said, "The angel has a letter." So Stephen came in too, and they both peered over William's shoulder. He shrugged them off. "Two letters. And I'll read this one aloud." Miles disappeared into his carrel and began droning over his books. He was not interested.

"This is what it says. It is from my uncle who is good to me. 'York. The Tuesday after Mary Magdalene. To the learned Bachelor in Arts William: greetings and a purse.' "

"Ha!" Stephen clapped him on the shoulder. "My good friend!"

William glowed. "The learned Bachelor of Arts." He had finished his course in June, though he had still to pass the formal determination. That was not until Lent. "But wait. Where's the purse! Miles!"

"Oh aye. I forgot. I will get it for you. A moment."

"He forgot." Stephen put his tongue in his cheek.

"The rest I am too modest to read you," said William, "for it is in praise of myself."

"Then why mention it at all?" Miles flung the purse at his head and went back to his droning.

"But he ends, 'I have sent another letter to Robert de Treng two weeks since, in which, together with some matters of my own, I have reminded him of you and recommended you to him once again. I am certain that you stand well in his eyes. Keep yourself clear of mischief, and we will see you at Merton before the year is out. The Holy Spirit have you in governance. Roger.' "

But Stephen was counting the purse money. "Excellent uncle! Kind benefactor! Let me calculate how many cups of ale this will purchase at the Prelate. Let's see. He sent fifteen shillings! And I have eightpence. William! Together we have fifteen shillings eightpence!"

Uthred pointed at the letter. "Look, there's something written along the side there. Did you see it?"

It was a scrawl. "Feast of St James. Nephew, I have just had the news. It is a great grief to me. Requiescat in pace."

"What?" said William. He read and reread the scrawl.

"What is it, Angel?"

William stood still. "Will you hand me that other letter?" he asked quietly. Uthred obliged. William took it and went into his study.

It was short. The hand was like a child's, big and painstaking.

"Brother. This is your brother's wife who writes this. What woe is in me to write this, you may guess."

William did not come out and he did not come out, and no sound came out either, so Uthred, worried, put his head in and said, "Angel?"

William started.

"William?" said Stephen.

William stood up. "I must meet Agrestis." He picked up the *Sententiae*, a costly book he had borrowed from Agrestis, and walked out of the room, pushing the letter under his belt.

He wandered into the Cornmarket and watched the haggling. From there he drifted through the drapery and into the cordwainers' row. He found himself before the widow's stall. She was there by herself, biting off a length of tough black thread. She looked up at him, cold sea green. "Yes? Can I serve you?"

He said, "My mother is dead."

She laid her work in her lap and crossed herself. "God rest the lady," she said, and took up her work again. Her eyes did not care.

"Please," he said. "Please." But he did not know what he was asking for.

She put down her work again. "If you will come in, I will fix you something to eat."

He followed her blindly. He heard her say, "Drew, mind the shop." He let her sit him down in the kitchen and watched dully as she cut into a wheel of white cheese. She poured him a cup of cider and set it before him. He took the cheese and put it into his mouth, but it turned to paste, and he could not swallow it. So he put his head in his hands, Judith did not know what to do. Joan, her eldest, gaped. Little Dickon played noisily under the table.

"I am sorry," William said at last. "I don't know why I came here. I will go home."

But as he said so his voice fled away from him and the room went white.

A distant woman commanded, "Sit!" and her hand pushed his head to his knees. He was in a little, low room, close and hot, on the floor. Green eyes, troubled, looked down on him. "Scholar? You fainted."

"I used to do that," he murmured. "I haven't done it for a long time. I'm all right now." He sat up and stared vaguely. She knelt beside him on the floor and put her arm around his shoulders. She put a wooden bowl to his lips and tipped it. "Drink that." When he had drunk, she put the bowl aside and wiped his chin with a cloth. "There," she said, "there." And then he was kissing her feverishly on the mouth. Startled, she did not stop him. Then she pushed him away, saying, "No, no, you can't have that."

"I'm sorry."

She stood, brushing her skirts. "Rest a while. I'll send Drew to Kibald to fetch one of your friends."

"No. No friends. I will go back now. I am well." He got up. The floor was unsteady. "I am sorry."

"Sorry for what?" she snapped. "Nothing happened." She followed him out of the house. John Hand the journeyman was in the stall now. He narrowed his eyes at William, but William did not see him. He went to the Puking Prelate and sat in the dimness.

When he had drunk enough, he made his way back to Chimney. He took a short way through a narrow alley. The houses there sagged anciently into one another, low, with sinking roofs. The gutter took up most of the street; it was necessary to dodge sogged cabbage leaves and decaying fish parts. It was one of the worst places in Oxford. John Hand followed him there.

"I think you left something with my mistress, clerc," he said.

William swung around in dead panic. Agrestis' *Sentences*! John Hand held it aloft.

"Give it me!" William snatched. "That belongs to a scholar of Merton!"

"Does it now?" John tossed the book from hand to grimy hand. William lunged for it. "Oops," said John casually, and dropped it into the gutter.

William cried out and bent, reaching for the book. John trod on his hand, and on the book, grinding hard; and tramped back down the alley, satisfied.

William stumbled back to St John street, his hand pressed in his armpit, the book in his elbow. Agrestis, stamping angrily out of Merton gate, sighted him and shouted, "You dog! I've waited for you half the morning! Where the hell have you been? You're staggering like a gaseous sheep." He took a second look. "Holy Mother of God!"

"Agrestis, I've ruined your book."

Agrestis rushed over. "What's wrong with your hand?" He grabbed it and stared. "Jesu! What in God's name?"

Agrestis brought William back to Chimney hall. He said to the gawkers who had gathered, "Our friend's been hurt. What are you staring at?"

Uthred pointed at the warped and reeking book in William's lap. "Warden Treng lent you the money for that book, Agrestis."

"Treng'll get his money." Agrestis made William lie down. "And then I'll kill that townie."

"No, it's my fault," said William. "I'll pay for the book. It's all my fault."

Agrestis turned back to the observers. "And I'll kill anyone who tells Treng about this, or anyone else at Merton. Bachelor or master, I'll kill him."

✳ 88

Kelda
July 1348

Gervase made Nicholas and Marion take the great bedchamber because after Maudlin died he did not want to sleep there any more. It was strange to Nicholas, sleeping in her bed. All night long he lay awake and saw images of days before he even went to Helmsley, days long forgotten when he played on the floor with William under his mother's loom, nights of women's voices and firesides and baths in a bowl.

Over the rim of the windy moor, over Old Keep and the walls of the little orchard, dawn was blowing moist, quiet light against the two tall windows. Between the windows was a wooden chest built into the wall, and a hanging his mother had made, simply and elegantly woven, embroidered with a daleswoman's dearest leaves and flowers. Marion awakened and saw that Nicholas was mourning. He pretended to be asleep when she rose and left the room.

Later she came back, and Nicholas sat up, because she was carrying his son on her hip and leading his daughter by the hand. She put the baby in his lap, boosted little Maddie up, and sat herself beside him on the bed. Nicholas held Robin awkwardly, not knowing what to do about it. Robin was a fat, convivial, beaming baby, well pleased with everyone. He gazed jovially on Nicholas and grabbed his nose.

"Father, Bobbin likes noses," Maddie explained.

Nicholas self-consciously jounced Robin up and down. "Pumpety pum, pumpety pum," he heard himself say.

Robin grinned wide, screwing up his eyes and turning bright red. He chuckled deeply, hilariously. Nicholas attempted to conceal a smile. He jounced harder. "Pumpety PUM! Pumpety PUM!" Robin took in his breath, lifted his voice and shrieked, "BUM! BUM! BUM!"

Excluded, Maddie sat between her parents and watched sorrowfully. Finally she slapped Nicholas on the elbow and demanded, "Bumbiddy *me!* Bumbiddy*me!*"

So Nicholas got both of them up on his knees and did "Pumpety PUM! You're riding to WAR!" until they screamed so hard that they rolled around and he had to catch them from falling off the bed. Marion laughed as she had not laughed for many months, but then Alice came in and pointed out that Robin had wet the coverlet. She fetched the children away crossly. "Marry. Stealing the bairns from under my nose. Throwing them around the room. St William, he's like to kill them."

"BUM! BUM!" bellowed Robin as he and Maddie were borne away. And all the rest of that day when Maddie saw Nicholas she jumped up and down and shrieked "Bumbiddy, bumbiddy," which embarrassed him no end in front of Gib Faulkoner.

It occurred to him how Robin looked like William, and it grieved him that he never saw his brother any more.

Keldacross and Oxford
December 1348

Marion sat up terrified, fumbled to light a candle, and knocked it over in her haste. She could hear Nicholas gasping in the dark. She shook his shoulder. "Nicholas!" In the faint, white light that came through the narrow windows she saw his eyes open wide. He threw his arms over his face and rolled over, breathing hard.

"You were dreaming."

"It was an owl in the solar."

"It was a dream."

"There was an owl, big, black. Its back was to me, but there was blood—"

"No. Don't tell me." Marion covered her ears. She uncovered them and lay down again. "I used to have evil dreams when I was a child," she said, "but I don't have them any longer."

Nicholas rubbed his face in his arms. That great bird waiting. "Holy Rood," he muttered through gritted teeth, striving unsuccessfully not to fall asleep again. As he slipped off, a deep note of music sounded, and he saw a shadowy figure gesturing or pointing somewhere. Nicholas fell to sleep again with the sensation of sinking.

Something kept rousing William that same night. He slept and waked and slept again.

Stephen the novicemaster said to him, "For your penance you will scrub the frater floor."

"How may I do so? There are rats all over it."

"Who let them in?" Father Stephen handed him a sack.

William woke again. Vigils. "I don't have to do this any more." He dreamt again.

He rode in a cart beside a blurred, familiar villein fellow over a road up a steep green hill. The road ran alongside a vague mossy wall; on the other side of the road was a grey heath. A great white cloud was rising there. Up ahead, at the rim of the knoll, was mild blue sky. They came down to the top of the hill and saw the road wandering down below them, wide, smooth, tawny, over broad meadows. In the middle of the plain was a great church.

The villein said, "That's Canterbury town," but there was no town.

"I am glad my brother is not here," William told him, "for he would never ride in a cart."

Suddenly the villein reined in the carthorse and jumped down. Win Thornrigg the archer. He looked up at William and pointed to the east, where the cloud was covering the sky. William sat in the cart, looking down the broad, flat road and the plain. No. Why should he turn the cart into the clumps and bracken, eastward, where the cloud was growing darker and darker?

✳ 90

Oxford
July 1348

Agrestis came into the Puking Prelate, waving an old, tattered, volume. "Listen to what this old stoat has to say about our English cities. Jesu Mary, what a picture! Listen."

He sat down and flipped the book open. " 'Rochester and Chichester,' " he read, " 'are mere villages, and possess nothing for which they should be called cities but the sees of their bishops.' "

"True enough," said Uthred.

" 'Oxford scarcely, I will not say satisfies, but sustains its clercs.' "

"Amen!" Peter Ymer pounded the table. "That old fellow spoke true enough."

But Agrestis looked up at him evilly. " 'Exeter supports men and beasts on the same food.' What say you to that, Peter? Is it all true?"

"Why certainly. We feed our dogs only the best pheasant and venison."

" 'Nor will you select your habitation in Worcester, Chester, or Hereford—ON ACCOUNT OF THE DESPERATE WELSHMEN!' " Agrestis roared, so that Lyra and Cyan could hear it across the room. " 'The town of Ely is always putrefied by the surrounding marshes. At Bristol there is nobody who is not, or hath not been, a soap maker.' And Colin, this is for you. 'As for the West Country, every market village and town hath but rude and rustic inhabitants. Moreover, at all times account the Cornish people for such as you know the Flemish people are accounted for in France.' "

"I never met a Fleming I didn't like," the Cornishman replied. "But what says he of the North, Yorkshireman?"

"Nothing. Nothing at all."

"Aye, I'll wager. Let me see that. Aha! Here we are. " 'Nor yet will you select your habitation in the northern cities. Yea, for in Durham, Norwich, and Lincoln there are few of your disposition; you will never hear anyone speak French.' "

"Good!" Agrestis cheered. "I count that a blessing."

"And York—well, 'York abounds in Scots, and vile faithless men, and rascals.' "

"Scots? As if York doesn't spend half its days driving Scots from its gates! What an ignoramus."

Lyra got up from his corner and came over. "I am glad to see you all so merry." His voice was chilly.

"Oh aye, Lyra, we know you. You're the glummer the more merry others are." Stephen pulled a dour face.

"You may be less mirthful when I tell you that the sickness has crossed the water."

Cyan the Harp came and stood with Lyra.

"Aye, I knew it," said the Cornishman. "I had it yesterday from a Dorset fellow. It came to Melcombe Regis on the feast of the Baptist. Your patron, fellows," he grinned at the Mertonians. "Everyone in the port is dead."

"Nay," said Cyan. "Inflated rumor."

"I heard everyone."

"We heard 'many.' "

"It came over from France," said Lyra, "by way of Jersey and Guernsey."

"Ah." Agrestis tapped his skull. "I see it now. King Philip is avenging Crecy at last. His knights are too craven to come over, so he's sent this plague instead."

They laughed, rather too heartily.

"But listen here." Agrestis grabbed back his book. "Here is this Norman fool on Canterbury. 'If you should chance to land near Canterbury, avoid the city at all costs.' " They all listened intently, pushing back what they had just heard. " 'It is an assemblage of the vilest, entirely devoted to their—I know not what—but some archbishop, lately canonized.' "

"Thomas à Becket!" Uthred brought out.

"Brilliant, Uthred. 'And every day they die in the open streets for want of bread and employment.' " Agrestis raised his cup. "He forgets to mention the pardoners and relic mongers."

"Aye," said Peter Ymer, "for as much of the martyr's blood they sell there, he must have had enough in his veins to fill the Thames."

William said, "For as many pieces of Becket's skull they sell, he must have had a head the size of Westminster Abbey." He chose to forget a bit of skull he had once pronounced authentic in a ring.

They all laughed and called for more beer. Lyra and Cyan went out, shaking their heads.

Then William remembered something. He set his cup down.

"Your friend," said the Cornishman, poking Agrestis in the ribs. "What's wrong with him?"

"Stephen," said William. Stephen was gripping his mug tightly and staring at the wall.

Agrestis took a long swig.

William said, "Stephen's of Melcombe Regis."

✳ 91

Yorkshire and Oxford
May 1349

Yorkshire:

On the last day of December the Ouse had risen up over its banks and drowned the western parishes of the city of York. In Kingston upon Hull, the next month, was born a pair of joined twins. On the Friday before Palm Sunday the monks of Meaux were hurled from their choir stalls in a great quaking of the earth. On the twenty-first day of May, St Godrich's wakeday, the sickness came to York, and everyone was thrown into terrified confusion, though they had been expecting it for months.

Oxford:

The afternoon was quiet at Merton. Those who had not gone away for fear of the plague looked sidelong at one another as they passed on the stairs, in the hall, or in the quadrangle. William had not gone home because he did not think he was welcome there; Agrestis, because he saw no reason to leave Oxford. He came into William's room, where William was lying in his bed, trying to read.

"Friend," said Agrestis, "come with me to the river."

William looked up. "Why?"

"The day is hot. I want to wash my face."

"You can wash your face here. There is a bowl of water on the chest."

"No, the river. Damn you, Angel, are you going to read all day? You will grow pedantic, and then I shall have to kill you."

William said, "I don't want to go out."

"Please, Angel."

"I don't want to go out."

"Fool! What makes you think it can't get you in here? If I do not go down to the river, I shall stifle to death."

William hesitated. "Very well." He rose and, to keep out the breath of Death, wrapped a scarf around his nose and mouth as if it were January.

The meadow squelched underfoot, all riven with grass-thatched streamlets. The Cherwell flowed full and sweet, tugging gently at switches of green-nubbed willow. Small birds sang and chattered in the high boughs; geese honked and snapped among the reeds, and everywhere there were flowers.

They were, at the moment, the only two people in the meadow.

When they came to the bank Agrestis bent and pulled off his shoes. Then he began to take down his hosen.

"What in God's name are you doing?"

"I'm going to bathe. Do you object?"

"It's only May. You'll take cold." Why was Agrestis hot? It wasn't hot.

Agrestis laughed loudly. He threw off his tunic and went into the river in his shirt. William stood stiffly on the bank watching.

Agrestis floundered around in the water, ducking his head, splashing his arms and legs like an imbecile. Finally he stood, dripping, among the rushes, with a fierce expression on his face. He pointed a finger. "Repent!" he cried, "for the kingdom of heaven is at hand!"

William glanced around. "Stop acting like a lunatic."

"I'm only quoting our patron saint, the Baptist. Vox clara ecce intonat, obscura quaeque increpat, a thrilling voice by Jordan rings, rebuking dark and darksome things. You brood of vipers! Who warned you to flee the wrath to come? Even now the axe is to be laid to the root of the tree. Come, Angel, be baptized. Or am I unworthy to tie your sandal strap?"

William went rigid. "Don't blaspheme."

"Yes, Father Abbot, pardon." Agrestis clambered up the bank, slipping a little in the mud. "Help me up. Exsurge Domine; extolle manum tuam, rise up O Lord, and stretch out your hand."

William folded his arms.

"Damn you then." Agrestis topped the bank. He stood in the grass, tipping back his head to watch the sky. Then he dried himself on his gown and pulled his tunic over his sodden shirt. "Ah," he sighed. "Better."

"Shall we go back to college, then?" William stepped away a little.

"No. First I want to go to the Prelate."

"I won't go there."

But because it was Agrestis, he did go there. They hurried through the streets. William hunched his shoulders and turned his eyes on the cobbles. Agrestis kept his head up, looking about. He was, as always, interested.

A voice shrilled out of the shop they were passing. "Take your twopence and stick it in your arse! I'll not be cheated!"

"I was thinking," said Agrestis. "If we went to old Claws the bookseller we might be able to get something good off him. Did you see that *Quodlibetal Questions* Peter Ymer bought yesterday?"

William shook his head.

"He got it for a shilling! Of course it wasn't from Claws, but from a fellow who was running away from town. Angel, why do these people run away home? Do they think that Death will be courteous and not disturb them in their own home? And see what they're missing: Duns' *Quodlibets* for a shilling! It's a beautiful book, too—clearly copied, hardly soiled, well bound. Angel, do you notice how cold it's suddenly become?"

In a gable over their heads a child was moaning. They hastened across the street, into the dimness of the tavern.

Five black monks of Gloucester college sat at a table casting knucklebones. Agrestis stared at them. "Benedicite, brothers! How good it is to see you here, pleading thus earnestly with God."

A couple of them fell silent, but one, a dark, hairy fellow, raised his hand and replied, "Maledicite, fili. Mors tecum." Death be with you.

"Our prior died today," another explained.

"You must have loved him dearly." Agrestis chose a bench and seated himself. He was shivering with the sudden cold. "Bring us in gude ale, gude ale, and bring us in gude ale. Bet! For our Blessed Lady's sake, bring us in gude ale." He turned to William. "Remember the first time we brought you in here? Marry, it seems an age ago. Think of all that's happened since! But it's no more than—how many years?"

"Four years," said William.

"God, you were a sweet little fellow then. Pure as the angel Gabriel; white as the widow's bedsheets. And now look at you! A debauched and criminous clerc, sunk in all manner of depravity."

"Agrestis, lower your voice."

"Well I remember. A lily of a youth, golden haired and ruddy cheeked, fresh from Cîteaux, afire with lust for learning. Standing on a table, singing lewd songs with blasphemous refrains. Where could you

have heard such things? And remember? That sour faced Austinfriar—
what's his name?"

"Lyra."

"Lyra came and chastised us. What a Pharisee."

Bet came with their ales. William fidgeted. Agrestis raved on and on.
Aside from Bet, no one else except the monks was in the tavern. The room
seemed smaller to William, the ceiling pressing down on their heads.

Agrestis began to explain some plan for the destruction of the Ockhamists. William listened fitfully. A fly buzzed round and round his head.
The monks began to quarrel. William listened to Agrestis again.

"Do you remember the first time you came here? Afterward we all
went down to the Cherwell and lay in the meadow till Vespers."

Agrestis' eyes burned like fire.

"I have always loved my friends. I love you, Angel. When I am chancellor of this university, I will do great things for you. Will you do the
same for me?"

William whispered, yes.

"After I have been chancellor, we'll leave this town of Oxen and pay
a visit to the city of St Thomas the Dumb Ox. Together we'll cow these
French modernists at the Sorbonne. Come now. This place has got stifling
again. Let's go down to the river."

William said, "We've been to the river."

"No. Thames this time." They hurried again through the streets.
"Think!" Agrestis said. "The Thames here is the same river that flows
through Scumdon town."

"Yes."

"But *conceive* it. The water here is the *same* water that will flow, some
hours hence, under London Bridge. But *think* about it. If I pee in the river
here, tomorrow some laundress may wash the king's sheets in it. I feel
noble. Perhaps I shall be admitted to the Order of the Garter, and fight
beside the Black Prince. Stop a minute, Angel." Agrestis leaned against a
wall. "It's so heavy," he said. "The day. Aren't you hot, Angel?"

"No."

"If you threw a wooden shoe into the Thames, you could ride hard
to beat it, and stand on London Bridge and watch it float under."

"Agrestis, let's return to college."

"Swale isn't like that. He tumbles over rocks, and flows under no
great bridge. Look, the sheep are coming down the fells."

"Agrestis, let's go back."

"Why are you hurrying me, friend? I'm hot." And suddenly Agrestis
slid down against a wall with his legs buckled up under him.

353

"William!" he cried, reaching out his hands. "It cannot be so!" William fled.

All men are faithless

All of them lighter than the wind

✳ 92

Oxford
May 1349, the same day

William ran into a church. In his confusion he did not know which church it was. Three blackfriars were saying Vespers. William crept in and knelt in the back, on the floor. He mouthed the psalms with the friars and thought, In a moment, in a moment. In a moment I will go back to him. Give me a moment. And his mind kept saying this over and over. The sun fell pale through the deep, small windows; the church was poor; its glass was not colored. The friars ended their office and filed out. A few minutes later one of them returned, vested to say mass. Two women huddled at the rail. William's eyes strayed from roof to floor to window to wall, everywhere except to the priest and what he was doing at the altar. He saw a man laid out flat on the flags, face pressed into the stone, fists under his chest.

Give me a moment. One more moment and I'll go back to him. The priest lifted the circle of bread. William quickly shifted his eyes from the Host. I was not with him. I do not know the man.

The man on the floor groaned. William nearly got up and ran again, but one of the women looked round, and William saw that it was Judith. He stayed. After the priest finished mass, he came down from the sanctuary and bent over the man on the floor, whispering a question. The man answered, "No, I am only praying." Judith came down the side aisle. She stopped when she came to William. "What are you doing here?"

"My friend is sick," said William loudly. "I am praying for him. Do you care?"

She shrugged and went out, followed by her friend the weaver's wife, who glanced back at him angrily.

After a moment William got up and trailed after her. When he came to her house, she was just closing the door after her. The weaver's wife had gone along home, and the stall was empty and stripped of wares. Judith did not finish closing the door. She looked at him through the crack.

"Where's John Hand?" asked William.

"At his mam's. His stepfather died, and she was all alone. What's it to you?"

"I do not want to go back to Merton."

She hesitated. "Do you want to come in here, then?"

He nodded.

She hesitated a little longer, then swung the door wide. "Well, come in then. Don't stand there. I haven't all day." She slammed the door after him.

They made a meal of cold, gray mutton that night, and stale bread and strong beer. Joan, the eldest, held little Dickon on her knees and made a great show of feeding him, though the child was more than four years old and well able to fend for himself. But he played the infant, making baby noises and drooly eyes at his mother. The middle boy was not there, the boy who liked sweets, because he was apprenticed to their friend the webbe. Judith's prentice sat silently on his stool, eating and watching William.

"Joan," said Judith, when they had done the washing up. "You and Dickon sleep in the loft with Drew tonight."

"Why, mam?"

"Do as I say."

"*Why*, mam?"

"Do as I say."

William gripped the table.

"Drew, lock up the house. Make sure the fire is out. Do not snuff the candle with your shirt." These were the things she always said.

Joan took her brother and scooted him up the ladder ahead of her to the loft, where hams and garlics hung in pungent darkness over the low cots, and where rats sometimes squeaked and scuttled in the night.

"I have to go now." William tried to stand up. He bashed his knees against the table and sat down again. "My friend is sick."

She dried her hands on her apron, holding herself stiff. "Do what you like." She lit a tallow stub, stuck it in a candlestick, and went up the three steps to her room. She pushed aside the wooden curtain and disappeared behind it. He got up and followed her there.

Inside was warm and dark. Her candle lit up a cradle piled with mending. She set the candle down and held out her arms, saying something in a voice he had not heard before.

"I have thought it all along," she said. "You are the sweetest golden angel all along. I have thought it from the beginning."

When Lyra returned to the Austinfriars' from a walk he had taken for air, Stephen of Melcombe was standing before the door. "Lyra!" he cried, and the sound of his voice was so accusing that Lyra could not at first understand what he was saying. "Agrestis is dead!"

Rain came down, running off the edge of Stephen's hood and down his long nose.

"Come inside," said Lyra. It was impossible to imagine loud Goodram Scarra dead. "What did he die of?"

"What do you think he died of?"

"I saw him hale yesterday morning."

"So? So did we all. He died overnight. What would you have me do about it?"

"Did he have a priest?"

"How should I know? I wasn't there. He did not even die in college. He died in the street. I don't know why. I went out looking, and found him this morning."

"Where is he now?"

"In the Mob quad. The swine won't take him in or do anything for him. May God curse them. May they die in agony."

"Hush, man. Isn't there enough death?"

Stephen leaned his forehead against the wall.

"Look you, man, what of your friend William?"

"I can't find him. I thought he might be here. I even went to that widow's, but she said he wasn't there. Curse her. Curse all townies. May they all die in agony."

"Hush, I said! He doesn't know what he's saying," Lyra said to no one in particular. "Go back to your hall," he said, "and rest there. I will find Cyan, and we two will see Goodram buried. I think you have had enough."

"Aye," said Stephen wearily. "Aye." Lyra helped him down the street.

William lay with Judith every night in the close, dark room, and he said, "I love you, I love you," and put everything else out of his mind. One afternoon he walked over to Merton, but he came away again quickly. Most days he sat in Judith's shop while she worked, staring at the walls in a yellow stupor, thinking how he should go back to college for his books. But he never did go back. He could not help Judith with her chores, because he did not know how to do anything useful. In the dark he said

"I love you, I love you," and in the dark she replied, "Thou angel." Until the night when he awoke with a pain in his groin, crying, "Agrestis!" Then she called her children down to her, and put William up in the loft.

It grew worse, always. Magister Alexander died. Stephen and Uthred crouched in their room. Miles droned over his books as if nothing were any different. Every morning Stephen woke up weeping, which made Uthred weep too. Then the two of them drew straws for who would forage up their bread and cheese. The streets stank.

Days passed. Lyra woke from a strange dream, and for some reason it was strong in his heart that he must go and look for William of Kelda. He resisted it angrily, but when morning came he gave in and went to Merton first, to be certain, but William was not in college. A man passing in the hall said that he had not been there for more than a week, and even then he had only stopped at the gate to ask after Agrestis. So Lyra went out to the cordwainers' row and asked for the house of Judith the widow.

"Who's there?" said a voice behind the door.

"A friend of William the clerc. Is he in there?"

"He's sick. They're all sick in here."

"May I come in?"

"If you don't mind getting sick."

"Let me in."

The door opened. A thin girl of ten or twelve stood there. "He's up in the loft. He's had it three days." Lyra avoided the sight of a boy spread out whimpering by the fire and followed the girl through the kitchen. "Up there," she pointed.

Lyra climbed halfway up the ladder, then down again. "He's not dead up there, is he?"

"No. It's the stuff that comes out of you when you've got it. It stinks."

Lyra gagged, "Jesus," and climbed the whole way. Later he looked down and told the girl he would give her a farthing if she would run and tell the Austinfriars that William of Merton was sick and that he was staying with him. The girl nodded. She caught the silver coin and looked at it for a second in the palm of her hand. Then she made a fist over it and ran off. Lyra did not think how it might have been better not to send the Austinfriars a messenger from that house of plague.

William was in great pain and covered with filth. He did not know Lyra at first, but then he wept, "Lyra, Lyra."

"There, that's a good man," said Lyra, though he could hardly stand the look of him. He breathed through his mouth, stopping his nose. It was the common kind, the kind with boils. Lyra climbed down to get a jug of water and rags from the kitchen. There was no water in the buckets so he had to find the widow on her bed and ask where was the well. Staring at the ceiling, she told him. He brought her a dish of water, and one to the boy by the fire. But the boy was too weak to drink and spilt most of it down his front.

"Well, man," he said, when he got back to William. "What you have may not kill you, they say. But look you. I can give you the sacrament. Not everyone has that privilege lately."

"I can't, I can't. O God, have mercy on me."

"I will hear your confession, man."

"I can't. God, have mercy on me."

Lyra said, "Nonsense, man. Accept grace when it is offered you."

But William would have none of it and would not make confession. So Lyra washed his face and arms and legs, but the parts that needed it most he could not wash, because William screamed at the touch. So he stripped the cot and threw all the bedding and the clothes William had been wearing into a heap on the floor. "Better to lie in straw than in those," he said, and took the bundle down to the kitchen fire.

He came back up and bathed William's face again. "Truth to tell, man, I doubt you look much worse than you did after your bout with the journeyman. You smell a little worse, is all."

William laughed, a rasping sound. Lyra started. He had not expected that. "That's a good man," he said.

Everything was terribly white to William. The sun grew bigger and bigger and burned him with its whiteness. "Close the shutter," he begged, but Lyra closed the shutter and it did no good.

"I will go down and see to the others now," said Lyra.

Then William cried, "Lyra! Forgive any wrongs I have done you."

"You can begin by calling me by name, and all else will be forgiven."

"I have forgotten your name," William said slowly, and everything turned into excruciating whiteness again. O dear Christ, it was knobs in the armpit, burning seeds, black peas, burning berries.

"When I come back perhaps you will receive the sacrament. It is God who needs to forgive you."

William opened his eyes wide. Wilfrid priest seemed to be standing over him with a bowl of mead. "You know better than to muck about in the rain," he scolded. Rain! Catch it on your tongue.

"Here you are, man." Blue eyes. "Iago!" William said. "Iago ap Rhys." Sweet wetness rushed into his mouth. He grasped the wrists that held the bowl.

"There! You remembered."

"Sing me," said William.

"No, man." Wry laughing. "I don't think you want that."

"Sing me."

A tuneless voice. Quemadmodum desiderat cerva rivos aquarum, as the deer longs for running water, so my soul longs for you, my God. Sitit anima mea Deum, Deum vivum, my soul thirsts for God, the God of my life. Quando veniam et videbo faciem Dei? When may I come and see God's face?

William wept and burned. The white light came and went and came again. It seared his face, burned out his eyes.

Gurges gurgitem vocat, deep calls to deep in the roar of your cataracts . . . All your tides have passed over me, all your waves . . .

Caedmon, inquit angelus, canta mihi principium creaturarum. Et statim, Caedmon, said the angel, sing me the beginnings of creatures. And suddenly . . . "Go on," said Wilfrid priest. "Read." It was Christmas. The lights burned red in the sanctuary, the voices rose and fell. Voices from the white faces, and from the brown carven ones on the misericordes. Hodie, hodie. Today.

Quare deprimeris, anima mea? Why are you sad, my soul, sighing within me? Hope in God, for I shall yet praise him again.

"I shall lie down and take a rest," said Lyra, after many years. "Call if you want anything."

The white light came and went again. More years passed. Was it Vespers? The voice was saying, Audi, Domine, hear O Lord. Do not hide your face from me.

It was Vespers. William answered, "My days vanish like smoke. My bones burn in a furnace. My heart is withered like dry grass."

Lyra said, "I am like a pelican in the desert, a night owl among the ruins."

William answered, "My days are like a shadow at sundown. Like grass, I wither away."

"He has worn out my strength on the road; he has shortened my days."

"Do not take me away in the midst of my days, when yours endure for all ages."

"You are the same. You never end."

If only he could tear away those knobs that screamed. Many years passed.

Why are you sighing? "It hurts," William cried. "Bring me water!" Where was water?

"I am poured out like water, and all my bones are out of joint. My heart is like wax; it melts within my breast my strength is dried up like a potsherd my tongue cleaves to my jaws." No water, but a voice singing, "If I climb to heaven, you are there. If I lie down in Sheol you are there. If I take the wings of the Dawn, if I fly to the uttermost west of the Sea, you are there."

Like a strangled goose. Ergo, Lyra.

"If I say: At least let the darkness cover me—To you Darkness itself is not dark; the night shines clear as day. To you the Darkness is Light."

"Lyra!" William called, much later. "Lyra!"

Nobody answered him. His throat was like dust. A voice was saying something he could not understand. "Stop!" he cried, but the voice went on. It was coming from the floor, beside the bed. Toneless. Welsh. Their kind are great singers. Except Lyra.

The voice from the floor was gone. Other voices. He opened his eyes and saw clearly. Men were standing there talking quietly. Grey men, cord belted. One said, "Good Austinfriar, he came to this house to help and has been here all this time. Who shall tell his brethren?" The other answered, "Has he any brethren now?" William closed his eyes. When he opened them again the grey men were gone. He sat up to look, but his muscles fluttered like birds, and he fell back. He went to sleep.

When he woke, the grey men were back. "Who are you?"

"Alive," they said, and one of them crossed the air over his head.

Later he heard noises in the street. A man was saying, "Come, sweetheart, come, darling." He thought briefly of Judith. He lay and stared at the wall. Leaf and light patterns were moving on it.

No greater love hath a No greater love hath

The house was silent. The man and woman outside moved away, and there was no sound in the house at all but for a mouse or a rat chewing and scuttling in the wall.

A man than he lay down his life No greater love hath

"Lyra!" William called, understanding, and great misery overcame him.

The thirst was driving him mad, and he must go down the ladder. He rose slowly, shaking all over his body. He was naked; he could not find his clothes. He started down the ladder backward, but it lurched, and he had to put it back and bump down on his hindquarters. It was dark below. Thin lines of pale light showed around the shuttered windows. The whole place smelt of pestilence and of the decaying fly-swarmed food on the kitchen table. He made his way along the wall to the water bucket. What was in there was warm and filthy, but he knelt and put his whole face into it. Then he lay down and shut his eyes. The dimness was close and hot around him. The thickness buzzed with flies, and with the drone and gabble of his long, senseless thoughts.

Once he heard glass breaking. He puzzled over it, naggingly, for hours.

He slept, and when he woke, a terror was on him. There was no light around the shutters now, and no sound of flies. He lay with his face against the rough wood of the water bucket, his eyes screwed shut. There was something in the house. He could feel it in all the corners. It must not see him. It must not know he was alive. His back, turned toward the empty room, burned and shivered. The panic tightened in his chest. Jesu God, Jesu God, Jesu God, until all of a sudden he sat up gasping,

"Jesu God!"

and the terror left him. He sat with his head on his knees. Cool sweat broke out all over him. He whispered, "Jesu God."

Then he screamed. Something had touched the back of his neck.

It was a woman's shape standing there. It was Judith.

"I thought you had been dead." His heart pounded in his head.

She stood there silently. Then, "I have no children."

They made a meal of old bread and hard cheese and slept back to back on the kitchen floor for company. The next morning they ate again, Judith finding the will to cut down a ham from the rafters. They had cider too, and the next afternoon William felt strong enough to say, "I will go find my friends."

"You'll come back?" She held his wrist.

"Aye."

She went and fetched him shirt and hosen and jerkin and shoes from her dead husband's things. He had forgotten that he had nothing on.

The light and air in the street made him dizzy. He made his way with his shoulder against the house walls. Once his knees gave out. A man on a cart cursed him, and nobody lifted a finger to help him. He got up and stumbled on. It was sweltering, and the light made his head ache like the sickness again.

An arm went round his shoulders. "Whoa there, don't fall on your face in the street. Tell me where you're bound, and I'll help you there." It was a sober eyed greyfriar.

"Chimney hall in Kibald street. Gratias."

"Just along my way. Come slowly now."

William laughed wanly. "Where I come from we have a dance called 'the friar and the nun.' Here's a new one: 'the friar and the ghost.' "

"Are you a ghost? Here, watch that hole now. You're a Yorkshireman, aren't you? I'm of the holyfolk myself." By which he meant he was from the Bishopric of Durham.

"Aye," said William faintly. "I'm of Rievaulx."

The friar made an exclamation and turned William's face with his hand, peering. "Have I not—"

William said, "Bonaventure."

"Helmsley. The little Rewley fellow."

"Merton, now."

"Christ, you've changed."

"So have you."

"Strange. The world is too strange." They went on in silence. "God give you good grace," said Bonaventure when they came to Chimney, and left William on the steps.

Miles was in the hall.

"Holy Rood," he said. "It's the Angel."

"God be with you, Miles."

"I hope you're not coming for me, Angel of Death."

"I was looking for Stephen."

"Well, you are somewhat late for that, Angel of Death. He died with Uthred the Puler, locked up in their room, three days since."

William sat down on a bench and said, "I will go home."

Misit tenebras, et facta est caligo, He sent darkness, and all was mist.

✳ 93

Keldacross
June 1349

When the Scots heard of the plague that was scourging the south, they decided that if God were whipping the English back to hell, they would lend him a hand. The word flew down to Yorkshire from the high marches. "Scots! To arms!" And men who could still stand prepared to join their lords.

The Death had not come to Keldacross. But Marion felt a terrible dread when Katharine, who had come up with Sir Henry for the Tewisdale muster, said that she would return to Emberthwaite as soon as the men departed.

"Katharine, why must you go? Can't you stay? Or may I not take the children and come with you to Emberthwaite?"

"You are mistress here as I am there. You must take care of Kelda. Remember my mother's words."

"Your mother. She died, but she didn't have to sit there waiting for everyone else to die around her. I wish she were here to help me."

"Don't be a fool. Cuth and Gib are here. John Bailley will return from York any day now, and you have Alice and no end of women to help with the household."

Marion tried to calm herself. "Perhaps the Scots will go away and the sickness will not come here."

"That's as God wills," said Katharine. "Now, pull yourself up. Act like a woman, not a child." Marion, shamed and intimidated, said nothing more.

But the panic overtook her in the night. She shook Nicholas awake and begged him not to go to the borders with his father.

"What are you talking about? I am called to Lord Ros!"

"Many men are going to Lord Ros. But I am alone here."

"Mother of God, calm yourself. I need my sleep."

Marion began to gasp hysterically.

"Mother of God!" Nicholas sat up. "What is all this? I need to sleep!"

"You will leave me alone, with nobody? You will leave me alone with this Death coming?"

"Either I go up to the marches or we're all carrion for the Scots. Is that what you want?"

Marion grew still. She heard herself say to Nicholas in a calm, cold voice, "You think the Great Host of the North would miss the arm of one petty knight from Kelda?"

Nicholas stared at her, dumbfounded. Then he hit her hard, across the face. He got up from the bed and dragged the coverlet after him to sleep on a bench in the hall. There he could not sleep at all, not because of the discomfort, but because of the shame and horror of what he had just done. But his pride was too great to go back and repair it, especially when she had been so insolent.

In the morning he stood bleary eyed in the courtyard while his new squire Richard of Tunnersgil buckled on his sword. He had some trouble mounting Archangel. Marion was not in the court with the other women. Katharine saw this and strode through the hall into the solar where Marion sat twisting and untwisting a strand of spun wool. "Marion," said Katharine grimly. "Come out and give my brother your blessing."

Marion shook her head, lips tight.

"Girl!" Katharine hauled her up and shoved her in front of her like a servant. "You would pout and sulk and weaken him with another worry at a time like this? You fool! Come down with me now, or I'll sweep you into the fire with the rushes, I swear it."

Terrified, Marion ran out into the court. The men were all mounted, horses stamping and champing at the gate. Gervase glared impatiently, beating his gauntlet against his thigh. Nicholas played with his reins.

Alice was there. She held little Magdalen up for Nicholas to kiss, then Robin. Robin clutched one creased hand to Nicholas' neck and pulled on Nicholas' nose with the other. "Bumbiddy," he said.

"Father rides away?" Maddie was demanding again and again in a piercing voice. Words jammed in Marion's throat.

"Well, God keep you," said Nicholas. He could not say anything more in front of the men.

The others waited, but nothing came out of Marion's mouth, so Gervase wheeled around to go. Sir Henry followed, and Sir Ralph and Sir Geoffrey, and the men at arms. Nicholas sat there on Archangel, chewing on the corner of his mouth, looking at Katharine. Then he turned Archangel and went clattering out of the court, into the shadow of the gate and into the dull sunlight beyond. The women, except for Marion, went up on Old Keep to watch them ride over Kelda. Marion stood on the spot, staring at the gate through which Nicholas had gone. Alice came back down and led her inside by the arm.

Katharine returned to Emberthwaite that very afternoon. She drew on her gloves and her brown hood and fastened her cloak pin. She bent and gave Maddie a dry peck. "When your father comes home, we'll have a feast down at Emberthwaite, and you will see your cousins. Will you like that?" Maddie nodded fervently. "Good," said Katharine. She took her leave and rode away. Alice stood beside Marion, but Marion did not feel her there. She stood helpless, all alone.

94

Keldacross
June 1349: two days later

John Bailley came back from York crack-lipped, fire eyed, bearing the sickness. It took him three nights to die of the raging fever and bursting boils, and Alice stayed by him the whole time. "You poor old badger," she said, weeping. "St William and St Cuthbert, who'd ever have thought you'd be the first to go from this cloddy vill?" He told her that they needed to plough more land.

Marion tried to come in and relieve Alice, but Alice screamed at her from the bedside. "You stay outside the door! You come no further in! St William, I'll throw this filthy water in your face!"

"How dare you speak so to me?"

"I'll call you every name I learned in the streets of York before I'll let you come one step further!"

Marion retreated and went down for Oswin priest. Alice would let *him* come in, of course, and for a short moment John was right enough in his mind to try to confess his sins. Even now it was difficult for him to think of any. "I have worked only for the prosperity of my master and the good of the village," he said.

"Yes, John," Oswin urged him gently. "But perhaps you have sometimes been too hard a man?"

"I hope," John muttered, "God will show his mercy."

"Oh yes," said Oswin. "His mercy is unbounded."

But men are less forgiving, and as soon as the villagers knew that John was dead and that he had brought the sickness to them, some of them, headed by Wat Cottar, stormed to the outskirts of the village to burn the bailley's thirty acre field, a rich assart that they themselves had hacked out of the gorse while he watched them with beetling brows. Even though he wouldn't know it, they'd have their vengeance on him. Marion had to rush out with Cuth Constable and the parson to stop them.

"You villein jackass!" Cuthbert bellowed at Wat from the great height of ancient Maccabeus. "Snuff that brand before I snuff you! Simon Thornrigg, put that pitchfork away. You don't scare me any more than a pissing grasshopper."

"Don't burn good barley out of spite, Wat Cottar," Marion pleaded.

"Listen to the lady," said Oswin. "The bailley may be out of the way, but winter will still come."

"I care for no lady," Wat shouted. "Did God make her any better than me?" But he doused his burning stick in Keldabeck. The others did likewise and followed him sullenly homeward.

"I'd truss 'em up in the cellar, lady," said Cuth. "They damn near did arson on half our barley crop."

"No. They thought better of it. They don't know what they're doing."

The hell they don't, thought Cuth to himself. But he looked at Marion's drawn, white face as she sat on her mare and said, "Lady, you've a gentle soul. May God reward you for it." And they rode back to the manor house.

Then it was as if some unseen and terrible principality had been granted leave to ravage the village like fire through dry thatch.

In the second week of the death, several of the women who were still able came to Godrich's porch, where Oswin met them on the steps. He said to them, "It's well you are here." He did not know what else to say, nor did they know what it was they wanted of him. Finally he asked, "Do you want the body of our Lord Christ?" He asked it in a shy, formal voice. These were women who rarely received except on great feasts, because they were humble and did not presume.

They shuffled their feet expectantly, so he led them into the darkness of the church for the eucharist.

Afterward they went out and stood on the porch again, waiting for him to do something, anything. Oswin spoke to them. "Why should you be afeared?" he asked them. "See the heaven helm above you: it will vanish like smoke in high summer. See the brown earth beneath you: it will wear into dust like the clogs on your feet." The women stared at him. He had addressed them from holy scripture often, but never with any eloquence, for he was a clumsy man with words. "But hear the voice of Isaiah," he went on. "He cries in the byways of this place, Turn to me, my heart, for I am God, and there is no other like me; I call you by your name."

Some of the women began to cry noiselessly. Win's widow Mary said, "Parson, we are still afraid."

They turned and went back to their work in the fields so that any of them who might live would have food to eat in another season.

Two women grinding grain together
One is taken and the other left.

And still the fieldwork must go on at Kelda, for the harvest must come in even if it were the world's last days.

95

Keldacross
June 1349

In the third week of sickness Simon Thornrigg looked up from his hoeing and saw four or five riders coming over the rigg of Kelda. The sun was in his eyes and he squinted. He could not recognize the colors. "Hoy," he said, and pointed. Mary Thornrigg was on her hands and knees weeding the next strip. The earth was dry and brittle from drought. She looked up at Wat's call, shading her brow. Two more riders joined the first number, and they began to descend the slope.

"St Godrich!" cried Simon.

Mary stood up, wailing, "Scots! Scots!" She began to run in the direction of the church.

It was not Scots. It was Hugh Cliderhou and his brother Walter and some of their kinsmen from Eskmere.

When they rode into the courtyard, Marion came out of the hall and stood on the steps between Cuth Constable and Oswin priest. The men and maids in the yard stood back warily. Mark the fletcher disappeared into Old Keep with Gib Faulkoner; they fetched bows and set themselves to watch at the slits. Hugh swung off his horse. He came forward, extending his hand. "God give you grace, lady. We have come to see Sir Gervase, if he will see us."

Marion said. "I thought you would know. Sir Gervase is in host, on the marches."

Hugh looked back at his companions. They sat, still, on their horses. "Pity, Walter. Sir Gervase is in host." He turned back to Marion. "Well, then we'd see my friend Nicholas if he is here."

Marion said, "My husband also is in host on the marches. I thought you would have seen him there. What is the news?"

Hugh answered, "Poor wee lady, left alone with so much death abroad."

Marion shook her head. "Not alone. Haven't you been in the north? Are the Scots defeated?"

"We have had a long ride today, lady. If you will bid someone take our horses, and give us the comfort of your hall, we would be most grateful."

Cuth said in her ear, "No!" But she did not know what else she could do, so she nodded, and Watkin and the grooms came forward to take the horses.

The knights dismounted and followed her back into the hall.

"Doubtless you've had your dinner long since, lady," said Hugh, "and it is early for supper. But we've et nothing all day, we were so eager to set off. So if you would have them set up the trestles for us we would be forever at your service."

"It is no trouble." She called Alice. "Tell them in the kitchen."

"Poor wee lady," said Hugh, again. "All alone."

"Not alone," said Marion. "You can see I am not alone."

Cuth stood near; Gib had come down from the Keep and joined him. Alice came back with Joan and served them wine.

"It's terrible, this death, isn't it, Dame Marion? There has never been the like since the plagues of Egypt. That's what the priests say, don't they?" He jerked his cup at Oswin priest. Oswin hung his head and mumbled, "Aye."

"It's as ugly as Sin, isn't it, lady? Any man left hale thinks he can do whatever pleases him. No one is safe anywhere, lady."

"I have heard it is so in the towns," Marion replied. "But here we do the best we can."

"You are fortunate, Dame Marion. Isn't she, Walter?"

Walter grimaced at her. He was a very young man, newly belted, with a broad, high forehead, and pimples. He had killed Rab Torbeck; Nicholas had made him eat dirt.

Marion turned her cup in her hands. "What news from the marches, Sir Hugh? When will the others come home? Have you driven the Scots away?"

"It's a pity with this sickness," said Hugh. "Every man does just as he pleases. Some will not do their service. Some even turn the troubles to their own advantage."

Alice called from the dais, "The supper is ready."

"Ah, good." Hugh patted his belly.

"Whew," said Walter. "What a ride."

"Shame." Hugh shook his head. "We rode so hard, so eager were we to see my dear friend Nicholas, and alas, he isn't home."

"He will be home any moment, since you are already returned from the war," said Marion, leading them to table.

"God willing, if he isn't dead. These Scots wield a powerful sword, Dame Marion, and I say it who hate 'em like gall."

"God protects the just man," said Marion.

"Oh, aye," said Hugh. "So he does."

The knights ate and drank, talking loudly among themselves and laughing. Their cups ran empty, and Marion had to call for more wine. When they had finished, they looked long into their cups. At last they said they were weary, and might they not roll up around her fire?

When they were settled, Gib Faulkoner took her into the solar and said, "Lady, this is not good. Dame Magdalen would not have let them in."

"I don't know what to do. I can't think how to make them go away."

"Lady, Sir Nicholas made Walter Cliderhou eat dirt." He did not say, he defiled Hugh's wife and humiliated him in combat, but what he did not say, she knew.

"How could I have stopped them? The gate was open. Maybe they mean us no harm. They came to see Nicholas. Since he is not here, they will go away tomorrow."

Gib frowned and took her hand. She looked at him surprised, but seeing his kind intent, she did not pull away. "Lady," Gib said, "it would be good if I slept before your door tonight."

She agreed quickly. "I will have Alice and the bairns in with me too."

Cuth Constable and Oswin priest also slept in her chamber before the door. Nothing ill happened that night. In the morning Marion came into the hall with Robin in her arms and asked the Cliderhous if they had passed the night comfortably. They said, oh yes, lady, most comfortably. She asked if they would take breakfast. Yes, lady, they had a long ride ahead, and it would be good to set out with something in their gut.

So they sat down to table again, over bread and cheese and apples and small beer. Marion sat in Sir Gervase's chair, holding Robin in her lap.

"That's a fine fair boy you have there, Dame Marion," said Hugh, over an apple.

"Yes," said Marion.

"What's his name?"

"Robert."

"Ah, Robert," Hugh nodded. "Poor old Rab Torbeck." Walter shifted on his bench and slid his eyes from Marion to Hugh and back to Marion again.

Marion set her mouth.

Hugh leaned toward her, grinning at Robin. "Well, good morning sir. Are they not pretty, Walter? Robin and Marion, no less. Hey, Robin, art thou a fine strong fellow? Wilt thou draw a bow in thy lady's defense? Art thou a help to thy mother?"

Robin beamed and said, "Aye."

Little Magdalen came up behind and hung on Marion's sleeve, staring with big eyes at Sir Hugh and cramming her fingers into her mouth.

"And here's another bairn," said Hugh. He looked up at Marion. "She's like you: dark but fair." He laughed at his joke. "Eh, Walter, dark but fair."

"Aye," said Walter. "Right dark and right fair." He bared his teeth.

Marion rose. "I must go and give my son to his nurse. I fear he is dirty."

"For shame, Sir Robin." Hugh got up as well. "You're too big a fellow for that." Walter rose, wiping his mouth on his sleeve. The others rose behind him.

"He's only two years," said Marion stiffly. "He hasn't learned." Her legs were shaking. She turned and walked slowly, Dame Magdalen-like, down the hall. She barely kept herself from running. She called, "Alice!" and then Hugh was right behind her. She stopped dead. "Cuth! Gib!"

The two were on their feet already, running across the room. "God damn you, Sir Hugh!" Cuth pulled his knife. "Touch her and I'll kill you."

Hugh's kinsmen all laughed. Hugh looked round at them, offended. "What's the fuss? What's the pother? I only want to see my dear friend Rab's little namesake a bit longer. Rab and I were lads together at Helmsley, and I miss him sorely." He pulled Robin out of Marion's arms and held him by the armpits. "It's a fine, fair lad, isn't it, cousins? I wonder where he got his pretty hair. My friend Nicko is no flaxen head."

"His Uncle William has that same hair." Marion reached for her son. "And now Robin must be changed. He's dirty."

"I make bad dirt," said Robin cheerfully. "Alice says, 'Pugh.' "

Hugh handed him to Walter. Walter held Robin in one arm, around the chest. With his free hand he pulled out his dagger.

Hugh said in a quiet voice, "Now. There'll be no screaming, and no fighting, and no calling on fat constables or anybody else." Everyone in the hall, men and women, stood in their places like stones. "Anybody make us any bother, the child's finished. Is that understood?" He turned to Marion politely. "Lady, is that understood?" She could not breathe. Little Magdalen dragged on her arm. "Mother, bid them goodbye now. Bid them goodbye." Walter set his knife against Robin's belly. "I'll slit him like a pig," he said. Robin began to kick and scream. Marion's voice came out harsh and strange. "No, Robin. Hush!"

Robin hushed, staring at her, red faced.

Her breath came short. She spoke to Hugh. "You must go away. You must not do this. It is evil."

"Evil, is it? Was it virtuous when Nicholas smutched my wife? Was it chivalrous when Nicholas made my brother get down in the dirt and eat muck?"

Walter said, "If we cannot foul Nicholas, we can befoul his wife, and that will serve."

"In Jesus' name, no," said Marion. "In Jesus' name."

"If you mislike me," said Hugh, "you may do as your friend Eleanor has done, and pretend I am someone else."

When they had ridden away, Alice came and held Marion, who stood in her arms like a post, dumb and wooden, her own arms hanging limp at her sides. Alice wept and cursed.

"Those rotten stinking swine. Those cowards. God damn them all. God damn them to everlasting torture. Those stinking rotten sons of pigs. May the Devil gnaw out their guts. Poor sweet girl who never hurt a soul, what did you do to deserve this?"

Then Alice, struck by the silence and the woodenness and the splintered face, cried out in anguish, "My darling, you did nothing to deserve it! It wasn't your fault. Holy Mother of God! It wasn't your fault!"

✳ 96

Northumberland, out of Hexham, by Hadrian's Wall
June 1349

The Tewisdale knights straggled along the green spine of fells that upheld the Old Wall. They had ridden out of Hexham that morning because a party of Scots had been seen riding over the riggs in the direction of Aycomb. The English knights had passed that village an hour ago and met no enemy. All that afternoon they peered over the empty, random sweeps of land and saw no sign of Scot or any other man, save an occasional spare shepherd and his thin flock.

The Old Wall climbed before and behind them, riding and dipping over the fells, as far as the eye could see, east or west. Every so often in the wall rose the distant shambles of an old guard tower. The Wall did not seem to guard anything any more save the wild, bright silence of that place. Great, flat bottomed clouds towered on the horizon, but no rain fell. The men were dry. The sun beat down and glared off their armor until Nicholas squinted with the pain it made between his eyes. Archangel's footing slipped a little, and a clod of earth went tumbling and scattering down the high bank of the wall mound. A strange crag loomed about half a mile ahead of them; a small, pale mere gleamed at its feet.

Richard Tunnersgil rode up beside Nicholas. "I hate this," he muttered.

Nicholas nodded. He did not like the Old Wall, nor its sense of ancient menace, nor the way the moors stared bright and desolate. They were nothing like the moors at home.

Apparently others felt the same as Nicholas and Richard. Sir Gervase cantered back from where he'd been riding with Geoffrey Scarface and said, "We're turning back to Hexham, thank God. Either that runner told false or else the Scots changed their mind, craven as they are. Tomorrow we'll ride for Berwick."

Nicholas' flesh sweltered and prickled beneath his mail. Good, he thought. I had not wanted to be caught here at twilight.

The company gathered and headed back toward the steep grey town of Hexham. Foreboding and desolation hung over them, and they did not talk or sing. Hexham, too, made Nicholas feel strange. The abbey church loomed over a cobbled square across from the squat, square tower where the knights were billeted. It was a church of heavy, bulky pillars and low, round archways. The monks there were not like the ones he knew at Rievaulx or Fountains. They were as grey and dour as their ancient church. More than once the Scots had burnt their house; more than once the monks had raised it again. Because of the Scots, there was always rubble about for rebuilding.

After supper, Nicholas, free of duties for the moment, went alone across the common to the abbey. Odd he should be thinking of Wilfrid priest this afternoon. He remembered the old man saying about Hexham, "God's people have worshiped there since before the days of Bede the Venerable." Nicholas climbed the steps of the holy place and went into the dusk inside. He blessed himself with the water by the doors and went down on one knee before the sanctuary—gestures of habit, but invested here with a special weight and solemnity.

A monk with the stern mouth of a warrior noticed Nicholas standing near the east wall, close to the high altar, gazing at a small stone font curiously carven with whorls and birds. He came over silently and stood by, wordless. Nicholas ducked his head. "I wanted to see St Wilfrid's throne."

The monk pointed to a carven chair. "There it stands. There sat Wilfrid the bishop. There were crowned all the Christian kings of Northumbria."

372

Nicholas swallowed. A tremor went through his joints and made him urgent. "Sir. Father. Hear me in this place."

So Nicholas was shriven before the chair of Wilfrid the bishop who had baptized his ancestors. He left the abbey with deep wonder on him.

Out in the sunlight again, he crossed sloping cobbles to the yawning gate of the keep. Geoff Wydclif was standing there with some companion of Emberthwaite. He half turned his back when Nicholas came up, but Nicholas said gently, "Hoa, Geoff, how goes it?"

Geoff kept himself turned, but when Nicholas started to walk by, he had to say, "You should rather ask how does my sister Eleanor."

Nicholas stopped and said, "How does your sister?"

Geoff muttered something unintelligible. Then he could not forbear to ask, "How are you served by Richard Tunnersgil?"

"He's green, but he does well enough. How is serving at Emberthwaite?"

"Well enough."

"Aye? That's good."

They stood there not quite looking at each other until Geoff's friend grew uncomfortable and said, "Good thing you came back now, Sir Nicholas. They're dropping t'portcullis in a moment."

Nicholas nodded and went away from them into the keep.

"Did'ye know he struck his lady the night we came up to Kelda?" Geoff's friend remarked. "He who's supposed to be so soft on her."

"What?" Geoff's heart, which had just begun to open, shut fast again, like a trap.

"Aye. I heard Dame Katharine tell Sir Henry. That's why they were acting strange in Kelda courtyard. Didn't you notice?"

"I never went into the court. I waited outside," Geoff replied coldly. He bit his lip; tears sprang to his eyes. If he had been there—! He never would have allowed discourtesy against her. Never!

Nicholas dreamt he woke outdoors and a man was sitting by him cros-slegged with his yew bow in his hand. His face was vague and blurred, but his villein's voice was kind and full of compassion—as at Neville's Cross. "Edwin!" cried Nicholas, and woke.

"Sir!" Richard Tunnersgil was saying. "Is all well?" Dawn was breaking through the slit windows of the keep. Gervase was sitting up and stretching. "Don't worry, squire. Sir Nicholas dreams sometimes." But he looked at Nicholas askance, for his son had tear stains on his cheeks.

"It's nothing," Nicholas said curtly, wiping his face with his arm. "I don't remember what it was."

The English rode down from the marches unbattled. There had been skirmishes with a few unusually well horsed Scots raiding parties, but that was all: the Scots were dying in their camps. The Helmsley knights rode heavily southward. They did not like the pestilence doing their work for them. They felt cheated, baffled, full of dread.

On their third day they came to the wold of Durham. "Look, sir," said Richard Tunnersgil, for the sun had broken through a wrack of dark clouds, setting long yellow bars against the great towers of the church above the River Wear. Nicholas nodded, unseeing. He was pondering what he would say to Marion when he met her. Dear friend, I am sorry to have struck you. You must know in what esteem I hold you.

✳ 97

York
June 1349

William passed over the Great North Road in half-delirium; he spurred Arrow northward without consideration for the beast's suffering; he traveled often after eveningfall and did not care if he fell prey to felons.

The road went on, eternally, through a yellow fog.

One evening he passed the knoll of the great beech, where he and his brother and his brother's wife once had paused in pilgrimage. Another man's life. Hic, nunc, hodie. Sorrowing Geoff, griping Alice, and Edwin the archer with his bright bow of yew.

On another day, far north of there, he made a strange side journey to a house of Cistercian nuns in Hampole outside Doncaster. She had said the hermit Richard lived there, had she not, his brother's wife? The road to the priory was green and wet, full of singing birds. The priory gate stood open; no portress was there to admit or forbid him; he entered the church through the laymen's door.

Inside was silence. Silence of the wrong kind.

Silence black and gaping, no hope of voices nor song of redemption. Behind the screens the stalls yawned vacant.

It was some time before he noticed that the sanctuary was stripped bare and that the sacrament was absent.

He wandered into the nuns' cloister. You could see that women had lived there. They had made larkspur grow up against the walls and had trained roses to follow the arches of the cloister walk. The roses ran yellow and rangy now, mingled with high weeds. In the middle of the cloister stood a stagnant fountain, green with slime.

William left the priory and returned through the gate to the road back to Hampole. A few yards before him on his left, a filthy, scabrous villein was slowly crawling, pulling up thistles with rag bound fists. His back was to William; he wore a black hood. William went by wordless, but the man turned up an ancient face and said something that, by reason of dialect or defect of speech, William could not understand. William inquired, "Do you work for the nuns?"

The man mumbled toothlessly, and William thought, He's gibbering. "Where are the nuns?"

"Gone," said the man. "Ista come to pray?"

"Does not a solitary live by here? A man named Richard?"

The villein smiled again, his broken mouth a tombyard hole. "Gone," he said. Then he reached up and grasped William's hand so that William, despite his revulsion, must pull him up from the roadside. Standing up on bowed, palsied legs, the villein pointed to his pile of up-rooted thistles. "Ee, t'thorns," he said.

In York William stayed at St. Peter's Keys. After supper he went to the cathedral close to look for his uncle. Two chantry priests standing on the west porch answered him at once. "Roger de Wherne? Dead."

"Dead two weeks."

"No, not that long."

"Yes, two weeks. I remember. Feast of St. Barnabas."

"You're thinking of Canon Dacre."

"No, Wherne."

William left them arguing. He went back to The Keys and lay on his bed.

He closed his eyes, and green eyes stared at him, frantic, witchy. How had he ever thought them beautiful? I have said I'm going home, and I mean it. I've left money on the table for you; it will help. Green eyes watching. I have no children. Clopping down the gray, empty street, her voice behind him, bereft, alone.

He sat up. "No!" He lay down again. But a crowd of guilts whispered in his mind. Why had he left those books? They were Wilfrid priest's; he had no right to leave them. He had not been able to face Merton again. To face Judith had been enough.

Arrow, fly me swiftly home.

He closed his eyes again. Uncle Roger, I was at Merton by Easter, as you said. For four weeks I was at Merton, and then I fled, leaving my books behind me. He slept again. He tossed and turned. He heard bells in the streets. Hollow they echoed, and from no side were they not coming. Whatever gate he turned down, they were never far away. Faceless people scurried by, never catching his eye, never saying a word. He saw the minster towers rising above crazy roofs and steeples. St Peter's church. He ran down twisted lanes, through bare, deserted courts. The streets twisted in on themselves and the faceless people scurried by again and again.

The minster! William ran to the great south doors and threw himself against them. Who shuttest and no man can open. Who shuttest. One was standing between the doors holding keys, a saint in a shadow. He banged and pounded on the minster doors, and the faceless crowd was drawing in behind him, whispering, "I do not know the man." He grabbed for the foot of him who stood between the doors. He would hold the stone foot, and the saint would make him safe. Then a cock crowed and the saint was only a man of flesh crouching with his arms wrapped around his head, rocking himself and keening, and suddenly there was no difference between the two of them at all.

William sat up covered in sweat. He tried to speak to the man who shared his bed, but his mouth felt as if it were bleeding. He waited until daybreak, then found his way into Goodramgate.

Adam Scawe opened the door.

"I am Sir Nicholas' brother."

"I remember you, sir. My master is upstairs." Adam let William into the hall. Alice's brother Martin was there, polishing the long table. Nan was sweeping out old rushes. The house looked peaceful and well ordered.

William asked, "Is your mistress well?"

Adam replied, "She is with God."

They went upstairs. Andrew was looking over his accounts. His face was drawn and grooved. He greeted William with an apprehensive smile. "Have you brought me news from Keldacross?"

"No, Master Comyn. I am come straight from Oxford. I thought you might have news for me."

They each knew what the other meant.

"Last I heard," said Andrew, "my daughter was well and her children and your father and brother also. But that was two weeks since. Your father and brother have ridden to the borders. The Scots have come down again."

"Is the sickness there?"

"The sickness is everywhere," said Andrew. "There is nowhere the sickness is not."

"I have ridden through towns and villages it has not touched."

"It will touch them."

William looked around Andrew's counting room. The whitewashed walls gleamed; the windows shone. There was the wool hanging woven brightly with pictures of the life of St William of York. William remembered it as something Marion had shown him in those first days of the pilgrimage. And he remembered the other hanging: a picture of moors and woods and fields, cliffs and a sea with a ship. There was an abbey tower, several little manor houses and tiny thatched villages. Little bowmen, little haymakers, small knights riding in a band, and, larger than all of them, a wool merchant on a horse.

"My wife," Andrew was saying, "got down on her knees and did as they told her. Ora pro nobis, ora pro nobis, ora pro nobis. You can see what good it did her." Andrew sharpened his pen. "It's for our wickedness," he said.

✻ 98

Keldacross
June 1349

Alice knelt in the windows of the solar, listlessly rubbing at the glass. She saw a few stragglers plodding in the summerfield, and Oswin digging his garden. A boy ran across Mucklebridge, across the common, and called over the churchyard fence. Oswin rose slowly, brushing his knees. Alice went back to gazing over Kelda. She caught sight of something small and black moving over the haunch of the fell. She dropped her hands into her lap. "Joan!" she called sharply. "Somebody's coming over Kelda."

Joan Faulkoner was laying the fire. A look of strained hope crossed her face. "Is it Sir Gervase? Have they come back?"

"Just one man. I can't see. The sun's behind him."

Joan came over and watched. The rider made his way down the steep bank. It could not be anyone from the neighboring manors. There was nothing beyond the fell for miles but the moor and the high, lonely road. The light lay pale and yellow over everything. The rider came under the shadow of the alders and wayfaring trees at the hill's foot. When he emerged into the light again, Alice reached behind her and clutched Joan's hand. "Quick! Fetch the lady!"

Alice rushed into the courtyard just as William came through the gate. A stablegroom stepped forward to take Arrow. William dismounted and looked dazedly around him.

"Master William!" Alice wept. "Oh, Master William, look at you. Look at your eyes. Look, you have a beard." And she led him into the hall.

Marion stood on the dais with her hands folded before her.

"Sister?" William stopped short. Was it she? She was so different.

"Welcome, brother," she said in a stern, distant voice. "Don't come near me," she said.

When William drew close, she shrank away; he was a man.

The baby, Robin, whom they had used to force her, had died the night before, covered with sickness, and crying.

William, having learned from Alice more than he could bear, wandered aimlessly down to Godrich's church. The horrors he had seen at Oxford, along the gray North Road, and now here at home, blended into a yellow haze around him, a miasma that nothing could penetrate. He could understand neither God nor the Cliderhou knights.

On the floor of St Godrich's was a new brass. William looked down on it and saw an image of his mother, long and cool, with a gown that folded at her feet and her hands pointed in prayer.

Magdalena Vernae uxor nobilis et fidelis Gervasi Celdacrucis militis mcccxlviii, Magdalen of Wherne, noble and faithful wife of Gervase of Keldacross, knight, 1348.

Verna? thought William. Keldacrux? How laughable to Latinize such English names as Wherne and Keldacross. How pompous are clercs; how ridiculous the entire race of men, and worthy of extinction.

He looked up and saw the seraphim on the walls. "You too," he told them. "You too will come to nothing." He walked out of the church and across the churchyard and into Wilfrid's house—for so he still thought of it. He stood in the middle of the front room. It was sunny and quiet. It smelt of onions and cabbage and cooked collards. Two rectangles of light lay on the swept floor, one long, from the open door, the other short, from the little window where Wilfrid had kept his books. Oswin kept but one book. It leaned against the great Bible that belonged to the cottage and to whatever priest who lived there. William went across the room, moved by a dull, habitual curiosity about books to see what it was. It was the *Incendium amoris* of Richard the hermit. William took it and sat down on the neat bed (for Oswin was a tidy fellow) and began to read.

Oswin came in with a bucket of milk and found William outstretched on his bed, holding the book at arm's length above him and reading up into it. The look on his face was so intent that Oswin made a little grunt and began to back out the door. But William sat up and said, "Forgive me, parson. I was reading your book." He laid it gently on the bedside bench.

Oswin cleared his throat. "I'm no learned fellow, sir. I keep that book because it moves my heart is all." His big face creased with humility and resentment. He set his bucket, sloshing, on the scarred oak table. Wilfrid's table, where William had taken his lessons. "I'm no scholar," Oswin said.

William suppressed a surge of irritation. "Yes, yes."

"He says in there," said Oswin, "how his book is not for philosophers and wise men."

William quoted, " 'Not for great theologians, bogged down in their interminable questionings.' The hermit knows what he's talking about. He was at Oxford once. But don't fret, parson, I am by no means 'a great theologian' or any theologian at all. I won't pollute your book."

Oswin took a dipper of milk.

William said, "When I was at Oxford I was blind."

Oswin wiped his mouth, shaking his head. "No sir. Busy, I'm sure, and young, but not blind."

William suppressed more irritation. "I said I was blind."

Oswin bowed his head.

William picked up the book again and opened it randomly. *My soul pants for you*, he read. *My whole being is athirst for you. Yet you will not show yourself to me; you look away; you bar the door; shun me, pass me over. You laugh at my innocent suffering.* "Hear that!" William said, but Oswin did not know what he was talking about, because he had not read it aloud.

"He says in there," said Oswin, "that an old woman can love God better than your theologian with all his studying, because that's for vanity's sake and not for God's."

"For Jesus' sake, parson, show some charity. You do not know that."

Oswin scowled. He was weary. He had passed all the morning tending the sick and the dying. Martha Reeve had given him this milk, and he wanted to sit alone and quiet, drinking it with a slice of brown bread. "You can borrow my book if you want," he said in a sullen voice. "You can take it up to the manor house."

"No, I thank you," William replied. "I do not borrow books." He went to the window and set the *Incendium* in its place.

"What says the blessed Job?" Oswin demanded, out of nowhere:

I have spoken of great things that I have not understood. But now I
see thee with mine own eyes, Therefore . . .

William said hastily, "I will go up to the house, to see if they want
me."

Therefore I melt away.

✳ 99

On the moor
June 1349

The Helmsley knights parted with the westbound knights at Rich-
mond and made southwest over the moor with the men of Bransdale and
Pickering. They sweltered as they rode, morose and silent. The hooves of
their horses were muffled in heat and deep turf; they made no sound but
the creak of their gear. High above them a great, hunting peregrine hovered on the air, its wings edged with light. It was not until they had left
the Bransdale and Pickering knights behind, and come within sight of
Drumm Tor, that the thing happened. It happened under a narrow rigg
crowned with a dark line of trees; rowan in snow white bloom and dwarfed,
wind embattled juniper.

Geoff did not know which came first, the whizzing from the trees or
Nicholas' face looking at him frowning, an arrow in his neck quivering
between the links of his mail. Horsemen crashed down from the trees at
the top of the rigg; one rode before the rest, swinging a spiked flail. Eskmere colors. Geoff, hesitating less than a moment, felt his bitterness slide
from him like a skin, leaving raw love only. He charged his horse between
Nicholas and the great destrier that bore down upon them. Hugh Cliderhou, you coward, you murderer.

Gervase roared. He wheeled his horse. Caught fast in a tumult of
enemies and friends, he could not reach his son.

Nicholas fell and lay choking in his own blood. The sky burned high
and hot above him; the sun was white fire in his eyes. All was gaudy sight
and no sound. A figure lay beside him on the green turf, its arm in a yellow
sleeve stained red. He turned his eyes sideways to see the face belonging
to the arm; it was Geoff's, dead. He rolled his eyes skyward again. A
shadow was on him. Broad shoulders blocked the sun. A visor went up

like a beak, but the face inside was black like an owl's against the fiery light.
A sword upraised. It was all dazzling slow. Where was that other bird that
hovered on the wind?

The bow he breaks.

The spear he snaps.

He burns the shields with fire.

"Jesu," said Nicholas. "Mercy."

Mercy stooped, swift and fierce.

At Keldacross nobody had seen Garth Shepherd for a long time, so
William and Thomas Reeve climbed Kelda looking for him. They found
sheep straying aimlessly over the moor and some lying on their sides,
bloated, tongues out, stiff.

"St Godrich!" Thomas mused. "It's got the sheep too, has it? Poor
Sir Gervie. Well, the rich suffer with the poor this time." Not without
satisfaction. He looked at William sidelong, defiant, but William only
said, "Hush, reeve. Keep looking."

But they did not find the shepherd.

Coming down from Kelda, they saw people knotted about the
church, and warhorses untethered grazing on the common, and a figure
running toward them, clambering up the Knee.

"Eh?" said the reeve. "They're back."

William had forgotten how much he loved his brother. He had not
known he would never see him again. He knelt by the body on St Godrich's floor. Dry sobs wrenched his innards. Gervase kept pacing back and
forth uttering strange, harsh, wordless noises. The knights stood around
him. Sir Ralph flung his arm out toward his friend and groaned aloud,
"Gervie, Gervie." Marion stood with Alice and said nothing. Sir Henry
put his hand on her shoulder, but she wrenched away. Then Oswin priest
had to pull back the sheet to do the anointing. Marion said, "Oh, his
face," and Gervase stumbled out of the church. Nicholas had no more
face.

The Watchers watched, and watching, burned.

Everyone forgot about little Magdalen. She took up her apple head
doll and went into the solar because the windows there made sun diamonds on the floor and she could play a hopping game on them, making
patterns with her eyes and well placed straws. Hop that diamond, skip
those three. Hop, hop, skip. Missed. But then it grew cold in there, so she
went out through the hall, through the courtyard, and into the stables.

The horses were warm; they stamped and made whuffling sounds with their lips. If Robin were there, they'd have played horses, pawing their feet and whinnying. But Robin was gone. Maddie saw Cuth Constable crouching on a sack in the corner of the stable with his face on his knees. His big shoulders heaved; his huge voice was cracking. But she had seen too much of that lately, so she put it out of her sight and sat in her own corner and held her doll. She listened to the horses and smelt their rich horse smell and drew comfort.

In the middle of the night Gib Faulkoner heard a noise in the solar and so went in with a lantern. Sir Gervase was standing there barelegged in his undertunic next to Dame Magdalen's loom. When he saw Gib he cursed. "Go roust Master William out of bed and get him down here, now."

William was lying in one of the high, bare rooms of Old Keep. By the time Gib had brought him down, Gervase had pulled on his coat and boots. He stood with his battered green hat pulled over his eyes and his face stubbled and hard in the lantern light. He barked at William, "I am going to stay with Ralph at Torbeck. I am leaving you the key to my strong-box. Look to everything."

In dull disbelief William protested, "Father, I have no experience of stewardship. Why do you lay this on me now?"

"You're a learned clerc, aren't you? You can scribble? You aren't fully useless, are you?" Gervase spoke harshly, but his face crumpled. He shut his eyes and, reaching out to steady himself, gripped William's arm. When he opened his eyes he searched William's face. "You put in his Helmsley spurs with him?" William nodded. And the old best hawking glove. And old Dragon's halter. When the time had come Gervase would have none of it; he had stood outside with his back to Godrich's church. Now he said, "Oh, William, my Nicko's brother." He wept briefly, openly, still gripping William's arm. William was dry of weeping; his lungs burned; he could say nothing but "I will do what I can." Then his father turned quickly and strode out of the hall.

William went back to Old Keep. In his high, bare room he lay sleepless because of Nicholas, and his father, and because of her whose pain he could not bear to face. Will you be a coward forever? She sits alone right now, and you will not go near her.

He forced himself up. He walked on cold stone until he arrived at her door. A line of orange candlelight shone under it. "Sister," William said, so she would know who it was. Marion's voice answered, flat, "What is it?" He said through the door, "May I come in?" After a while she replied, "I don't care." He opened the door.

She was sitting in one of the dark windows, wrapped heavily in Dame Magdalen's best embroidered coverlet. At the foot of the empty bed, little Magdalen was cramped up in her old cradle, for lately she would sleep nowhere else. She slept open mouthed with her doll under her chin.

William stood in front of the door with his hand on the latch behind him. Marion kept her face to the window. At last William said, "Sister, we are the only pilgrims left."

"Alice," Marion rejoined abruptly, still looking into the window.

It took William a moment to understand. Then he said, "I meant those of us who are gentlefolk."

"I am not gentlefolk. I am Yorkisfolk."

William was silent. Then he said, "You are fairer and gentler than most gentlewomen." As soon as the words were out he wished them swallowed back in the dark idiot place they had come from. A man did not speak to a violated, widowed woman of her fairness.

She turned her face and looked at him from a terrible distance. He quailed and fumbled at the latch. Before he could leave, she stunned him. "I will go to hell."

William thought she must have said this because she hated Hugh Cliderhou, so he answered, "You cannot help it." His voice shook; he covered his eyes with his hand.

Marion turned to the window again. She felt sorry for William, but everything was dim to her now and far away. "I did not give your brother my blessing. I could not—would not—speak to him before he left me, forever. If I had, he might have lived."

Astonishment gripped William, then rage. "Woman! How could so much depend on you? Do you think that punishment follows sin? I tell you, there isn't that much sense or reason in the world."

"Don't say that. I don't want to hear it."

William collected himself. "Just don't think these horrors come because of your little sins. Your sins count for nothing, just as your virtues count for nothing. These horrors do not come because of you."

"Then tell me why they come, since you are learned," Marion asked him from the cold, flat distance of her anguish, and meant no harm. But William, stung by what he thought was her scorn, answered ruthlessly.

"He hates what he has created. It offends God that we exist at all."

Marion drew the coverlet tight around her shoulders. Finally she said, "You have said a stupid thing. God cannot hate his very flesh."

"I do not know that." Cold and bitter. "I do not know anything."

"Then why do you say so much?" Marion turned back to the darkness of the window.

After William had gone from the room she laid her head on her knees. "Jesus," she said. "O Jesus God."

Says the one who hangs on the bloody tree, Heart's flesh, my very self, behold my answer. But she could not yet make out the sound of his voice.

✳ 100

Keldacross
July 1349

A fortnight passed, and Marion lay in the bed in the great chamber, listening to William pray his beads for her sake. The prayers washed over the room like waves of quiet sea water; where one slid back, hushing, the next swelled up and overtook it. Marion did not think of the words, but only of the sounds, and of the sound of her own breathing. Alice had borne away bloody rags and thrown them onto the pile of such things that lay beyond the orchard wall waiting to be burned. William would not let them be burned, because he thought the smoke might spread the sickness. Now Alice stood in the doorway with a basin of clear water in her hands. Marion had made her confession. "I would not give Nicholas my blessing." Now she closed her eyes and said, "Sing me." William got up from his knees and sat on the bed. "What shall I sing you?"

"A prayer."

William laid his beads in his lap and, for her sake, chanted mechanically.

Domine noli me arguere in ira tua
nec me corripere in furore tuo,
Do not rebuke me, Lord, in your anger.
Do not punish me in your wrath.
Have pity on me Lord, I am so sick.
Heal me, Lord, my very bones are in pain . . .

Marion frowned. "No. I want Master Richard."

"Which of Master Richard?"

"Mine," she said. "I showed you." With the straw in the book.

He tried, but he could not remember.

She choked. She tried to say its name, but no one heard. She shut her eyes. Her lips came together like old leather. She put out her tongue and tasted sour blood. The whole room changed; she could see it behind her eyelids.

She sat up and clung to William. There was retching and blood. The black stuff caked in her hair; it ran down her breast and spattered over William's hands, onto the beads in his lap.

Alice dropped her basin. She put both hands over her face.

Marion was brittle now and hollow. There was nothing left of her. Her chin was on William's shoulder. He comes in cloud. He rides like dawn. A tree stood in the deep of the forest and she could no longer resist the sound of the Voice. The cloud rose over the edge of the world, setting it afire. She ran through the burning grass and was not burnt.

Alice ran her fingernails down her cheeks. "There is no God," she said.

William set down his beads. He went to the churchyard and fell on his face by the well. The well was deep and full of darkness. A breeze came and scattered old yew berries on the water. William, drowned in darkness, struggled, and did not stir.

✳ 101

Keldacross
September 1350

For more than a year there had been no manor lord but William. He pored over the ledgers and records and held manor court. The villeins found him fair, sympathetic, and quick to catch them in dishonesty. He would not let them cheat his father.

Thin low clouds oppressed the moor; days were breathless, rainless. In the morning under the veiled and sweltering sun William went down from the manor house to do sexton's work for Oswin, bearing corpses out of cottages and digging graves. There were still a number of able bodied villeins who could have done it better, but William said, "They have corn to get in."

Oswin stood and gaped at the gentleman working below the grass of Godrich's yard, throwing wormy earth up with a shovel. Cuth Constable and Gib Faulkoner could not understand his doing villein's work; they thought it signified befuddlement on William's part, and they worried about the shrewder villeins who might take advantage.

When William finished his work this morning he propped his shovel against the trunk of Godrich's yew and wiped his face on his arm. "Call if there's need, parson." Oswin nodded wordlessly.

William toiled up the track to the manor house with clods on his shoes and black soil under his nails. Sweat fastened his clothes to his back. Thomas Reeve saw, and followed him up the hill.

"Master William, I have to tell you that the freemen will not work without a better wage. They've become too few, and the labor is too heavy."

William answered patiently, "I have told you before that I do not have the means to give them a better wage."

"Then you must look for no more boonwork on your strips from either free or unfree, Master William, if we are to get the harvest from our own."

William stopped in his tracks. Thomas regarded him politely. The man had lost his Martha in the horror; half his friends had gone under Godrich sod, but his outward manner had not changed. There he stood, ruddy, pleasant, smiling. But as William hesitated, a hard, cynical look showed behind his eyes, and William could read his thought: The gentleman is lying about the state of his coffers.

"Villein!" William snapped, angry at last. "It is for you to help with the harvest, not hinder it." He felt heavy, sodden with sweat, unclean. He wanted only to bathe and to rest in the cool, bare room in Old Keep.

The reeve continued smoothly. "There's some, sir, that's talking about going off to work on other manors. They say Farndale way the evil's struck worse than here, and the gentlefolk are paying a fair wage."

William shook his head. Weariness made him sharp. "Thomas, think a little about what you are saying. You are threatening to abandon Kelda to starvation unless I pay you a wage I do not have. My father's flock is ruined, Thomas; you have seen it with your own eyes."

Thomas ignored the last remark. "Well, sir. Folks are needy. For instance, sir, I need to use your father's roan bull on my cows, Byre and Brackenback, but there's the matter of fee, sir; it's hard . . . "

"So! Good!" William exclaimed. A vulgar humor seized him, and he laughed in Thomas' face. "Take the stud, man, and service all the cows in the village, and the ewes and nannygoats too, if you like. Use him to service the geese and ducks while you're at it."

"Sir—withouten fee?"

"Oh, yes, 'withouten fee.' Go, take your bull. Enjoy yourself." As soon as the words were out, William regretted them. After all, the man had suffered. He spoke again more gently. "Reeve, if it were mine to give you, you could have the manor house itself. I'll give you the coat off my back if you ask for it honestly. You have only to ask in an honest manner, and I will give what I have at my disposal. I can do no more."

Thomas looked at him askance as if he did not know what to make of him.

William turned again to climb the hill. God, for water, cool and cleansing. He entered the house and called for Gib to pour him a bath in the solar. Little Maddie ran up, babbling earnestly. William waved her back. "No! This is bad dirt. Remember, I have told you not to touch me until I've washed."

"When will we go see Alice? When will we go see my grandfather in York?"

"I don't know, child."

Gib hauled the barrel tub into the solar and poured the water. He laid William's clean clothes on a bench and set a folded towel on top of them. "Thanks," said William, and dismissed him. He pulled his capuchon over his head and his shoes from his feet, and peeled off the rough tunic and hose. He stepped into the bath and took up the lardy soap and the harsh cloth. He heard Maddie playing some little game by herself out beyond the screens. Without warning his heart was wrenched for her.

A black wave of rage and guilt and dread swept toward him. Over the past year of misery and hard labor, he had learned, when this happened, to let the wave swell over and past him. He sat in the cold bath for many moments, pressing his hand against the uneven wooden edge of the tub. A crowd of faceless terrors mumbled from the corners of his mind. But something deeper than the wave was welling around him and he knew he must surrender. He sat a long time doing nothing until at last a will of love was worked in him that he could not name or understand, nor ever dare to hope repeated.

After a time he got out of the bath and dried himself. He put on the clean clothes and ran his fingers through his hair. He felt his face and wondered how many days it was since he had last shaved, and thought how a man should not go about looking like a hollow eyed, grizzle cheeked penitent. He went out into the hall and said, "Maddie mine, will you tell Gib to bring uncle's razor and glass. Then you may hold the mirror while I shave."

Maddie hopped up and down as if this were the best thing in the world. She looked at him with her Nicholas eyes, her obliging sweetness like Marion.

"Go then. Let's see how fast you can gallop."

Maddie tossed her head. She pawed the rushes, whinnied, wheeled, and pranced down the hall with her fat brown braids bouncing behind her. A word pierced William's breast and spoke there.

I am knit into all your wounds.

Maddie came flying back with Gib Faulkoner pacing behind her, bearing bowl and razor. Maddie threw herself at William and crushed the mirror against his chest.

"Whoa, Magdalen! You're a palfrey! We'll have to change your name to Wutherwind!"

"No, I'm a peregrine," she said. "I'm Windiscry."

William laughed and hugged her tight to him, kissing the top of her head. "You're a sorceress, and if you keep shifting your shape I'll have to call you Maddie le Fey."

✳ 102

Keldacross
October 1350

Maddie awakened early, before cock, before bell, before leaves and fields outside had color, and she climbed out of her bed and went padding across the long dark hall with its people and dogs snoozing, and she pulled open the little door to Old Keep stairs. She ran up to where her uncle slept in a high, bare room with a slit window. He was already awake, sitting up in his bed, doing the quiet thing. She climbed into his lap, and he held her under his chin and rocked her, and it was warm. When he was finished with the quiet thing he kissed her and tried to put her aside, but she hung on his arm. "I will go with you where you are going."

"Your Aunt Katharine comes today," William said gently. "She will stay a fortnight perhaps, and then you will go with her to Emberthwaite. You will see the other Maddie, your cousin. Will you like that?"

"No," said Magdalen. "I want to go with you."

He did not answer. They went down the stairs, planning their breakfast. "Green gooseturds," said Magdalen.

"Fried cowpats with gooseturd sauce," said William, "and rabbit beads for comfits."

"Comfits for *breakfast?*" said Magdalen incredulously, and hung harder on his hand.

Katharine arrived shortly after dinner. She took some beer and cheese and went up Old Keep stairs with William. They scaled the short ladder at the very top, climbed through the trap, and stood outside by the battlements. William leaned over, looking out and down. Katharine watched him. A long, amber light lay over everything. A breeze stirred brown leaves far below.

"It is good of you to take the child," William said.

Katharine replied, "She reminds our father of Nicholas. To see her gives him too much pain."

"Yes. It's good of you to have her at Emberthwaite."

"Nay, she won't even be noticed."

William bit his thumb. Perhaps that was not such a good thing. "I reckon she could have gone to her grandfather in York. Alice is there, who loved her mother."

"What? God, no. I'll not have the child raised a tradeswoman."

The breeze became a wind, and the whole moor sighed.

Katharine frowned. "You'll miss being our father's steward now that he's returning? You've done your work well."

"No, I won't miss it," said William.

"Not much left to be steward of, eh, brother?"

"Enough," William said drily.

"But it's still Kelda." The name was sacred.

Keldabeck glimmered palely under scarlet berried whitbeams. A hawk circled over the common; at the pond crazy old Hereswith watered her geese. Simon Thornrigg and Wat Cottar plodded behind their oxen, turning brown earth in the rusty fallow. Old Hawisa, grim, slow, and limping—but living, because Simon was living—came across the common with kindling on her back.

After a while Katharine burst out, "Father will die and the manor will escheat to Helmsley! How can you do this to us?"

"Father will marry again. He will not forfeit Kelda."

"He is like a feeble old man! He who rode in Middleham lists and was never unhorsed!"

"Jesus-God, Katharine. Give him time."

"Time! Why do you think God let you leave the abbey? Why do you think he let you live through the Death in Oxenford? So that you could keep Kelda for us, that's why. Stay here. Marry. Get children! Does Kelda mean nothing to you?"

William said, "You know better."

Katharine clenched her fists. She would have liked to hit him. "You are *not* doing God's will. You think you are, I can see it, but you are *not*. You must do as I say."

William looked her in the eye. "If only I knew God's will as well as you do, Katharine."

Her knuckles whitened in the folds of her cloak. "Don't mock me. Don't ever mock me." Her voice dropped and broke. "Isn't it enough that they all should die?"

It was impossible that Katharine should cry. Her mouth worked, then set like flint. All the years of Keldacross looked out of her grey eyes: ancestors, men and women, children long gone, villeins with their ploughs. After a while, William said, "Sister." He reached for her hand.

"You," she said bitterly. "You were always running away."

"No longer," he answered; and she left him. He heard her clamber down the ladder. Her steps echoed, down and down, in the stairwell.

Out on the fell, Mary Thornrigg struggled with Molly cow, who was loath to give up the last green grass between the thickets of the russet season. Straddling the steep path and tugging the beast by the halter, Mary glanced over her shoulder at the village, and saw Hawisa crossing the common with her back bent under a load of kindling.

Mary gave the cow the freedom of the fell and hastened down the path over the Knee. She caught up with Wisa just as she reached the pond. "Let me take your load, mam. Save your back."

The two of them rounded the common in silence, picking their way carefully around the rim of the pond, where the geese dropped their green slime unmolested now that the thatcher's wife was dead. Thinking of the dead, Mary remembered that there was something she ought to tell Wisa. She had known for days that she ought to tell but had kept it back for fear of saying it wrong. How was a woman to speak of such things?

They turned down the path to Wisa's cottage, and Mary thought, "It's now or not at all." She stopped in her tracks and blurted it all at once. "I dreamt of Win a few nights back."

Hawisa looked up sideways, as she must, so bent was her back these days. "I never dream of Edwin." Her voice was dull beyond bitterness.

"You know I never did till now."

"Did he speak to you?"

"No, mam. The dream were little to speak of, except it was him. I thought you might be glad of it."

"Glad."

Mary screwed her brows, struggling for words. They came out

390

strained and halting. "You think . . . you've always thought him worms-meat only; but if he were wormsmeat only, mam, it were all for nowt."

Hawisa said nothing.

Mary raised her voice in urgency. She clutched Hawisa's wrist. "If even one of them were only that, it is all for nowt. Don't you see?"

"I see," said Hawisa, "that I need more sticks for my hearth. Will you help?"

Mary nodded, subdued. "I'll fetch your axe." She walked up the path and disappeared into the cottage.

Hawisa remained outside, her eyes bent to the earth. Tears stung in the furrows of her face. Oh Win, she thought, I don't know what you are.

Mary came out with the short-handled axe, and the two of them walked back across the common to the beck. There, but for the bickering of squirrels in high branches, the wood stood quiet. Keldabeck flowed silent over round, smooth stones.

Whither shall I flee from thy presence?

If I say, Let only darkness cover me,
    and the light about me be night,
Even the darkness is not dark to thee,
    the night is as bright as the day;
For darkness is as light with thee.

PSALM 139

Blessed be God, who lives forever.

✳ 103

Rievaulx Abbey
March 1370

Epilogue

Katharine of Emberthwaite was fifty years old. She had borne eight children, she had seen two pestilences, and she was still alive. She rode her grey mare, accompanied by her niece Magdalen and one manservant only, into the long forest vale of Rye. Ice lay on the river in patches; the water flowed out from under the ice, melting it, tumbling over stones with the cold, brisk sound of March. The voice of a woodlark echoed in the trees. Within the abbey walls, someone was singing: Flecte quod est rigidum; fove quod est frigidum, bend whatever is stiff; warm whatever is cold. Without the walls, above grey branches, a single thread of blue smoke curled up into the sky. Under the branches was a house, and in the house a woman was baking bread.

Katharine ordered her niece, "Smell that."

Freckled Gilbert the hospitaler met them at the guesthouse gate. He smiled at Katharine and said, "I will see if I can rout him out for you. He's always in demand, your brother, always sought after."

Katharine sounded amazed. "Well, Holy Death of God." Then she inquired of Gilbert. "Have you still that pear orchard behind the hospital?"

Gilbert answered yes.

"Good. Tell him to meet us there." Katharine nodded at Magdalen. "We'll stretch our legs."

Gilbert went into cloister. He found he must wait for William to finish private speech with one of the novices.

In the small parlor where they sat, the novice was muttering, red faced, "I've been a fool."

"Aye, well," William replied, "in your case that's nothing strong victuals and strong cider won't cure."

The young man blushed deeper.

"A day or two's lambing with the laybrothers might clear the cobwebs, what think you? It's helped me more often than not—March wind, spring sod, and fresh muck."

"You'll ask this for me?"

"On condition that you'll indulge in no more secret fasts and penances, and promise to enjoy at least one full night's sleep."

William dismissed the novice and came out into the silence, where Gib met him, signing to him that guests awaited him in the orchard. Two kinswomen.

William found them wandering under bare branches. The orchard was grey and green; the grass was up but the buds not yet out. William walked quickly, delightedly, over the grass toward them. Katharine examined him. He looked worn, she noticed, but merry. She embraced him. "Well, brother."

He chose a bench by a sunny wall, and they sat down. "Maddie," said William, holding out his hand, but their niece would not sit with them. She stood to one side, stiff and painful, staring at the grass. She did not know how she was supposed to act with this uncle whom she loved but had not seen for years. The uncle who had left her when she was small and orphaned and all alone.

Katharine spoke of Keldacross, now blessedly safe from escheat, of their father's widow, of their three stepbrothers, fierce young swaggarts all, and of the good match made for their stepsister Nicola—surprisingly good, since she was the youngest of Gervase's four daughters. "But she is well favored," said Katharine, "as are our father's kin. And the flock increases year by year, so her dowry was not meager." Then she said, "Magdalen here is for Rosedale Abbey. But I reckon she's told you that in one of her letters."

William nodded.

"Nuns at Rosedale are glad to get her. They've never made up for what they lost during the Death." Katharine looked Magdalen up and down. "Always was like her mother—fey and useless. Perhaps they think she'll prove holy and bring 'em in pilgrims and money."

William laughed out loud. He hit his knee with the heel of his hand. Magdalen looked up, startled, and then down again. Katharine frowned a little. She had not thought it so funny. She coughed. "Well, I know not why else they'd want her."

Magdalen looked at the shadow branches on the grass.

Katharine said, "In any event, she wanted to come see you before we packed her off. So I said, what the hell, why not, I'll go with her and see my brother."

William said, "I'm pleased."

Katharine snorted. Then she continued. "I have something to say to you. I do not know why I have never told you. Will you forgive me?"

He crooked his brow at her. "What is it?" She looked grave, and to his astonishment, fearful, so he asked, lightly, "Is it my business not to forgive you?"

"I hope you don't make it your business. It concerns our mother."

His face was still humorous. That irked her. This was a grave thing. "It was when our mother was dying. Our brother's wife said, 'Dame Magdalen, will you not forgive your son William?' Our mother could not speak; she was too ill. But I was close to her. I saw her eyes. They changed."

"I am happy," said William, after a pause. His voice was steady, but his face drained of color.

"I should have told you before now," said Katharine.

He shrugged. If he spoke, he would rebuke her, and he had no business to rebuke.

"Do you forgive me?"

He nodded, reached out, and grasped her hand.

"It would have made you happier earlier."

Now he could speak, and honestly. "See it this way: I am happier for having waited for it longer."

Katharine stood up, embarrassed, and dusted her hands. "Well. That's that then. I'll leave you to young Magdalen, if that's well." He smiled and said nothing, so she bent and kissed him on the forehead. "God be with you, Pimple. I will trouble you no longer."

"Kate, for some strange reason known only to God, you are no trouble."

"Ha, you liar." She kissed him once more, turned, and stepped briskly across the grass, frayed hems trailing, hawk-stained cloak billowing, back straight as a lance. At the orchard gate, she turned and commanded, "Pray for me."

"I will. And you for me." He raised his hand in farewell. After she was gone he turned to Magdalen, who was still watching the grass.

"Well," he said. "Tell me. How is life at Emberthwaite?"

She shrugged. "All right."

"Your Uncle Henry, that kindly man, Katharine said nothing about him. Is he well?"

Magdalen mumbled, "Well enough for being so old."

"I'm glad," said William, "but will you not sit down?"

She shook her head and twisted her fingers.

"I have enjoyed your letters," he told her. "I hope mine have not been altogether worthless."

She lifted her head and looked him in the face. He had forgotten that she had Nicholas' eyes, and that jarred him.

"Magdalen, sit by me."

She obeyed.

"You are like your father. Do you remember him at all?"

"A little."

William waited for her to say more; then he said, "You're a woman of few words! Can't you be a little more garrulous? I don't have much chance to gab in this place, and silence does not come natural to me."

"It doesn't?" She looked astonished.

"God, no! Give me a moment's leave, and I go on interminably. They hate me in chapter house."

"Well, I have no one to talk with at Emberthwaite or at Keldacross. All they think about is arms and tourneys and such, and I don't give a mare's turd about it."

William grinned and threw his arm across her shoulders. "You think like your mother, but you talk like your aunt."

Magdalen blurted, "My mother was a sweet lady. All my life I have wished she were with me. I don't know why the Death had to take her, and I don't know why you had to leave me when I was so little, all alone in that evil time. I don't see how you can be so serene and full of good humor as if you had done nothing wrong."

William withdrew his arm.

"You asked me to talk. I'm talking." Her voice was too miserable to be insolent.

"I did ask you. Only I never thought to be accused of excessive serenity. Do I seem complacent to you? God forbid. I'm sorrier than I can say."

Magdalen looked unconvinced, so William told her, "Perhaps it was wrong for me to leave you at that time. Even now, I cannot know for certain. At the time, it seemed that I must not wait."

"I think it was wrong of you to leave me, and if we do ill we should suffer for it."

"Whether we *should* is not for you or me to determine. That we *will* do in some way is unavoidable. Do you want me to go around looking like a death's head to prove it? Will that help you? It has never helped me. Look, Magdalen. There is One who bears all our agonies within himself. That one sorrow is enough."

"I try to believe it."

"That's all that's needed. Faith is an intention of the will and not necessarily accompanied by movements of the affective faculty."

"Speak plain English!"

Silently, William reproved himself. Ass, she doesn't need your little lectures. He joked again, "Plain English! Are you John Wyclif now? Will you have me Englishing scripture and preaching at market crosses?"

"I know nothing of this Wyclif. I know nothing of anything. God is farther from me than Orion, and sheds less light."

William looked at her, and a great sympathy of recognition went out from him. He said, "Like shooting arrows into fog, Maddie. It's the most we can do in this life."

The bell rang for Sext. William rose. Magdalen stood up hastily. "Uncle, will you still write me when I'm at Rosedale? I'm sure I don't know what you mean by this 'fog,' for I don't see how it can be a good thing. Yet I want to see." She met his eyes.

They walked together to the orchard gate. At the gate William blessed and kissed her. He did not answer her about the letter, but his cheek was rough and kind, as in the old days.

"My dear uncle," said Magdalen. "You are a good man."

"Cowpats," he told her, and she felt the blunt humor of it like a friendly blow. He kissed her again, and they said farewell.

He went to sing Sext. After Sext he went to the cloister walk with pen and ink and paper. He sat in one of the carrels they had lately built there. He thought for a moment with his pen in his mouth—for he still enjoyed chewing on pens. Then he set down a greeting.

"To Magdalen, my brother's daughter and mine, God's peace. I trust you will have had a good leavetaking and a happy homecoming. Warn your prioress that if I hear she has not given you good welcome I shall come and beat her with a stick. Otherwise, blessings on her and all her house."

A few more pleasantries and he got down to business. Plain English, he told himself sternly.

"You are puzzled," he wrote, "by this 'fog' I spoke of. The idea seems dreary to you, and I am not amazed that it should seem so. On my part, I am awkward and confused in writing of it. And this itself is a joke, for the heart of the matter is simple enough for an unlettered villein. Believe me, a cow could understand it—though this doesn't prevent learned scholars at Oxford from quibbling over it as if it were an obscure idea from the Subtlest of Doctors."

William dipped his pen in and out of the inkwell, considering.

"How can I best explain this 'cloud'? A wise man wrote about it in ancient days. His name was St. Denis, and when I was young I fought him tooth and nail, until, I think, he must have felt sorry for me and prayed to get me a little understanding. This is an understanding that comes from 'unknowing' everything it thinks it knows about God, until it comes to a place where there is nothing left to un-know. Then it is left naked in blind darkness, and by darkness I mean an absence of knowledge, or feeling, or any sensation or image of God. To a soul newly met with this darkness it will seem empty indeed. But it is in reality a sacred and living darkness, for it surrounds the Unknowable God—God not as we think he is, but as he really is.

"I hear you say, 'How can I, a sinner, approach this Hidden Divinity?' I can only answer this. Love with desire. Love with a desire that forgets whether you are guilty or innocent, learned or ignorant, worthy or unworthy. Love with a longing that forgets all thought of hope or consolation. Desire nothing of God, but only God himself. Pierce the dark cloud of unknowing with the sharp dart of longing love. For by love alone is Love caught and held. No thought, no deed suffices."

William read what he had written. He wondered about the prudence of writing anything at all: these ideas are so easily misconstrued. He considered for a moment and decided to send the letter. He prayed at least that it would do Maddie no great harm. He added one last thought.

"My dear niece, can you see what I am trying so clumsily to say? If so, for the love of God make up with your courage what I have always lacked in mine. For this work of love is the labor of the whole creation, who groans and pants in the fulfillment of her redemption. It is the work of consummation for which the world was made."

There was a yew in the center of the cloister, a tree like the one by Godrich's well. Its roots buckled the cloister pavement so that the monks had to mind not to stub their toes against the cracked and upturned flags. The roots descended deeper than the abbey cellars, cracking the floor in the abbey crypt, tangling in the dark with earth and stones and blind, white worms. In one season the tree dropped bloody berries; in another season it tipped its dark branches with new leaves like green fire.

A Word went out of that place and pierced the world's dark heart.
Flesh of my flesh and bone of my bone.
In truth there is no distance between the two of us at all.

William folded the letter and sealed it. On the cover he wrote, "To Magdalen of Rosendale be this delivered." He nowhere signed his name, which was "Gulielmus Rivallis." William of Rievaulx.   ◊

MAJOR CHARACTERS:

Manor families:

Keldacross:

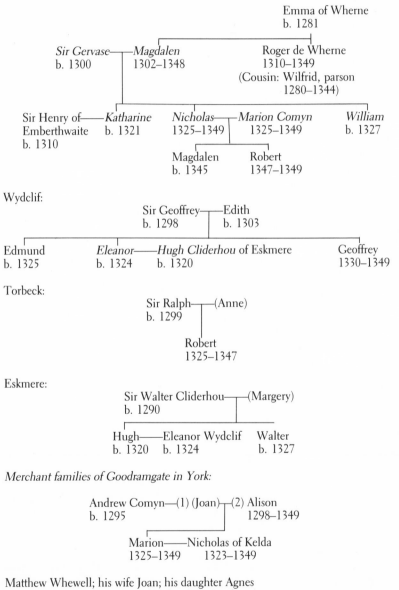

Emma of Wherne
b. 1281

Sir Gervase——Magdalen   Roger de Wherne
b. 1300   1302–1348   1310–1349
                                (Cousin: Wilfrid, parson
                                      1280–1344)

Sir Henry of——Katharine   Nicholas——Marion Comyn   William
Emberthwaite   b. 1321   1325–1349   1325–1349   b. 1327
b. 1310
                           Magdalen   Robert
                           b. 1345   1347–1349

Wydclif:

Sir Geoffrey——Edith
b. 1298   b. 1303

Edmund   Eleanor——Hugh Cliderhou of Eskmere   Geoffrey
b. 1325   b. 1324   b. 1320   1330–1349

Torbeck:

Sir Ralph——(Anne)
b. 1299

Robert
1325–1347

Eskmere:

Sir Walter Cliderhou——(Margery)
b. 1290

Hugh——Eleanor Wydclif   Walter
b. 1320   b. 1324   b. 1327

Merchant families of Goodramgate in York:

Andrew Comyn—(1) (Joan)—(2) Alison
b. 1295   1298–1349

Marion——Nicholas of Kelda
1325–1349   1323–1349

Matthew Whewell; his wife Joan; his daughter Agnes
Thomas Noye; his wife Anne; his daughter Cecily